FINDING FAITH

FINDING FAITH

KIM PRITEKEL

SAPPHIRE BOOKS

SALINAS, CALIFORNIA

Finding Faith
Copyright © 2020 by Kim Pritekel. All rights reserved.

ISBN - 978-1-952270-16-1

This is a work of fiction - names, characters, places, and incidents are the product of the author's imagination or are used fictitiously. Any resemblance to actual persons living or dead, business, events or locales is entirely coincidental.

All rights reserved. No part of this publication may be reproduced, distributed, or transmitted in any form or by any means, including photocopying, recording, or other electronic or mechanical methods, without written permission of the publisher.

Editor - Heather Flournoy
Book Design - LJ Reynolds
Cover Design - Fineline Cover Design

Sapphire Books Publishing, LLC
P.O. Box 8142
Salinas, CA 93912
www.sapphirebooks.com

Printed in the United States of America
First Edition – November 2020

Want a free book? Sign up at Sapphire to get yours.
www.sapphirebooks.com

Dedication

To the love of my life.

Chapter One

Faith Fitzgerald stared at him, not entirely sure she'd heard correctly. Finally, she cleared her throat, getting a modicum of her composure back in place. "Um, Devon, as in Devon Mitchell? Four-DUIs-last-year Devon Mitchell?"

"Eh, we all make mistakes," the older, well-dressed man sitting across the large desk from her said, waving his hand. The stone on the gold pinky ring he wore caught the light coming in from the large window behind him, one of many in his corner office. It was the office of Gordon Scott, one of the founding partners of Abbott, Scott & Jones.

She cleared her throat again, a hand coming up from where it rested in her lap to push long, blond hair behind an ear, a nervous tick she'd had since childhood. "I was under the impression that the promotion would be going to me, sir," she said, trying to keep her voice calm, even. "That's what Ned indicated to me last month after I won the McHale case for the firm."

"Yes, you were great as support representation on that," Gordon said, removing wire-framed glasses before he brought out a small bottle of cleaning solution and silk cloth to wipe down the lenses.

"Sir, I was lead counsel, and I brought in nearly thirteen million dollars with our win—"

"Of which, you got a nice bonus," he responded,

glancing at her from beneath bushy gray eyebrows as he continued to clean his glasses.

She crossed one leg over the other where she sat, straightening out her skirt before responding. "Yes, I was able to put an extra month's worth of rent in savings." She managed a small smile. "Just in case."

"See that?" he asked, brows lifted and arms opening wide in dramatic gesticulation. "What boss would pay his employee's rent unless she was awful good using something other than her brain?"

She found his laughter disgusting and the comment degrading. As usual. "Mr. Scott, if I wasn't called in here to get the promotion, why was I called in here?" She steeled herself, trying to keep her professionalism in place even as sweat began to gather under her arms and between her breasts. Gordon Scott had always made her the most uncomfortable of the partners, but he seemed to have kept most of his inappropriateness for the carousel of receptionists that paraded through the firm on what seemed like a monthly basis.

"Glad you asked," Gordon said, tossing his newly cleaned glasses to his desktop before stashing away the cloth and cleaner. "I need you to give Devon your notes on the Bastian case."

She stared at him for a moment. "Wait, what? You mean, the Bastian case I've been working for the past thirteen months? That Bastian case?"

"Yes. Devon has now worked his way up to such a case with this promotion, so he'll need your notes," the older man said, as though the reason for his request was self-evident. He gave her a wide smile, bleached teeth unnaturally white. "When you're here a few more years, you'll understand that."

"Mr. Scott, Devon Mitchell has been here four

years." Her shock and disgust were beginning to flare into anger.

"And, you've been here, what? Two? Three?"

Incredulous, she looked down at her hands, which were now wringing in her lap. "Eleven," she said quietly, knowing to argue was useless. It was done. Not wanting to hear another word, she pushed up from her chair, not even bothering to fix her skirt even as she could feel it riding up a bit on her left leg. "I understand," she said, voice flat.

"I knew you would," the older attorney called after her, along with an invitation to join him personally for the celebration for Devon Mitchell's promotion at his place.

She ignored everyone and everything, encased in tunnel vision as she headed to her desk which was wrapped in her cube which was wrapped at the center of the cube maze that was her seven levels of hell.

Reaching her cube, she plopped down in the desk chair and rattled the mouse to wake the computer screen. Clicking through her files, she found what she was looking for.

"Hey."

She glanced up at the whispered voice, its owner peeking over the wall of their shared cube. "Hey, Marge," she whispered back.

"How'd it go?" the other attorney asked, six years and four divorces ahead. Her heavily lined brown eyes flicked toward the area where the partners' offices were before returning to their initial target.

"Not how, *who*," she responded.

"What do you mean? The who is you, that's who," Marge said, her hands joining her face as her fingers rested along the top of the dividing wall.

"No." She snorted. "The who is Devon Mitchell, that's who."
"Faith!"
"Marge!"

Marge looked as though the air had been knocked out of her. "You are fucking kidding me." With a slew of undistinguishable curses, the older woman disappeared back into her cube.

Slightly amused, she returned to the file she brought up on her desktop. She couldn't help but wonder if her sorrows would wind up in Marge's prayers at the bottom of a large glass of red that night with husband number five.

Tucking her bottom lip into her mouth so she could chew on it, she studied the little file icon before her, titled simply, *Case # F552-9—Bastian, Dale.* She considered what was in it. More than a year of her hard work is what was in it. Her anger began to burn hot again, thinking of her entire career with the Manhattan-based firm. Eleven years, that's what she'd given to them, doing nothing more than being an errand girl for the male attorneys. She did the legwork, asked the hard questions, only for them to take the glory when the judge ruled in their favor. Never was it taken into account that two of the biggest cases the firm had won had been from her work, including the McHale case, which she'd handled on her own when the attorney she'd been partnered with had to drop out when he was forced into rehab for his cocaine addiction.

She'd won that case—*she* had—yet there she sat like a good little monkey in her cage as the boys congratulated themselves on promoting yet another of the breed to the Boy's Club at the top.

She glanced toward the opening of her cube and saw Devon across the way, in his cube, packing a box so he could move into the office at the end of the hall. Yes, it was a tiny office; yes, it typically smelled like urine because it was right next to the bathrooms and there was a plumbing issue; but damn it, it should have been hers.

Devon looked up from his packing, the softball trophy that had always graced his desk in his hand. He raised it in salute as he met her gaze. She quickly looked away, disgusted. She highlighted the file and right-clicked on it. Her options box opened and she zoomed down to *Send to*, which she knew would offer her up the option to zip it up as a compressed file so she could email it to him. Another option caught her eye, too.

She chewed on her bottom lip.

The little white arrow tormented her, waiting there patiently for her to move it, to decide her fate.

She glanced over at Devon again. He was laughing with one of the other attorneys, no idea what they were laughing at. She could guess, however, as the young man who'd joined Devon at his cube was moving his hips in a suggestive way, not difficult to discern what he was pantomiming. The two burst into boyish, locker room laughter.

She tore her gaze away from them. She could hear her heart pounding in her ears, a tiny person inside her head banging on the inside of her skull with a ball-peen hammer with every beat.

Send to...
Delete...

Her decision made, she finished her task and shut down her computer before grabbing her purse, keys, phone, and the small cactus that sat on her desk. She hurried down the narrow aisle between cubes as quickly as her four-inch heels would allow, finally making it to the elevator. She dropped her badge and main office key into the potted fern placed against the wall beneath the panel with the two buttons for the two elevator cars: up or down.

The shiny stainless steel doors whooshing open, she stepped into the car and looked out over her workplace of more than a decade. "Fuck you all!" she cried just as the doors whooshed shut again, leaving her shouting at her own reflection.

※※※※

"Son. Of. A. Bitch!" Eyes closed, Faith let out a long, guttural groan as her head fell back. "How did I do that?"

Angry with herself, she tossed the belongings she'd carried with her onto the tiny end table that rested between the small couch and the front door in the postage-stamp-sized living room in her slightly-larger-than-postage-stamp-sized apartment in the Flatbush area of Brooklyn. $2,200 a month for 470 square feet of private paradise.

She engaged the three locks on her door, chilled through the thin material of her blouse, her winter jacket left hanging on her chair in her haste to make her dramatic—yet sadly anticlimactic—departure from the office. Her thirty-five-minute subway ride had been filled with angry thoughts and silent rants, Faith far too busy in her own head to realize how cold she was.

Shivering in the frigid November night, she hurried over to the tiny kitchen tucked into the corner off the living room next to the bathroom. She reached into the fridge to grab the large can of Folgers and set it on the small square of counter space. As she reached into the cabinet above for the coffee filters, it finally hit her.

The tears came hot and fast. She dropped the bag of filters and buried her face in her hands, salty wetness sliding through her fingers, no doubt leaving behind gray trails from her mascara.

"Damn it." She sniffled, looking at the mess, chuckling at herself through her tears. She reached to turn on the hot water tap when there was a knock at her door. "Crap," she muttered, ripping off a sheet of paper towel from the holder to scrub at her eyes and face as she hurried to the door. Looking through the fisheye peephole, she groaned when she saw a distorted image of one of her bosses. "Crap," she said again, this time in a whisper.

Shoving the used paper towel into one of the pockets in her skirt, she squared her shoulders in a feigned display of confidence before unlocking the door and pulling it open. Dressed in his ever-present overcoat and fedora, Ned Tuttle stood out in the hall. He had her coat slung over his arm.

"Hey, Ned," she said, her tone a bit sheepish. "Thanks," she murmured, pulling the coat off his offered arm. "You didn't have to bring it all the way over here."

"No, but since I never see you wear any other coat, I figured it's the only one you've got." He nodded at the small living room behind her. "Mind if I come in for a sec?"

She stepped aside, allowing him to enter. They

remained silent for a moment until he stood at the center of the room, fedora in hand. The overhead light shone down on the top of his scalp through his thinning brownish-gray hair.

"Did you have to delete all your files?" he asked quietly, a bushy eyebrow raised. Though his tone was serious, Faith could see the amusement that she appreciated in his deep blue eyes.

She tossed her coat to the love seat, the only thing that would fit in the small room and which wasn't a whole lot bigger than a glorified chair. "It was a little drastic, I know." She let out a breath, meeting his gaze. "I just had enough, Ned. Tired of being shit on by a man who doesn't appreciate anything or anyone but what benefits his sexist, misogynistic, narcissistic perception of the world."

Ned nodded, shoving his hands into the deep pockets of his London Fog. "You know, Gordon and I went to Harvard together. Long time ago, certainly, but, though he was always a narcissist, he was smart, a good lawyer, and a decent human being." He shook his head and shrugged. "Somewhere along the way it all got mixed up in his head, I guess. He became the bastard you described so eloquently and accurately." He smirked. "He was so angry that you deleted everything, he threatened to sue you for the cost of retrieving it with IT specialists."

Faith felt her blood go cold. "Oh god."

"Don't worry," he said, waving off his own words. "I won't let that happen." He studied her for so long, she began to feel uncomfortable. "What are you going to do now? If you like, I can introduce you to—"

"I'm going home, Ned," she said softly, surprised the words tumbled out of her mouth. She hadn't even had enough time to consider what came next. "Yeah," she said, nodding. It felt right. "Going home."

"Colorado, right?" Ned asked, lightly tapping his hat against his side.

Faith nodded. "Yeah. Littleton."

Ned nodded and let out a heavy sigh. "Well..." He reached into his overcoat to the inside pocket of his suit jacket and pulled out his wallet. "Here."

"No," Faith said, raising her hand to stop him. "No, Ned. What I was going to use for a rainy day, well..." She smirked. "I just stepped out into a downpour."

"Doesn't matter." He stepped up to her and held out a stack of hundred-dollar bills. "I've watched you grow from an awkward, unsure duckling just three years past the bar exam to a beautiful swan, eleven years later, who is one of the best damn lawyers I've ever seen." He wiggled the bills until she took them.

"Ned, no, I can't take this," she said, breathless. "There's five thousand dollars here." She looked up at him with wide eyes.

"I know, sorry about that. It's all I could get my hands on tonight." He grinned. "Damn convenience stores just don't carry much cash these days."

She grinned, shaking her head. "Cute, but I can't take this." She tried to hand it back to him, but he stopped her, wrapping his large hands over hers.

"Gordon told me you were at the top of his list for that promotion. That jackass Devon Mitchell wasn't even on the list, so no clue where he pulled that one out of. You call Tisch in payroll tomorrow and give her an address you plan to be at, and I'll make sure you get your final paycheck and all your untaken vacation and personal leave liquidated. Okay?"

Faith nodded, stunned and greatly relieved. "Okay." She met his fatherly gaze. "Thanks, Ned."

"You got it." He put his hat back on his head with a flourish and walked past her to the door, turning to her once he'd gotten there, Faith meeting his gaze. "Go find yourself, kid. And," he added, pointing a finger at her. "Don't give up on the law. You're too damn good at it." With a wink, he left, closing the door softly behind him.

Left standing alone in her living room, Faith forgot all about her coffee and her tears, and went to her tiny bedroom, not much bigger than a prison cell, and booted up her laptop. It was time to make some plans.

❧❧❧❧

The heels of her boots sounded hollow on the aged hardwood floors, the dull thuds echoing strangely in the empty space. She'd donated or sold all her furniture and anything that wouldn't fit into the 2003 Honda Element she'd picked up for forty-eight hundred bucks. One thing about living and working in New York—a car wasn't necessary.

As she walked the empty rooms, arms crossed over her chest, she knew she wouldn't miss the crappy windows that let in far too much cold. She wouldn't miss the creepy dude who lived across the hall and somehow "magically" would leave and arrive home at the same time she did at least four days a week. She wouldn't miss the noise, the never-ending business of the City, and she sure as hell wouldn't miss a thing about the firm.

She considered for a moment: just what *would*

she miss after her eleven years living and working there? She smiled as she considered the pastries. Ultimate Bakery, just down the street, had bread to die for and pastries to kill for. Yeah, she'd miss those.

She ran a finger along the windowsill in the bedroom, the only decent-sized windows in the place. Many a plant had gone there to die before she'd given up, admitting her green thumb was a figment of her hopeful imagination.

The thing that struck her in that moment, however, was that, other than perhaps Ned, there wasn't a single person she'd miss, not even Marge. In eleven years, she knew more about Julio, the guy who ran the front counter of her favorite sandwich shop, than she did about the person who'd occupied the cube next to hers for six years. She'd learned early on working for the firm that any sort of private life wasn't in the job description. Her time, day or night, was expected. So, after a handful of dates, she'd given up and had dedicated herself to her job and her vibrator.

She let out a heavy sigh, part sadness and disappointment of the corpse that had become her hopes, but also a bit of relief. She had no clue what was ahead, but she knew for sure it was the open road. According to her GPS, she'd have twenty-eight hours of driving time to figure it out.

Chapter Two

Fingers tapping on the steering wheel, Faith nearly gritted her teeth as she tried to distract her need, which was quickly becoming urgent, with loud music. No good. It had been several miles since she'd passed any sort of sign advertising anything useful for a woman who needed to empty her bladder soon or things would get messy.

Reaching a point of desperation, she took the next exit that she came upon, no clue where it led. At that point, she didn't care. If nothing else, she'd be able to find somewhere more private to squat than the shoulder of I-80 West.

The snow-covered banks off the interstate turned into large expanses of snow-covered fields, the occasional farmhouse dotting the landscape off in the distance. Somehow, by taking that exit, she'd stumbled upon even more desolate territory than she had seen cruising along I-80.

"Crap," she muttered. "I think this was a baaaaad idea."

About to give in to the call of nature and pull over, she became distracted as the road wound around from open farmland into foothills, and finally opened up into a little town nestled in a little valley, a breathtaking view of the snow capped Rockies just beyond that left Faith's mouth open and eyes wide.

"Did a Hallmark movie land in Colorado?" she

muttered, the long, curved road straightening out into what looked to be the main street of the town.

On either side of the street was a line of buildings, very narrow alleyways between them, some separated by mere inches. Some of the buildings were made of wood siding while others were brick, tall and short. Running along all of them was a wooden sidewalk, something she'd expect to see as she was about to step into an Old West saloon.

She chuckled when she saw an old man coming down the street toward her in the opposite lane driving a sleigh, the type that she'd seen in Central Park during the holiday season, a single beautiful brown horse pulling the load. She followed the old man with her eyes the entire way, returning his wave as they passed each other.

"What the hell?" she muttered with a grin, noting the sleigh's unique tracks in the snow-covered street, clearly not as heavily traveled as the interstate was to clear it of snow.

The charm of the tiny town that seemed to expand out beyond the main street faded away as the reason she'd stumbled upon it hit her once again—straight in the bladder. She tore her gaze from an adorable and what looked to be old, simple white church to her left, and looked anew for somewhere to stop. She spotted a café just up ahead.

"Thank god." She pulled into the small parking lot next to the single-story building, which was offset from the row of buildings that formed the block. It definitely looked to be a newer addition—perhaps built in the thirties or forties, judging by the style of architecture—the brick aged, a few missing or smashed where they had been placed. The sign above the door read *Pop's*.

Pushing the glass door open, Faith was presented with an aged and somewhat run-down café. The four-sided tables that littered the dining area were made of wood scarred from years of use and abuse. The wooden chairs tucked beneath looked uncomfortable, some a bit rickety. The linoleum that was the floor looked like it had been ripped directly from the hallways of an elementary school, and was stained and bubbled in some places.

A few patrons sat at tables. One man sat alone in one of the three booths lined up against the wall opposite the lunch counter, where chrome-ringed stools were bolted to the floor in a line along its length, ending at a cash register that looked like it belonged in 1972. An ancient man sat in front of the cash register reading a newspaper, his reading glasses perched at the end of his bulbous nose.

Gaze moving away from the counter, Faith spotted a dark hallway at the back of the building, a teenage boy mopping nearby, though she was sure he was more flipping through the options in the old jukebox than doing any cleaning.

Hurrying down that way, she found what she was looking for, but nearly cried in desperation when she found the women's room door locked, a sign posted that declared she must order food to gain entrance.

"Fuck!" Stepping out of the hallway, she looked to the man at the register. "Sir?" As if in slow motion, which she didn't even think was possible, the man's eyes slowly, oh-so-slowly, moved up from the paper to meet her desperate gaze over the rim of his glasses. He said nothing. "Can I please have the key to the restroom?"

"I don't recall you ordering anything," he muttered.

"I will, I swear. It's..." A bit embarrassed, Faith glanced at the teen who was looking at her, then hurried over to the lunch counter. "It's a bit of an emergency, sir," she said quietly, for the old man's ears only.

He continued to meet her gaze, seeming unmoved.

"Oh, Pops, be nice."

Hearing a woman's voice, Faith turned to see a petite redhead standing in the doorway between the area behind the lunch counter and the kitchen, the metal swinging door halfway pushed open. She held a tray loaded with plates of food balanced on a hand. Her deep auburn hair was pulled back into a short ponytail, tied back with a turquoise kerchief that matched the color of her eyes.

She hurried over to the counter, the tray barely moving as she bent down to reach under the counter, her hand coming up to reveal a key chained to a two-foot piece of wood. She handed it to Faith with a wink before hurrying off to one of the patronized tables.

Barely able to manage a thank-you, Faith took off. Ten minutes later, and feeling admittedly better, she pulled the bathroom door closed, making sure it was locked, and made her way back to the lunch counter.

In the time she'd been using the restroom, the jukebox had been commissioned, Patsy Cline's "Walkin' After Midnight" playing, and a pair of old men had taken seats at the lunch counter down by the cast register. They were chatting loudly with the man the waitress had called "Pops." She saw the same waitress standing at the large coffee maker on the counter that ran along the outside of the kitchen, her image reflected back in a distorted way from the stainless steel diamond plate that covered that wall.

"Thanks so much," Faith said, setting the key and its long stick of wood on the counter several stools down from the pair of old men. "I really appreciate it." She slid onto the closest stool, prepared to honor the requirement to use the café's bathroom.

The waitress glanced over her shoulder from the coffeemaker, the tip of her ponytail whipping her cheek with the movement. "No problem. Y'all feelin' better?" she asked with a small smile, Faith noticing for the first time a bit of a southern accent in her words. "You were lookin' pretty desperate."

Embarrassed, Faith reached a hand up to rub at the back of her neck. "Yeah, well..." She grinned. "Been driving for quite a while, now."

"Oh? Where from?" The waitress finished her task at the coffeemaker, which whooshed to life before she turned to face Faith, grabbed the key, and absently tucked it out of sight beneath the counter before placing a menu in front of Faith.

"New York, though I'm actually from here. Littleton."

The waitress nodded as she wiped her hands on the white apron tied around her waist over faded blue jeans. Her blouse had capped sleeves and bright flowers all over the yellow background. "I've been here for about six years now, I guess," she said, resting her weight on her hands, which were flat against the counter. "We came up from Athens, Georgia."

Faith stared at her for a long moment, surprised. "You're kidding. I graduated from UGA."

It was the waitress's turn to look surprised. "Well, I'll be." She grinned. "Grew up in Savannah."

Faith jumped at the sound of the cash drawer being slammed into the cash register. She glanced over at the old man behind it to see him glaring at the waitress. Getting the message, Faith grabbed the menu placed before her and began to peruse it.

"Any recommendations?" she murmured, scanning the lunch options.

"Well, our special today is the grilled cheese and homemade tomato soup," the friendly waitress said. "More of a tomato bisque," she explained. "Good stuff."

Faith nodded, handing the laminated menu over. "Sold. And a Coke."

The woman pulled a small pad and a pen out of one of the pockets of her apron, scribbled down the order and, with a smile, disappeared into the kitchen.

Left alone, Faith took in more of the place, now able to concentrate as her eyeballs no longer felt like they were floating. Her fingers absently tapped on her thigh to the Patsy Cline classic. She noted with amusement that the old man at the register was partially smiling as he once again read his newspaper.

"One Coke."

Suddenly a glass with the carbonated drink was in front of Faith, as was the waitress. It was then she noticed the name tag attached to her blouse. "Wyatt. That's your first name?"

The waitress glanced down at it before grinning with a nod. "Well, see, they thought I was gonna be a girl, and my daddy had a penchant for Westerns and characters of the Old West. So, it was either gonna be Wyatt or John Wayne. Mamma, on the other hand, had a penchant for serial killers. She didn't want me to get teased."

Confused, Faith cocked her head slightly to the side. "Why would they tease you?"

"Our last name was Casey."

It took a second, but then Faith's head fell back as a bark of laughter erupted from her lips. "Oh my!"

"So, Wyatt it was," the waitress finished with a charming grin.

"Wyatt Casey," Faith said with a nod. "Definitely a, shall we say, safer-sounding name?"

Wyatt grinned. "I'd say. But that was my maiden name, so no worries now."

For a strange reason, Faith felt the slightest sting of disappointment knowing the beautiful young waitress was married, as foolish as it was to care. She'd never be back in the tiny little town that didn't seem to have a name, so it mattered not. "I certainly hope your husband isn't an Earp," she added, eyeing Wyatt as she tore the paper off the straw and pushed it into her drink.

Wyatt looked away and shook her head. "No, but he is a lawman."

There was a loud *ding* from a bellhop's bell and a man's voice calling out, "Order up!"

"Be right back," Wyatt said, heading into the kitchen. A moment later she returned with Faith's lunch, dropping it off with a smile before running back to pick up another order.

Faith was left alone at the counter to eat her lunch—which was a hell of a lot better than she'd expected—as Wyatt performed her work duties of cleaning, waiting on patrons, and disappearing for long moments into the kitchen. She checked in from time to time as any good waitress does before zooming off again.

Finally, she finished her meal and it was time to hit the road again. Sliding off the stool, Faith grabbed the ticket Wyatt had left for her with a small wave and wishes of safe travels, and headed to Pops, who flipped through the newspaper as though making sure he'd read every last word.

"Enjoy it?" he grumbled, not bothering to look at her as she stepped up to the cash register, her wallet in hand.

"I did, thank you." She handed him a twenty-dollar bill and waited for him to slowly—good lord he was slow—ring up her ticket and take her money and return her change.

He eyed her over the tops of his half-moon reading glasses. "Wanna own a piece of Wynter history?" he asked, voice deep and grumpy.

She looked at him, confused. "Excuse me?" She was startled when suddenly a laminated page was presented before her eyes. It looked to be the same lamination style as the menu—crappy, with bubbles and some of the paper still uncovered.

Taking it from him, she quickly read the short missive:

Church Steeple Raffle:
$10 buys you a ticket and a piece of Wynter history.
Drawing March 3.

Glancing down at the change in her hand that the old man had given her, she handed him the two five-dollar bills. "Why not?" she said with a smile, which wasn't returned as he snatched the money and the laminated page from her.

"Wyatt! Raffle," he called out, a roll of raffle tickets appearing on the counter next to the register as he returned to his paper.

Faith looked at him in surprise, wondering if he did anything but ring people up, read the paper and, it seemed, complain. Her thoughts were interrupted by Wyatt breezing through the swinging door with the grace of someone on roller skates.

"Sorry," Faith muttered, knowing her raffle ticket was taking Wyatt away from far more important duties.

"S'kay," Wyatt said with what Faith was beginning to understand was her signature smile. Wyatt truly was a lovely woman, looked to be in her early thirties perhaps. Her turquoise eyes, striking in color, held such warmth and kindness that fell into that smile. She couldn't help but return it.

Faith watched as Wyatt tore off the two-part raffle ticket from the roll, sliding it on the counter in front of her along with a pen.

"Go ahead and write your name and phone number there," the waitress instructed, tapping the tiny bit of space provided for the information. "I'll give you this side of the ticket." She tapped the other part of the ticket, which just held a five-digit number and could be torn away from the other part with correlating numbers and her contact information along the perforated line. "If your ticket is drawn in a few months, we'll give y'all a buzz."

Faith nodded, taking her part of the ticket after she finished writing her information. "What's the raffle prize?" she asked, glancing at the number on her ticket before carefully tucking it into a pocket in her wallet.

"Honestly, I have no idea," Wyatt said with a shrug, dropping Faith's stub into a jar she'd taken out from beneath the counter with others. "The town commission just came in one day and told us what to say and what to collect."

"Of course they did," Faith said with a chuckle. "Well, good luck with this." She indicated the jar with a wave of her hand. "Sounds like it's going to a good cause. Happy New Year to you."

"And you," Wyatt said. "Take care, now."

Chapter Three

Thump, thump, thump, thump.
Faith's eyes blinked open.
Thump, thump, thump, thump.
Looking around, nothing in the dimness of the basement room she was in gave any clue as to what that unending sound was.
Thump, thump, thump, thump.
Sitting up on the mattress she'd slept on, placed on the floor of her stepmother's "fitness area"—a.k.a. a room with cement floor and walls filled with exercise equipment covered in a layer of dust—she looked around. Finally, the thumping came to a shuddering stop and the loud, shrill *buzzzzzz* following made her realize that she wasn't under attack, but rather the laundry room was next door and had been busy.

Rolling her eyes, she shoved the sheet and quilt off her, revealing the sweatpants and sweatshirt she'd worn to sleep. Though the subdivision in Littleton, an upper-middle-class suburb of Denver, was only twenty years old, she wasn't convinced the basement had heat. Shivering, she felt around in the dim room, the one small window covered by closed blinds, until she found her shoes. Her toes were frozen, even covered by wool socks.

"Jesus," she muttered, irritated as her teeth began to chatter now that she was no longer buried beneath a heavy quilt.

Shoes on and tied, she pushed up from the mattress and hurried to the doorless doorway, noting that, sure enough, the laundry room shared a wall with the small room she'd been given, a heap of floor rugs waiting to be washed on the floor in front of the washing machine, the dryer full of the load that had just thumped its way to dryness.

Running her hand through long, blond hair, Faith trotted her way up the stairs, the air getting warmer with every step up. She damn near moaned in pleasure when she pulled the basement door open, the warmth from the main floor enveloping her like a blanket.

She heard the murmurings of the TV in the kitchen and smelled coffee. She made her way in that direction, stopping at the bathroom in the hallway to do her morning business. She washed her face and brushed her teeth with the couple toiletries she'd been allowed to leave there. Finished, she looked at her reflection, noting that her hair was a mess. She studied her reflection for a long moment. Large brown eyes—she was once told she had Judy Garland doe eyes, whatever that meant—looked back, long blond hair colored to perfection. She felt like she was looking at a stranger.

Reaching up, she tried to finger-comb her hair into some semblance of order, mentally computing the thousands of dollars she spent every year on expensive Manhattan salons trying to turn herself into what she was expected to be. The facials, mani-pedis, let alone the tens-of-thousands-of-dollars-worth of clothes, all to impress the partners and clients alike. Since her talent, intelligence, and skill as an attorney wasn't getting her anything except a bigger workload, she'd tried to buy her way into the club she thought she wanted to be part of.

Now, as she stood there in front of a mirror in the downstairs guest bathroom of her father and stepmother's house, a thirty-nine-year-old woman without a job, without a home, and without a clue who she really was, she began to cry. The tears came fast and hot, but she tried to keep them silent, a trick she'd learned during eleven demeaning years of frustration.

Tugging a wad of toilet tissue, she wiped at her eyes and face before she blew her nose, the tears coming to an end…for now. Blowing out a breath to give her the strength to face her stepmother Carrie, she turned out the light and opened the bathroom door.

"Well, there she is!" Carrie's ever-present high-pitched exclamation-point-filled tone grated on Faith's nerves as ever. "Hope the wash didn't wake you," she continued, slowly stirring her coffee with a spoon, a bottle of creamer sitting on the counter next to her. "I was going to wait but it was getting late, so…"

A surreptitious glance to the clock on the stove showed Faith that it was eight minutes until seven in the morning, but she said nothing. "It was fine, thanks. A little cold, but fine."

"Cold?" the older woman said, her bottle-bleach job on full display as her locks nearly glowed in the early morning dimness of the kitchen lit by the flickering TV and the dated light fixture over the sink. "I told Dawson to turn on the heat down there. Darn him."

Carrie's poker face was complete, so Faith wasn't sure if she was being her normal bitchy self, or earnest. "Where is Dawson? I haven't seen him in a few years. I wasn't aware that he'd moved back home." Her twenty-seven-year-old half brother was Carrie's precious, fragile little egg.

"Oh, that fell through," Carrie said, waving off the notion. "He never moved out. He had it all planned out with his buddies, and wouldn't you know it, they went and got a place in Arvada."

Faith stared at the older woman who had been in her life since Faith was ten years old. "I don't follow. Why couldn't he move in with them?" she asked, walking over to the large pot of coffee sitting on the coffeemaker's hot plate. "May I?"

"Help yourself," Carrie said, pushing away from the counter to take a seat at the table in the built-in nook in the huge bay window. "Dawson works at Albertsons, as you know. Can you believe he's going on three years? We're so proud of him."

Her back to Carrie, Faith rolled her eyes. *I've had bras longer than that.* "That's great," she managed, pouring herself a cup of coffee.

"You'll have to tell him that. I have to wake him up here in a couple hours for work, so... Anyway, so his friends get this place in Arvada, which is like White Trash Alley of the Denver suburbs, and that would be a forty-minute drive for Dawson! Can you imagine?"

Faith took a deep breath to steady the rising annoyance as she stirred in the flavored creamer before turning to face the older woman, coffee mug in hand. "Well, sometimes you do what'cha gotta do," she said. "I had a thirty-five-minute train ride to and from work when I was in New York." She shrugged, sliding onto the bench seat across from Carrie. "He has a car, right?"

Carrie took her mug in both hands, her already-thin lips pursing into a slash across her face. "He's your baby brother, Faith," she said, tone flat. "I thought you'd be more sensitive to his needs and the unfairness of the decision his friends made, without talking to us, no less."

"I actually think it was smart. I mean, Littleton is really expensive, downtown Denver is pretty much out of the range, too, so Arvada, Aurora..." She shrugged again. "A few friends could make it happen." She brought her mug up to her lips and muttered, "And, he's twenty-seven."

Their attention was drawn by the hard, thundering footfalls coming down the stairs, appearing in the kitchen moments later in the shape of her half brother, light brown hair sticking up in all directions with an overgrown beard wearing a T-shirt and boxer shorts. He was barefoot and looked grumpy, more like a sixteen-year-old boy than a man of almost thirty.

Faith hissed in pain as her shin was kicked hard by Carrie under the table in her haste to scramble out of her chair and over to her son. She glared at the woman's back.

"Honey! Oh no, were we too loud?" she gushed, reaching for Dawson, her hands gripping a somewhat scrawny arm. "I was just telling Faith over there that she needed to quiet down. I'm sorry, sweetheart."

Faith gasped as she stared the older woman down. Before she could say anything, Dawson glanced over at her and nodded, his silent *Yo* loud and clear. "Hey, Dawson."

"What are you doing up?" Carrie asked, hurrying over to the cabinet above and next to the sink, grabbing a drinking glass. Faith watched, amused as the mother tried to beat her son to the fridge, which he reached first. Carrie's face and her hand with the glass fell as he grabbed the gallon of milk and drank straight from it. He let out a loud, disgusting belch after recapping the jug and plopping it back in its place.

"Fuckin' Jose called. Gotta go into work early," he explained, tossing the tub of cream cheese to the counter next to where his mother had just placed two sliced bagels into the toaster. He nearly hit her with it.

Faith sat where she was, stunned as she watched the events unfolding before her like a fly on the wall, as neither paid her any mind. She couldn't believe the way Dawson talked to Carrie, and she couldn't believe the way Carrie coddled Dawson, which no doubt circled back to why he treated her the way he did. It was mind-boggling. Carrie would have slapped the living crap out of her had Faith dared talk to her the way he was.

"Where's Dad?" he demanded, reaching into the large ceramic cookie jar shaped like a grinning pig on the counter. He retrieved a handful of what looked to be homemade chocolate chip cookies. "He said he'd give me some fucking gas money today," he said around a mouthful of cookie.

Faith was disgusted, watching as a large crumb fell out of his mouth. He looked down at it, then kicked it with his bare big toe. She took a drink from her coffee in order to not yell at him to pick it up and throw it away.

"Where else?" Carrie smirked, handing him the first of two bagels slathered liberally with the white spread. "The office."

"Fuck!" Dawson roared. "Mom, how the fuck am I supposed to get to work? I'm on empty."

"Don't worry about it, baby," Carrie said calmly. She handed him the second bagel before placing her hands on either side of his face, his gaze meeting hers. Faith watched, a bit creeped out at the obvious connection the two had. "I'll get you gas money. Come on."

"Where we goin'?" he asked, tearing off a piece of bagel with his teeth as he followed her out of the kitchen, neither giving Faith a second look.

"Raid the stash your father doesn't know I know about," Carrie said, her voice trailing off as the two headed up the stairs. "Faith," Carrie called, her voice sounding like it was from the top of the stairs.

"Yeah?" Faith called back.

"I forgot to tell you. Your father wants you to stop by the office today."

"What time?"

"How the hell am I supposed to know? I'm not your goddamn secretary," Carrie hollered, her voice moving farther away.

Faith smirked. "Yeah," she murmured. "But you are Dawson's bitch."

She sat where she was, stunned and disgusted. She quickly scooted out of the little eating nook and hurried downstairs to the basement to get dressed.

∾∾∾∾

Knees bobbing with the nervous tapping of her heels, Faith waited. She sat uncomfortably in the comfortable chair, one in a matching trio in the small lobby area of the architectural firm of Fitzgerald & Associates. She wanted to bring her hand up to chew on a fingernail, but she forced her hands to stay put in her lap, not wanting to resume a childhood habit she'd dropped in law school.

"Faith?"

Faith turned to look at the receptionist, an elderly woman who had worked at the firm for nearly thirty years, who was just replacing her desk phone in its cradle.

"Go on in, hun."

Faith smiled at her and nodded, pushing to her feet. She took a deep breath before shoving her hands into the deep pockets of her coat before making her way to the closed office door with Ogden Fitzgerald's name on it. Taking another deep breath, she reached up and turned the doorknob, pushing the door open.

As she remembered, the overhead light was off and the blinds were pulled on the two large windows, creating a dim, cave-like atmosphere. The only light sources in the room were the light table with blueprints rolled out over it, the opened laptop on the desk, and a small Tiffany lamp which illuminated the organized chaos that was the top of the large desk's surface.

The man sitting behind the desk had aged so much since she'd seen him last. He hadn't been part of the reluctant welcoming party the evening before, and she hadn't seen him in going on seven years.

He looked up from the book he had open in his hands, his light blue eyes looking small and beady behind the thick lenses of his round-framed glasses. His ever-present beard was trimmed as usual, but snow white, just like his full head of hair. Last she'd seen him, there had been some light brown mixed in, the same color as Dawson's hair.

"Hey, Dad," she said, her voice low and quiet, keeping in the feel of the dimmed room. "How are you?"

He pushed away from the desk, tossing the book atop a stack of papers and rolled blueprints. He looked like he belonged buried in the stacks of a library or academia with his sweater-vest over a crisp white buttoned dress shirt, replete with bow tie. He certainly didn't look like he was the brilliant architect he was.

"Hello there," he responded, large hands shoved into the hip pockets of his loose-fitting corduroy trousers. "Good trip home?"

She nodded. "Long, but good."

The two stood in awkward silence for a moment before Ogden finally made his way around his desk and offered a quick one-armed hug, which Faith returned.

"Let's sit," he said, moving away from her and indicating the old, tattered couch that she remembered in the den of their house when she was a kid. Now, however, it was tucked into the corner of the office and was covered with papers as well as a wool blanket. He moved everything aside to create a space for them to sit.

"How're things?" she asked, not sure what else to say. The energy in the room was stale, uncertain.

Ogden nodded, reaching up to run a hand over his beard. "Finished up the project down in Albuquerque I emailed you about last year. Been working really close with that young architect we hired on in May, Tammy. She's doing a real fine job."

"That's great. I'm glad you picked a woman." Faith gave him a shy smile before turning away, eying all the framed awards that filled half the wall space across the room from them.

"How about you? What's your plan? Is the guest room okay for your needs?"

She glanced over at him, wondering if he was being facetious. Nope. Serious as a heart attack. "Um, well, I'm appreciative for the space in her exercise room," she began, feeling a bit uncomfortable as she didn't want to come off as unappreciative. "It was fine," she finished lamely.

"What?" he exclaimed, the most fire she'd seen in him in years. "Exercise room?" Muttering to himself, he pushed up from the couch and stormed over to his desk. Opening the top drawer, he rifled through some things before producing what looked to be a hotel keycard. "Here," he said, holding it out in her general direction.

Surprised, Faith also stood and walked over to him. She took the card and looked at the plastic, credit-card-sized object before looking at him in confusion.

"We hold this room at all times," he explained. "We so often have designers and such come into town to work on projects with us that we found it cost-efficient to keep a few rooms booked at all times. Plus," he continued. "Tom used it during his divorce, and lord knows I've used it a time or two to get away."

Faith was saddened by the resigned tone of his muttered words. "Thanks." She pocketed the keycard, extremely grateful.

"What about work?" he asked, clearing his throat and adjusting his glasses as he met her gaze. "What will you do? Do you need money?"

"No, I'm okay." She shook her head. "I've got a little for now, but I intend to pick up whatever I can, be it McDonald's or Walmart, whatever, get some money coming in until I decide what I'm going to do."

Ogden studied her for a moment before he nodded. "A plan is good."

※ ※ ※

"Heaven," she muttered. "Pure heaven." With a dramatic flair, she spread her arms and legs wide, neither hand nor foot able to reach a corner. "I am definitely investing in a king-sized bed one day."

Sitting up, Faith rested on her elbows as she looked around the beautifully appointed room at the Hyatt Regency in the heart of downtown Denver. She climbed off the bed, still made to perfection, though the comforter was wrinkled from her tumble upon it, and walked over to the sitting area where some of her boxes had been stacked with the help of a well-tipped bellboy. There was no way she was going to leave her car a target of a break-in because it was loaded with earthly belongings.

She grabbed the large duffel bag that held some of her casual clothes and dug out a simple outfit to put on after she took a long, hot, soothing shower. She needed to wash off the road and the slimy feeling she had every time she saw Carrie, even though she had dinner at her father's house coming up in a few hours. Driving to the hotel, she'd noticed a business a few blocks away that she planned to visit, a change long overdue needing to be made.

※ ※ ※

She'd never been a fan of science class, always feeling sorry for the little mice sent skittering through the maze to try to find the cheese at the end or the beautiful butterfly pinned to the board and placed under glass. That was precisely how she felt in that moment, though she'd have given anything to go skittering off through a maze right now, only to never come out.

"What?" Faith asked, feeling the wall kiss her back as she took a step backward.

"Who the hell you think you're supposed to be?" Dawson laughed, crumbs from the handful of popcorn he'd just thrown into his mouth falling into his unruly lumberjack beard. Faith was disgusted.

"Or maybe she was going more for Winona Ryder." Carrie smirked from near the table as she began to set it for dinner, finally moving out of Faith's personal space.

"Who?" Dawson asked, looking over at his mother as he stuffed more popcorn into his mouth.

"You went back to your natural color," Ogden said softly, entering the kitchen. He looked at Faith, who eyed him warily considering the reception she'd been given from her stepmother and half brother. "It fits you better," he added with a nod. "Your mother was a brunette."

Feeling a bit shy, Faith brought up a hand and ran it over the dark brown pixie cut she was now sporting. "Really?" she murmured. So few memories of her mother, and somehow, all the pictures of her had disappeared years ago. Faith had always suspected Carrie of being responsible for that but had no proof.

Her father nodded at her question. "You look so much like her like this."

Faith could only stare at him. She'd never heard him talk about her mother, not since she'd been eight years old. Swallowing, a bit due to nerves and a bit due to surprising and confusing emotions, she nodded. "I needed the change."

"Can we end the lovefest here and be productive? It's hair, Ogden. Goddamn hair," Carrie complained, hand on hip as she glared at father and daughter. "Ogden, get the damn wine. Faith, get glasses from the china cabinet in the dining room."

Ten minutes later, the four of them sat at the kitchen table in silence, dinner sounds abounding: silverware scraping against a dish, small belch, drinking, the small thud of the dish of cream corn being put back on the table after a second helping was doled out onto a plate. Faith sipped her wine, eyeing the other three over the rim of her wineglass as she did. The food wasn't bad, Carrie being a half-decent cook when she wanted to be, but the company was anything but pleasing.

"So," Carrie finally said, her own glass of wine in hand as she studied Faith. "Have an eye on where you want to go, yet? Job?"

"Well," Faith responded, letting out a tired sigh. "Dad was kind enough to let me stay in one of the rooms at the Hyatt—"

"What?" Dawson asked, looking from Faith to his father. "Seriously? She can't hack it in New York, so you let her stay there?"

Cool as a cucumber, Ogden met his gaze. "She gave eleven years of her life working for a couple of misogynistic, ineffectual attorneys who denied her what was rightfully hers due to her hard work, dedication, and commitment."

"Are you serious?" Dawson said, turning his ire on Faith. "You came back here with your fucking tail between your legs because of that?" He slammed his hands on the table with a dramatic groan. "For fuck's sake, Faith! Three years I've put up with Joel Sandburg chewing my ass out because the traffic is so goddamn bad that I'm late. Have you seen the fucking traffic here?" he exclaimed, eyes wide. "Am I right, Mom?"

"Pretty bad," Carrie said with a nod just before putting a forkful of chicken casserole in her mouth.

"Do I quit? Fuck no." He slammed his palm on the table again, his fork nearly jumping off the table in the process. "I stick it the fuck out." He shook his head and grabbed his can of beer. "Pathetic," he muttered.

"Dawson, the two are hardly comparable," Ogden said in his quiet, calm way. "This is a career she worked very hard for, top of her class at the University—"

"Oh, I get it." Dawson slammed his beer can onto the table. Faith watched with wide eyes, wanting desperately to hide under the table. "I went to college, too," he roared. "But you don't care about that do you, *Dad*? All you care about is that fucking degree hanging on the wall. The what, what they call it, the fucking goat's skin? Well, fuck you!" He slammed back from the table, startling Faith, and even his mother looked alarmed. "Fuck you all!" He slammed out the front door, the sound of a car starting following moments later.

"Nice, Ogden," Carrie said, her voice deadly quiet. "Real nice." She, too, pushed up from the table and disappeared upstairs.

Left alone with her father, Faith had no idea what to do, what to say. She wasn't even sure if it was wise to breathe.

After a long moment, Ogden muttered, "I'm going to the office," then scooted away from the table and left the house via the inside garage door.

Shaken, Faith looked at the empty seats and half-eaten dinner and let out a long, shaky breath. "And they wonder why I never came home," she whispered. After a moment, she got up and put the leftovers into containers in the fridge, then took care of the dishes and pans before wiping the counters, stove, and table down with a dish towel. Finished with that, she quietly left the house.

Chapter Four

She looked around, ducking her head into the attached bathroom. The room was furnished with the bare-bones basics: bed, nightstand, and a tall, six-drawer dresser. There was room over by the window if she decided to buy a chair of some sort to relax and read.

"You said there's some storage space in the basement, too?" she asked, glancing at the cute little blonde who stood in the open doorway, casually leaning against the doorframe.

"Yup," she said, running a hand through her short, shaggy hair, making Faith itch to do the same. Though it had been a week since she'd cut hers, she still wasn't used to bringing a hand up to find most of her hair gone. "If you want to see it, Cam said I could take you down there. You can see whatever you want," she finished with a grin.

Faith gave her a shy smile in return. She'd thought the younger woman was cute when they'd met in front of the house she was looking to rent a room in, the house belonging to the woman's sister. She'd thought perhaps the taller blonde was flirting with her, but Faith was so out of practice with dating or even flirting, she figured it was more likely just in her head filed under "W" for wishful thinking.

"Yeah, I'd like to see that. And, the storage is included with utilities in the rent price you and your sister quoted me, right?" Faith asked, hands on hips as she gave the room another once-over.

"Yup. All part of it, along with helping out with the dog," the other woman replied.

"Right. Bruno, we met in the backyard," Faith said, eyeing her companion, who nodded. "And, she's okay with me going month-to-month, right? You told her?"

"Yup," the woman said, holding up her phone to show a text message conversation on her screen. "Cam said so right here."

Faith nodded, turning her thoughts away from the cute young blonde to the situation at hand. She chewed on her bottom lip as she considered the money she had in the bank and what she'd be making on her first check at her new job as a receptionist in a Realtor's office. She felt comfortable that she could make it work. She wasn't too keen on renting a room in someone's house, but didn't want to get into a tight financial spot with her own place or buying something until she had a better idea of what was next for her.

She glanced back at the other woman, who returned the look with what seemed to be hope in her hazel eyes. "Show me the storage area," Faith said with a smile.

※※※※

"Hello, hello?" Faith growled as she punched another button on the desk phone base. "Hello? Mr. Swanson? Oh, Mrs. Graves. Yes, ma'am. I'll get you to Jill in a jiff." Her eyebrows fell when suddenly a dial tone was in her ear. "Hello?" She growled again, doing her damndest to keep her composure as she cradled the phone. "Son of a…" She glared at the phone before letting out another breath, trying to calm her nerves. "I got this," she said, blowing out another deep breath. "I got this."

Suddenly, Faith was mortified to realize she wasn't alone in the glitzy reception area of the somewhat over-the-top Realtor she was working for. Sitting in one of the stylish yet terribly uncomfortable chairs provided for those waiting to meet with the agents was the woman she'd come to know was named Trista. The one and only time she'd seen her was two weeks ago when she'd given Faith the tour of what would become her new home. Dressed in casual attire that day, today Trista was dressed in a security guard's uniform.

Running her hand through her short locks, Faith gave her a sheepish grin. "How long have you been sitting there?"

Trista pushed to her feet and sauntered over to the receptionist's desk, a grin on her face. "Long enough to see how adorable you are when you're flustered."

Faith looked away, knowing damn well she was blushing a bit. She cleared her throat and forced herself to look up at the woman who stood on the other side of her desk. "I swear I'm not this stupid," she said, indicating the complicated desk phone. "I passed the bar my first try, for crying out loud!"

Trista gave her a side glance, an eyebrow raised. "A lawyer, huh?"

"Yeah, well, one on vacation, anyway." Faith sat back in her chair and chuckled. "What are you doing here? Are you waiting for Jill or Stephanie?"

"Nope, waiting for you. Cameron just so happened to mention where you work, and I just got off work, so I figured I'd swing by and see if you had dinner plans."

Faith studied the adorable younger woman for a moment, slightly cocking her head to the side. "Just so happened, huh?"

"Well." Trista grinned, resting a hand on the desktop. "There might've been some money exchanged, I just can't remember."

A bark of laughter burst from Faith's lips. "I see. Only problem is, I don't get off until five."

"Fine, I'll pick you up at seven," Trista said, pushing away from the desk and sauntering toward the door in the same amusing fashion she had made her way over. "After all," she added dramatically. "I know where you live." She flipped non-existent long hair and pushed open the tinted glass door before exiting the building.

Faith laughed again, shaking her head as she dug out the owner's manual for the phone.

☙❧

"What do you think?" she asked, turning from the standalone mirror she'd bought to the dog, who lay on her bed. "Necklace or no necklace?" Her response was a wide and noisy yawn before Bruno rolled over from his left side to his back, the brown-and-white Boxer making his Boxer sounds. "Very helpful bud. Very, very helpful."

Turning back to the mirror, Faith took in her reflection. She'd gotten home in enough time to grab a quick shower, not that her job was all that physical, but still. She wasn't entirely sure what Trista's intentions were for dinner, though she assumed it was likely not exactly going as friends. Faith was nervous about it, as Trista was ten years her junior according to her sister, who had mentioned it in passing conversation as they'd gotten to know each other. Not only that, but she hadn't been on anything that resembled a date in more years than she had fingers on one hand.

"Okay," she blew out, thinking she looked okay, dressed casually, but nice. It was a cold late-January night, snow expected the following day. Reaching up to do a few light touches to her hair, she was ready.

≈≈≈≈

"Thank you," Faith said to the host, who seated the two ladies.

"Your waitress will be with you shortly," he said with a smile and a menu to each of them.

"So, you were saying?" Faith said, glancing across the table at her companion as she opened her menu. "Youngest of six kids?"

"Yes, ma'am," Trista said with a sigh, opening her menu. "It's funny, even though Cameron is the second to the oldest, she and I are the closest."

"All girls?" Faith asked, trying to imagine growing up with so many siblings. She felt like she'd largely grown up as an only child, considering Carrie all but had Dawson hanging off her teat his whole life.

"One boy, the oldest." Trista smiled up at the attractive young woman who stepped up to their table. After they both ordered drinks and an appetizer to share, the waitress left them alone and Trista looked to Faith again. "What about you? Your family?"

Faith spared the cute blonde a brief glance before

looking back to her menu. "My dad has been married to my stepmom since I was a kid," she said softly, not entirely sure why she told her only part of the story.

"Divorce," Trista said, shaking her head. "Hard on kids. But," she added, her finger pointing up to emphasize her point. "I honestly think if my parents had split years ago, it would've made life easier on everyone."

"Why didn't they?" Faith asked, glad to have the spotlight taken off her and a subject she wasn't fond of.

"Catholic," Trista said simply, waiting for the waitress to get their drinks settled and leave again. "Honestly, they claimed to have so many kids because of their religious beliefs, but I truly think they kept pushing out kids to keep their marriage together."

"Marital problems are never a reason to have kids," Faith said, shaking her head. "I think that's where my half brother Dawson came from. One day I'm pretty sure Carrie, my stepmother, is out, the next she's whooping with joy that she's pregnant. Now, here we are with her kid, almost thirty and living with Mommy and Daddy's money." She shook her head again. "Just…damn."

"Assholes like your brother give us Millennials a bad name." Trista added with a sheepish grin, "No offense. But, it seems like we fall into one of two categories." She brought up a hand and ticked the first off on her fingers. "Either they're like my sister, Cameron, the overachieving doctor, or like me, working two jobs to make it work. Or." She ticked off a second finger. "They're living with their parents, maybe working, maybe not working, but definitely not adding anything useful to society."

"Dawson is definitely in the second camp," Faith said. "To my knowledge, he doesn't pay rent. I'm pretty sure they bought him his car. I mean," she added, leaning forward slightly in her disgust. "His mother gave him gas money, for crying out loud."

As dinner continued and their food arrived, Faith found she was enjoying the company. She was amused by Trista's stories of being a security guard at an area hospital, and how often she was mistaken for a cop.

"You've seen me in my uniform," Trista said, pushing her plate away, mere scraps remaining of her dinner. "Other than being a hot lezbo living a stereotype, I'm clearly not a cop."

Faith laughed, enjoying Trista's self-deprecating humor. "Well, hey, if you're living a stereotype, they say the ladies like a girl in uniform. Maybe it's not so much mistaking you for a cop, but liking the idea of dominance."

Trista sat there for a moment, eyebrows drawing as if in thought. Finally, one raised, and she eyed Faith. "I like the way you think."

Faith grinned. "Hey, this noggin gets used for more than hats."

"What about you?" Trista asked, her tone taking a decidedly sexy turn as she leaned forward a bit.

Faith felt her stomach flip and breath slightly catch. The look in Trista's hazel eyes was pure sex, and she wasn't entirely sure how she felt about that. "What about me?" she managed.

"You like a girl in uniform?" Trista's tone was clearly that of a woman fishing for information.

Faith realized that the younger woman wasn't entirely certain if she was a lesbian or not. Was she so out of practice that she came off as, god forbid, straight? "I like a girl in uniform," she admitted quietly, holding Trista's gaze. "Or nothing at all." There. Can't get any clearer than that.

A slow smile slid across Trista's adorable features. "As I said, I like the way you think."

An hour and a half later, Trista pulled up in front of her sister's house. She put the car in Park and cut the engine, which made Faith's heart skip a beat.

"I really appreciate you being so understanding about cutting the evening short," Trista said, releasing her seat belt as she turned slightly in her seat to face Faith more full-on. "The five a.m. shift sucks."

"I'm sure, and I completely understand," Faith responded, also releasing her seat belt. "I appreciate dinner. I went fully expecting to pay for my own ravioli."

Trista chuckled. "Yeah, but what kind of date would that be if you paid for your own? I mean, I gotta impress you somehow."

Faith smiled, amused, even as her stomach flipped again as the energy in the car began to shift. "I see," was all she could say.

"So, you wanna go out with me again?" Trista asked, her hand reaching over, fingers absently running in random patterns on Faith's thigh down by her knee.

Instant tingles flew through Faith's body, landing squarely between her legs and making her want to squirm. Somehow, she managed to stay put. She met Trista's gaze through the dimness of the car, only lit by the streetlight down the road and the porch lights of the houses around them.

"I really want to kiss you right now," Trista said

softly, her fingertips becoming a bit more bold as they trailed up a bit to mid-thigh, then slowly back down to Faith's knee.

"You know I'm, like, ten years older than you, right?" Faith said, a little breathless as her arousal—and nerves—kicked in overtime.

"So?" Trista smirked. She leaned in a bit, her hand drifting up from Faith's thigh to cup her jaw. "Doesn't matter."

Faith held her breath, her heart racing and eyes sliding closed as Trista neared. The first touch of those inviting lips was heaven, a forgotten softness and a forbidden delight due to her self-imposed exile from the touch of a woman. She sighed into the kiss as it deepened a bit, Trista's lips opening slightly to invite a deeper connection.

Trista's hand slipped into Faith's hair, the move used as leverage to pull them closer together as just the barest touch of a soft tongue glided against Faith's. A thrill of sensation shot through Faith like a silver bullet, leaving a trail of fire in its wake. That fire ignited her as much as it brought her back to reality, a reality she wasn't ready for just yet.

Pulling back, Faith turned her head, breasts heaving with her heavy breaths. "I'm sorry," she murmured, a hand coming up to her chest in an attempt to calm herself, ground herself to the car in which she sat and the cold night that surrounded the vehicle. Taking several deep, cleansing breaths, she finally met Trista's gaze.

"Too much?" the younger woman asked, her hand resting once again on Faith's thigh.

"Too soon," Faith responded softly.

"Did I screw up?" Trista asked. For the first time,

she seemed unsure of herself. That made Faith sad.

"No," she said, shaking her head. She took the hand that was sliding off her thigh and held it in both of hers. "No," she said again. "It's just been a really long time." She studied the adorable security guard for a long moment before smiling. "Give me a call or a text and let me know what your upcoming schedule is. Okay?"

"Yeah?" Trista asked, eyes brightening and her confidence seeming to slide back into place as she sat up a bit straighter.

"Yeah." Faith leaned toward her and left a lingering kiss on Trista's lips before letting herself out of the car.

Chapter Five

"This looks amazing, Jill."

Faith smiled over at Stephanie, who was grinning ear to ear at the plate of food that had just been set before her. She sat in the dining room of her bosses, who to her shock had been together for nearly twenty-five years, married for six. Working for the duo, she'd had no idea they were anything more than business partners.

Looking at them now, it was easy to see, even as different as they were. Jill Boise was fifty-nine and very old-school lesbian tonight in her casual high-waisted jeans with belt over a tucked in polo shirt, as opposed to her women's suits tailored with a masculine bent at work. Her short hair was left to go naturally gray.

The complete opposite side of that coin was Stephanie Jerkins, with makeup at work that looked as though a professional artist had done it mere moments before, shoulder-length stylish black hair, and wicked-sharp polished fingernails. She looked far more like she'd been a single career woman eating men alive for thirty years than in a happy, monogamous lesbian relationship for a quarter of a century.

To see the two at home, relaxed—Stephanie in a pair of flannel pants and slippers, a comfortable-looking Mickey Mouse sweatshirt, no makeup, and hair pulled back in a ponytail—it all made sense. The two looked like they absolutely belonged together. It was clear, in their beautiful home in Highlands Ranch, that the two were still very happy together.

"Thank you," Faith said as her food was placed before her, the steak cooked to perfection and potatoes and greens fragrant and gorgeous.

"You got it," Jill said, taking her own plate from the top shelf of the small cart she'd rolled in from the kitchen before taking her seat next to Stephanie, across from Faith. "Anyone need anything before I dig in?" she asked, looking over at her wife and then Faith, eyebrows raised in wait of a response.

"Nope. Everything's lovely, baby," Stephanie said.

"Good here," Faith agreed. She began to cut up her steak into bite-sized pieces and glanced up at the two. "Why do you guys keep your relationship a secret?"

Jill eyed her as she used her fork to stab some asparagus and scalloped potatoes on the same bite. "We don't."

"I mean in business. I've been working for you gals now for, what, about a month or so, and I just found out you two were not only a couple, but have been together for a really long time."

The two women exchanged a glance, the kind of silent communication of two people who had been connected for a very long time, before Stephanie began to explain. "When we started our real estate company seventeen years ago, we considered catering to the LGBT community, as there was very little like that in the area at the time, but we decided to keep it on the down low when we realized there's an almost..." She looked away from Faith, as though trying to think of something specific.

"Almost like an underground railroad," Jill supplied.

"Yes! Exactly. Word of mouth spread in the shadows about business owners like us," Stephanie said, indicating herself and Jill with the motion of her hand. "So, while in the light of day you get to sell houses and buildings to good ol'-fashioned straight people—"

"I sold an apartment complex for one of those dipshit MAGA people," Jill exclaimed with an evil grin. "Dude was too far into his own bigotry to realize he was giving an absolutely beautiful commission check to a pussy-eating dyke."

"Jill," Stephanie admonished, a minor look of disgust on her face.

"Sorry."

Faith watched the two, amused by their behavior and clear connection. She was astounded how they were able to hide it at the office yet radiate it in their home.

"But, we also gathered quite the large 'family' clientele, as it were," Jill added. "It's hard to look at us, especially her, and know we're not gay." She chuckled, nodding toward her wife. "But people see what they want to. It's helped us build a very successful business."

Which," Jill said, setting her wineglass down after taking a sip. "Now that you've mastered the phones, we wanted to let you know you're doing a fantastic job for us."

Faith brought a hand up to cover her face, embarrassed. "Yeah," she said from behind her hand. "Your phone system was nearly the death of me." Grinning, she allowed her hand to drop into her lap. "But, I prevailed."

"And got a steak dinner for your trouble." Stephanie laughed, a forkful of food halfway to her mouth.

"We just wanted you to know you're doing a great job and we appreciate you," Jill said, cutting up more of her steak. "Now that you've been with us a full forty-five days, well, as of Tuesday, anyway, we're giving you a raise."

"Typically, we wait until ninety days," Stephanie added. "But we're making an exception for you."

Faith looked from one to the other, stunned. "You're serious?" At the nod she got from both women, her surprise grew into a smile, feeling pretty damn good about herself. "Thank you. Wow." She sat back in her seat, basking in the feeling of being appreciated, a very new one for her professionally. "Thank you," she said again.

"So, speaking of couples," Jill said, leaning forward slightly as she pinned Faith to the spot with brown eyes. "How's it going with that cute little blond security guard?"

Faith smiled, the face of the woman she supposed was her girlfriend flashing before her mind's eye. She preferred to think of her as the woman she was seeing. "It's going okay. Only been a handful of weeks, so…"

"She good in bed?" Jill asked, popping her last bite of steak into her mouth.

"Jill." Stephanie shot her wife a look. "That's rude."

"What?" Jill asked, glancing over at her wife before looking back to Faith with an expectant gaze. "They're young. Probably screwing like bunnies like we used to."

"Uh, well," Faith sputtered, clearing her throat as she shifted slightly in her seat. "I uh, I don't know.

We haven't had sex yet."

It would have been comical how both of them looked at her, eyes nearly bugging out of their heads, if Faith hadn't been so embarrassed by their reaction to such a personal decision.

"What?" Jill gasped. "What do you mean? She cold, or something?"

"Not even on Valentine's Day?" Stephanie added.

Faith cleared her throat again, looking down at her plate, which suddenly didn't look so appetizing. These were questions she'd been bothered by, too. "No."

"Are you not into her, Faith?" Stephanie asked gently. "She's certainly attractive."

Faith nodded. "She is, absolutely. And, yeah, I like her." She let out a long breath and shrugged. "I don't know. It's been a really long time for me. Guess I'm just nervous."

"What, you haven't been laid in a long time?" Jill asked with her ever-present directness.

"Or, have you not dated in a long time?" Stephanie's tone was a bit more understanding and gentle.

"Yes," Faith said, forcing a smile and not at all enjoying this sort of spotlight being shone on her. "Back in New York, I really just had to cut any sort of personal life out." She shook her head. "Just wasn't conducive to what I was trying to achieve professionally."

Sadness in her light blue eyes, Stephanie shook her head. "No job's worth that, sweetheart. You're human, too."

Faith nodded, sending a smirk her way. "Yeah. Too bad it took me until I was nearly forty to figure it out."

"Eh," Jill said, waving off her words. "You're still young. I will say, however," she added, a finger raised to emphasize her point. "The fact that you haven't jumped that hot little mamma tells me somewhere inside you know she's not right for you."

"Jill, that's not fair," Stephanie chided. "Leave her alone to make her own choices and figure out what's right and not right."

༄༄༄༄

Driving home, Faith considered the conversation with her bosses, their input on the situation, and her own feelings about things. Truth was, she'd been trying not to think too much about her relationship with Trista, specifically the lack of physicality between them. They kissed from time to time and Trista was affectionate with her, would grab her hand or put a hand on Faith's thigh while they were in the car. But, Faith struggled with her own acts of affection.

Growing up, her father had been less than affectionate, and while Carrie had offered it, it had largely been weaponized. So many times, if Faith had done something to anger or simply displease her stepmother, Carrie would give her the iron silent treatment. This consisted of ignoring anything Faith said, talking to her incredibly sparingly, or talking to her through Ogden or Dawson and pouring the sugar extra sweet on Faith's half brother. He would get even more hugs, even more kisses, even more praise, and even more attention.

Eventually this behavior from Carrie had not only pitted sibling against sibling and caused a permanent fracture in their relationship, but it had also taught Faith not to trust affection and those who offered it.

Faith slowed her Element as she neared a yellow traffic light that she knew would be turning red any second, pulling up to a stop next to a red pickup truck. She glanced over at it and saw a man behind the wheel and a woman as his passenger. She was laughing as the man was talking in an animated fashion. Faith smiled simply at the obvious joy the woman was getting from whatever he was telling her.

Turning away from them, she stared straight ahead waiting for the light to change again, once more getting lost in her morose thoughts of her own shortcomings when it came to affection. Like anyone, she wanted affection—in fact, desperately needed it—but struggled mightily giving or receiving it.

Once nice thing about having Bruno in the house: she absolutely smothered the dog because she had so much bottled up affection to give, and animals were the best to give it to. They'd never turn you down, never turn their backs on you, and never punish you with it.

Ten minutes later, she was giving loves and baby-talking to the dog in question. He whined and pranced, excited she was home. His mommy, Cameron, was working as the ER doctor on the overnight shift, so Faith had promised to be home in plenty of time to make sure Bruno was taken care of for the night.

"You hungry, big guy?" she asked, giving his large head one more rub before making her way from the front door—as far as he'd let her get—through the dark house to the kitchen, flipping on the kitchen light once she entered the room.

Getting his dinner ready after she unlocked and

opened the back door for him to run out into the backyard to do his business, her thoughts turned to Trista. She agreed with Jill's assessment of the younger woman: she was cute, she had a hot-as-hell body, and, what her bosses didn't know, she was clearly willing. She'd made it very obvious that all Faith had to do was say the word.

So, why hadn't she?

She let that question marinate in her brain as she finished her nightly routine after getting Bruno fed and settled. She washed her face, brushed her teeth, and changed into the tank top she slept in and cotton pajama pants. She lay in bed, the bedside lamp spreading a warm, buttery light on her thoughts. She stared up at the ceiling of her bedroom, not seeing it but instead seeing sexy, hazel bedroom eyes. She was imagining how small, soft hands felt on her breasts.

A little thrill went through her at the thought. Faith could feel her nipples tighten and, upon slowly sending a hand beneath the covers and under the waistband of her pajama pants and panties, gasped at the amount of growing wetness she found there. She closed her eyes, caught between pleasant surprise and disgust with herself for being so weak.

Her eyes shot open at that last thought. "No," she muttered, shaking her head where it lay on the pillow. "I have the right to want to be touched." Just like her therapist had told her.

Sitting up, Faith didn't allow herself to think, but instead reached over and grabbed her cell phone from where it lay by the lamp. Taking a deep breath, she dialed and waited for the call to be answered.

"Hey," she responded when it was. "What are you doing right now?" Heart pounding, she forced herself to say, "Your sister's gone all night. Wanna come over?"

Twenty heart-pounding minutes later, Faith's breath hitched when she heard a car pull into the driveway, the headlights washing across one of the windows of her bedroom. Taking a deep breath and swallowing hard, she positioned herself in the bed on her side, head held in the palm of her hand as she stared at the opened doorway of the bedroom, Bruno running to the front door barking.

She heard a key slip into the lock of the front door, then the door open and an excited Bruno greet the visitor before the door was closed and locked, footfalls making their way back to Faith's bedroom. Moments later, Trista appeared in the doorway dressed in track pants and a hoodie. She stood there, looking at Faith.

"Um," she hedged, looking behind her then back to Faith. "Is this what I think it is?" she asked, teasing in her voice.

"What do you want it to be?" Faith felt a bit coy, even as her nerves plagued her.

Trista gave her a sexy grin before she reached down and whipped off her hoodie, revealing a T-shirt as she tossed the heavy jacket to the floor on her way to the bed. She startled Faith by jumping on it, landing on the comforter next to her, their faces mere inches apart.

"Fantasy come true?" Trista murmured.

Faith ginned, meeting her gaze, her body warming substantially with Trista's closeness. "Could be."

Trista unceremoniously removed her tennis shoes with violent shoves and pushes from the opposite foot, the shoes falling to the floor one at a time with a thud. Once they were off, Trista moved more fully on the bed, partially on top of Faith, the thick layer of covers between their bodies.

Faith allowed herself to get lost in the passionate kiss Trista initiated. She buried her hands in short blond hair, pulling the younger woman closer. After a long, breathless moment, Trista pulled back, both breathing heavily. She looked down at Faith with eyes that were on fire.

"Jesus, I fucking want you," she growled.

"I want you, too," Faith whispered back, her gaze falling to Trista's lips as the words left her own.

※※※※

Faith was brought into the early morning reality by the feel of a hot, wet mouth wrapped around her right nipple. Her eyes remained closed as she relaxed into the sensation, her hips moving slightly of their own accord.

"Sorry," Trista murmured around the nipple before her tongue flicked it and that mouth moved up to Faith's neck as her body moved atop her. "I gotta get going, I got work early," she continued, insinuating a thigh between Faith's spreading legs. They both moaned as she pressed into Faith's growing wetness, Trista's thigh instantly painted by Faith's wet heat. "But," Trista explained, moving against that thigh. "I needed to make you cum once more time."

Faith said nothing, simply reached down and squeezed Trista's gorgeous ass as it moved. She raised her thigh just a bit, pressing harder up into Trista's need before her hands ran up a smooth, strong back and around to cup small, firm breasts. Trista's body was very much that of an athlete, perhaps a soccer player.

Trista's quickening breaths were hot against Faith's neck as they moved faster together. Faith moved her hands from soft breasts to wrap her arms up and over the back of Trista's shoulders. She wasn't going to last long, her orgasm hurtling forth at breakneck speed. Finally, she cried out, Trista following half a second later.

Both panting heavily, they held each other for a moment before Trista pushed up and off of Faith. Cheeks flushed, she ran a hand through her hair, making it spike. Faith grinned at the hairdo.

"I really gotta get," Trista said, leaning down and leaving a quick kiss on Faith's lips before climbing off the bed to gather her clothes and carry them to Faith's bathroom, closing the door behind her.

Feeling good, and certainly sated, Faith reached over and grabbed her phone to check the time. It was nearly six, and she knew Trista had to be at work by seven thirty. With getting home and traffic, it would be cutting it close. Luckily, it was Saturday morning.

Noting she had an unheard voice mail, she dialed in her code and listened to the first one, which was Jill reminding her to come hungry the night before. She chuckled at the useless message, which she'd never gotten before arriving at her bosses' house for dinner. The second message played:

"Good evening. This message is for Faith Fitzgerald. This is Wyatt callin' about the raffle you entered. Wanted to let y'all know the ticket was drawn, and it was yours! Please give me a call back at your convenience for details. Bye, now."

Chapter Six

The familiar scenery passed by as Faith and Trista cruised along in the Element, now emptied of her earthly belongings, unlike the first and only time she'd taken this route. There was a bit less snow as they'd had a smattering of warm days over the past few weeks in this area of Colorado, just shy of two hours from Faith's residence in Aurora.

"So, let me get this straight," Trista said, glancing over at Faith from the passenger seat. "You stumbled into this place to pee and ended up winning something in a raffle, and that's why we're wasting an entire Saturday for this?"

"For the third time, yes, and for the fourth time, you didn't have to come today, Trista." She glanced over at the other woman, giving her a hard glance. "I told you I was fine to do this alone."

"Yeah I know," Trista said with a sigh. "Wynter, huh?" she asked, grabbing her phone from the cup holder she'd set it in. She activated the touch screen and began to swipe and tap on the screen until finally she smirked. "Wynter, Colorado, even spelled with a 'Y' instead of an 'I.' Cute."

"Probably named after somebody," Faith said absently as she glanced in her rearview mirror to make sure she wouldn't run into anyone as she went to switch lanes.

"Okay, here's what it says. 'Wynter, Colorado is

a small mountain town located—' blah, blah, blah," Trista muttered. "We know where the hell we are. 'In 1872, Jeramiah Isaiah Wynter entered the valley from where he grew up in Indiana, raised by incredibly religious parents—' blah, blah, blah. Ah, here we go."

Slightly amused at Trista's antics, Faith listened, curious about the little town they were soon to reach.

"'Wynter discovered a vein of silver ore in 1874, just two years before Colorado got its statehood. A boom ensued and the town of Wynter was established officially in 1890. A mining town for many years with a population reaching nearly 12,000 at its zenith, Wynter had to transition from the mining industry to the lumber industry when the mine ran dry in the early 1900s. By 1910, Wynter and the surrounding area provided nearly one-fourth of the building materials for the booming city of Denver.'"

"Wow." Faith spared a glance at her passenger. "Interesting. I love hearing how things like that get started."

"Well." Trista met her glance briefly before returning her focus to her phone screen. "Says here that, by the late 1980s, they'd bled this place dry. Totally deforested the area and the wood mill had to close down in 1994." She put her phone back in the cup holder. "After that, the place pretty much went to shit. Says by 2016, the population had dropped down to just over three hundred people living here."

"Holy cow." Faith shook her head. "Like a bunch of locusts, coming through and raping the land of all its resources, then once there was no use for the town, abandoned it." She felt Trista's gaze on her. "What?"

"That is so utterly depressing."

"But it's true," Faith argued.

"Yes. Yes, it is true."

Hearing the short history of the town gave Faith a bit of a different perspective as they entered the little place tucked into a valley. As she drove along the main street, she imagined the hustle and bustle of horse traffic, people traffic, excited miners ready to celebrate a hard week's work. No doubt there were brothels sprinkled throughout the town, right alongside saloons and—

"God, this place is a dump."

Trista's muttered observation pulled Faith out of her thoughts. She looked around, seeing the same buildings in the same condition and the same empty streets as she did when she had been there a couple months before. She didn't respond as she pulled the Element into the parking lot of Pop's, as Wyatt had instructed her to do when they'd spoken the previous weekend when Faith had returned her call regarding the raffle.

There were about four cars in the parking lot, which was about three more than the last time she was there. "Okay, let's do this," she said, cutting the engine and pulling the key from the ignition.

Climbing out of the vehicle, she noticed the guy from last time, sitting in the driver's seat of his sleigh as his horse lumbered its way down the street. To her surprise, he pulled over at the edge of the parking lot.

"You friggin' kidding me?" Trista murmured, partially laughing.

Faith sent a glare her way before smiling up at the man, who she was now able to get a better look at as he sat looking down at her. He looked to be in his seventies or eighties, his skin more like grizzled leather than the skin of an elderly man. His hair was snow white; at least, that's the color she saw from what was sticking out from the gray woolen flat cap perched on his head. He had a whisper of a mustache. She couldn't tell the color of his eyes, nearly hidden beneath the white caterpillars that were his eyebrows, but could tell they were on her.

"Hey there," she said, raising a hand in greeting. "Beautiful day for a ride," she added, indicating the sleigh and horse, which was a beautiful mare of brown, her white patches having grown over time with her age.

He said nothing but looked past her at whatever or whoever was behind her. Turning, Faith saw Wyatt hurrying from the "Employee Only" entrance to the café. She was wrapped in a winter coat and held a huge bag of something on her shoulder, holding what seemed to be a very heavy load steady with her hand. It brought to mind the observation during her first visit that Wyatt had incredibly strong arms. They didn't look like the arms of anyone who works out, lifts weights, or any such thing, but the arms of someone who lived a very active lifestyle, perhaps like a farmer or rancher whose body was the other tool in the pasture or field. In her free hand was a Styrofoam take-out container.

She smiled at Faith before doing a double take as she hurried by her to the sleigh. "Good mornin', Mr. Billy!" she exclaimed, holding out the Styrofoam container up toward him.

"I can't take this, Wyatt," he said, trying to push away the container. "It's too much."

"Now, Mr. Billy," the waitress scolded. "Mamma taught me that a gift is a blessin'. So, don't you go rejecting my blessin', now."

With a heavy sigh, just this side of annoyed, the older man took the container and set it on the seat next to his blanket-covered legs. "Thank you, Wyatt," he grumbled.

"Why, of course," she said, heaving the heavy sack onto the floor of the sleigh, the thud when it landed denoting the weight she'd been carrying on her shoulder. "Now, Mr. Billy, I want y'all to meet Faith Fitzgerald," she said, indicating Faith with a wave of her hand, "And, her friend—"

"Girlfriend," Trista interrupted, taking a slight step closer to Faith, who wanted to roll her eyes but didn't react or say anything.

"My apologies," Wyatt said with a warm smile. "And, this is Faith's girlfriend, Trista. This handsome fella here is William, though some call him Billy." She walked over to the horse, who instantly took to nuzzling Wyatt's hair. She giggled, sounding like a little girl as she rubbed the horse's nose. "And this feisty lady is Stella, twenty-one years young."

Faith smiled. She knew nothing about horses, had rarely been around them in her life, but thought they were beautiful and majestic animals. "It's certainly nice to meet you both," she said. Trista said nothing, though William studied Faith with hard eyes for a long moment before he looked away, clearly getting ready to leave.

The pretty young redhead and older man chatted quietly for a moment. Then, with an encouraging shake of the reins and click of Billy's tongue, Stella began to move, pulling her passenger and his load back onto the snow-covered street.

Faith watched him go, for some reason fascinated by his mode of transportation. She was brought out of her reverie when she felt a tug on her jacket sleeve.

"Come on, let me get you ladies out of the cold," Wyatt said, hurrying back toward the building and the doorway she'd exited from, ushering Faith and Trista inside ahead of her.

They were led through the kitchen of the café, the two men dressed in white aprons and caps glancing their way as they prepared orders. The kitchen was hot and smelled of various foods, from frying bacon to freshly cut onions to baking bread. Racks were placed strategically, the metal shelves filled with pots and pans, three stacks of clean plates and bowls and plastic buckets of clean silverware separated by purpose.

Wyatt unzipped her jackets as they made their way through the maze of racks and cabinets. "Go on out that door," she directed, pointing to a metal door with a portal window. "It'll take ya to the hallway by the restrooms." She stopped at a door that opened to a tiny office. "Be with y'all in a sec."

"When the hell did we leave Colorado and enter Country Bumpkin land?" Trista asked as they made their way down the hall and past the jukebox, which was silent. "That chick with that thick-ass accent then the dude on the horse?" She grinned and shook her head as they walked to one of the empty booths. "Crazy town."

"Be nice," Faith said, beginning to regret inviting Trista on her trip. She turned away from the younger woman and saw Wyatt tying her apron into place as she pushed through the swinging door to the area behind the lunch counter. Catching Faith's eye, she grabbed the coffee carafe and raised it in question. "You want some coffee?" Faith asked Trista, who glanced over to see what had caught Faith's attention.

"Yeah."

Faith raised two fingers, Wyatt nodding in acknowledgement before fulfilling their request. She glanced across the table at Trista, who was staring intently at something. Following her gaze, she saw that it was pinned squarely to Wyatt's incredibly shapely behind. Faith had to admit, nobody wore a pair of Levi's like Wyatt did.

Clearing her throat, she looked away, feeling as though she was ogling the waitress who had no idea she was being visually eaten alive by the lesbians at table three.

Minutes later, Wyatt carried a tray over to their table, which surprised Faith, as a tray shouldn't be needed for two cups of coffee. When she reached their table, she lowered the tray to reveal not only the two cups of coffee and a bowl of little creamer containers, but also two plates with huge, mouthwatering sweet rolls on them.

"I know y'all didn't order these," she explained, placing a cup on a saucer in front of each of them before a plate of warm, gooey goodness. "But I just made these fresh this mornin', so wanted to treat y'all."

"Oh my god," Faith muttered, eyes huge and her mouth literally beginning to water. "Looks like heaven on a plate."

Wyatt grinned as she set the bowl of creamers down on the table between them. "I hope you enjoy. I'll be right back to chat."

Faith began to dig in, unable to keep in her moan of pleasure at the first bite. She glanced up at Trista when she heard her speak.

"Where the hell is she from? Texas?"

Faith shook her head and swallowed the chewed food in her mouth before responding. "No, and I think she'd probably throw you around like that sack earlier if she heard you say that."

"Where's she from?" the younger woman asked, using the side of her fork to cut a bite off the sweet roll.

"Georgia." She took another bite, preparing her coffee as she chewed.

"What about Georgia?"

Faith looked up to see Wyatt step up to the table, untying her apron as she did. It was clear she planned to sit, so automatically Faith scooted over, reaching up to the table to move her plate and cup with her.

Wyatt gave Faith a smile of thanks as she sat down in the booth next to her, her beautiful turquoise eyes studying Faith's face and hair. "You have changed, I must say."

Initially confused, Faith realized that the last time they'd met she'd still had long, blond hair. "Ah, yes," she said with a shy smile, reaching up to lightly run her fingers through the short, dark brown pixie cut she sported. "Guess so."

"I like it," Wyatt said softly. "Suits you."

"So, what's up with this raffle thing?" Trista asked, garnering the attention of both the women sitting across from her.

"Well." Wyatt reached down into the pocket of her jeans and withdrew a single key, the size and look of one that would fit a heavy-duty deadbolt. "I was given this and an address. So, when you ladies are finished with your breakfast, I'll take you over there." She looked at them both and shrugged. "Beyond that, I'm as in the dark as y'all. But breakfast, by the way," she added, "is on the house since you came all this way for God only knows what."

※※※※

The two-story building of whitewashed brick was across the street and two doors down from the café. The front door was large and imposing, looking disproportionate to the rest of the building and its attributes. Faith found that interesting. There were no windows on the lower level in the front of the tall, narrow building, but two large windows were on the second level.

As she and Trista stood on the wood sidewalk behind Wyatt as she struggled with the lock, Faith looked up the face of the building to those windows. She had the creepiest feeling that they were being watched.

"Voila!" Wyatt, using her full body, pushed the large door open and stood aside for the other two to enter before her.

"Why do I feel like we've been sucked into a bad B horror movie?" Trista asked, looking past Wyatt into the darkness inside the building. "Like, we were lured to this rinky-dink town on some raffle hoax only to get us inside here where the town's serial killer is waiting to kill us so you guys can chop us up and put us on the menu at the café?"

Faith stared at her girlfriend, mouth open, not entirely sure what to say. She glanced over at Wyatt, who was looking at the youngest of the trio pretty much the same way.

"Uh," Wyatt finally said, meeting Faith's gaze with a shrug. "Sounds like a hell of a movie, but I'm just not clever enough to pull that one off."

"Come on," Faith muttered, walking past the other two and entering the building. She had to admit, though, now that the lofty and dramatic plot was vocalized, she found herself looking around a lot more, trying to make heads or tails of the impenetrable shadows.

The main room had surprisingly high ceilings from what she could see by the light coming in through the opened front door. They were easily twenty feet high, and were covered with what at one time would have been gorgeous tin ceiling tiles forming an elaborate pattern. They'd clearly been painted at some point, though a poor paint job had been done, rusted tin showing in places.

The building went back deceptively far, a set of stairs at the very back of the giant open room. The last thing she saw before the outside light was shut out was that it was completely filled with junk. It wasn't bags of trash, it was just…stuff.

Faith jumped at the sound of the slamming door and a muttered apology from Wyatt.

"All right," the waitress said, her voice moving around in the darkness, disorienting Faith as it was nearly pitch-dark in the huge space. "Hang on, ladies. I saw a lantern over here."

Faith stayed put, worried about tripping over something unseen, just as it sounded like Trista did, a muttered curse following.

"Eureka!"

The place was suddenly lit by a battery-operated lantern of the sort used in camping. The bar light was blinding, and Faith brought up a hand to shield her eyes.

"Oops. Sorry, y'all. Guess that's a little bright." Wyatt chuckled, clicking something on the lantern which brought the beam down to more of a 40-watt level from 5,000.

The light revealed a cabinet surrounded by the piles of stuff, but it itself had been cleared off. A thick layer of dust covered what looked to be cherry wood, but Faith could easily work out an algebraic equation atop that cabinet. On the dust-covered surface was the lantern and a thick, sealed, business-sized envelope, Wyatt's name scrawled across its surface.

Wyatt set the key down on the cabinet and picked up the envelope, sparing a glance at Faith before she used her thumbnail to make a tear large enough to use to carefully open the envelope. She reached inside and pulled a folded bundle of pages out of it. She unfolded the bundle and began to read. After a moment, her eyebrows shot up and she met Faith's gaze.

"What?" Trista asked, standing just behind Faith, her hand on Faith's hip. "What is it?"

Without a word, Wyatt refolded the pages and tucked them back into the envelope. She grabbed the key and held it against the envelope with her thumb as she reached across the cabinet toward Faith.

Looking from Wyatt's hand to her eyes, Faith shook her head. "What?"

"These belong to you," Wyatt said softly. "The key to the building, and the deed to the building."

Chapter Seven

Faith chewed on her bottom lip, her foot tapping a nervous beat as she waited. She looked from where Jill sat behind her desk up to where Stephanie was perched on the side of it. Jill finished a page from the bundle Faith had received from Wyatt then handed it to Stephanie, who placed the newly received paper in front of the one she'd just read.

"Well," Jill finally said after what seemed an eternity. She handed the final page to her wife. "It looks legit to me, Faith."

Stephanie nodded as she continued reading. "I agree."

"I would, however," Jill added, sitting back in the large, black leather executive's chair behind her desk. "I'd go talk personally to that Barbara Steele person with the Wynter County Historical Society as the grantor."

"The last thing you want," Stephanie said, tapping the pages together on Jill's desk to make them neat and orderly before handing them back to Faith. "Is to make a decision with the property and perhaps invest money into it only to have a lawsuit on your hands or to find out that, even though the paperwork looks right, was notarized and all that jazz, it was made under fraudulent circumstances."

Faith blew out a breath and nodded as she looked down at the paperwork in her lap, held in her hand. "Great point."

"If it's all legit," Jill said, eyes bright as she sat forward, the look of a giddy teenager on the face. "What are you gonna do with it? Is it worth salvaging?"

Faith shook her head with an exaggerated shrug. "I have no idea," she blew out with a nervous laugh. "My dad said he's willing to check it out for me, see what condition the structure is in."

"He's an architect, right?" Stephanie crossed her arms over her chest as she casually began to slowly move her foot back and forth where it dangled over the edge of Jill's desk, the other one planted on the floor.

"That's handy," Jill added at Faith's nod. "Best of luck with this, kiddo. Let us know if there's anything we can help you with."

❧❧❧❧

If anyone wanted to know what it felt like to stand motionless in an honest-to-goodness creepy place and see how long they could take it without saying, "Uncle," Faith would gladly sell tickets to her building. She'd met with the Wynter County Historical Society and felt secure in the fact that it *was* her building, in which she stood at the moment.

Gloved hands tucked into the deep pockets of her wool peacoat, one wrapped around the small walkie-talkie she was given, Faith stood just inside the door, which was closed as it was bitterly cold and snowing outside. She could feel the immensity of the dark space before her, almost as though the space itself were looking back at her. If she didn't know better—

and she would fully concede the fact that she may not know better—she'd say somebody was standing at the back of the main floor watching her.

Bouncing lightly on the balls of her feet to stay warm, Faith nearly was in need of an adult diaper when the walkie-talkie in her hand squawked to life.

"Okay, try it," came the deep voice from her pocket.

Faith withdrew her hand and walkie from her coat pocket and turned blindly to her right where she knew her father had left the switch for the system he'd set up before he'd headed back outside into the storm.

An audible sigh of relief left Faith's lips as the four, industrial-sized floor lamps all erupted into a life of bright, luminescent glow across the entire expanse of the main level of the building. It was the first time Faith had been able to see just what all she was dealing with, at least on the first floor: a true treasure trove of junk.

The door opened and Ogden blew in, snowflakes stuck to his wool flat cap. He removed it and smacked it against the leg of his pants absently as he looked around. Replacing the cap, he turned to Faith. "Someone liked to collect," he said before walking over to the canvas backpack he'd left with Faith before heading outside to hook up the mobile generator he'd hitched up to the back of his truck before he'd driven himself and Faith to Wynter.

Squatting before the bag, he unzipped it and pulled out two white hard hats, replacing his flat cap with one and reaching back toward Faith with the other in his hand.

Walking over to him, she took it, looking down at it before looking around. "Do you think this place is dangerous?" she asked, placing the protective gear on her head.

"Not sure," he said, shrugging into the backpack, which she knew held his tools of the trade, from flashlights and a laser distance meter to notebooks and any other number of things she'd forgotten the name and purpose of. "We'll see." He reached into the hip pocket of his baggy cords and withdrew the walkie-talkie that was the twin to the one she held. "Stay in contact, and remember, if it—"

"Bows, bends, or rocks, stop," she said in concert with him.

Nodding, he headed off toward the stairs at the back of the room.

Left alone, Faith let out a long breath, feeling slightly overwhelmed. In the month since she'd been given the deed for the property, she'd tossed around in her mind what she wanted to do with it. Once she found out for sure it was hers, the thoughts had gone into hyperdrive. Keep it? Sell it? Finding out it was on the National Registry of Historic Places, she knew she couldn't knock it down, nor could she do much to change the outside façade. But no matter what she ultimately did, she knew she had to clean it out.

Removing the knitted winter gloves she wore, she replaced them with the pair of latex gloves she'd stowed in her coat pocket for the very task she was about to perform. Not entirely sure where to start, she walked farther into the building, her gaze scouring the heaps and stacks of stuff. Her goal was to try to identify things, and decide what to do with them.

Chewing on her bottom lip, she walked over to the first stack she came to and visually sifted through it. She saw papers, newspapers, some books that looked to be badly damaged by water or neglect. The entire pile, from what she could see, would need to be trashed.

Remembering that her father mentioned in passing he had a roll of large yard bags in his truck, Faith hurried out into the storm to grab them. Though she knew she had to have them, she regretted that decision almost immediately. The wind had picked up significantly in the time she'd been inside. It was more gusts, and they were stronger, nearly blowing her into her father's truck.

Reaching out to brace herself against it, she took a moment to try to catch her breath as the wind died down for a brief moment, blown snow stuck in her eyelashes.

As she spit the snow out of her mouth and tried to blink away the flakes, she saw a large truck making its way up the road. It was the type with the rumbling Hemi engine, the back tires double, the large body shiny black. The passenger-side window was closest to her, and she realized as the truck got closer that Wyatt sat in the passenger seat. She was clearly crying.

Stepping away from her father's truck and toward the road, Faith couldn't take her eyes off the pickup that was passing by. Wyatt never looked at her, never looked up from what seemed to be her lap as she cried. It wasn't sobbing, but the type of tears that just seem to flow no matter what you do. Faith couldn't see who was driving the truck, the larger figure not much more than a silhouette, but she assumed by the size that it was male, and he was gesturing wildly.

Instantly, she felt anger rising within her. She had no idea what was going on, but it looked as though Wyatt was being yelled at or lectured like a child. She couldn't imagine what a sweet woman like the waitress could ever have done to deserve such treatment. She followed the truck with her eyes until it pulled up in front of Pop's.

She watched as Wyatt opened the truck door and nearly fell out of the large vehicle, seemingly in haste to escape the tirade from within. She scurried around the back of the truck then stopped at the employee door, Faith just barely able to see her. Wyatt's back was mostly to Faith, but from the movements of her body and hand, Faith surmised she was wiping the tears away from that beautiful face, replaced by the warm smile that Faith had seen both times she'd seen Wyatt.

Faith watched as the waitress disappeared inside the building, the employee door slowly shutting behind her. She walked back to her father's truck, wind forgotten, as she wondered how many times Wyatt plastered that smile on her face. Had one of those times been when Faith was in the café? Or was it just a bad day in the world of Wyatt the Waitress that morning?

Deciding it was none of her business, Faith retrieved the roll of trash bags and headed back inside the building, a big job ahead of her.

Opening the trash bag with a violent shake, Faith set it aside as she began to make a pile that would be trash in the tiny bit of space she made by using all her body weight to move a four-foot-tall stack of newspapers over.

She put the old books she'd seen before in the pile, making sure none of them could be salvaged. The earliest date she came across on the endless supply of newspapers was 1992. She shook her head as she tossed the papers onto the pile. It was a damn good thing the place hadn't caught on fire, she thought. There was enough kindling to make a bonfire that could be seen from space.

After three hours, eight bags had been filled to bulging and dragged outside to sit in a line by Ogden's truck. Wiping her hands against each other, she headed back inside, her peacoat long discarded and laid over the cabinet Wyatt had used the day of the raffle prize reveal. She stood in the space she'd made, which was a good radius of about eight feet. Hands on hips, she looked around the entirety of the main floor.

"Only about eight thousand more bags of shit to go," she muttered, smirking at her own joke, though she wasn't entirely sure how far off the mark she was.

Turning to her left, she studied the long object that had begun catching her attention as she cleared more and more stuff out. It was about eight feet long and about three feet high, though it was settled on a folded set of risers, the type that when extended formed a multi-level platform on which a choir could stand and sing. This extra added height brought the top of the long object to just a bit taller than Faith. It looked as though there was some sort of cloth or something covering it, but it was so shrouded in dust that she couldn't tell what material it was, or even the color.

Making sure there were no spiders in the general area and with a grimace of disgust, she grabbed at the cover. Initially her gloved fingers slid right off the material, but finally she got a good hold on it and, careful should the thing topple, slowly pulled the cover off, her grimace growing as a layer of dirt, dust, and God only knew what else slid off the material to rain down on the ground and her boots.

"Crap," she muttered, watching the mess gather. She shook off her left foot, the stuff falling to the ground. Looking back up, she continued to pull the material and found herself looking into lifeless blue eyes.

Crying out, she jumped backward, eyes wide and heart racing, only to feel a hand on her shoulder, which sent her whirling around, crying out again.

"Jesus God, Dad." She gasped, hand coming up to cover her racing heart.

"Scared you, did I?" he asked, looking past her. "Oh, look at that. I haven't seen one of those in years."

Still shaken, she turned to see him step over to what she'd revealed. Rolling her eyes, she stepped up next to him. "What the hell is that thing?" she asked, staring into those blue eyes before looking away.

"Mannequin head," Ogden said simply. "Look, she's got holes in her ears. She's bald now, but back in her day, they changed her look all the time by changing her hair, probably modeled earrings."

Faith studied the head, which had a graceful woman's neck that spread out into a woman's décolletage, ending just below the collarbones. "Necklaces, too." She grinned. "Makeup looks like Joan Collins from *Dynasty*."

"Probably not far off on the time period." He took a step back, looking over the revealed object. "Display case. Pretty good condition, too." He reached over and rapped his knuckles on the glass. "Real good condition." He glanced over at Faith, who met his gaze. "Probably get a decent penny for it."

The thought hadn't even occurred to her as she looked it over then scanned the rest of the area that needed to be gone through. It was a daunting task ahead of her, but perhaps she'd find some treasures.

"Hungry?" he asked.

Taking inventory of her body's needs, she nodded. "Yeah."

❧❧❧❧

The café was busier than Faith had seen it during her previous two visits, but then it was lunchtime. She saw Pops sitting at the cash register, the old man absent the time she'd been there with Trista. Wyatt was standing at the swinging door to the kitchen, which she held open, yelling something back to the cook before buzzing off to a group of five sitting at two tables dragged together.

Faith led her father to a table back by the jukebox, sitting in the chair that faced the breakfast counter. She saw Pops glance over his newspaper and reading glasses at her before he returned to his reading.

"What can I get you to drink?"

Faith was surprised by the sudden presence at their table before she'd even shrugged out of her coat. It was the young man she'd seen the first time at the café who'd been mopping.

"Uh, Coke," she said, looking at her father. "Do you know what you want, Dad?"

"Coffee's fine," he said to the waiter, sitting back in the creaking wood chair, arms crossed over his chest. The two left alone again, he reached up rubbed absently at his beard. "Somebody loved that building," he began, nodding at his own assessment. "Foundation got some work thirty years ago or so I'd say. Solid as a rock. Plumbing's shot, electrical is shot, but I think that's pretty much neglect. Couple of the floors upstairs have a pretty nasty slant to them, but not due to any foundation issues, the wood has warped. Get some new subflooring in there and new floors." He nodded again, meeting Faith's gaze. "Good to go."

"That is excellent news." Faith placed her coat on the back of her chair, utterly relieved. "Maybe it won't be so hard to get rid of."

"Thinking of selling?" he asked, hand stroking his beard then reaching up to pluck his glasses off his face before he began to polish them with the tail of his untucked button-up shirt.

"I really don't see the use for it," she said, waiting for the waiter to leave after dropping off their drinks before continuing. "I have no connection to this town, no reason to be here, and it's just far enough from Denver to not even be remotely practical."

He nodded, bringing the glasses to his mouth to slowly blow hot breath over one round lens. "Entirely up to you."

Faith studied him, analyzing his face and all the tiny clues that one had to know to look for to understand Ogden Fitzgerald. "You think I should keep it."

He met her gaze. "I think that building was once loved, and it would be lovely to see it loved again."

※ ※ ※ ※

Lunch finished and Ogden hitting the men's room, Faith stood at the cash register waiting for Pops to acknowledge her. When finally he did, she smiled.

"Hey, Pops," she said, handing over the twenty-dollar bill Ogden had insisted she use to pay the bill. "Didn't see you last time I was here."

"Hemorrhoids," he muttered, punching in the correct buttons on the ancient cash register. "Witch hazel," he added, nodding as though he was giving her the advice she sought.

She stared at him for a moment, not sure what to say. Finally, with a polite smile, she took the change and walked back to the table to leave a tip.

When she got there, Wyatt was already clearing it off, the lovely redhead gathering their dirty dishes onto a large round serving tray, including their condiment items and sugar shaker. She had no idea what to say, feeling a bit uncomfortable as she remembered when she'd glimpsed Wyatt earlier that morning.

Apparently feeling she was being watched, Wyatt stopped and glanced over at her, a surprised look on her face. "Goodness!" she said, hand to chest. "Sorry. You downright startled me."

"Sorry," Faith said sheepishly. "I was going to leave this for the waiter." She held out a few bills. "Can you make sure he gets it?"

"Of course." Wyatt took the money and put it in her apron pocket. She met Faith's gaze.

As Faith studied her, she saw the same woman she'd seen before, just as beautiful as she'd thought she was before, but this time she saw something in those turquoise eyes that either wasn't there before or that she'd simply missed: a deep well of sadness. It struck her so intensely she was nearly left breathless.

"Everything all right?" Wyatt asked. "Y'all have a problem with your food or anything?"

Forcing a smile to her face, Faith shook her

head. "No. It was fine." Out of the corner of her eye she saw her father headed her way from the hallway with the bathrooms. "Well, guess we're going to go."

Wyatt looked from Faith to Ogden and back to Faith, giving her a small smile before walking away, taking the tray with her.

Chapter Eight

Sipping her cup of coffee, Faith sat on the couch in the living room, Bruno sprawled out on the floor in front of the gas fireplace, which glowed with warmth. One hand wrapped around the handle of her mug, the other using her laptop which was open on the coffee table. Her fingertip slid across the sensory pad, moving the arrow to a link that took her to another article on her building. Over the past week since she'd left the tiny little town the previous weekend, she'd contemplated her unexpected situation.

At work, in between calls, reports, notes, and putting together property brochures, she'd snuck glimpses at the pictures of her building from its beginnings, all the way back to 1894. It was the very first permanent building in the town, thus the brick used. She was utterly intrigued.

From where he lay on his back by the fireplace, Bruno's tail began a lazy thump, thump against the thick floor rug. Faith chuckled, glancing over at him.

"Really, dude? Your mamma's home and you're too lazy to go greet her?" He whined in response and his tail thumped a bit more enthusiastically.

Faith continued to do her research as the garage door was opened before it whirred closed, Dr. Cameron Todd's 4Runner tucked safely inside. A moment later the small garage door that led into the kitchen opened and, finally, Bruno jumped up and ran into that room, his nails scraping along the wood floor in his haste to get there. Faith was amused at the sounds of the near-nightly ritual.

The emergency room physician greeted her dog with loud, dramatic baby talk, inciting excited barks and whimpers that grew louder as the pair made their way to where Faith still sat.

"Hey there," Cameron greeted, plopping down on the couch a cushion away from Faith.

"Howdy," Faith responded with affection. She'd grown to really like and respect her landlady and friend. "How was it today?"

"Busy, but not as bad as overnights," Cameron said, blowing out a tired-sounding breath. She was still dressed in her scrubs. She glanced over at Faith, reaching up to tug her ponytail free. "Damn, you look hot, chica. Better keep you away from Damian."

Faith chuckled. "Oh yeah, I am so hot to trot after your boyfriend." She met Cameron's amused gaze. "Trista has been after me to meet her friends, so," she added with a big sigh. "I agreed to go out with them to some club downtown."

Cameron's eyebrows quirked. "Damn, you're brave. You guys looking to get serious?" She raised her hands in supplication as Faith felt herself closing down. It must have shown in her eyes. "Hey," Cameron said softly, reaching over to lightly touch Faith's knee. "Listen, I love my little sister, but relationships come and go, Faith. As long as you don't do anything shitty to her or hurt her on purpose." The doctor shrugged. "I'm not going to hold anything against you. If you guys work out, great. If you don't, life goes on. My friendship with you or if you rent from me or not has nothing to do with that. Okay?" She slapped Faith's knee lightly before taking her hand away. "Honestly, I kind of think she put you in a tough spot pursuing you while you're living here, but…" She shrugged with a smirk. "My parents both spoiled Trista rotten, trying to make her love them more. Really messed up behavior on both their parts, very selfish. Now, Trista can be a wee entitled."

"I appreciate that, Cameron," Faith said, relieved. "I truly do. Honestly, I'd rather be curled up in bed reading right now, but it is what it is." She shook her head. "Funny thing is, I wasn't into bars and clubs when I was in my twenties, let alone now, pushing forty. Too busy trying to build my career."

"Preach, sister." Cameron laughed. "Preach." She leaned over toward Faith to get a better look at Faith's computer screen. "Is that what it originally looked like?"

"Yeah," Faith said, grateful for the change in subject. She fully trusted what Cameron had just said to her, but at the end of the day, blood still was thicker than water. She moved the computer over on the coffee table to be more centered between the two women on the couch. "This was taken in 1894, when it was built to be a saloon and boarding house for the miners."

"Boarding house." Cameron grinned. "Or bordello?"

"Yes," Faith exclaimed, making them both laugh. "Look at this," she continued, serious again as she scrolled through the pictures from over the years and various incarnations the building had taken on, ending with what it looked like at present, a picture she'd taken with her own phone last time she'd been there. "The place is still trashed despite what I got out last weekend, but my dad said it has some good bones." She glanced over at Cameron when she remained quiet and saw the doctor studying the picture.

"That building needs some love," she said at length, meeting Faith's curious gaze. "It hasn't been loved in a long time and it longs for it. You can feel the sadness."

Before Faith could ask her what on earth she was talking about, she heard a car pull into Cameron's driveway.

"Your chariot awaits, milady." Cameron pushed to her feet. "You crazy girls have fun tonight, and call me if you need a lift if you guys decide to get bombed."

༄ ༄ ༄ ༄

The V was like the few other thumpa thumpas she'd ever been in with its dark, dramatic lighting, deafening music, expensive drinks, and cramped dance floor. Hand held in Trista's, Faith was led through the busy club to the smattering of tables along the back wall.

Faith looked around at the other tables, which were all full. Most had groups of people leaning in over the round tabletops to be heard over the music, while one table had only two occupants, two women who were trying to outdo each other in shoving her tongue down the other's throat.

Grimacing, she turned away and focused on the table they stopped at. There were four people already seated, all women, though one she questioned, as "butch" didn't quite encapsulate the woman's look. She looked more like a man than many butch women did, but strangely she had a tank top full of cleavage that threw off the entire picture. She introduced herself as "Blaise." Faith found the name both appropriate and entirely unhelpful.

Trista completed the introductions all around, and Faith endured the lecherous stares aimed her way. Dressed in a tight tee that had a lower neckline than she'd normally wear and a short, tight leather skirt, she knew she looked good, looked the part of the club girl with spiked hair and smokey eye makeup. Truth was, it wasn't her, and she felt very uncomfortable. She figured one night of this and Trista would get it out of her system and they could go on having a little fun together.

"All right, let's get some drinks!" Trista clapped her hands, looking at the group of women and taking orders, Faith's last.

"Just a water, Trista," Faith said loudly into the younger woman's ear. "That way you can drink and have fun with your friends, and I can drive us home," she explained at Trista's disapproving look.

"All right. Be right back," Trista said, one of the other ladies going with her, the two quickly disappearing in the throngs of people. Faith took the seat abandoned by the friend who had accompanied Trista to the bar and sat in silence as the other three friends engaged in spirited conversation amongst themselves.

Shrugging out of the jacket she wore, Faith placed it on the back of the chair. Tapping her fingers on her thigh to the throbbing beat of the song, she smiled as a woman walked up to her, asking if she wanted to dance. She politely turned the stranger down, when what she really wanted was to ask the woman to drive her home, please.

What seemed like forever later, Trista and the woman returned, each carrying six shot glasses filled with clear liquid that caught the rainbow of changing lights in the club. She looked at Trista, noticing the absence of her water. Trista met her gaze and grinned, wiggling her eyebrows.

The two women reached the table and set the shot glasses down, doling out two per woman. "Okay, ladies, let's get this party started," Trista exclaimed, sliding Faith's shots to her.

"Where's my water?" Faith asked.

Trista wrinkled her nose. "Water's boring," she explained, taking one of her shot glasses in her hand. "We're here to have fun with my friends. Don't be such an old woman."

Faith could only stare at her, mouth literally falling open. She nearly tossed the shot she was handed into Trista's face, but decided the scene and drama wasn't worth it.

Trista raised her glass, the group following. Faith simply watched, bracing herself for whatever liquid fire was about to pass her lips. She winced and a violent chill rushed through her as she threw the shot back on cue with Trista's lead. Not a big drinker in general, and certainly not a hard liquor drinker, she knew it would hit her fast.

"Yeah, ladies!" Trista yelled, slamming her empty shot glass to the table and grabbing the second. "We drink!"

Faith looked at the second drink set in front of her on the table and was very dubious. She glanced over at Trista to see she was watching her. She felt warm anger slither through her at the look of expectation on her girlfriend's face. She knew it was the alcohol raising her emotions, but she felt them regardless of the source.

Feeling angry and a bit manipulated by Trista's clear expectation for Faith to impress her friends, Faith gritted her teeth as she grabbed the second shot. It was one night, and then she and Trista would be having a discussion. A long one.

"Come on," Trista said, grabbing Faith's hand and tugging her toward the dance floor.

"Don't let her get you to the bathroom!" one of her friends shouted, the others laughing and cat-whistling.

Trista turned to the group and flipped them the bird, Faith watching the whole thing, her head growing more and more fuzzy as the alcohol began to set in. The two shouldered their way to the center of the dance floor where Faith was pulled in close to Trista, her body heat nearly incendiary.

Focused on Faith, Trista gave her that sexy little smile that Faith had grown to appreciate. "You look hot as hell," the younger woman said into Faith's ear, her breath sending a little thrill down Faith's spine.

She said nothing, but did return the kiss Trista initiated, wrapping her arms around her neck as Trista's hand roamed down to Faith's ass, pressing them together. As her buzz wrapped a nice warm blanket around her, she felt sweet arousal ooze through her like honey.

"Why don't we head to your place?" she asked into Trista's ear, knowing her roommates were out of town for the weekend. She buried her fingers in Trista's hair. "What do you say?"

Trista met her gaze, fire and lust burning in those eyes.

Again, Trista grabbed Faith's hand and tugged her back through the crowd, Faith nearly taking an elbow to the face by an enthusiastic dancer. Seeing they were headed toward the front of the club, Faith tried to get Trista's attention that she needed to go back to the table and get her jacket, her keys in the pocket. Trista ignored her, continuing to tug her along behind. After a moment of confusion when they walked right past a sign that indicated the exit was off to the left, Faith realized Trista was headed to the bathrooms.

"Wait, Trista—"

Before she knew it, Faith found herself shoved into a bathroom stall, the door not even securely locked behind them before Trista's hands were all over her, roughly grabbing her crotch after reaching up her skirt.

Her shock wearing off, Faith tried to push the aggressive woman away. "Trista, stop—"

"Fuck, you're sexy," Trista growled, attacking Faith's mouth with her own.

Faith gasped as she was entered around the leg line of her panties by two fingers. She squeezed her eyes shut in pain and shock at the rough treatment, Trista acting more like an unhinged monster than the lover she'd known over the past many weeks.

"You're so wet," Trista groaned, shoving a third finger inside. "Fuck yeah, baby."

Faith's shock and anger was replaced with shame when she heard giggles from a group of women who had entered the restroom.

"Yeah, someone's getting some!" one of them exclaimed.

That shame turned to fury and that fury gave

her seemingly inhuman strength. "Get the fuck off me!" She shoved as hard as she could, sending Trista backward out of the stall and flat onto her ass just beyond the door that flung open with her sudden expulsion from the stall. "Don't you ever treat me like that again!" Faith raged, standing over the stunned blonde.

Marching past the group of women who were clearly no longer amused, Faith made her way back into the club, the tears hot as they flowed freely down her cheeks. She made her way back to the table where the butch woman sat, the other three friends of Trista's gone.

"Hey, you okay?" Blaise asked.

Faith said nothing, simply nodded as she grabbed her jacket and shrugged into it. She reached into the pocket and felt for her keys. Relieved when she grasped them, she cried out, startled when she was grabbed by the arm and whirled around to face a very angry-looking Trista.

"What the fuck, Faith?" she demanded. "What the fuck's wrong with you?"

"Wrong with me?" Faith gasped, stunned. "You attacked me, Trista."

"You said you wanted it, Faith!" Trista yelled, shoving Faith by the arm she still held.

Faith was left utterly speechless by this side of Trista. She knew they hadn't been dating for an extremely long time, but certainly long enough to have seen this sort of behavior. She was disgusted and downright scared.

Yanking her arm out of Trista's grasp, Faith could only stare at the woman standing before her. She looked like Trista, had her hair, her sporty casual dress, but her eyes were not those of the woman she'd shared her time and her bed with.

"I'm going home," she said.

Trista burst into laughter. "How the fuck you gonna get there, bitch?"

"Trista, dude, chill," Blaise said, standing from her seat and walking over to the two arguing women.

"Fuck off, Blaise," Trista said, glaring at her friend.

"Dude, you know you get stupid when you get all liquored up. I knew we shouldn't have had those drinks earlier before you picked her up. You need to chill, dude."

Faith looked from Blaise to Trista. "You were already drunk when you picked me up? You could have gotten us killed!"

Trista smirked. "When the fuck are you gonna get that stick outta your ass, Faith? You act like a fucking old lady." Trista turned her hateful glare to Faith. "Who the fuck are you to judge me?"

"Okay," Faith said, shaking her head as she backed away. "I'm not doing this."

"Where you gonna go?" Trista asked by a bark of laughter. "I fucking drove your ass here."

"I'll drive you home," Blaise said, stepping over to Faith, a kind hand on her arm before she turned to Trista, a finger pressed into her chest. "You, sober the fuck up before you fuck up another goddamn relationship."

※※※※

Faith sat in the passenger seat of Blaise's truck. The tears had returned, slowly sliding down her cheeks. She'd never been made to feel so cheap, so used as Trista had made her feel in that club. Not even by her former bosses in New York.

After a silent drive, the red Tacoma pulled up in front of Cameron's house. Faith brought up a hand and wiped angrily at her tear-streaked cheeks. She smiled over at her savior.

"Thanks for the ride," she said softly.

Blaise nodded, giving her a sympathetic smile. "I'm really sorry she acted like that. I know there's no excuse for it, but she'll regret it in the morning."

Faith nodded, then let herself out of the truck and up the path into the house. She was grateful that Cameron was in her bedroom, as she had no desire to talk to her or to answer difficult questions that she herself hadn't even fully analyzed yet.

Closing her own bedroom door softly behind her, she leaned back against it, standing in the dark safety of her room. It was then the tears really came. She could still feel Trista's fingers inside her and felt dirty.

Pushing away from the door, she stripped out of her clothes and headed to her bathroom, wanting a shower.

An hour later, Faith lay in bed, freshly showered and dressed in a T-shirt and flannel pants. Normally she slept just in panties and a tank top, but she felt the need to cover herself more fully. She pulled the comforter to her chin, feeling cold despite the hot shower. The chill was coming from inside

She stared up at the dark shadows covering the ceiling. She reached a hand out of her cocoon to angrily swipe at another tear that insisted on escaping. Her mind went back to the events of the night for the zillionth time, and it hurt just as much and was just as confusing on the zillionth as the first.

She wasn't sure if she should ask Cameron about Trista's behavior. Did she have a drinking problem Faith wasn't aware of? Did she have a problem that was even more nefarious she wasn't aware of? Either way, the relationship was done, but no woman should ever have to be treated that way, should ever be made to feel as she did in that moment.

Wiping away one last tear, she turned to her side and curled up as she closed her eyes, hoping sleep would sweep her away to sweet dreams.

※※※※

The sky was a perfect blue, not a cloud to be seen. She felt a peace wash over her as she removed one of three clothespins from where it had been held gingerly between her teeth, clasping one side of the sheet in place where she'd just placed it over the clothesline. Holding the next section in place with one hand, she used her other to retrieve the second clothespin, pinning the freshly washed sheet in place and finally the third.

She'd always heard about people hanging clothes out to dry, and honestly it had never occurred to her that it was a viable thing to do in the age of the clothes dryer. But, as her wife had shown her, it was a wonderfully fresh option.

Speaking of, she smiled when two hands appeared at her waist followed by two arms as she was hugged from behind. She placed her hands over those clasped at her belly. She heard a contented sigh in her ear as a chin was rested on her shoulder. Her attention was grabbed by the musical sound of a child's giggle followed by that of a barking dog.

Heaven. She was in absolute heaven.

Chapter Nine

Faith scrolled through the newsfeed on her social media account, chuckling at some of the posts, rolling her eyes at some, and sharing others on her own page. Her hand reached absently for the sandwich baggie of baby carrots, her fingers digging their way into the soft, malleable plastic until they came into contact with the cold, wet veggie nubs. Bringing one out, she bit it in two as she raised her hand with the remaining half pinched between thumb and forefinger and waved awkwardly.

"Just made fresh coffee," she murmured around the food to her boss who had just entered the small kitchen-style breakroom at the office.

"You are all that is good and holy," Jill said, raising her travel mug in salute as she walked over to the coffeemaker placed on the counter next to the fridge. "You didn't happen to get the Sterling building brochures back from the printers yet, did you?" the older woman asked, dressed in a tailored women's suit, the pocket square her only nod toward her natural masculinity.

"Yup." Faith turned in her chair as she watched her boss fill her stainless steel travel mug with the fragrant brew. "FedEx guy dropped them off right before I went on lunch. They're sitting on the floor beside my desk."

"Excellent. This open house is a huge friggin'

deal. I know Steph's really worried about it." Jill brought the filled travel mug to her lips, taking an experimental sip before scrunching her nose and setting the mug back to the counter to add more sugar.

"Was this what you always wanted to do, Jill?" Faith asked, indicating the room around them. "Real estate?"

"No way," Jill said, shaking her head. She smirked as she glanced at Faith over her shoulder as she used a spoon to stir her coffee. "By now I would have thought I'd be chief of a fire department."

Faith stared at her, shocked. "Really? Wow. You wanted to be a firefighter?" She was intrigued.

"Since I was a kid. My folks have a Polaroid of me somewhere in my first firefighter Halloween costume." She grinned, testing her coffee again. Clearly satisfied with it, she twisted the lid in place before taking a seat at the round table made to seat four and eyeing the orange vegetables.

"How'd you end up selling houses and buildings?" Faith asked, reaching into her baggie for two more carrots, handing one to her boss.

Jill took it and grinned before biting it in half with straight white teeth. "Steph."

Faith chuckled, finishing the carrot she'd been eating before taking a bite of the new one. "Should have known. She always want to do this?"

"Oh, hell yes. Stephanie was born to sell. Her father was one of those traveling salesman types and her mom sold Avon back in the day before moving on to Mary Kay." Her grin widened. "She had the pink car to prove it."

"Impressive. Selling runs in Stephanie's blood, huh?" Faith popped the last of her baby carrot into her mouth, her lunch break nearly over.

"Yup. She talked me into starting a business, and here we are. Why do you ask?" Jill asked, taking another, smaller bite.

Faith shrugged a shoulder. Why had she asked indeed? She thought about it for a second, then responded. "I've had this dream three times this week, same cast of characters, same basic setting, though what I was doing varied. One night I was hanging laundry to dry outside, another time I was setting out a huge sun tea jar on the back porch, and once I was weeding a flowerbed, all at the same farmhouse." She chuckled. "I hate yard work, and I certainly never saw myself being a mother."

"A kid was in each dream?" Jill asked gently.

"Yeah. I never see her, just always hear her playing with the dog, singing little songs, or calling out, 'Mamma, watch this!'" She shook her head. "Definitely never wanted kids. There's always a woman, too, though I never see her, either. She's always around somehow, and I know we're a couple."

A small smile tilted Jill's lips. "How do the dreams make you feel?"

"Utterly alone and sad when I wake and realize it was a dream," Faith murmured, her gaze falling to her phone lying on the table, able to recall the heavy sadness she'd felt each and every time. She glanced up when she felt Jill's hand pat her own.

"Maybe it's your heart telling you there's far more to life than you ever planned for yourself," she said, pushing to her feet, travel mug in hand. "Listen to it." With a wink, she left the room.

Hands on hips, Faith looked around at all she'd brought in—over three trips—from the pickup truck she'd borrowed from Ogden. Before her was her sleeping bag, cooler with food and water, a kerosene heater along with a bottle of kerosene, box of trash bags, box of latex gloves, small port-a-potty that could be used in a camping-type situation, and the newest book she was reading.

Hoping she had everything she'd need for the weekend, she turned her attention away from her supplies to take a look around the top floor of her building. She'd only seen a brief glimpse of it the previous time she'd been there. Now, she intended to look the building over from top to bottom, not through the eye of her architect father but from the perspective of a woman who had to make some sort of plan for the place.

Kneeling by her backpack, which held various survival essentials, she took out a flashlight. It was long, heavy, and bright, similar to what police would use. She felt it would be good not only for its bright beam, but also as a weapon should she need any outside of the Taser gun and pepper spray she had in her backpack. Though she felt the building could be locked up securely, her father having replaced all the locks when they were there last, she didn't have a feel for the town and the type of people who lived there.

She'd arrived just after nine that morning so she'd have plenty of daylight upstairs to find out what was covering the main floor windows, or if they'd been boarded over, or what. Her backpack also held flashlights, batteries, a battery-powered lantern, and a headlamp for hands-free investigation. She'd not set foot in the basement, so she wanted to make sure she had plenty of portable light for that.

As her father had warned, there were areas on the second floor that were somewhat unusable with the drastic slanting of the floor. Though he assured her it was safe, it wasn't entirely functional. The upstairs was currently split into four rooms, two roughly the same size and square. She could imagine they were once offices or could work as bedrooms, though she'd not found any research on the place being living space—not since its earliest years, anyway. The third room was the bathroom. The toilet and sink were missing, the plumbing capped and sticking out of the wall, as well as an aged mirror, splattered with water and God only knew what else, left behind and mounted to the wall over where the sink once was.

The main room, and largest, was where she intended to camp for the night. It was a decent size, and she could easily envision it being an open kitchen-living room combo. There was a fireplace, though it had been bricked over long ago.

Truth was, it wasn't hard to see the upstairs as a cozy, nice-sized apartment. It could be reimagined in terms of bedroom sizes, and even the addition of a bathroom suite. The inside walls were brick, reminding Faith of her apartment in Brooklyn. People paid good money for the quaint feature.

One thing she found interesting, however, was the markings on the floor. She followed their lines with her eyes throughout the entire second level. They were lines of discoloration on the original hardwood where walls had once stood. They closed off two rows of very small rooms, reminding her of the size of a modern-day jail cell. No doubt it went back to the years this place was a "boarding house" and whatever else that entailed. She was surprised they'd been able to cram twelve rooms on the floor, a narrow hallway separating the two sets of six, the doors facing its twin across the hall.

"Wow," she whispered, taking it all in again. "What have you seen?" she asked softly to the building in general.

Flashlight in hand, she trotted down the long, narrow staircase to the main floor. Blowing out a breath, she assessed the mess before her. She'd made good headway during her last trip, but in a very small area. That cleared area stuck out like a smile missing a tooth, especially since what she saw depended on where she aimed the strong beam of the flashlight.

"Windows," she muttered, trotting down the last few stairs. "Wherefore art thou, windows?"

Raising her hand that held the flashlight, she slowly trailed the intense beam along the wall to her left that ran along the entire length of the building. She hadn't noticed it before, but there was a heavy black curtain that was drilled into the brick that ran along the entire length. It was about four feet long, more than enough clearance to cover the length of the windows that she'd seen from the outside.

"Good lord," she said, carefully and slowly making her way to it over and around piles of stuff. "That crap is on there to stay," she muttered, tugging at the heavy fabric, which for some reason reminded her of something that would be found in a funeral home.

Clearly somebody didn't want anyone peeking into the building. Looking around the room, she felt a bit of a chill finger its way down her spine, wondering why. What were they trying to hide?

Deciding to let that thought marinate for a bit, she made her way back toward the staircase, where the door to the basement was tucked underneath. It was accessed by a separate key, which her father had found sticking out of the deadbolt-style lock in the door. Unlocking it, she turned the knob and pushed the thick plank door inward into a pitch-black stairwell. She figured the door was likely original to the building, though it looked as though the doorknob and certainly the deadbolt lock were relatively recent.

The air that met her face was cool and dank, like a cellar. Aiming her flashlight beam to guide her way, she made her way down the stone steps, rounded and smooth from nearly one hundred and thirty years of use. The walls were brick, which she used to help steady herself on the uneven stairs, as there was no railing.

Finally at the bottom, she stepped down onto the cobblestone floor. It made her think of a street in Europe somewhere. The flashlight beam slashing through the blackness, Faith looked around. It was an open space that led to doorways—with no doors. One proved to be a utility room which once held a furnace and water heater, the moorings still there to stabilize them. Another room was filled with empty shelving units, some anchored to the wall, others freestanding.

Looking at the shelves, particularly the ones of wood anchored to the wall which she suspected were original to the building unlike the metal freestanding shelves, she could easily imagine the storage of canned and dry goods in large glass jars. They could have been products sold to customers, perhaps, or used in food prepared at the saloon or fed to the men who lived in the rooms upstairs. The cooler temperatures would have been perfect for a root-cellar-like environment to store grain, or whiskey for the miners.

She smiled, almost able to hear the sounds of a bartender or barmaid bustling around gathering goods to take upstairs. She'd never had unfettered access to such an old building, and she found it deeply intriguing. From listening to her father over the years, she'd learned to look for the beauty of a building, its soul. Her father truly felt they all had one, a sentiment that Faith once found ridiculous. Exploring this one, she was beginning to understand that a little.

She moved to a room farther back, a hallway separating it from the other rooms. The farther down the hall she went, the warmer the air seemed to get. She smirked, bouncing the flashlight beam over the walls and floor. "Did I inherit the Portal to Hell or something?"

Amused at her own joke, she ventured into the room at the end of the hall, which was roughly the size of a walk-in closet, with a door that had a rounded top made of the same thick wood plank as the door leading to the basement. This one, however, had iron ribbing for strength, reminding her more of something out of a medieval castle than a nineteenth-century saloon. There was no door handle, only an iron tab hinged onto the door below a keyhole that was long, the type that would accommodate a large, iron key—nothing remotely current.

The tab squeaked as she lifted it, using it to tug on the door, which didn't budge. Locked.

"Lovely," she murmured. "Can't exactly get a locksmith for this puppy."

Letting the hinge fall back against the door, she shrugged and turned around to head back upstairs to grab the trash bags and get started once more on sorting.

With her phone connected to a small speaker bar, she blasted music as she worked, hips moving to the beat as she got lost in her task.

Hours and bags of trash later, Faith had run across a handful of antiques that she set aside, intending to have them looked at. Some were beautiful pieces of old furniture, while one was the type of radio a family may have used for entertainment in the 1930s or 1940s, beautiful ornate wood body and tubes inside. Not all the guts were there, but perhaps it could be sold for a decorative piece or parts.

With a grunt, she dragged an old tire off a surface it seemed she'd finally reached, the tire bouncing once on the floor before it fell over, missing her foot by a few inches. It looked as though it had once been on a pickup truck by its size.

"Yikes," she muttered, looking down at it, out of breath from all her exertion. She noticed three more tires that mated the one on the floor that were leaning against something, all in a line. She was ten, maybe twelve feet from the wall, so clearly wasn't that.

Grunting as she rolled the tires out of the way, she was puzzled when she saw a metal pole that looked like it was on its side and raised a few inches above the ground. Copper? She squatted down, wrapping her knuckles against the cold metal tube, realizing that it was attached to something.

"What the hell is this?" she wondered aloud, pushing to her feet again to look at the surface that was revealed when she removed the tire.

Reaching up, she aimed the light attached to the adjustable band around her forehead so she could see better the wood surface. She ran her hand over it, eyebrows knit together. It was smooth, yet clearly years of use had left its mark, literally. She lightly picked at a deep scratch with a fingernail before moving on to a few more.

Backing away a foot, she took in as much of the revealed picture as she could, then gasped. "Oh my god! It's a bar."

She grinned as she began to move things off as much as she could. Sure enough, it was what had once been a gorgeous bar. From the pictures she'd seen, she suspected perhaps it was original from the days of the saloon.

She glanced toward the massive front door of the building when she thought she heard something. Unsure, she walked over to her phone and turned off the music. The instant silence was deafening. She waited. Sure enough, a knock sounded.

Turning the stiff deadbolt her father installed, Faith pulled open the door, only to find Wyatt wincing, the large paper bag she held pushed out in front of her. Confused, Faith realized she'd just blinded the poor thing.

"Sorry," she said, reaching up and tugging the headlamp off and switching it off.

The bag was lowered to show a rapidly blinking redhead. She shook her head as though to clear it, then smiled warmly at Faith. "My, my. Quite the welcome from y'all." She lifted the bag again, though this time in offering and not as a shield. "I brought you and your daddy some food."

Surprised and touched, Faith smiled. "Well, I'm on my own today, but thank you. That's incredibly kind."

"Oh." Wyatt lowered the bag, chewing on her full bottom lip for a moment before her smile returned. "Well, if you leave the second lunch out in the truck, it should stay cold enough for breakfast."

Faith chuckled and moved aside to make room for Wyatt to enter. "No, I have a better idea. Come in, join me if you've got time."

Wyatt suddenly looked shy, flashing those gorgeous eyes at Faith. "I don't want to impose, Faith."

"Absolutely no imposition. Come on in. The company would actually be really nice."

"All right. I've got a little time." Wyatt's smile was bright and so welcoming, Faith felt like it held the warmth and comfort of the most beautiful fire in a fireplace.

"Let's head upstairs," Faith said, pulling her gaze away from that smile. She flicked on her headlamp and, held it in her hand, raised it to use as an ordinary flashlight in the darkness of the main floor as she closed the front door behind Wyatt. "Want to follow me upstairs, or want me to follow up with the light to guide your way?"

Wyatt looked from the light in Faith's hand over to the stairs at the other end of the building then at Faith. "Guide me, won't you?" she asked shyly.

Faith grinned and nodded, indicating with a wave of her hand that Wyatt should head for the stairs. She was close behind with her headlamp back in place around her head. "Can you see okay?" she asked, following the waitress.

"I can."

The pathway to the stairs was fairly unfettered with trash or objects, so Wyatt had a straight road to get there. She began to climb the stairs, Faith not far behind. And, her gaze was very much glued to Wyatt's behind. She had never seen a woman wear a pair of jeans the way this woman did. She forced her gaze away, feeling like a cad, and focused on making it upstairs.

"Goodness!" Wyatt gasped when she reached the top of the stairs, the dying light from the sunset outside the windows showing the large, open space. "This could make a wonderful apartment."

Faith smiled, clicking off her headlamp and tugging it off her head before walking past Wyatt to turn on the lantern that would give them plenty of light as the sun would be gone soon. Already feeling the temperature dropping, she grabbed her bottle of kerosene. "Make yourself comfortable, Wyatt. Sorry I don't have a table or chairs or anything. I guess pick your square of floor." She grinned at the other woman over her shoulder before returning to focus on getting the heater filled and started.

"I have to say," Wyatt began, the sounds of her removing Styrofoam containers from the large paper bag filling Faith's ears. "I was mighty pleased to see your father's truck here this mornin'. I honesty figured by now you'd sell this place and be done with it."

Faith remained silent in what she was doing for a moment, considering what she'd been told. She used one of the long stick matches she'd brought with her and lit the pilot light on the kerosene lamp and waited for it to catch before turning to Wyatt.

"You know, I considered it." She pulled her legs up to sit cross-legged across from Wyatt, two take-out containers sitting stacked between them as Wyatt continued to empty the paper bag. She removed two Styrofoam cups with plastic lids, placing one in front of Faith and the other next to where she sat, and two straws. Packets of ketchup, mustard, and mayo followed before she handed Faith one of the containers. Taking it from her, she added, "But after spending some time here last time, getting the okay from my dad, I've decided to get this place emptied out then make a plan."

"What does your daddy do?" Wyatt asked, sticking the straw in the hole created when she peeled the flimsy plastic tab back on the lid.

"He's an architect." Faith fixed her cheeseburger the way she liked it with the provided condiments, tossing the spent packets into the empty paper bag. "Thank you so much for this, Wyatt," she said, tossing a French fry into her mouth. "I'll stop at the café in the morning and pay for this."

"You'll do no such thing," Wyatt said, glaring playfully at Faith. "It's the least I could do." She grinned, bringing her burger up to her mouth. "After all, you've given the town something to finally talk about."

Chapter Ten

Faith came to wakefulness just in time for her back to begin screaming its displeasure at her. Wincing, she slowly rolled from her side to her back, staring up at the ceiling. The sun was just beginning to creep in through the large windows, glazing the ceiling with its golden tribute to a new day.

She'd slept surprisingly well considering she was in a sleeping bag on a hard floor. She'd turned off the kerosene heater around midnight when her phone alarm woke her to do so. She didn't want to chance a horrible accident happening. It was definitely cold in the upstairs of her building now, however.

After a few lazy moments, she sat up and scooted over to the heater to light the pilot light and get things warmed up. Mission accomplished, she lay back down, cuddled up in her sleeping bag, and considered the previous night. She'd gotten a lot of work done, completely filling the bed of her father's truck with trash bags and broken furniture and other such random items. She'd completely cleared off the bar, delighted by what good shape it was in. It certainly needed some restoration work, but it wasn't a far cry to imagine the beautiful splendor it once was and could be again. The pole-type structure she'd found attached to the front of it that ran along the floor was something men standing at the bar could rest a booted foot on, the metal still scuffed.

Over the two days she'd dedicated to cleaning up the main floor, she'd cleared about a fourth of the space. Just getting the trash out made a huge difference. The lion's share of what was left was in the back across from the stairs and against the wall with the windows. The piles of stuff towered over her head, stacked so high. She'd opted to start on the other side of the room first so she'd have space to bring some of the trash and items down from the rafters. That was her plan for the day, to get started on the right side of the main floor.

Warming, she pushed the sleeping bag down a bit and brought her hands up to rest behind her head on the pillow. She glanced over and noticed the large paper bag left behind by Wyatt the previous afternoon. That brought a smile to her face.

Wyatt hadn't been there more than twenty minutes before claiming nervously she had to "be on time," whatever that meant. Be on time for what? Her break to end? A certain patron of the café? One moment they'd been laughing, sharing stories of cramming in delicious feta fries at The Grill in Athens, Georgia, and the next Wyatt had glanced at her phone and nearly whimpered in distress as she threw the uneaten bit of her lunch into its container and had scurried away with a yelled apology trailing behind her. She hadn't even waited for Faith to light her way, she'd just been gone. Poof!

Sitting up again, she glanced over at the cooler she'd brought, picturing the single-serve bottle of orange juice and wrapped Danish she'd brought for breakfast, then glanced over at the paper bag and thought of a nice big plate of waffles, scrambled eggs, and sausage. Decision made, she climbed out of her sleeping bag.

※※※※

Baseball cap pulled down over her messy hair and a quick change into fresh clothes, Faith had used adult wipes to clean up a bit before heading across and down the street a bit to Pop's. There were several cars in the parking lot, as well as two sheriff cruisers.

Hands tucked into the pockets of her loose-fitting track pants, she made her way inside. Expecting to see Wyatt behind the lunch counter, she was surprised to see an older woman with a hideously bad dye job, the black hair dye even staining her forehead at her hairline. The tables were pretty full, a couple families, but mostly older people chatting loudly, the volume in the café turned up and lively.

As she made her way toward the lunch counter, she saw two men in Sheriff's Department uniforms. The older one looked to be in his later fifties or sixties with salt-and-pepper hair and matching beard. The younger of the two was an extremely handsome man with raven hair and blueberry-blue eyes. What she noticed most about him, however, was his size. His forearms were nearly the size of Faith's thighs, his knees spread wide to avoid banging up against the underside of the table.

The huge younger one nodded acknowledgement at her and the older one spoke. "You the little gal that won the old Stringer building?" he asked, one hand absently using a spoon to stir his coffee.

Faith nodded with a shy smile. "Yes I am. In a bit over my head, but here I am."

He smirked and nodded. "G'luck to ya. Let us

know if you get any problems."

"Thank you, Sheriff. I appreciate that." Faith gave both men a final smile before continuing on her way.

Making her way to the lunch counter, she slid onto a stool, a man who looked to be in his sixties sitting one stool over. He glanced at her and gave her a smile and welcoming nod before returning his attention to his breakfast.

She grabbed one of the menus tucked between the sugar shaker and ketchup bottle and perused the offerings.

"What can I get'cha?" the waitress asked as she stepped over to Faith. Her hair looked even worse up close, as though she'd dunked her head in a vat of tar before ratting the hair up on her head.

"Uh." Faith forced her eyes off the hairdo disaster. "Wyatt not working this morning?"

The waitress glanced over at Pops, who was at his regular seat at the register. He met her gaze, looking at her over his glasses. He gave her an almost imperceptible shake of his head, his eyes boring into the hazel ones of the waitress.

Recognizing the silent communication for more than Pops telling the waitress Wyatt wasn't in, Faith looked between the two, concern filling her heart. No, she didn't know the younger woman well, but there was something about her, a frailty, perhaps, that made Faith feel a bit protective of her.

Disappointed but letting it go, Faith ordered all that she'd been craving when she woke up, and waited for her food as she sipped the coffee that the waitress Wanda—so said her name tag—had brought her. Wincing at the strong brew, she added more cream.

Her attention was garnered by the low but seemingly upset voice of a man coming from the booth nearest the jukebox and bathroom hallway.

"Mr. Carter, I explained to you over the phone what our needs were and sent you pictures of the church," an older, balding man in a Presbyterian clergy collar said, his voice imploring the man sitting across from him in jeans, work boots, and a flannel shirt.

"Father, I understand that, and I honestly don't mean to be disrespectful to you or your church here, but the damage to the steeple is far more than I was originally led to believe. The materials alone will eat up the price you quoted me, and I still gotta pay my guys."

The priest nodded, giving the younger man a smile. "I understand." He reached into the inside pocket of his black sport coat and brought out a business card. "God be with you, and if you change your mind."

The man in the flannel shirt took the priest's hand and shook it before he stood. He looked down at the card that lay on the table and shook his head. "I'm sorry, Father," he said, regret in his voice. "I just can't afford to take this job. I'm sorry."

Faith could literally feel the heavy disappointment in the priest's sigh as he reached out and took the card off the table. Without thinking, she slid off the stool and hurried over to him before he repocketed it.

"Excuse me, Father," she said politely. "Forgive me, but I couldn't help but overhear your conversation with that man." She met his gaze when he looked up at her with surprised eyes behind his glasses. "May I have that?" she asked, indicating the business card.

Foot tapping in nervous energy, Faith lightly chewed on her bottom lip as she waited. A glance at the wall clock told her she still had time, but she hoped he'd hurry. She'd let him know she'd be dropping by. As if in response, the office door opened and Ogden and his associate Tom exited, the two men quietly continuing their conversation. Finally, Ogden glanced over at Faith as she pushed to her feet.

"Hello there." He walked over to her, Tom following. "Tom, you remember my daughter, Faith?"

"Of course," Tom said, giving her a quick hug. "So nice to see you."

She smiled at the man whom she'd known from her father's professional life since she'd been in college. "Hi, Tom."

The architect released Faith and slapped Ogden on the back. "See you tomorrow."

Left alone, Ogden turned to Faith. "So, what did you want to talk about?" he asked, leaning back against a half wall that served as a planter in the lobby of his firm.

Faith felt a wave of nerves wash through her and took a clarifying breath before speaking. "Do you remember over the years how you and your guys would do projects for people or situations where funds were short or just flat-out not there?"

He crossed his arms over his chest and smiled, nodding. "Yes. 'Pity projects,' as Carrie calls them."

"Yes, exactly, spoken with Carrie's usual grace and eloquence," Faith responded sarcastically. "So, there's a church that is falling apart. What began as a problem with its steeple has turned into the building being shut down because it no longer meets code."

Ogden nodded again, his eyebrows knit together as his gaze intensified on her with obvious attention to what she was telling him.

"The whole reason I have the building there is because of the raffle to raise money for the steeple. But," she added with a shrug. "The money raised is no longer sufficient for the amount of work that needs to be done. I spoke with the head priest about it Sunday, and they can't get anyone willing to help them, nor do they have any more resources to add."

He reached up and stroked his beard, the softest smile quirking his lips. "Didn't take you for the church type, *Faith*."

She grinned. "Yeah. Me, neither."

※ ※ ※ ※

"Excuse me, gentlemen," Faith said, pushing her chair back from the table. Her two male companions stopped their discussion and looked at her. "I apologize for interrupting, but Father, I'm going to get a refill," she said, placing her hand over her empty coffee cup. "Would you like one?"

"Oh, please," the kindly priest said, handing his empty cup to her. "Thank you."

"Dad?" She glanced at her father, who had been speaking animatedly to the religious leader. "Want me to tell them you want more iced tea?" she asked, unable to take his glass and the two mugs. At his nod, she took the two coffee cups and weaved her way through the café tables to the lunch counter.

She was stopped along the way by an older

woman who looked to be in her late fifties or early sixties. She had a sweet smile and, despite the large amount of gray in her light brown, bobbed hair, her blue eyes were filled with a youthful twinkle.

"You're the young woman who has the building just across the way, right?" she asked. Her voice was soft, but there was a quality to it that made the listener want to hear what she had to say.

"Yes," Faith said, nodding. She had no clue where this was going.

"You're also the young woman who's going to get our church repaired, is this also right?"

"Well," Faith said, glancing over at the table where the two men were nearly head to head as her father excitedly drew out plans for the church. "My father will handle that, if he takes the project." She returned her focus to the woman. "But, I suppose so." She grinned. "I drove him here, anyway."

The woman's smile was big and bright. "Bless you. You see, I've played the organ and piano at the church for the last thirty-seven years. That church has been a huge part of this community my entire life. It's not just a place of worship," the woman continued. "It's where we've met for weddings, funerals, and even a graduation or two." Her smile softened, sadness entering her eyes. "So, you can see how important it is to us." She glanced around the café. "Though there aren't a lot of us left here in town, it's still important."

Not sure what to say, Faith nodded. "We'll make sure it gets fixed," she said, no clue how on earth she was going to make that happen, but she'd do her best to talk Ogden into it if he turned the project down.

The woman squeezed Faith's arm then walked away, heading to the bathroom. Faith watched her go before blowing out a heavy breath, feeling the weight of her own words and promise on her shoulders. She continued her journey to the lunch counter, very happy to see Wyatt butt her way through the swinging door, a tray filled with filled dishes held high overhead. She smiled brightly when she spotted Faith.

"Be right with y'all," she said before hurrying over to one of the filled tables.

Sliding onto an empty stool, Faith set the cups on the counter in front of her, mindful of which was which. Tapping her fingertips, she watched Wyatt hurry back to the area behind the counter carrying the empty tray in her hand. She looked absolutely adorable, Faith thought, in her signature jeans and a short-sleeved women's button-up shirt. She wore a red bandana in her auburn hair, Rosie-the-Riveter style.

"Hey!"

"Hey, yourself," Faith said, unable to not smile when confronted with the warm, beautiful one the waitress sported. "How are you?"

"Lordy, I'm hoppin' like a frog in a hot pan," Wyatt said, glancing down at the two coffee cups before hurrying over to the coffee station to grab the carafe and fill them as she continued to talk. "I'm so glad you came in this weekend. I didn't feel right grabbing your number off your raffle ticket without permission." She set the carafe aside and leaned on her forearms on the counter. "I'm sorry I had to take off so quickly last time you were here," she said softly, looking Faith in the eye. "I'd like to make up for it."

Faith looked up into her eyes, and it was then that she noticed—though it was clearly fading—bruised skin around her left eye. From the yellow and greenish coloring, she guessed it was nearly a week old. She felt her stomach clench in concern, but something told her to not mention it. Instead, she focused on the beautiful eyes that studied her. "Okay," she finally said.

"Well, will you be down next weekend?" Wyatt asked, hope in her voice.

"I will. I've got an event for work tomorrow, so I'm heading back after an antiques dealer looks at some stuff at the building—"

"Bessie," Wyatt blurted.

"—later, and... What? Bessie?" Faith said, confused.

"Yeah," Wyatt said, pushing up on her tiptoes as she looked across the café.

Faith followed her glance and saw she was looking over at the table she'd been sitting at moments before. Before she could say another word, Wyatt had zipped over and grabbed a clean glass and was filling it with fresh iced tea.

"We always just refer to it as 'the building,'" Wyatt explained, setting the tea next to the two cups of coffee. "Sounds so cold."

Faith burst into laughter, shaking her head. She was utterly charmed. "Um, all right. So, an antiques dealer is coming to...Bessie today to take a look and see if anything can be bought or whatever, then I have to head back to Denver."

Wyatt's eyes widened. "Oh my! That's exciting." She smiled.

"We'll see. Hopefully, I can make a few bucks. It'll all go back into Bessie, but there's so much that needs to be done. So, what did you have in mind for next weekend?"

"Well," Wyatt began, once again leaning down on her forearms. "Lucas is going huntin' up at his cabin, so I thought maybe I could have you over for a proper, home-cooked lunch."

Faith noticed that, in Wyatt's current position, she could see just a bit of her cleavage in the open vee of the button-up shirt. Clearing her throat, she quickly looked away, knowing that wasn't Wyatt's intention.

"Well," Faith said, meeting Wyatt's gaze. "I was going to drive around town, see the area, take in the whole county."

"Oh, golly, I'm so sorry." Wyatt gasped, waving her words away as she backed up from the counter, seeming embarrassed. "I'm so sorry, Faith. Here I go again, pushin' in on your plans."

"Wait," Faith said, feeling panic slice through her at the thought of Wyatt being upset for any reason. "Why can't we do both?" she asked. "Why not pack up that lunch and go with me?" She hadn't even realized she'd been holding her breath until she saw Wyatt's smile. She let out a relieved breath and matched it. "I mean, you live here, so you can show me around. Right?"

Wyatt leaned against the counter again and nodded. "I can."

※※※※

Faith decided to kill two birds with one stone. Her father knew a lot more about antiques than she did, and given the way the man who had arrived at Bessie was looking her up and down, she opted to let Ogden deal with him. So, while they looked at the objects she'd dug out over her time there, she worked on the huge pile that remained.

She began to pull things off the pile, and realized that underneath the trash bags that seemed to be filled with paper and such, there were layers upon layers of blankets and tarps beneath that.

"What the hell?" she muttered.

She grabbed the end of the last layer of tarp and began to pull, gently tugging. More bags fell away, rolling harmlessly to the floor, until finally the tarp pulled free with a yank from her. Her loud gasp had her father at her side.

"What's wrong? What'd you find?" he asked.

"It's a car," Faith murmured, staring at the small portion of it that was revealed.

"Holy shit," the antiques dealer whispered, stepping up on the other side of her as he whistled through his teeth. "That's a 1915 Cadillac Type 51."

She looked up at him to meet his gaze. "Okay," she muttered, no idea what significance that had.

His smile was wide and a bit lecherous, though this time she had the feeling it had nothing to do with her. "You just won the lottery."

Chapter Eleven

"Destination on your left."
Faith looked over at the two-story house she pulled up to, foursquare in style, so called because traditionally the four rooms on the main and second floors were stacked perfectly on top of each other. The front door was recessed back into the shadows of the covered front porch that ran the length of the house. A detached garage sat back from the house at the end of a long asphalt driveway.

There was no car in the driveway, nor one parked in front. Faith checked the address Wyatt had texted her against the one on the mailbox, and sure enough, it was the right place. She reached for the key, about to turn off the ignition, when the front wood-and-glass door opened and Wyatt emerged, dressed for a casual fun day and carrying a large picnic basket. Her hair was down, the deep red in the auburn locks shining under the sun as she hurried down the walkway straddled by two neat patches of winter-yellow lawn.

Faith took in the shoulder-length hair which framed the face of an angel. "Good. God." Clearing her throat and her mind, she smiled through the driver's side window and returned the wave she got from an advancing Wyatt.

"My goodness, what a beautiful day," the waitress gushed as she opened the back door of the Element and settled the picnic basket on the back seat.

"Indeed," Faith muttered when Wyatt closed the door before opening the front passenger door to slide in next to her. She noticed how amazing Wyatt smelled, too. Harboring a lifelong weakness for a woman who smelled amazing, she knew it was going to be a long day closed up in a car with this particular woman. She was amused at her own predicament. "Okay," she said, hands on the steering wheel. "Where to?"

"Well, I figure we could start down by the old mines," Wyatt said, meeting Faith's gaze. "See where it all began."

"As you wish."

Faith drove along the tree-lined streets of Wynter noting the old houses, some not much more than shacks, others grand Victorian-style homes, though few had the love and care that once made them grand. They passed a closed-off road that Wyatt explained led to the old mines. They ended up in an area not far away that was row upon row of tiny identical square houses made of wood, thin, stovepipe chimneys protruding from the roofs of some while others seemed to sport a more traditional fireplace chimney.

"The single men that came into town to work the mines," Wyatt said softly. "They were expected to either board in Bessie or the other boarding houses in town that popped up, or they camped out in the woods," she added, indicating the wooded area nearby. "But these"—she pointed to the tiny houses—"were where the married men lived." She met Faith's gaze. "Can you imagine you and a spouse and ten kids crammed into one of those things?"

Faith looked back to the houses, trying to picture

just such a thing. She shook her head, looking back to Wyatt. "No. They look to be what, maybe eight hundred square feet?"

"At best."

"Do people still live in them?" Faith asked. "They look abandoned. Definitely in need of serious repair."

"No. The last person left a few years back. I think it's a cryin' shame," Wyatt said with a sigh. "Hits right back to the very beginnin' of Wynter's history."

"Those would make great cabins to rent," Faith muttered, not even realizing she'd said anything aloud until Wyatt asked her to repeat it. "Huh? Oh, uh, nothing." She gave her a sheepish smile. "So, where to next?" She was a little taken aback by the mischievous look she received. "What?"

"How do you feel about cemeteries?" Wyatt asked.

※※※※

The two passengers were jostled as the Element climbed its way back up into the woods, the tires gripping on gravel, rocks, and rutted ground with wild vegetation.

"You were not kidding that this place is off the beaten path," Faith muttered, knuckles white as she gripped the wheel hard to keep them from falling into a rut or off a large boulder.

Wyatt chuckled. "You're doin' great." She patted the side of Faith's leg for good measure.

Faith grinned but said nothing more until finally up ahead she saw a wrought iron gate appear. "'Miner's Hole Cemetery,'" Faith read aloud, the letters part of the elaborate iron work in the arch. She looked to Faith, eyebrows drawn. "Miner's Hole?"

"This entire area was referred to as Miner's

Hole," Wyatt explained, indicating the surrounding woods. "All the way down to the mine and the miners' houses."

"Okay, so that was actually kind of a term of endearment for those guys?" Faith turned off the ignition and released her seat belt. At Wyatt's nod, she turned back to take in the old gate that was clearly rusted, some leaves and debris stuck in some of the curlicue decoration.

They climbed out of Faith's car and met at the front of it, Faith feeling a bit uncertain. The place was creepy, overgrown with huge, ancient trees sending their winter-bare branches to the sky like the bony fingers of skeletal hands, even as some of those fingers were beginning to bud with spring growth. The headstones within were hidden in places by overgrown foliage, a few toppled over or partially sunk into the ground.

She felt part amused and part embarrassed as her expression was so readable based upon Wyatt's next amused-sounding words.

"I know you think I just led you to the backyard of the Addams Family, but I assure you I didn't."

Faith met her gaze and gave her a sheepish grin. *Busted*. "Well, as long as Uncle Fester doesn't saunter out from behind a tree, I think we're good."

"I'll protect you," Wyatt said sweetly, a mischievous twinkle in her eye.

The two headed up the slight incline to the gate, which was rusted ajar, the two women just barely able to squeeze through the space. A larger person would have a harder time entering. Once inside, Faith was amazed at how everything seemed so quiet; even the birds that had been singing in surrounding trees had stopped. She subconsciously moved a bit closer to her companion, who seemed oddly at peace in the cemetery. As though able to hear Faith's mental musings, she began to speak, her voice soft, almost reverent, as they walked down what had once been a stone path but now was clogged with weeds, mud, and vegetation. The whiteness of the football-sized stones peeked out from time to time like the bleached ends of bone poking through skin.

"When I was a little girl, my mamma used to take me to the cemeteries around Savannah," she began. "Daddy found it creepy," she added with a chuckle. "So, he refused to go with us. Fine by us, honestly." She shrugged. "Just kinda became our time together."

"What do you like about them?" Faith reached up to push some vines hanging down from a tree out of her face as they passed. She managed to keep her instinct to recoil and shudder at bay.

"Honestly, the peace, the calm energy. The history. Like this fella," Faith said, stepping off the "path" to a nearby headstone, aged and weathered, though still mostly legible. "Thomas Whitley, died in 1897." She looked at Faith, who had stepped up beside her. "Only twenty-two when he died. Did he die in the mines? Did he fall sick? Did he die in some silly brothel brawl?" She grinned. "The possibilities are endless and can be so scandalous," she whispered dramatically, making Faith smile. "But in seriousness, I find it so fascinatin' that he died when Wynter was in its mere infancy, only a few years old."

Faith looked back down to the grave with a new perspective. It had never occurred to her to think that way. Like many people, she looked at cemeteries as a creepy place for dead bodies and ghosts to hang out.

"Do you like history?" she asked, allowing herself to relax as she felt the calmness and relaxation radiate off Wyatt's body as they continued their slow stroll.

"Love it," Wyatt said, brushing her fingers over the top of a slightly cockeyed headstone they passed. "Mamma taught history in primary school for several years. Though she was fairly limited in the scope she could teach for her students, she saved her best lessons for me." Wyatt's smile was proud, yet she carried an air of sadness behind the memory. "She loved to learn, loved to teach what she'd learned. Yup," she added with a more peaceful smile. "She loved history."

"And serial killers," Faith added, remembering her very first conversation with Wyatt, who burst into laughter. The sound was like music to Faith's ears. It had the clarity and purity of wind chimes tinkling in the breeze.

"Yes," Wyatt amended. "And serial killers."

Faith shoved her hands into the pockets of her jacket. Though cooler due to their elevation, it was truly a beautiful day. "You keep talking about her in the past tense," she said gently, hoping she wasn't inadvertently wading into unwelcomed territory.

Wyatt let out a heavy sigh before she nodded, reaching up to brush some fiery strands out of her face as a light burst of breeze swept across them. "Yeah. My parents were murdered on my husband's twenty-eighth birthday."

Faith's breath caught at the unexpected information. "Oh god, Wyatt. I'm so sorry. You don't have to—"

"No," Wyatt said, shaking her head and looking over at Faith, who was surprised when suddenly Wyatt moved in next to her and slid her hand into the bend of Faith's arm. She thought perhaps Wyatt needed personal contact for such a difficult subject. "It's not an easy thing to talk about, but I feel if you're gonna tell somebody's story, you gotta tell the entire story."

Faith nodded, though said nothing. She decided to leave it to Wyatt to decide what she wanted to say. Instead, she allowed herself to enjoy the warmth and closeness, Wyatt's perfume wafting to her from time to time. As though in silent agreement, they walked over to a stone bench which, with a quick swipe of the hand to wipe off dead leaves and some dirt, was perfectly suitable.

"So, at the time, we were still livin' in Savannah. Lucas was a state trooper and I was waitressin', of course," she said with a small smile to Faith before she looked out over the cemetery again. Faith forced herself to look away from Wyatt's profile. "I still had my car then, so the three parties—me, Lucas, and my parents—were all gonna meet up for dinner, then Mamma and Daddy were gonna come back to our place so the boys could watch college ball while, ironically, Mamma and I probably went to a cemetery."

Faith wanted to smile at that, but the churning in her gut and lump forming in her throat wouldn't let her. "What happened?" she asked softly.

"My parents were stopped at a stoplight waitin' for the green, when out of nowhere two shots rang out." Wyatt sighed, her shoulders slumping slightly, seemingly with the weight of the memory. "They were pronounced dead at the scene."

Faith was silent for a long moment. Needing Wyatt's warmth, she moved her leg just enough so her thigh barely touched Wyatt's. "I have no words, Wyatt." She was quiet for a moment, trying to imagine what that must have been like, the pain and the loss Wyatt felt. Since she never spoke of any siblings, Faith guessed Wyatt was an only child. Clearing the emotion out of her throat so it wouldn't end up in her words, she asked, "Is that how you ended up here?"

"No. They never caught who did it, and between never really feelin' safe and just too many painful memories, we moved to Athens when Lucas got a job with the police department. Couple years later, he heard about the opening with the Wynter County Sheriff's Department after Miss Vicky's husband died of a heart attack, so…" She shrugged, looking around before meeting Faith's gaze. "Here we are, six years on."

"Who's Miss Vicky?"

"You met her last weekend at the café. She plays the organ and such at the church. Sweetest lady ever. I felt guilty about Lucas taking her husband's job after he died, but she was so supportive of him, took me under her wing. Heck," she added with a warm smile. "She talked Pops into giving me my job."

"She seems like good people," Faith said, remembering the kind lady from the previous weekend. "You know, there's just something about this place," she added, looking out over the headstones and overgrown foliage and seeing the tiny, injured town beyond. "There's so much more to it than meets the eye." She looked over at Wyatt. "Isn't there?"

"I think so," Wyatt said after a moment, her phone chirping to life. She pulled it out of her coat pocket as she added, "The people here are some of the kindest I've ever known." Wyatt looked at the phone screen and saw who her caller was. She quickly pushed to her feet and walked away from the bench as she answered her call.

Opting to give her even more privacy, Faith stood and walked in the opposite direction, noting the stones she passed, finding it sad that one simply said, *Baby O'Brien, Aged 1 Day*. She couldn't imagine losing a child, which brought her back to Wyatt's loss, and that of her own. With her new friend being so open with her, she felt she should do the same. It wasn't something she thought about often, and certainly never spoke about. But of anyone, she felt Wyatt would understand.

"I'm really sorry."

Faith whirled around, startled at the touch to her upper back and the voice. She gave Wyatt a sheepish smile. "No worries. I hope everything's okay?"

"Eh," Wyatt hedged. "It was Lucas. Apparently, he managed to hunt and kill something, so he's coming back tonight instead of tomorrow." She let out a heavy sigh and ran her hand through her hair. Faith thought she seemed anxious. "I have to get home and find some damn tarp he can't live without." She looked at Faith apologetically.

Faith tilted her head slightly in confusion. "What does he use the tarp for?"

"Lays out his glorious, victorious bounty in the backyard until his buddy comes down from Denver to process it. I hate it," she muttered, uncharacteristically dark.

"It's no problem, Wyatt, really," Faith said, not wanting to add her disappointment of their truncated day to Wyatt's obvious discontent. "How about I help you find it?"

Seeming to brighten, Wyatt nodded. "Okay. Then we can eat our picnic lunch in my living room."

The two laughed before, once again, Wyatt's hand found the bend of Faith's arm as she led them back the way they'd come. "Do you come here often?" Faith asked.

"Sadly, no. I haven't been here in about three years," Wyatt responded as she squeezed through the space in the open gate.

"What?" Faith gasped, following suit. "But you seem to love this place so much."

"I do." Wyatt took a last look at it before opening the front passenger-side door, finishing her reply once they'd both climbed inside. "But, in his infinite wisdom, three years ago Lucas decided we had too many bills, so we sold my car."

Faith said nothing, simply stared at Wyatt, who was buckling herself in. Finally, she looked away, getting her own seat belt on before starting the car. "I see," she said quietly, keeping it simple so she didn't say what she really thought and had no right to say.

"So," Wyatt said after a long pause. "I've seen your daddy a couple times now, were you always close? Are you close to your mamma?"

"Funnily enough, I've seen my father more since I won Bessie than I have in nearly fifteen years." She grinned over at a surprised-looking Wyatt. "We're not close, never have been."

"Why?" Wyatt blurted, quickly apologizing for what she called rudeness.

"No, it's okay. Short answer is, he'd never allow it," Faith said simply. "And, as for my mother, the story of her somewhat answers the question of my father. My mom took her own life three weeks before my eighth birthday." She heard the loud gasp and spared a glance to Wyatt, surprised to see tears in her eyes. "Truth be told," she continued, her eyes moving back to the road. "I don't really remember her. I think I have images or maybe a memory or two, but I'm not entirely sure how much of that is real and how much of that are the fantasies of a little kid."

"I'm so sorry," Wyatt said softly.

Faith gave her a smile in acknowledgement of her kindness. "I don't really know anything about their marriage before she died, but after, it wasn't long before my father remarried and then they had my little brother, Dawson." She felt Wyatt's gaze on her and turned, bursting into laughter at the expression on Wyatt's lovely face. "Honestly, I don't think there's anything nefarious about it. I just think my father wasn't equipped to be a single dad. I mean, he was a shitty enough dad when he *was* married, so…" Faith slowed the car to a stop as they pulled up in front of Wyatt's house.

"I was twenty-four when I lost my mamma, I can't even imagine being just a child." Wyatt met Faith's gaze for a long moment as they sat in silence. "My heart goes out to you, and to your daddy."

Faith smiled. Somehow the soft lilt of Wyatt's southern accent made the earnest words have that much more impact. She felt them in her chest, which threatened to tighten with long-repressed emotion on the subject. "Thank you."

Wyatt reached over and grabbed Faith's hand, squeezing it for a moment before releasing it as she climbed out of the car.

The storage shed in the large backyard was at the back of the property, which was largely natural, covered in mountain sage beyond the small patch of grass past the screened-in back porch. It was about the size of a one-car garage, though more square than rectangular. It was filled with neatly stacked boxes and plastic tubs, easily accessible by aisles. Smaller boxes were placed neatly on shelves mounted to the side of the permanent structure. At the back of the shed was a tall, narrow gray box with a combination panel built into it.

"What's that?" Faith asked.

Wyatt glanced over to where Faith pointed. "One of Lucas's damn gun safes. Hate those things. He collects them."

Faith met her gaze, eyebrows raised. "Guns, or gun safes?"

Wyatt grinned. "Yes."

"Okay, what are we looking for?"

"Okay," Wyatt said, hands on hips as she scanned the contents of the shed. "It's a dark brown tarp with little gold eyelets on the four corners. Oh!" She brought her hand up as a thought seemed to hit her. "You know what, I'll look for the tarp and why don't you look for the stakes he uses to pin the tarp flat to the ground. They look like tent stakes, know what I mean?"

Faith thought for a moment, but then remembered camping a few times as a kid. "Yeah, I gotcha."

"Great. Should be in a smaller box on that shelf, and the box should be open and they're on top. Lord knows he uses them enough," Wyatt muttered with a sigh. "Most of the boxes should be taped up, stuff we don't use or get into. Sound good?"

Faith gave her a grin and stood straight, heels clicking together as she gave her a salute. "Aye aye, Captain."

Wyatt grinned and waved her away. "Goof."

Faith headed in the direction she was instructed and began to scan boxes as she went, looking for ones whose flaps weren't taped shut. Even though many were larger boxes stacked atop others on the floor, she could take a quick peek inside to make sure nothing got missed. Easier to do it once than backtrack, was her theory.

No luck there, she moved to the shelves, eight in total, four in a row with an additional four mounted a couple feet above. She saw an untaped box tucked between two taped boxes on the higher level of shelves, so she reached up to grab it. As she pulled it down, another box whose loose tape was stuck to the first came with it.

"Oh crap," Faith exclaimed as she caught the first box, the other tumbling to the ground, smacking into her shin in the process.

Heart racing, she looked down at the scattered contents, grateful when she heard nothing break but shocked to see a mini-library of trade paperback books. She knew many of the titles and authors, having read most herself, including the collection of lesbian erotica anthologies in the mix.

"Are you okay?" Wyatt asked, hurrying over to her. She stopped short.

Faith glanced back at her to see Wyatt staring down at the books, her mouth open. She met Faith's gaze then quickly looked away, embarrassment seeming to color her cheeks. Understanding that this was apparently a stash of reading material Wyatt hadn't intended Faith—or, she assumed, anyone—to find, Faith said nothing. She simply placed the box she'd caught atop another one before squatting down and gathering the literary treasure into a neat pile before turning the toppled box right side up and placing the books back inside.

She got to her feet and gently set the heavy box of books on another box. "Do you want me to put these back there?" she asked gently.

"Nah," Wyatt said, her back to her as she seemed to uselessly fumble with the tarp she'd found. "Y'all can just throw 'em away."

"Now, why would I do that?" Faith asked, eyebrow raised and a playful tone in her voice. "Why would I throw away perfectly re-readable books? Hell, that one in there, *Zero Ward*, is one of my favorite books of all time. And the *2012 Lesbian Erotica Collection*...come on, girl." She grinned when Wyatt spared her a shy glance over her shoulder. "Hey, it got super lonely in New York."

Wyatt burst into laughter, a hand coming up to wipe at the tears that had sprung to her eyes. Faith suspected they were tears of shame. She walked over to the other woman, softening her tone.

"Listen, I don't know if you've heard, but I own this beast of a building named Bessie, and it's like, twenty yards from that place you work." She shrugged. "Hey, I used to love to read during my dinner break at the law firm." She gave Wyatt her most winning smile, trying to calm her embarrassment and shame. "Bessie has plenty of room for great books."

With a quiet sob, Wyatt threw herself into Faith's arms. Though she was initially startled, Faith wrapped her up in an embrace.

"It's no big deal, Wyatt," she whispered, allowing her friend to take whatever she would out of those words.

"Thank you," Wyatt whispered back.

Chapter Twelve

Like a caged lion, Faith paced, back and forth, back and forth. For a moment, she had an idea what an expectant father must feel. She was in the small room created for people like her in the warehouse that was Jack's Antiques and Auction in Boulder, a gorgeous town at the foothills of the Rockies that was the home of the prestigious Colorado University, or CU, as it was more widely known.

The room was the size of a small bedroom with comfortable couches, a self-help coffee bar, and a little refrigerator filled with bottles of water and cans of soda. She tapped one such water bottle against her thigh as she paced. A flat-screen TV was mounted to the wall with closed-circuit video playing of the auction in the main warehouse area. She was able to forgive Jack Tejon when he wrote her a $4,500 check for the antiques he bought from her, all mined from Bessie. She'd had no idea that an old clock could be worth nearly two grand all by itself, let alone the odds and ends.

The reason she was there now, however—and about to have a coronary—was because of the 1926 Brough Superior SS100 snuggled between the Cadillac she'd uncovered and the wall. The strange-looking motorcycle was apparently rare and, according to Jack, who looked as though he were about to orgasm when he saw it, very valuable, just like the car.

Her gaze never left the screen or Jack, who held a microphone to be heard by the entire crowd of wealthy collectors who stood holding white placards with large black numbers printed on them. Jack and the bike, currently covered with a black cloth, stood on a dais in front of a large screen that currently read $0.00.

"And now," Jack said, his voice echoing through the room as he spoke into the microphone. "The first of our two special beauties for today!" He pulled the cover off the motorcycle, and Faith had to laugh as a round of *Ohhs* rippled through the crowd of mostly older men.

She continued her pacing, listening as he went over all the specs and history of the bike, which she would normally find interesting, but in that moment all she wanted to do was throw up. After Jack finished with the bike details, he explained how the auction worked, and that full payment of items was due within one day or the win would be null and void and the item would go back up for auction.

"Well, that's good," she whispered. "At least the torture is only twenty-four hours' worth at most."

"So, with that, let's begin," Jack exclaimed.

Faith's heart nearly leapt out of her chest at those words, crazy nervous that the bike wouldn't sell. *No, stop.* It was no skin off her back, she had no money invested in it; in fact, it had been dumped in her lap with Bessie. Still, a girl could hope. Jack had told her that the bike could easily bring in four hundred thousand dollars or more. She thought that was insane for a simple motorcycle, but who was she?

The bottle of water tapped harder against her thigh as her anxiety level increased for the first few minutes when nobody was making any bids at all. Finally, finally a man in the back wearing a straw cowboy hat broke the ice.

"One fifty!"

Faith listened as Jack began his crazy auctioneer drone, which sounded more like he was talking in tongues than verbally caressing bids. Unable to keep up with him, her gaze became glued to the screen behind him, which changed with each advancing bid. She was beginning to sweat, feeling it between her breasts and under her arms. She felt lightheaded when the bid hit two hundred and fifty thousand dollars.

"Holy shit." She shook her head, eyes never leaving the screen behind Jack. She nearly jumped out of her skin when the door to the room opened and Lynette, Jack's wife entered, hugging a clipboard to her chest.

Smiling, Lynette closed the door behind her. "Exciting, isn't it?" she asked, indicating the screen behind Faith.

"Heart-attack-invoking, more like it," Faith responded. She was a little concerned to see Jack's wife and business partner walking over to her, worried there was an issue with the auction.

"I wanted to talk to you about something unexpected that has come up in the last little bit," the attractive African American woman explained. "I received a phone call from someone who often deals with Jack, so we know he's legit. Now, normally we don't do this—once the auction for an item is set, it's set. But, he saw the Cadillac online on our website, and he wants it."

Faith felt her heart skip a beat and her breath catch. "Okay..."

"So, here's where we stand, Faith," Lynette explained. "We can continue with the auction to follow the bike there, and we're estimating you'll get a great return on it, likely up in the low million range."

Faith's eyes popped open, her legs suddenly feeling a bit weak. She reached out with the hand not holding the water bottle to brace against the wall. "Okay," she managed. Jack hadn't given her a number, had only told her he felt they'd "do well."

"Now, this buyer doesn't want to deal with the auction nonsense—his words—and prefers just to buy the car and be done with it. Said he's been looking for this one for twenty years. If he can buy the car today, he'll give you a cashier's check for one point nine."

Her brain foggy, nothing computing as it should, Faith shook her head. "One point nine?"

Lynette nodded. "One million, nine hundred thousand dollars, cashier's check—Faith!"

The last thing Faith remembered was everything going black.

※ ※ ※ ※

She'd only had it for three days, so was still learning all the buttons and gadgets of her brand-new Toyota 4Runner SRS Premium Edition, shiny black with all the bells and whistles. The dark gray leather interior creaked pleasantly beneath Faith as she adjusted in the comfortable, heated seat.

She was jamming to Within Temptation's "Faster" as she cruised along, head bobbing to the fun beat and heart swelling with the incredible vocals of Sharon den Adel, the Dutch band's lead vocalist.

Getting a little too into it and nearly running off the shoulder of the road, Faith slowed and turned the music down as she neared her exit. It was late in April and an absolutely beautiful day with sunny skies, which she figured would melt the snow from the last spring storm on the ground, especially noticed as she veered off to take the exit that would lead her to Wynter. She was heading to town for a short trip, a single purpose in mind.

Passing the farmer's fields, she saw the white church. Over the two-week period since work had begun, scaffolding had grown up around the building, and she couldn't help but grin, proud to have been a small part of the reason behind how that had happened, even though it was her father's resources and connections doing the work.

She slowed the large SUV even more as she entered the snow-covered main street of the town proper. Without even realizing it, a smile spread across her lips as she saw the long row of buildings, now so familiar, including—and especially—Pop's. The smile slid from her face as guilt began to gnaw at her gut so much that she felt nauseous.

Ripping her gaze from the café, she focused on the slow, measured turn into the small space in front of Bessie. She wasn't used to maneuvering such a large vehicle so it took some focus, but eventually she got the sleek black SUV parked.

Cutting the engine, Faith sat there for a moment staring at her building. Her heart was beating quickly, and again guilt began to gnaw at her. Pushing it aside again, she pulled her keys from the ignition and searched through the collection until she found the right one for Bessie. Blowing out a breath, she grabbed her phone from the passenger seat and climbed out of her new ride.

Unlocking the door and stepping inside, Faith was excited to see the newly installed light switch right next to the door. It was part of the basics the electrician had done; who knew what ultimately the building would be used for or would need, so she had put off any decisions regarding outlets and such. The guilt returned as the thought haunted her that it wouldn't be her who was making those plans. Not anymore.

Hitting the switch, she was delighted when a sea of bare lightbulbs all flicked on at once, strung about ten feet up and illuminating the entirety of the main floor. After discovering the car and the motorcycle, they'd needed to clear out the rest of the junk and goods in order to get them out. Now, it was completely clear, save for the bar, which Jack had wanted to buy from her. She'd flat refused, feeling it belonged with the building, and certainly hoped whoever bought Bessie would feel the same way.

She wandered around the main floor, the square heel on her boots thudding with every step on the expansive wood floor. She took in the high ceilings almost like seeing them anew with the original tin tiles, which would definitely need to be replaced. They'd removed the black funeral curtains, letting the natural light come in, though the place was set up in such a way that the windows didn't do a ton. It would always need supplemental light. She walked over to the bar and ran her hand along the dusty mahogany of the bar top, noting again the beautiful craftsmanship in the carved front that the brass bar ran along.

Stopping her progress about halfway down the length, she looked around the room, hand resting on the cool wood. It wasn't hard to imagine cowboys and miners sitting around tables laughing or fighting, playing cards. She could see the saloon girls wandering, perhaps pulled into the lap of a lonely miner who bought her a drink if she'd keep him company during the poker game.

She smiled, swearing she could hear kitschy piano music coming from the back of the room over by the basement door. She swore she heard the thud of hard-soled boots walking to and fro. She swore she felt life in the room. She could easily imagine life in Bessie once more.

Shaking off where her mind wanted to go, she slapped her palm on the bar top before bringing her phone up to switch it to camera mode.

Taking pictures of every wall, room, ceiling, and floor of the basement and main floor, Faith headed up to the second floor. She knew the ladies would want to see every nook and cranny in the place. When she reached the top of the stairs, she stopped, a smile instantly coming to her lips.

A small bookcase had been placed against the wall next to a large beanbag on the floor with a wool throw folded neatly and placed atop it. The bookcase was filled with all the books that had been in the box Faith had taken for Wyatt from her storage shed. One of them, *Zero Ward*, sat on the floor next to the beanbag, a bookmark tucked between its pages about a third of the way through the thick paperback. Clearly, Wyatt had used the key Faith had mailed her at the café and had taken her up on reading breaks.

Faith ran a hand through her short dark hair, that guilt returning to her gut again. Letting out a heavy sigh, she brought her phone up once more for pictures.

"Wyatt, I just wanted to drop by and let you know that I'm abandoning Wynter." Faith's eyes squeezed shut, her hands covering her face. "Clearly not the thing to say," she whispered into them. Hands dropping to her lap, she stared out the windshield at Bessie, not seeing the large building but the beautiful face of her friend instead. "Listen, to my shock, all that stuff sold for a lot of money, and I've decided I need to find myself, so I'm gonna abandon you. Damn it!"

She lightly smacked the steering wheel. Truth was, Wyatt probably wouldn't give two cares, regardless of what Faith told her. They'd known each other a very short time, and Wyatt had her life there with her job, her husband, and friends of Wynter.

"I'm totally projecting my guilt," Faith murmured, head resting back against the headrest. "What the hell am I guilty of, though?" she asked, hands flopping down to her lap. "I got my dad to help with their church. That's good, right?" She met her gaze in the rearview mirror. "Right? Cleaned this place out. Also a good thing. Place was a mess," she added, self-righteous even to her own ears.

Without another word, she inserted the key into the ignition and started the SUV. Resolving to be a big girl and face her own decision, which a long chat with Cameron and her boyfriend the night before had helped her make, she glanced into her side mirror to make sure she wouldn't plow back into anyone passing by.

Her hand reaching down to put the 4Runner

in Reverse, she noticed tracks in the snow that she hadn't noticed a moment before, though they had to have been there. She knew Stella wasn't quite *that* fast.

She tapped her fingers on the steering wheel for a moment, trying to decide what to do. To the left of her across the way was the café and Wyatt—if she was there. To the right would be the direction Stella and Mr. Billy had gone in the sleigh, the double narrow sled tracks telltale along with Stella's hoofprints.

She had no idea why, but suddenly a deep curiosity consumed her and she found herself going right. Part of her wondered if she was just being chickenshit and avoiding the café, but the bigger part of her genuinely wanted to know where Mr. Billy went.

Nobody behind her, she drove slowly, following the tracks, which wound their way up toward the old mine past the miners' houses and to a thick wooded area in the middle of nowhere. Finally, she saw an old barn built in a cleared area, though it hadn't been cleared much, one tree looking as though it was one good snowstorm away from falling over onto the structure. She noticed that just behind the barn was a pole that extended far above the treetops with what looked to be some sort of solar panels mounted to it.

Faith pulled the SUV to a stop, noting the sleigh tracks went right into the barn, which had two huge doors that looked like they swung outward from the center. To the right of the big door was a smaller, human-sized door. The barn was weathered wood, two-story, as she saw a window up top. Looked like perhaps it was a hayloft, but it had glass.

Shutting down her vehicle, she climbed out, looking over the structure as she did. She noticed a beautifully carved owl that perched on a branch mounted to the side of the building not far from the smaller door. She walked up to it, admiring the artistry. She gasped and jumped back when a voice came out of it.

"Come in, Faith. I've been expecting you."

Though she'd only formally met him the one time and only heard his voice that one time, she knew it was Mr. Billy. "Um," she said stupidly, looking more closely at the owl and realizing that there were lenses behind its eyes, and she figured there must be a camera in there along with an intercom system. "Okay."

She found the door unlocked, so pushed it open and entered, closing it behind her. Instantly, the smell of fresh hay met her nose and she saw that the main area of the barn looked like she imagined any stable would. Stella stood in her stall munching from a bale of hay. She noticed a bag hanging from a thick square pole at the corner of Stella's stall. It looked very much like the one Wyatt had put into Mr. Billy's sleigh. She realized it was filled with oats.

She smiled and waved, feeling like an idiot, as the beautiful old mare glanced up at her. "Hey, Stella."

The sleigh was parked in a stall of its own. There were various things hanging from the walls that Faith figured were used to care for the horse. She knew nothing about the animals other than they were huge, beautiful, and majestic. Everything seemed to be neatly in its place.

Just past the sleigh was a wide, solid wooden ladder that was anchored to the wall and led up to the hay loft. The higher she climbed, the warmer it got, and she could hear the popping and crackling of a fire, which didn't seem like an entirely good idea in a wooden barn with lots of hay below. But, to her amusement and great surprise, the "fire" was actually an electric fireplace with a screen covering a very convincing rendition of the real thing.

The old hayloft had been converted into a cozy little living space that wasn't even as large as her bedroom in Cameron's house. There was a narrow bed against the wall, which wasn't much more than a mattress on a platform, three-fourths the width of a twin-sized bed. A recliner sat near a floor lamp, where Mr. Billy sat, his legs covered by a crocheted blanket. The electric fireplace was made into a small table, which had several books and journals stacked atop it. In the corner was a small kitchenette with a dorm-size fridge and a hotplate sitting atop a small microwave.

"This is a neat little setup," she said, impressed.

"Come sit by the fire," he said, smirking at his own little joke as he reached to the floor beside his chair and produced a fat throw pillow. He lightly tossed it to the floor near his chair and the warmth of the heater.

Doing what she was told, Faith lowered herself to the wood plank floor, parts covered in large area rugs. She looked at the electric fireplace. "This thing is pretty neat," she said, grinning up at him where he remained seated in his chair.

"My whole life I've had a fireplace," he explained. "This place isn't exactly conducive for one, what with a hundred-and-thirty-year-old barn filled with hay."

Faith smiled and shook her head, readjusting her sitting situation. "I suppose not."

"I knew you were the one," he said quietly, his gaze boring so deeply into Faith's it began to make her a bit uncomfortable. "That first day you came into town. We passed on the road, and you waved at me."

He smiled. "You had this look on your face…" He began to chuckle. "It was this mixture of wonder and utter bafflement."

Faith grinned. "That's fairly accurate. But, I was the one for what?"

"To save Wynter."

She stared at him. "What?"

"I once thought it would be Wyatt," he said with a sad sigh as he adjusted the blanket on his legs. "She spoils me, you know," he continued, affection in his eyes. "She made this for me. Insists on feeding me and can't seem to deny Stella of her beloved oats."

Hearing all the wonderful things Wyatt did for the old man put an instant smile on Faith's lips. She remembered that day, her friend's insistence that he take the take-out container. "Yes," she said softly, finding it entirely too easy to see Wyatt's beautiful face before her mind's eye. She shook the image loose. "She's a sweet woman."

"When she showed up five or six years ago, I thought, 'There she is, the one who can bring life back into this town.'" His smile faded off his grizzled face, replaced by pure distaste. "Then I met her husband." He shook his head, once again messing with the crocheted blanket. "I knew he'd never allow it. So, I kept it locked up, a mystery kept safe by my dear friend Barbara at the Historical Society."

Faith gasped. "Oh no! Bessie is yours?"

Heavy eyebrows fell. "Bessie?"

"The building. Sorry, Wyatt's nickname for it. Oh my god, I'm so sorry. I can give you the money. It's okay, give me enough time to get back to Denver and to my bank—" Faith pushed to her feet, panicked. She was stopped by a surprisingly strong hand on her arm and his eyes boring up into hers.

"Sit, please," he said gently, lightly squeezing her arm before letting it go. He waited until she was seated again before continuing. "She kept that building safe under the auspices of an old, run-down building that the Historical Society just hadn't gotten around to, yet." He chuckled, seeming proud of his ruse. "I saw you that day, a young woman with life, a light about you, and I knew it would be you." With slow movements he pushed the blanket aside and got to his feet, walking over to the bed. A small wooden chest lay on the floor at the foot. "I loaded it with treasures that would help you on your journey," he explained, though each word confused Faith even more.

"What do you mean? Mr. Billy, I don't understand."

He grinned over his shoulder at her as he knelt down in front of the chest. "If you're going to call me Mister-something-or-other, call me Mr. Wynter." He reached inside the chest and rifled through what sounded like papers until he apparently found what he was looking for, because he removed his hand from it and closed the lid. He made his way back to his chair, a wrapped item in his hand. "My great-grandfather built this town, Faith." He slowly lowered himself back into his chair with a loud groan. "You've been chosen to bring it back to life."

Faith looked at the wrapped item he held out to her. She took the small, cloth package. "What is this?"

"Oh," Billy Wynter said cryptically. "It's the key to your success." He burst into laughter at his own words.

Confused, she unwrapped the material to reveal an oversized iron key.

Chapter Thirteen

Faith sat behind the wheel, looking at the key she'd been given, tapping it against the palm of the hand. Letting out a heavy breath, she looked out the windshield at Mr. Wynter's barn. "What the hell did I just promise?" she whispered. "Shit."

Rewrapping the key in its cloth, she set it on the passenger seat, started her 4Runner, and backed away from the barn to leave the property.

Feeling a bit shaken by what the old man had told her, as well as an enormous weight on her shoulders, Faith decided to drive around a bit to clear her head. Once she got back to a road that was closer to the town proper than Mr. Wynter's property was, she drove aimlessly, taking random turns onto random streets.

She found herself near the old school. The neighborhood contained houses that were perhaps just barely pre-WWII, all dilapidated. They were still occupied, it seemed. Or, at least some of them. She had to slow down as the asphalt was in horrible condition, huge potholes dotting the street, and if someone wasn't paying attention, it would be easy for their car's alignment to be completely knocked out.

Finally, she pulled over at the curb in front of the school. It was a single-story brick building that had once held K-12, though from what Wyatt had said, there had been plans at one time to build a separate high school. That never came to fruition and the entire Wynter school system was shut down, kids bussed to another town.

Cutting off the engine, Faith climbed out and walked over to the school property. It literally seemed that in the ten or twenty minutes she'd been driving around, the nice, sunny spring day had clouded over, the sky gray and cold. She hugged herself as a cold breeze whipped past her.

She looked at the building, noting many of the windows were boarded over, a couple broken. The parking lot was a mess, in places chunks missing, weeds growing through all the cracks. Next to the school was what she assumed was once a large open grass space, probably used for recess and gym class, and then for the neighborhood kids to come and play after school hours. Now, it was overgrown, trash and discarded machine parts littering it.

"These kids deserve better than this," she whispered. Turning in a slow circle to take in the entirety of the neighborhood, she shook her head, resolve in her voice. "They all do."

༄༄༄༄

They walked in silence, Faith holding tight to Bruno's leash as they made their way around the neighborhood, the Boxer a happy boy as he trotted along, stopping to sniff some unseen mystery now and then. She'd been surprised when Ogden had called, asking if he could come over and discuss the progress of the church with her, but she'd acquiesced as long as he was okay with joining her while she walked the dog, which had already been her plan.

Finally, he spoke. "Some great people there, aren't

there?"

She glanced up at him before returning her focus to the curious dog, who was tugging at the leash to head toward yet another mailbox. "Wynter? Yeah. There really are." She smiled, Wyatt's laugh and face immediately coming to mind. Just as soon as it did, then it was Pops, then Mr. Wynter and Father Brandon and some of the others she'd seen so often in the café. Of course, it circled back around to Wyatt.

"So, we're making great progress on the church," Ogden began, unwittingly knocking Faith out of her thoughts and musings. "I'd guess another few weeks and we should finish up."

"That's really wonderful," Faith said, a genuine smile of pleasure spreading across her face. "Father Brandon is over the moon, I'm sure."

Ogden grinned. "They all are." They walked in silence for a few houses before he spoke again. "Have you decided what you're going to do with…what does that little gal at the café call it? Bessie?"

Faith smiled. "Wyatt."

"Oh, sorry. I thought it was Bessie."

Her smile widened. "It is Bessie, Wyatt is the 'little gal at the café.'"

"Oh, okay. Wyatt. That's unusual," Ogden said thoughtfully.

"And, as for Bessie, I want to renovate her. I have no idea into what, but I actually was thinking about talking to you about this," she added, glancing up at him as they continued their walk. "Have you taken a good look at Wynter? Like, driven around and seen what bad shape it's in?"

Ogden nodded. "I have. And, Father Brandon and Vicky had spoken to me about it at length."

"I want to do something to help, feel like I *have* to do something," she said. She considered telling him about her visit with Billy Wynter but opted to keep it to herself. Perhaps she'd talk to Wyatt about that. For now, she simply said, "Should I build a McDonald's? Something?"

"Well, what good is a Big Mac if people can't afford one?" Ogden countered.

"Good point," Faith muttered, watching as Bruno stopped to sniff a rolled newspaper that a delivery person had thrown terribly, the paper halfway on the sidewalk and halfway on the lawn. "So, what do I do?"

"Well, whenever we get a project, be it a building, a house, renovation, whatever, we always begin by talking to the client about what their needs are. For instance, what good is it if we build a grand staircase when the client has bad knees and can no longer climb stairs, and what they really needed was a main floor bedroom added on?"

"Ohhh," Faith said, nodding. "I get it. Maybe I can gather the mayor, city council members, folks like that."

"I think that's a fantastic idea. Certainly a great place to start." Ogden stopped their progress with a hand to Faith's arm. "Um, I think the dog took those people's newspaper."

※※※※

Wyatt: Gooooooood morning! Pops said everyone will be there and I got coffee and sweet rolls ready! See you soon...

The boisterous text message was accompanied by a picture of a grinning Wyatt holding up a carafe full of coffee. Faith smiled, taking in that beautiful face and thinking that smile would be something mighty nice to wake up to every morning, just as she'd awoken to the message and selfie that morning.

She pulled her new SUV into the parking lot of the café, noting a smattering of cars, much like other times she'd been there. Cutting the engine, she grabbed her belongings and opened the door. Her smile was instant when she saw Wyatt step through the employee side door. Her smile grew when she realized the waitress was beckoning her over.

"Hey there," Faith said.

"Howdy, stranger." Wyatt reached a hand out, grabbing Faith's to tug her inside the building. Once they were tucked into the tiny hallway that led to the kitchen proper and the door was closed behind them, Wyatt took a surprised Faith into a quick but tight hug. "I'm so glad you came back."

Faith looked at her, confused. "Came back?"

"Well," Wyatt said softly, giving her a shy smile as she stepped back out of the hug. "I'm not so sure I woulda stuck around after makin' that kind of find."

Instantly, guilt flooded Faith and she brought a hand up, running it over the back of her neck. "You knew about the stuff in the building?"

Wyatt shook her head. "Not until after. Mr. Billy told me about it." Her smile returned "I was so worried y'all would leave, I'd never see ya again." Wyatt shrugged, biting her bottom lip. For a moment, she looked like a shy little girl. "I felt like we'd started a real friendship, and I don't wanna lose that."

Faith's heart melted. "Me, neither."

The smile those two words earned her was more reward than any dollar figure in her bank account ever could be. "Everyone's here," Wyatt added after another tight hug. "I'll get the coffee poured."

Faith nodded, nerves totally overtaking the warmth Wyatt's hug had filled her with mere moments before. Doing a bit of positive self-talk, she made her way through the kitchen to the dining room, expecting to find a firing squad of city officials. Instead, she found three old men sitting at a four-top table, a handwritten name plaque sitting before each, the fourth and empty spot with her name written in the same bold, all-caps writing.

A couple of the men she recognized from other trips to the café, but the oldest one with a full Santa Claus beard she'd not seen before. Stepping up to the table, she heard them talking about a golf game that seemed to have gone terribly wrong when sprinklers were turned on.

"There she is," one of the men said, the one she'd seen the most, his blue eyes kind. He pushed back from the table and stood, reaching over in a gentlemanly gesture to push her chair out.

"Thank you," she said, feeling completely in over her head as she lowered herself to the chair and scooted it toward the table, three pairs of expectant eyes on her. "Um, well, I'm Faith Fitzgerald, and I appreciate you gentlemen meeting me. Uh..." She looked around the café, noting nobody seemed to be paying them a bit of attention except for Pops, who sat in his usual spot behind the cash register. "Are we awaiting anyone else?"

"Let's see," Santa Claus said, opening a red folder that had been lying on the table before him. He removed a few sheets of paper stapled together. He pulled on the reading glasses that had been hanging around his neck on a thin chain, glancing over the top of them at Faith. "I found the minutes from our last meeting."

Faith glanced past the sugar shaker at the pages lying on the folder to see the date, March 5, 2003. "Your last city council meeting was in 2003?" she asked, looking at the men at the table, who then looked at each other before meeting her expectant gaze.

"Guess so," one of them said.

"Okay, shall I take roll call?" Santa Claus asked, eyebrows raised as he took the pages in his hand. With no response, he began. "Mike Sills."

"Present," one of the men at the table said, raising two fingers.

"Lionel Custer," Santa said, pointing to himself. "Present. Ted Martinez."

"He died what, four years ago?" Mike said.

Lionel glanced at him over his glasses then turned back to his paper. "That would explain why he never returned my email," he muttered, fetching a pen from the front pocket of his flannel shirt. He clicked it into life before drawing a line through a name on the page and tucking the pen away.

"Here we go, y'all," Wyatt said, lowering a tray filled with steaming cups of coffee, Faith's fixed just how she liked it, and four plates of Wyatt's homemade cinnamon rolls.

Faith's mouth instantly began watering. "Oh my."

Wyatt grinned down at her as she placed a plate and silverware rolled in a napkin in front of her. "Enjoy," she said softly, giving her that little grin that

Faith was beginning to love and look for every time she saw the waitress. At the moment, as Wyatt had leaned in close to set her breakfast down, Faith was in a cocoon of competing heavenly smells: Wyatt's perfume and freshly baked cinnamon roll.

"Thanks," she managed to say, almost grateful as Wyatt moved away to serve the men so she could catch her balance.

"You gents being kind to our Faith here?" Wyatt asked, one hand resting on Faith's shoulder while the other held the empty serving tray down by her leg.

"Well, of course," Mike said, beginning to dig into his food. "You know us better than that, Wyatt."

"Indeed I do," Wyatt said with a wink. She gave Faith's shoulder a light squeeze before she moved on from the table.

Still able to feel the warmth from the beautiful redhead's hand on her shoulder, Faith tried to shake it off and return her focus to the business at hand. "Okay, any more?"

"Yup," Lionel said, sipping is black coffee. "Andy Frank," he said, glancing at the third man at the table, who simply nodded. "And, finally, Samuel Popperton."

"Present."

Faith was surprised to hear the fourth voice come from far behind her. She glanced over her shoulder to see Pops, still reading his newspaper. She smirked. "Well, I'll be," she murmured to herself.

"Mister Secretary, we are all present and accounted for," Andy said. "Except for Ted. He seems to be deceased."

"So noted," Lionel responded, scribbling a few notes on his paper.

Faith watched this, feeling like she'd fallen down the rabbit hole. "Okay. Um, great. Is the mayor coming?" she asked, looking at each man, who looked back at her in turn as though she had three heads.

"Mayor?" Mike reached up to stroke his walrus of a mustache. He looked to Andy, who adjusted his flat cap. Something about him reminded Faith of the late actor Jack Lemon. "We didn't vote anybody else in after Martin, did we?"

Andy shook his head. "Nope, and we took the vote to boot him...When was that, Lionel?" he asked, glancing over to the heavily bearded man.

Lionel scanned the second page of his small packet. "March 5, 2003."

"You guys haven't had a mayoral election in almost twenty years?" Faith said, forkful of breakfast paused halfway to her mouth.

"We were going to," Lionel said, eyebrows drawn. "Why didn't we?"

"Ted died," Andy supplied, sipping his coffee.

"Right."

Faith, again, found herself feeling like she was having an out of body experience. "Perhaps you guys should have one, get somebody in charge to try and make things better, here."

"Well, isn't that why you're here?" Andy asked, giving her a kind smile.

"That's a fine idea, Andy," Mike added. "Why don't you do it, missy?"

"Do what? Organize a mayoral election?" she asked.

"No, be our interim mayor," Lionel explained.

"Whoa," Faith said, putting her fork down and raising her hands in supplication. "I don't even live here, gentlemen."

"Good point, good point," Mike admitted, nodding as he dug into his roll.

"She owns property here," Pops added, prompting all four of them to look his way. Never turning from his newspaper, he continued. "I feel that makes her a viable candidate."

"All in favor say 'aye,'" Lionel said, followed by a chorus of ayes.

"Wait—" Faith sputtered, scooting her chair back from the table.

"And, all in favor of Miss Faith Fitzgerald taking the Office of Interim Mayor, say 'aye,'" Lionel continued.

"Whoa! Hold on—"

"Aye!"

"Ayes have it," Lionel pronounced, tapping his coffee cup to the table like a gavel. "Measure passes."

Faith blinked at him several times, utterly confused and feeling lightheaded. She turned to see Wyatt leaning on the breakfast counter watching, that same, soft smile on her lips. "What just happened?"

※※※※

Faith paced in front of the bar, hands tucked into the back pockets of her jeans. Nerves causing her to chew at her bottom lip, she brought her hands up and ran them through her hair before she blew out a loud breath.

She made her way over to the bar and leaned back against it, a booted foot resting on the brass bar that was there for that purpose. Finally, the door opened and Wyatt appeared. She gave her a small smile and wave.

"Hey. Thanks for coming." Pushing away from the bar, she waited for the waitress to make her way over to her.

"Hey, darlin'," Wyatt said, giving her a tight hug, which Faith happily returned. "I'm sorry it took me a minute to get away."

"It's okay," Faith said into the hug, her eyes sliding closed in relief of the warmth and comfort of her friend. "I appreciate you finding time away."

"Of course." Wyatt gave her a tight squeeze before releasing her and taking a partial step back. "You look more stressed out than a long-tailed cat in a room full of rockin' chairs." She smiled and reached out to take Faith's hand. "Come on, now. Let's go upstairs and sit."

Nodding but saying nothing, Faith followed along until they were on the second floor. Wyatt walked over to the beanbag and grabbed the folded throw off it, using it as a pillow before patting the bean bag.

"You take the seat of honor," she said invitingly.

Faith smiled before lowering herself into the comfortable piece of furniture. "I'm not entirely sure how you haven't fallen asleep in this thing," she said, patting the side of the bean bag, which had spread out under her weight. "So comfy."

"Who says I haven't?" Wyatt's grin was wide. "So," she said, sobering. "Tell me what's goin' on in that pretty head of yours?"

"I think I'm just a little overwhelmed by what happened at the café," Faith explained, again running a hand through her hair. She felt it sticking up a crazy way on the side but didn't care at that moment. "Why did they do that?"

"Do what?" Wyatt asked, pulling her legs in to sit cross-legged. "Nominate you to take control of this town?"

"Yeah."

Wyatt smirked. "Because they sensed there's finally a damn adult in the room, I'd wager." Faith wasn't amused, and she assumed her expression showed as much when Wyatt scooted closer to where she sat, placing her hand on Faith's knee.

It was clear Wyatt was an affectionate person, but she was also an extremely beautiful woman that Faith found herself attracted to, which certainly made it slightly awkward at times. She said nothing as Wyatt continued speaking.

"Faith, the people in this town have given up, that's clear as day. Though I didn't know it before, Mr. Billy has been lookin' for somebody to give a flyin' whoops for years."

"Why doesn't he? Clearly he had the resources. Why does he choose to live in a barn when he has access to funds to do a lot of good?" For reasons she couldn't quite put her finger on, Faith felt a flash of anger at her own words. A man who'd loved the town his own ancestors founded had done nothing as it fell to pieces and began to die. She was about to say as much when Wyatt's soft voice stopped her in her tracks.

"Mr. Billy is dyin', Faith." Wyatt looked away, her hand sliding from Faith's knee to join her other hand in her own lap.

Faith could feel the sadness rolling off her friend in waves. She grunted as she struggled to sit up in the quicksand that was the bean bag, but finally succeeded.

She felt it was her turn to reach out. Placing a hand on Wyatt's own knee, she said gently, "Tell me about him. Who is Billy Wynter?"

"Mr. Billy left here in 1942 to go fight in the war," Wyatt began. "Him, a brother, and a sister went. He was the only Wynter brother to survive, and he fell in love with the order of the military, so he stayed in and his sister Bethany returned. He fought in Korea, then Vietnam. He retired as a general, and then finally he and his wife Gretta returned in the eighties. Over the years and in the countries he'd been stationed in, they made some smart purchases and investments." She shrugged. "By the time they returned, this place had gone to pot over the fifty years he'd been gone. He tried hard to revamp this place, and it even started to, but then the markets fell in 2008, and that was pretty much the death knell."

Faith listened, fascinated, growing a brand-new respect for the man she'd only spent any real time with once. "Wow."

Wyatt nodded. "After Gretta died, he sold everything they had—their house, cars, all of it—and turned the money into what you found in Bessie." She smiled. "Typical of his generation, not all that hot on banks, so figured whoever he chose would get far more bang for their buck today once the treasures he hid in here were liquidated."

"How long has he had this planned? To pass the mantle off," Faith clarified.

Wyatt smiled. "A long time. A long, long time." She reached down and covered Faith's hand with her own. "So, *Mayor*, what'cha gonna do now?"

Chapter Fourteen

She was nervous. A look at Wyatt standing behind the bar filling cups of coffee helped ease her anxiety, as well as the smile sent her way, but she was still nervous. She was set up at the back of the main floor of Bessie with a small table provided by Pops where the karaoke machine was set up, microphone in her hand. They thought the simple speaker system would be plenty for the size of the room she was trying to reach.

"Come on in, everyone," she said, waving those in who were lurking at the front door. She saw the three city council members milling about, which made her feel better, especially since they'd helped her put this town meeting together in the first place. Her father stood over by the wall with the windows, along with Tom and a few other associates of his architectural firm. She saw a few other faces she recognized, including Father Brandon and Vicky and some other folks from the church. A moment later, Pops and Mr. Wynter entered together. She was stunned, as she'd never seen Pops actually up and moving.

"There's coffee over at the bar, folks. Please help yourselves." She blew out a nervous breath after she lowered the microphone. She watched as Lionel "Santa Claus" Custer wobbled her way, his cane tapping the staccato progress like Morse code. "Good morning, Mr. Custer," she greeted, forcing a smile.

"'Mornin'." He gave her a winning smile. "You ready?"

"I hope so," she said with a nod. "I wrote myself a few notes last night, but I'm not so sure how they're going to take any of this coming from me, a stranger, an outsider."

"Well, I thought perhaps I'd introduce you. You okay with that?" he asked, indicating the microphone in her hand.

She nearly shoved it into his large belly. "Take it."

He broke out into laughter, taking it from her. "I'm giving it back, you know."

Faith smiled, taking a deep breath. She glanced again over at Wyatt to see her give her a thumbs-up before pouring more paper cups of coffee from the huge industrial pot she and Pops had brought over from the café. Wyatt had also shown her the large college-ruled notebook she'd brought—to take notes, she'd explained.

At Faith's look of surprise, Wyatt had quipped, "This country girl has more skills than merely pourin' coffee, darlin'."

"I bet you do," Faith muttered to herself, a small internal smile at her own naughty thoughts, which she quickly pushed away. She was surprised and excited to see Jill and Stephanie step in, Jill walking over to grab her wife and herself a cup of coffee. Faith raised a hand in acknowledgement that she'd seen them.

She'd spoken to the two women about her idea the previous week, and truthfully, from the skeptical look on Stephanie's face, hadn't for a second thought they'd want any part of it. Yet, there they stood, back by the door.

"Okay, boys and girls." Lionel's voice boomed out over the room, which was filled with the chatter of the people that had come to the meeting, which from Faith's naked eye looked to be more than a hundred, perhaps a hundred and thirty. "Get yourself a cup of coffee if you haven't yet and let's get settled, please."

Faith watched as, just as Mr. Custer had requested, people began to settle down and find places to stand to listen. She was impressed.

"Okay, now I know you are all wondering why we called you here. Well," he said, placing a meaty hand on Faith's shoulder. "This little gal is going to talk to you for a minute. Now, I had every single one of you in my biology class at Wynter Mountain Middle School, and I fully expect you to give her the same attention you gave me. Okay?"

Ahhhh, okay.

"So, without further ado, I introduce to you Mayor Faith Fitzgerald!"

Faith cringed at the title of mayor, still not even positive that was legal, but from the hoots and boos she got, her stomach dropped.

"Why do we need another one?" someone yelled.

"No more politicians!"

"The last guy ruined the town!"

"Okay, okay," she said, taking the microphone hesitantly from the older man. She raised her free hand in supplication. "Everyone, please calm down. Okay? Listen, I'm not a politician, I'm actually a lawyer." Faith jumped behind Lionel Custer when a paper cup came flying at the little dais they had set up. "Not that kind of lawyer!"

Suddenly, a loud whistle rent the air, instantly quieting the room down. Faith peeked out from behind the big man just in time to see two of Wyatt's fingers lowering from her lips.

"Hey!" she called out after the shrill whistle. "All y'all calm yourselves down and have some manners." When the place was totally silent, she turned to look at Faith and smiled.

Bemused, Faith took a deep breath and surveyed the crowd once more, all eyes on her. "Listen," she began gently. "I don't know a lot about what's happened here, but it's obvious to anyone with eyes that Wynter has been abandoned by those who were supposed to protect her and protect you guys. What I said is true, I'm not a politician. Yes, I am a lawyer, though right now I'm not practicing."

"Yeah, ain't you that big shot outta New York?" someone called out from the crowd, causing a few anxious rumblings.

"Hold on," she said, raising her hand again to stifle anymore upset. "Hold on. Yes, but let me tell you a little bit about me before you get any ideas in your head that just aren't true." She walked over to the stool that had been placed on the stage in case she wanted to sit down, and she decided to, perhaps to give off a more casual, I'm-not-your-enemy air. "I worked in Manhattan in mostly corporate law. Now, my dream was to be a big-shot lawyer, you bet. But, after eleven years of being taken advantage of, watching my dream given to other people time and time again, I decided I'd had enough."

She looked around, seeing understanding on some faces, particularly those of the women, though many of the faces were still guarded and seemed unsure. She continued on.

"I quit my job, I packed up my car, and I drove

home. Yes, this," she said, pointing down at the floor which she stood. "Colorado is home. I grew up an hour and a half up the road from here." She was pleased—and relieved—when she heard some surprised sounds from those gathered, a few words of approval. "Do you want to know how I ended up in Wynter?" she asked, feeling a bit more comfortable as she looked around the room, meeting a few gazes. "I had to pee." She shrugged, noting the few chuckles and smiles she got. "To make it worse, Pops over there," she said, pointing at the man in question, "wasn't going to let me go. Really? Doing the pee-pee dance here, and I had to buy something first?"

She was glad to hear the round of laughter that story got; clearly the people of the town had been submitted to the same treatment. She lowered the microphone, waiting for them to quiet again. She noticed the door to the building open and the huge sheriff's deputy she'd seen a time or two at the café walk in. He was in full uniform, and walked over to Wyatt.

Turning back to the crowd, Faith pressed on. "Needless to say, Wyatt had mercy on me and gave me the key to the ladies' room, but yes, I did buy lunch." She grinned after another round of laughter. "And, a raffle ticket." She indicated the building around them. "That's how we're all standing here right now. Look, folks," she continued, her voice taking a more serious note. "I know most of you don't know me from Eve, but obviously this town has been done terribly wrong. Look at the state of the roads, the state of the houses, the school." She paused as she let what she'd said sink in, noting the nods and looks of angry disgust on the faces of the townspeople. "The fact that there hasn't been a duly elected mayor in nearly twenty years tells me a lot. The last guy, from the little I've heard, was a real piece of work. Took money—"

"And my wife!" someone yelled from the crowd.

"Ouch," Faith said, shaking her head. "Well, I can assure you I'm not here to take your money, and I'm definitely not here to take your wives."

Laughter erupted in the room, along with scattered applause. Faith felt a gaze on her from off to the right and glanced over toward the bar to see Wyatt grinning at her, clapping. She returned the grin before looking back out on those before her.

"I want to help you," she said, the laughter dying down. "See, the money that was being raised from the raffle, as you all no doubt know, was to replace the church's steeple. Unfortunately, the work that needed to be done far exceeded the steeple repair, as well as the funds that the raffle raised." She looked over at Ogden, who leaned back against the wall watching. Dare she say she saw pride in his eyes? "You've all seen that the church is all but being rebuilt, so I'm sure you're confused since I just told you not enough money was raised." She pointed over at her father. "That man, Ogden Fitzgerald, is my father, who has been an architect with his own firm in Denver since I was a kid. He volunteered his time, knowledge, and resources to rebuild it." The room erupted in applause aimed at her father. It was her turn to feel proud.

Faith stood on the dais, her heart full of conviction behind every word she was about to say. "Now," she said loudly to be heard over the clapping and whistles, which began to die down. "Now, here's what I *do* want from you." She waited to make sure she had everyone's attention. Bringing up a hand, she ticked off each point with the lowering of a finger. "Your heart. Your talent. Your skills. Your time."

Confused looks abounded from her words, some quiet chatter and shrugged shoulders.

"Father Brandon has agreed to donate the unused steeple fund to put toward buying materials. I'm going to use some of my own resources, and I'm in talks with some folks back in Denver who have interest in investing in Wynter." She looked around, able to see the uncertainty and distrust returning. "So," she added. "If you're a plumber, we need you. If you're an electrician, we need you. Builders, we need you. If you have a truck and are willing to lug people and materials to the various worksites, we need you. If you can slap two pieces of bread together and make a sandwich for the workers, we need you. Let's rebuild this town!"

The room erupted as realization of what she was saying hit in full, the townspeople cheering, some crying. As Faith stood there, her heart raced in her chest. She had no idea how on earth she was going to pull it off, she just knew she had to.

She glanced over at Wyatt again, hoping to share that moment with her, but instead she saw the sheriff's deputy looming over her, almost menacing. Considering he had about a foot of height on her and easily a hundred pounds, she didn't understand his need for such intimidation. She nearly flew off the dais when she saw him grab Wyatt's arm with a huge hand that squeezed. The look on Wyatt's face told her that she was in pain.

"That was amazing. Just amazing!"

She turned to see a very excited Lionel standing before her. She lowered the microphone and smiled.

"I hope so. We need these people to buy in if this is going to work."

He nodded. "I agree. I'll send out an email, as we discussed, for people to let us know what they can do, skills, all that, as well as the worst areas in town to start. That way, we can formulate a plan of attack."

Faith was bounced from group to group, many of the people wanting to meet her and several with questions. Clearly, those present had contacted others who began to arrive in droves, all with questions. Bessie had more people in her than she'd probably had in a hundred years.

Not only had she not expected to see Jill and Stephanie again until she arrived at work Monday, she sure as hell hadn't expected to see them in deep, in-depth conversations with the townspeople of Wynter. Jill was talking with a tall man who looked more like a lumberjack than anything, while Stephanie gesticulated wildly in conversation with a group of three women.

Moving from the group she'd just spoken to, Faith was stopped by Andy and Mike. "Hey, gentlemen."

"Nicely done, little lady," Mike said, Andy nodding in agreement. "We wanted you to know that we did a little asking around and, well, after everything happened with Martin, the government of Wynter basically abandoned their posts, leaving us fellows in charge." He indicated himself and Andy.

Faith chuckled, nodding. "Oh boy."

"Which is precisely why we pass the job onto you," Andy added, holding out his hand, a silver key laying in the palm. "We have the authority to put someone in place. You!"

She looked down at the key. "What's this to?"

"Your office," Mike explained. "May be a little dusty, don't think anyone's been in there in years."

She studied the key for a moment before, with a deep breath, took it. "I guess we'll see. Thanks, guys."

Andy tipped his flat cap before the two men moved on.

Finally, she was able to make her way to Wyatt, who still stood with the deputy, though he was talking to a man she recognized from the café. It wasn't hard to see that the light that was usually in Wyatt's eyes was missing.

"So," Faith said as quietly as she could and still be heard over the den of the crowd. "A little birdy told me you like a certain cemetery nearby, and that you don't get to go all that often." She smiled when she saw a bit of that light return to those gorgeous turquoise eyes. "Think you can get away after this?"

Wyatt gave her a little grin. "I think I can sneak away."

"Excellent."

"So," came a deep, booming voice from far above Faith's head. "You're the little lady causin' all this dustup, huh?"

Faith looked up to find herself looking into the deep-set blue eyes of the deputy. His black hair was cut just so, neat in a style known as a fade. He gave her a charming smile, his huge hand extended toward her in greeting. She took it, finding her own hand absolutely dwarfed and engulfed.

"This is Faith Fitzgerald," Wyatt said, her voice sounding almost as though she was nervous or uncomfortable, Faith thought. "Faith, this is my husband, Lucas."

Instantly feeling anger fill her, Faith swallowed it down, though she had no doubt it was in her eyes. "Oh, you're her husband?" she asked, feigned surprised in her voice. "Because the way you were manhandling her earlier, I thought maybe you'd mistaken her for a suspect of a crime or something." She couldn't believe she'd said it, the words falling unchecked out of her mouth. Though she was definitely angry at this man, the truth was, it wasn't her business.

The deputy stilled their handshake for a split second, his grip tightening before he released her hand. "Well, ma'am," he said, standing to his full height, no doubt trying to use his size to intimidate her as well. "Any communication between my wife and I is no concern of yours."

"It is when it's on my property," Faith quipped nonchalantly. A voice deep inside was screaming at her to shut up and stay out of it, but her anger overrode her common sense. "I would expect nothing less than kind and gentle from a southern gentleman."

He gave her a chilling smile as he placed his uniform hat atop his head, the wide brim shadowing his face entirely. "I think you've been watching a bit too much *Gone With the Wind*," he said, his southern accent accentuated. "Have a good day now, ma'am." With a tip of his hat's brim, he turned and walked away.

Eyes sliding closed, Faith took a deep breath, a bit shaken by the interaction. She wasn't one for confrontation, but she just couldn't help it. Opening her eyes, she saw Wyatt studying her. "I'm sorry," she said, more of a whisper than anything.

Wyatt smiled, reaching out and resting her hand on Faith's shoulder before letting it slide down the length of her arm until it reached Faith's own hand, which she squeezed lightly. "Give me a couple hours, then I can slip away, okay?"

Faith nodded, feeling like a real ass.

≈≈≈≈

"This thing drives so smooth," Wyatt said, awe in her voice. "I can't believe you're lettin' me drive it."

Faith chuckled. "Why? It's not like it's a gold-plated Rolls-Royce."

The waitress spared her a glance. "Hey, I make less than three bucks an hour. For me, it might as well be."

"Simple then," Faith said. "Don't crash." She laughed at the glare that earned her. She looked around them, not recognizing the route they were taking to the cemetery. "This is a different way then you had me go last time."

Wyatt nodded. "It is. I love this part of town. These beautiful old homes."

"Looks like they were probably in the rich part of town at one point," Faith observed. "And, that's basically because they had more than one bathroom and more than two bedrooms." She smiled. "You know, it's so funny how what would've been considered a mansion once is considered a normal home today. Like, have you ever been into the Molly Brown house in downtown Denver?"

Wyatt shook her head. "Nope."

"Well, you think Molly Brown's husband came into tons of money so they built this ginormous house to be part of the upper crust society. At the time, they did and it was massive, but the rooms are teeny tiny.

Today, our standards are just so different, what we consider huge, livable. Like, the houses we drove by last time. They weren't a lot bigger than my apartment in New York, yet just me living there, I thought I was in such a tiny space."

Wyatt smiled as she nodded, keeping her eyes on the road as she drove along the winding roads, the houses getting farther and farther apart. "I know. We're such a selfish, wasteful culture."

"We certainly can be," Wyatt agreed, slowing the 4Runner as she neared a stop sign.

Faith glanced over to the left, her gaze instantly caught by a beautiful two-story farmhouse-style home perched atop a bit of a hill set back from the road. It looked to have a wraparound porch, or at least partial, and a couple of outbuildings.

"Wait," she said softly, reaching over and placing her hand on Wyatt's arm. "Would you drive over there, please?" she asked, indicating the house with her finger.

"Of course."

The large SUV turned off the main street and onto a narrow side road, whose sole purpose seemed to be to access the property, which was gated off by an old split rail fence. Wyatt pulled up and Faith ran out and unlatched it, pushing the wide gate open so they could drive through. It was clear the property was neglected, the big yellow foreclosure sign visible from the road.

Wyatt drove up the private dirt road that stretched out into a large parking area as opposed to a formal driveway. The house looked as though it were built at the turn of the century, perhaps even in 1900 itself. It had white siding, though it needed a paint job. The yard that spanned around three-quarters of the house was massive and definitely overgrown, though it didn't look decades-neglected like some of the town was.

Pulling to a stop, Wyatt cut the engine and the two climbed out. Faith shielded her eyes with her hand as she looked up at the peak of the roof and took in the upper floor. It looked as though there might be an attic as well, and ground-level windows denoted a basement.

"Can you see anything?" Faith asked Wyatt, who had climbed up the stairs to the porch and was looking into the windows available on that side of the house.

"Nah," Wyatt said, backing away from the window. "It's pretty dark in there from what I can see. Looks like most of the curtains are still there and closed."

Faith noticed a porch swing and walked over to it, testing to see if it would hold her weight by gingerly lowering herself onto it. When it held, she smiled, lightly pushing the swing back and forth as she took in the scenery around the house. "So beautiful."

"This is God's country right here," Wyatt responded softly, lowering herself onto the swing next to Faith. "When we first moved here," she began, her voice just as soft. "It was so strange seeing the mountains all the time. I remember the first time it snowed," she recalled with a laugh. "It was what y'all call a 'glazing,' not even a full inch, and I was just in awe as I rushed to the window in the café. Miss Vicky was there and she said, serious as a heart attack, 'Honey, this isn't snow, it's fluffy rain.'"

A bark of laughter burst from Faith's throat.

"Fluffy rain. I love it." She glanced over at Wyatt, studying her profile. Such a beautiful, beautiful woman, she thought. "I'm really sorry about earlier, at the meeting."

Wyatt met her gaze for a long moment before the barest of smiles crossed her lips. "Don't be."

"It's absolutely not my business or my place to say anything to Lucas. I really hope I didn't get you into trouble."

Wyatt let out a heavy sigh. "You know, Faith," she began, resignation in her voice. "The way I see it, nothin' can happen or everythin' can happen and Lucas will get mad or he won't. Ain't no rhyme or reason as to why." She gave her a sad smile. "Truth is, it was kinda nice to have someone step in. Nobody's done that since Mamma died."

"How did you end up with him?" Faith asked, far more vitriol in her voice than intended. "I mean, how'd you meet him?"

"At a football game, of all things. You see, in the south, high school and college ball is king, not the pro stuff. Even so, I hated sports then and not a fan now. Back then I was all about my horse, Lady Belle." She smiled and met Faith's gaze. "She was my best friend. Anyway, when I was sixteen, my friend Laurel begged me to go to the game with her, the guy she liked played for our school, and she wanted to go watch. I literally ran into Lucas heading down to get a seat."

Faith nodded. "Was he a student there, too?"

"Lord, no. Lucas was twenty-two. He was there with some friends to watch a little brother."

Faith's eyes popped open. "You began dating a twenty-two-year-old when you were sixteen? How on earth did you get away with that with your parents?"

Wyatt's eyes darkened as she was silent for a long moment, seemingly lost in a bitter memory. "Mamma hated Lucas from day one," she finally said, voice flat. "Daddy drooled all over him, insisted I accept Lucas's phone call, Lucas's request for a date, Lucas's hand in marriage." She shook her head. "Mamma didn't want to see me settle down young like she did. I don't think I ever saw my parents fight like they did the night of my weddin'."

Faith looked down at her hands, which fidgeted in her lap. Finally she said, "I'm so sorry."

The air between them got heavy for a moment until finally Wyatt smiled and slapped her hands on her thighs. "So," she exclaimed brightly, obviously forcing herself out of her memories, which Faith felt terrible for sending her back to. "What'cha gonna do about this place?"

Faith let out a heavy sigh, looking out over the house and the yard. "I don't know." She met Wyatt's gaze. "What? What's that grin for?"

Chapter Fifteen

Pushing open the glass door, Faith stepped into the lobby. It was the same as pretty much every public government building: polished floors; the cool, sanitary smell of circulated air; blah-white walls; and the ceiling lights a staccato line of halogen bars. In this case, however, many of the lights were burned out, leaving entire corridors dim or even dark.

All the windows she passed, where normally a person would be behind the glass with a speaker inserted for the two parties on either side to hear each other, were closed, metal shutters pulled down in front of them. She followed the signs on the wall that finally led her to the part of the multi-purpose building where the mayor's office was.

Making her way up to the second floor via a wide set of stairs, she headed down the hall, all the office doors she passed closed, the signage announcing the offices of various government officials hanging silent, every door locked on a Monday morning.

Finally making it to the mayor's office, she saw that, again, it was a closed door. She had the key she'd been given over the weekend in her pocket, but it would do her no good as the lock required a combination on the push-button pad attached to the door.

"Well, crap," she muttered, turning to look behind her, whimsically hoping that someone would suddenly appear to help her. That did not happen.

An exploration of the third floor proved the same result—a ghost town—so she headed back to the main floor. The front doors were open and lights were essentially on, so that had to mean someone was in the building.

"Hello?" she called out, headed to the area that housed Wynter's DMV. There was a lobby with several rows of metal and plastic chairs, all unoccupied, and a wall with three windows, much like the others she'd seen. Two were shuttered and, to her delight, the third was open. She could hear soft country western music emanating from the room beyond the glass.

Walking over to it, she peeked inside and saw a woman sitting in a chair staring back at her, her lips closed but jaw moving as she chewed on a piece of gum or something. She was a Hispanic woman with oversized glasses on and looked to be in her fifties. Her hairstyle looked as though she first got it when she was in her thirties, and just now it had traces of gray running through it.

"Good morning," Faith said with a smile, bending down a bit to be closer to the round speaker in the window. "I need to speak to someone about getting into the mayor's office."

The woman looked up at her. Now closer, Faith realized she was filing her nails with an emery board. "You need to go to Window D down the hall and around the corner," the woman said, her words clipped by a Spanish accent. She pointed in the direction she wanted Faith to go. "Somebody will show up and help you. Ring the doorbell thing on the wall."

Faith glanced in the general direction, feeling doubtful, but nodded. "Okay, thank you. D, right?"

"Yup," the woman said, her attention already returned to her nails, even as a hand absently reached to the small radio on her desk to turn up the volume.

Summarily dismissed, Faith turned and headed back down the way from which she'd come, turning the corner as her eyes began to scan for Window D. Sure enough, at the very end of the corridor was a set of shuttered windows, the last one with a "D" painted on the window fame above. And, again, sure enough there was a small glowing yellow doorbell button, which she pressed with a finger.

Toe tapping, Faith waited for what seemed forever. She was beginning to think her friend in the DMV was full of crap and there was nobody in the vicinity. Letting out an irritated sigh, she was about to walk away when suddenly, and with a violent metallic grinding sound, the shutters were yanked open, like miniblinds pulled up fast and hard. She was bemused to see herself staring into the large brown eyes of the DMV lady again.

"Uh..." Faith blinked a few times, then gathered herself together. "Okay. My name is Faith—"

"I know who you are, Mayor Lady. Didn't Mike give you the key I gave him?"

"Well, he did," Faith said, fishing it out of her pocket. "However, there's a door with a code lock on it that this will do nothing for."

The woman muttered something in Spanish, then the shutters slammed down. Faith jumped back, startled by the move and loud clang that followed.

Unsure what to do, she stood in the hall, looking both ways for an inkling of inspiration of what to do. The decision was made for her when she saw the woman wheel around the corner and head for the stairs. Assuming she was to follow, Faith hurried to catch up with her.

They walked—or, more aptly, marched—to the mayor's office in silence. The woman punched in a five-digit code, then stood aside after turning the handle and pushing the door open, her arms crossed over her blouse-covered chest. Initially, Faith thought the woman's attitude was just that—attitude. But now, as she passed her to enter through the doorway, she could feel the woman's contempt for her, seemingly aimed *at* her.

Deciding to take a more diplomatic stance rather than telling the woman to screw herself, as was her initial instinct, she turned and faced the woman. "Listen, I can see that you're leery of me—"

"Lady, you're a politician. I don't trust you as far as I can throw you," the woman exclaimed, eyeing her.

Glancing behind her, Faith saw that it was a reception area of sorts with a few chairs and a receptionist's or secretary's desk. She looked back to the angry woman. "Will you sit down with me for a minute? Answer some questions?"

Without a word, the woman stepped around Faith, her arms like a shield in front of her, crossed so tightly. Once past Faith, she reached out and flicked on the overhead lights then chose one of the chairs, looking expectantly up at Faith where she stood. Clearing her throat, Faith walked over and took a seat.

"So, what do you want to talk about, Mayor Lady?"

"Faith."

"I ain't here to preach to you! You believe or you don't."

Faith's hands shot up. "No, no. No." She took a breath and tried again. "My name, Faith Fitzgerald. Please call me Faith, as opposed to Mayor Lady."

The woman sitting next to her eyed her again before nodding, almost imperceptivity. "Ana Lucero."

"How long have you worked here, Ana?" She was hoping that this feisty lady could give her some answers or fill in some blanks.

"If I were to be staying, twenty-seven years in September," Ana said, raising her chin slightly in a look of defiance.

"What do you mean, if you were staying? Are you leaving?"

"Look around you, Faith," Ana said, indicating the empty room they sat in, including the desk with nobody manning it and the closed door farther back in the room, the sign reading "Mayor" mounted to the wall next to it. "Do you see anybody else here? After what that man did? That man who called himself a mayor? A leader? All he did was bleed the town dry for his own pockets and those of his friends in Tunston, inept, corrupt, and downright estupido," she added, throwing her hand up in a wave of dismissal. "You'd think Donald J. Trump was here ruining this town before he ruined the country!"

Faith hid her smile, but just barely. "How did it happen?" she asked softly, easily able to see the pain in the woman's brown eyes, let alone the anger in her voice.

"Slowly," Ana said, re-crossing her arms over her chest as she crossed her skirt-draped legs. One sandaled foot swung lazily over the other. "He was in office for eight years, slowly changing things here. At first he gave the excuse that the school needed to be fixed, so the kids had to be bussed to the Tunston schools. My daughter-in-law taught at that school, Faith. Taught fifth grade for years. Suddenly, before we knew it, she's out of a job. No fixed school. No explanation. Next, the roads stopped being maintained. The traffic light down on 3rd Street has been blinking yellow since God was a boy."

Faith shook her head, disgusted. "Wow."

"But then, when it really got scary, suddenly a deal was cut with the Tunston Sheriff's Department. You see, now they would take care of all our problems here, too. Wynter Police Department gone." She ran her finger across her throat in a slow slashing motion.

"There's a police department here?" Faith asked, shocked. She'd never seen a single police car in all her time there, only the two sheriff's cruisers.

"The empty building sits right next door to this one here," Ana said, hitching a thumb in the general direction. "Empty jail cells right next to the firehouse. When it went dark, then my own son was out of a job. All he wanted to do since he was a boy, be a fireman. They had no choice, Julio and Stacey. They moved to Colorado Springs and took my grandbaby with them." She looked away for a moment, shoulders drooping. "They hate it there, but they're doing what they have to do."

Faith reached over, placing a hand on the older woman's knee briefly in sympathy before removing it. "I'm sorry."

"So now," Ana continued, meeting Faith's troubled gaze again. "Instead of my son living across the street from the house he grew up in, instead of Sunday barbecues with my husband, his father nearly burning down the house. Instead of afternoons making tamales," she said in a breathless rush, her voice rising in volume and anger. "Now, Jose and I have to drive three hours to see my grandson, and that's one way," she spit out, raising a single finger. "How unfair is that, Faith? And it's not just our family. Born and raised here, Jose and I have seen so many of our friends and neighbors have to leave just to survive. Or," she added with a smirk. "They get jobs in Tunston and live in houses here that are falling apart, streets that are dangerous to drive on."

"How far is Tunston?" Faith asked, almost afraid to hear the answer.

"Forty-seven minutes away by car," Ana said. "Forty-seven minutes is the soonest you'll get groceries for your family, gas for your car, see a movie, anything."

Faith nodded in understanding and acknowledgement of Ana's pain. "Why do you stay here?" she asked gently.

"Wynter is our home. And, unlike many, we're lucky. Jose has worked for the railroad for thirty-three years and has a good retirement and benefits. I stay here," she added, tapping the arm of the chair she sat in. "Because everybody left. People still have needs here that must be processed here in Wynter."

Feeling overwhelmed, Faith sat back in her chair and ran her hands through her short hair. She stared up at the ceiling for a moment before she glanced over at the woman sitting next to her. She felt so sad, as Ana, clearly a strong woman, looked so defeated.

"Ana, if I can promise to you that I'm going to do all I can to untangle the mess the last guy left, will you promise to stay on? I need people like you, people who have been here through it all, know their jobs, and frankly, know this town and her people." She held Ana's gaze for a long moment, making sure she had her full support. "Would any of the others be willing to come back? Repopulate this building again?"

Ana met her gaze, skepticism behind those glasses, though her voice held a bit of hope. "You gonna open up the cops and fire department, too?"

"Absolutely. It's absurd for this town not to have its own services. I plan to do what it takes to undo what has been done. Okay?" Faith said, a tentative smile on her lips. She knew she couldn't pull this massive task off without the backing of the townspeople.

Ana extended a hand. "Shake on it?"

Faith's smile opened into a grin. "Shake on it."

Ana headed back downstairs, leaving Faith to her task of going through an absolute disaster of an office. Ana had told her that, once the breadth of Martin Lowry's corruption was discovered, he fled the country with what was left of Wynter's taxpayer's money and Albert Schulz's wife.

The office smelled stale, a literal snapshot in time, as it had been locked up since the day he left. She said the town had been so shocked that local officials had decided to take some time for everyone to absorb what had happened, but that time had spread from days to weeks to months, then finally, years. Their inaction to right the horrible wrongs had nearly brought the town of Wynter to its knees.

Drawers had been flung open, one completely pulled out of the desk and left open-side-down on the floor. All the filing cabinets had been rifled through, some folders strewn across the floor while others were haphazardly tossed in an open drawer.

The place was dusty, the berber carpet filthy with stains and what looked to be a few holes created by cigarettes or cigars. The one window had miniblinds covering it, but they were bent and snapped in places, also filthy.

"Jesus," she whispered, standing at the center of the smallish office, hands on hips. Even the chest-high bookcases, filled with volumes and notebooks, were caked with dust.

She saw the ancient computer on the wood desk, the monitor so big she wouldn't even be able to get her arms around it or carry it. She wasn't even sure if the thing worked. Wishing she had some latex gloves or hand sanitizer, she pushed the power button and waited as she lowered herself slowly into the chair, which looked as rickety as the desk. While it booted up, she searched the remaining drawers in the desk.

She found a bunch of random keys, which she put in the same drawer for safekeeping, and pens, most of which no longer worked, she found as she tried each one on a scrap piece of paper. She grimaced when she found a used condom shoved to the back of one of the drawers. The contents were long dried, but it was still revolting. With the expression and sound one makes when finding a cockroach, she used two of the dried-up pens like chopsticks and dropped them and the condom into the wastebasket beside the desk.

"What an asshole," she murmured, remembering the stories she'd heard of the former mayor cheating on his wife with another man's wife.

Finally, to her surprise, she found a small steno-type notebook which contained an entire page of passwords, penned in sloppy pencil. Luckily, it stated next to each what they were used for. She snuck a glance at the progress of the old DOS program that had finally sprung up on the computer before she grabbed her phone to check the time. She'd promised Wyatt she'd stop by the café for lunch.

Blowing out a breath, Faith took the notebook in hand. "Here we go."

The birds were singing in the trees, their song making her smile. The porch swing beneath her swung lazily back and forth, the foot that wasn't tucked beneath her resting against the wood of the porch floor, giving just enough push to keep the swing moving. She looked out over the large yard, the grass emerald green. She knew it would be cool and thick under her bare feet.

A giggle caught her attention, that of a little girl that was five years, one month, and fifteen days old. It was off to the right. She laughed out loud when she saw the string of ribbons flying just above the tops of the tall sunflowers, which stood easily seven or eight feet tall. The ribbons bounced and bobbed with every skip of the giggling little girl who she knew was skipping, her favorite way to travel most days. She could hear the excited bark of a dog running along behind.

She felt satisfied. Truly satisfied.

She looked away from where the giggling and barking came from when she heard the shrill squeak of the screen door squeal open, then close with a little snap of wood against wood.

"I need to fix that," she said, bracing the swing

with the foot on the porch as the weight of another person was added, the woman she loved. She smiled when she felt gentle fingers in her hair, nails lightly running against the back of her neck.

Her eyes slid closed and her head fell to the side, into the hand.

"Darlin'?"

"Hmm?" she murmured, *letting out a sigh of pleasure at the touch.*

"Darlin'?"

"Yeah?" Faith sighed.

Still feeling the fingers in her hair, she reached over and cupped a soft cheek, moving her head over until her lips pressed against the softest lips she'd ever felt. The lips were unmoving for a moment before they grew pliant, their softness responding, lightly pushing back against her own for a moment before they were quickly taken away.

With a gasp, Faith's eyes flew open, horrified to see Wyatt leaning over her.

Chapter Sixteen

She couldn't believe it, absolutely could not. She sat behind the wheel of her 4Runner but leaned over to rest her hand on the empty passenger seat as she stared out the open passenger window. The once vacant and overgrown park next to the school had been plowed over by a local and his riding lawnmower, and was now filled with row after row after row after row of pallets of bricks, Sheetrock, shingles, tar paper, sheets of plywood, five-gallon buckets of construction mud, and endless other types of building materials. There was also a virtual lumber yard that had been delivered.

She was in awe. From what she'd been told, this was only one such materials dump site around town. She'd spent the previous three weeks working with the Colorado Governor's office to help untangle the massive web left by Mayor Lowry.

Lawyers had been called in and were involved, and it was taking the jaws of life, but they were successfully removing themselves from their dependence on Tunston, getting their rightful place back as the County Seat, as well as getting tax money issues resolved. Sometimes Faith felt like climbing out of quicksand would be easier, but the lawyers assured her Wynter was in the right.

So, while she'd been dealing with that mess, her father had offered to take care of coordinating everything for what had been dubbed The Big Build. She'd made several phone calls herself to big box stores to see if they could get any discounts on materials or even donations, and a few had made promises, but she'd been nervous they'd come through.

As she looked over the shrink-wrapped pallets, she saw tags marking the pallets with the logos from almost every company she had called as well as a few she hadn't even thought of. But, she knew the lion's share of this had been Ogden.

"It may have taken almost forty years, Dad," she whispered. "But you finally came through for me." He'd managed to turn every dollar into about three with the steep discounts he was able to get from vendors he used on his own projects when his firm didn't just design, but built, as well. He had partial interest in a construction company out of Boulder.

Readjusting so she was sitting correctly in the driver's seat, she let out a long, steady breath. The day was only a partial success so far; yes, the construction materials had all arrived and all the plans for the dozens and dozens of projects to be done had been drawn up and mapped out. Now the huge question mark that remained was if the workers would show.

As she drove through the quiet town headed to Bessie, she thought back over what Lionel had told her. He'd only received a handful of emails and offers to help from skilled workers locally, though he'd gotten several more from people willing to help however they could. That was definitely good, but they needed skilled workers—plumbers, electricians, framers, etc. In short, people who knew what they were doing. Ogden had said he had a few people he was going to check with, but he hadn't given her any solid numbers last they'd spoken.

She pulled into a spot in front of her building, a few other cars parked around, and a handful more in the parking lot of the café. As she cut the engine, she let out a heavy sigh, her gaze glued to the small eatery and the redheaded waitress she knew was inside. She and some of the other townspeople were busy putting together sack lunches for the workers that everyone hoped showed up to help. Faith didn't know that firsthand, but rather because Mike told her when going over the details for the day. She hadn't gotten the details from Wyatt personally because she hadn't spoken to Wyatt in nearly a month.

Closing her eyes, she covered her face with her hand for a moment, the sadness washing over her, a familiar feeling of late, before she shook it off and climbed out of her car. She had a lot to do.

It was an absolutely gorgeous day, she noted as she made her way to the front door of the building. She even wore what normal people called capris, but she referred to as hobbit pants. It wasn't quite nice enough for shorts, in her estimation, but pants would be a mistake once she got moving and working.

A few more people had shown up at Bessie since she left it a half an hour before. The group was about twenty or so people strong, mostly men, and they stood in small clusters chatting or just wandering around, looking like they were waiting to be given directions. It was great to see everyone, and she smiled at and exchanged a few words with a few, but the one she hoped would be there was not.

She sent off a quick text message to Ogden with three simple yet deeply heartfelt words: *Where are you?*

When she heard no response within a minute or two, she brought her phone up, prepared to call him when the front door opened and he strolled into the room, hands tucked into the pockets of his baggy cords. He looked like a man without a care in the world. She rushed over to him, grabbing his arm and shaking it slightly in her anxiety. "Is he coming?" she demanded.

"Who?" he asked, removing his round-rimmed glasses to clean them on his shirttail.

"The guy! The guy you said would come help," she exclaimed,

He let out a heavy sigh as he shook his head. "No, I'm sorry. Ron and his crew couldn't make it today."

Faith felt her heart drop and tears of profound disappointment prick the backs of her eyes, her anxiety level rising to the point of making her want to lose her breakfast. She gasped, eyes wide. "What, what are we going to do?"

He said nothing, merely raised his glasses up to the light as if to look for spots or smudges on the lenses.

She was about to roar at him to care about her panic when her voice was caught in her throat at the sudden sound of insistent car horns, not just one, but several.

Releasing him, she walked over to the door, almost as if in a daze, the others in the building following her. Opening the door, she was stunned to see a parade of trucks, vans, cars, even a motorcycle or two. Each van, truck and car was packed to capacity with yelling, whooping men and women, each one with a large poster board announcing the skillset of its inhabitants either affixed to the side of the vehicle or one of the passengers holding it and waving it proudly.

ROOFERS, PLUMBERS, ELECTRICIANS, BRICK GUYS, LANDSCAPERS

On and on they came. One truck filled with men wearing hardhats and toolbelts, most standing in the bed of the truck, was shooting bright orange strands of silly string at the crowd that had gathered from Bessie and Pop's.

Faith's eyes filled with the tears that had been threatening, now tears of shock and pure gratitude. She did, however, burst into laughter at the van driving slowly by in the stream of workers that boasted it was filled with beer.

"You were saying?" Ogden said loud enough to be heard over the cacophony.

She looked over at him, her mouth still hanging open. She watched as, just as calm as before, he stepped into the street and meandered across between two trucks. Faith was speechless. She yelped out, startled as a long bit of silly string headed her way and caught her across the forehead.

Snapping her out of her shock, she reached up and began to peel off the wet, stringy goop. She felt eyes on her and glanced across the street and down just a bit. Wyatt stood with the onlookers on that side of the street and was staring right at her.

Faith felt her stomach hitch and, with a small nod, she turned and headed back into her building. After all, there was work to be done.

"Is this where you want it?"

Faith chewed on her bottom lip as she studied the placement of the bucket that was to represent the commode. "And, the sink would go there?" she asked, using the pen she held to point at the tool box that had been set down to represent the fixture in question. At the plumber's nod, she considered. "Yeah, I think it makes the most sense in this small space." She met his gaze. "You think?"

"With the laws of Colorado, the inches between sink and toilet and all that, I think it's really your only option," he said, rubbing the back of his neck with a big, calloused hand.

Faith nodded. "Okay, sounds good, Robert. Thanks." She turned in the small, framed room that was the newly imagined upstairs bathroom. One had already existed, though it had been moved over a bit. She headed toward the stairs when she heard her name called out from the first floor.

"Yup," she replied, trotting down the stairs to see another of her plumbers waving her over to the basement door. "You ready?" she asked, reaching into one of the many pockets on her cargo-style hobbit pants. She retrieved the oversized iron key given to her weeks ago and led the way down into the basement.

Truth was, she'd forgotten about the key Mr. Wynter had given her, as things had quickly exploded in her world from unemployed attorney to sudden owner of a random building to becoming mayor and savior of a little town that was nearly strangled by its own umbilical cord.

"Damn, it's getting hotter," he said, his heavy work boots making loud thuds on the stones as they made their way down the narrow hallway to the locked door. "Is there a boiler in there?"

"I honestly have no idea," Faith said, slowing as they reached the door. "I've never been beyond this point, so..." She grinned over her shoulder at him, the single naked bulb above masking the taller man's face in eerie shadow. "Lucky you."

He grinned back, the shadows turning an innocent expression of amusement into the garish smile of a monster.

She inserted the large key into the keyhole and, with some effort, turned it in the lock. She took hold of the iron tab and pulled, her companion reaching around her smaller frame to help her pull the door open. Stubborn at first, finally it began to give. With a little grunt, Faith pulled the door fully open and both she and the plumber gasped in surprise at the wave of warm, moist air that hit them.

"What the hell?" the plumber muttered from behind her.

Faith pocketed the key and pulled out her cell phone, activating the flashlight feature. She aimed the beam out into the space beyond the door. The beam revealed a set of stone stairs that went down and down and down, the beam not strong enough to reveal what was at the bottom. Aimed up, the ceiling looked like that of a cave, stone carved out into a cavern from water and time.

"What the..." she murmured.

Suddenly, her surroundings burst into the light of day as the man standing behind her clicked on a flashlight with a beam that seemed to go for miles, which was good, because the cave seemed to, too.

Down the stairs, which seemed to be nearly a

full story tall, was shimmering water, a huge pool of it. Faith could see the steam emanating from it. She was stunned. "Did you know about this?" she asked softly.

"Nah," he said, his quiet voice just a matter of inches from her ear as she could feel him leaning slightly over her to look past her. "Lived here all my life and I've never heard of anything like this. What the hell is it? I mean, look at them tiles down there, along the water. An indoor swimming pool?"

Faith shook her head as she looked around for a railing or something to hold on to before preceding down the steps. "No. I think it's a massive natural hot spring." She saw a thick, thatched rope tied taught and affixed to the stone wall. She grabbed it and gave it an experimental yank. Confident it would hold tight, she took a step. "Be careful, I imagine these steps are a bit slick."

They made steady but careful progress down the stairs, the air getting heavier and hotter as they went. It wasn't unpleasant at all, and if dressed in shorts and a tank top or bathing suit, it would be pure heaven.

Hitting the bottom of the stairs, Faith looked around, aiming her phone flashlight all along the stone floor, noting once again the tile work that had been done who knew how long ago. It was chipped and looked as though some of it had come loose, a few squares missing altogether.

"You know," she said, glancing over to where her companion was squatted next to the water, shining his flashlight down into the depths, which only seemed to be about four or five feet deep. "This place used to be a brothel. Maybe this place was saved for the big spenders." She grinned.

He met her gaze and let out a bark of laughter.

"Sooo, was this like the hot tub at Playboy Mansion, then?"

"Ew," Faith said, half grimacing, half laughing.

"Can you imagine?" he said, pushing to his feet. "Some lady getting preggers by a dude who's been dead for a hundred years?"

"Okay," Faith said, raising her hands in surrender, laughing. "Enough."

The "pool" itself was large enough to easily accommodate a large number of reclining adults, still and enjoying the warm, bathtub-like water, or a few dozen playing children.

"This place is amazing," the plumber said, shining his light up to the tall ceiling far above their heads and along the stone walls. "It's a self-contained cave. Wonder where the source of the spring is."

Question hanging in the thick, humid air, Faith roamed around the pool until she spotted a small crevice in the wall. "I think it's right here," she said, aiming her phone flashlight at it.

"I believe you're right," he agreed, walking over to her.

Faith looked around the massive space, myriad questions and concerns whirling through her head. "What on earth am I going to do with this?" she murmured.

"Can't answer that for ya, Mayor, but I know the community would sure love it."

She met his gaze for a long moment before looking away with a sigh. "I was worried you'd say that."

≈≈≈≈

It was nearly ten o'clock when Faith pulled up to the gate. She could see lights on upstairs in the house and was glad her father had made it back safely. She opened the gate and pulled through before closing it behind her and driving up to the old farmhouse. She'd gotten the keys the week before and had moved in only the essentials, a couple mattresses on the floor for herself and Ogden to sleep on, as her father was staying with her during the massive town renovations. She'd brought the recliner she'd bought while living at Cameron's and had a couple folding camping chairs and folding TV tray-type tables next to the chair.

She pulled up into the driveway, Ogden's truck parked off to the side. She sat for a moment admiring the wraparound porch and the swing she and Wyatt had shared together, and couldn't quite believe the house was hers. She cut the engine of her SUV and climbed out, slamming the door shut behind her. For not the first time, she was amazed at just how quiet it was on the hill. Coming from the craziness of New York to the slightly-less-craziness of Denver and now to the outright still calm of Wynter, she certainly felt she'd made a good choice in purchasing the old farmhouse. The bank had been so grateful to get it off their hands that she'd gotten it and the surrounding acres for next to nothing. Though sorry to see her go, Jill and Stephanie had been impressed by her find and were in the middle of making purchases of their own all over the tiny mountain town.

The front door was unlocked, so she locked it behind her and didn't bother to turn on any lights as she made her way through the large open space that was the foyer to the stairs that led to the second floor. The strange layout of the first floor bemused her, with its large open foyer but closed-off dining room, kitchen, living room, and sitting room. She intended to open it all up one day.

Her boots thudded dully on the wood steps as she made her slow way up, her body tired and hurting and desperately wanting a long, hot shower.

She passed by the bedroom Ogden had been using the past few nights and stopped at the open door. He was sitting on the mattress on the floor, neatly folding clothing that was being packed into a duffel bag.

"Hey," she said, lifting her hand for a small wave when he glanced up at her. "Leaving tonight?"

"No, but I plan to be on my way early," he said, setting aside the white undershirts he'd just folded to begin on a pair of his ever-present cords. "I got you a dinner to go from the café," he said. "It's in the fridge. Wasn't sure if you'd managed to stop for lunch after your big find this morning."

Faith blew out a long breath, running a hand through her hair. "Yeah. About that. When are you coming down again?"

"Soon. I'll be back real soon. But for now," he said, rising to his feet and walking over to her. "You look like you're about to fall over." He cleared his throat, suddenly looking unusually shy. "I um, I had one of the guys go into Tunston today to the store and pick you up some of those bath bomb things you've mentioned you like so much." He nodded in the direction of her bedroom and connected bath. "I left it for you in your bathroom."

Truly touched, she smiled. "That is so sweet," she said quietly. "Thank you. That sounds absolutely heavenly right now."

"All right. Well, I'm going to get some sleep so I can be up and at 'em early." To her surprise, he leaned over and left a quick, tight kiss to her cheek, the grizzle of his facial hair tickling her skin. "Proud of you," he said.

So tired that her emotions were a bit more surface than they'd usually be, she felt the tiniest bit of emotion prick the backs of her eyes. "Thank you." She pushed off the doorframe to head to her bedroom. "You know," she added, looking at him. "How sad is it that your guy had to drive all the way to Tunston just to pick up a toiletry product?"

Ogden met and held her gaze, a little soft smile on his lips. "So change that. Mayor."

≈≈≈≈

Though the hibiscus bath bomb made it look as though Faith were reclining in the middle of a slaughter, the red-tinted water smelled amazing and she couldn't help but close her eyes and breathe in the hot, fragrant water that filled the old, claw-foot tub.

She'd owned the house for two weeks but had only really been in for a week. She'd wanted to get things settled back in Denver, squared away with Cameron and Jill and Stephanie. The first time Faith had stepped into the house, let in by the bank, she'd known instantly that it was meant to be hers. Yes, it needed work, yes much of it was outdated or simply rundown, but that didn't matter to her. She knew she had the time to work on it slowly, to turn it into the house of her dreams—literally.

Though she'd had very little time to enjoy the house, and certainly no time to do anything to it but bring in the basics, she already loved it. The only thing missing was...

Faith's eyes opened and she let out a long, slow breath. No, she wasn't going to let her mind go there. She couldn't. Instead, she looked around the bathroom attached to her bedroom. It was a decent size but looked as though it had been updated about thirty years ago, and even that had been shoddy work with mismatched tile and areas where the grout had been sloppily applied.

She tried to force her mind into what she wanted to do to the bathroom, what sort of tiles and color scheme she'd bring in, what sort of updated vanity, etc. If she could do that, she could keep her mind off of what she was so acutely missing. Well, not what, but who.

Chapter Seventeen

Faith's eyes snapped open, her heart lurching at being startled. Lying on the mattress plopped in the middle of her bedroom floor, she raised herself to her elbows, looking around the sparse space as she listened, trying to figure out what had awoken her with such a start.

The amount of sunlight shining in through the many windows in the large master bedroom alluded to the fact that it must be at least eight or so in the morning. She should be alone in the house. She thought perhaps she'd dreamt it until, with a gasp, she shot up into a sitting position when she heard a thud from downstairs followed by soft cursing.

Eyes wide, she slowly pushed the sheet and blanket off her bare legs and feet, revealing the mesh shorts she slept in as well as the tank top that covered her torso. Tucking her bottom lip beneath her top teeth in a nervous gesture, she looked around the bedroom to see what she could use as a weapon.

She saw the one thing that was left in the house when she bought it: the antique tool set for the fireplace in the master bedroom. Trying to be as quiet as possible as she scampered over to the fireplace, she winced when she stepped on a squeaky board. She silently cursed the fact that she hadn't yet learned its whereabouts to avoid.

The cold, hard poker in hand, Faith made her

way to the closed bedroom door. She pressed her ear against the cool, white-painted wood and listened. She heard nothing. She grabbed the doorknob and slowly turned it, pulling the door open just enough to peek out into the long hallway that led to the stairs, straddled by the open doorways of the two other bedrooms and guest bathroom. Nothing. No noise, no movement. Then suddenly, the long, slow sound of ripping.

"What the hell?" she whispered.

It had sounded like it came from downstairs, so she pulled her door open a bit more and stepped out of her bedroom, her weapon held up like a baseball bat. She slowly made her way away from the safety of her bedroom and down the hall, glancing into the spare bedroom where her father had been staying. To her surprise and confusion, his duffel bag was packed full and zipped on the floor next to the mattress. The bedding had been made up like a bed, replete with the sheet folded down just so over the top of the blanket.

Lowering the poker just a slight bit, Faith continued on, still mindful that something could be wrong. She made her way down the staircase, her bare feet making her steps silent like those of a cat.

Flexing her fingers around the cold metal of her chosen weapon, she creeped around the banister and tiptoed her way through the dining room that would lead to the kitchen, the two rooms separated by a swinging door with a portal window to ensure nobody bashed the door into someone coming on the other side.

She raised up a bit to get a better view through the round window and looked into the kitchen beyond. Her relief was complete when she saw her father. Blowing out a breath, she rested the fire poker against her shoulder like a shouldered rifle and pushed through the door, letting it swing behind her.

"What are you doing?" she asked, watching as he continued to peel wallpaper off the wall on the other side of the room, closer to the eat-in nook by the bay window that overlooked the front of the house.

He spared her a quick glance as he continued his task, a pile of peeled strips of the dated wallpaper on the floor at his feet. "Getting rid of this atrocious wallpaper," he said simply, as though that explained everything. "This was the room you wanted removed, correct?"

She glanced at it and nodded. "One of many, but I figured you'd be long gone. You said you planned to head out early."

Ogden was quiet for a long moment as he carefully picked some old wallpaper glue off his fingers. Finally, he met her gaze. "I've decided I'm not going back," he said quietly.

Stunned, Faith literally took a step back, her back coming into contact with the fridge. "What does that mean?"

He was about to shove his hands into the pockets of his cords but realized they were still covered in the yuck attached to wallpaper that had been stuck to the wall for who-knew-how-many-decades. He walked over to the sink, squeezed liquid out of the bottle of dish soap Faith had bought for the odd and random dish she'd be using, and washed his hands.

He cleared his throat before he began to speak. "I filed for divorce from Carrie two months ago."

Faith walked farther into the room, setting the fire poker on the breakfast bar before leaning on it.

She watched him do his task. "Okay." She tapped her fingertips on the gold Formica countertop. "Why now?"

He snorted, never looking at her. "Indeed. I filed to end a marriage that never should have existed to begin with."

She was surprised to hear the honesty come out, a subject he never would talk about, so said nothing for fear her words would jolt him out of his train of thought.

"Faith, watching you these past many months, taking on a seemingly impossible task for no other reason than it needed to be done, has inspired me greatly. Initially I helped simply because you asked me to, but as time has gone by..." He smiled, drying his hands on a couple pieces of paper towel as he glanced over at her. "Lady Wynter has managed to seep into my soul, just as I suspect she has yours."

She met his gaze, a small smile and nod to his statement. "Yes."

"And," he continued, walking over to the breakfast bar and standing on the opposite side, the expanse of countertop between them. "For the first time in my life—since your mother died," He clarified with a raised finger. "I'm doing something for the very right reason."

Faith was surprised as he reached out and placed his larger hand atop hers where it rested. She glanced down at their hands before meeting his gaze again.

"If it's all right with you, I'd like to buy the little house by the lake I've been eyeing. I'd like to help continue to bring this phoenix back from the ashes."

Once again, just like the night before, Faith felt emotion creep up. She was touched by his little announcement. "You're a grown man," she said softly, her voice thick. "You don't need my permission."

"Yes, but I have so very much to make up for in regards to you, Faith," he said gently. "So very much for us to talk about. I don't feel I have the right to encroach upon your journey if I'm not wanted." He gave her a sad smile. "You'd have every reason not to want me here."

Faith used her free hand to reach up and swipe at the tear that was threatening to squeeze out. She shook her head, feeling happier than she had in a long time, if not completely confused. "No. I don't mind at all."

He smiled, a full-on smile with teeth and everything. He squeezed her hand before removing his own. "Why don't you go get dressed and take your friend there back to the bedroom," he said, tapping the fire poker with his knuckles. "I'll take you to breakfast and we can talk."

☙❧

As Faith made short order of her giant breakfast burrito, she noticed the people that came in and out of the café or who walked along the sidewalk—something she'd never seen in all her time in Wynter—were tired for sure after the incredible amount of work done over the past forty-eight hours, but had a twinkle in their eye, a pep in their step, and hope in their smile. So many made their way over to the table she and her father shared simply to say hello or shake their hands. One young couple even offered to pay for their breakfast, which of course they declined. It was a different town, and Faith loved it.

This was her first time in the café for a few weeks, and as she and her father talked in between interruptions, she had eyes in the back of her head. She had yet to see Wyatt. Part of her was sad about that, worried even, but relieved.

"Can I ask you something?" she asked, looking down at the mess she'd made of her plate.

"Certainly," Ogden responded.

Faith was silent for a long moment, feeling she had an opportunity here that she had never had with her father: to finally get answers. "Tell me about my mother's death. Why did she die? I mean," she added, setting down her fork and picking up her paper napkin. "I know she took her own life, but why?"

Ogden sipped his coffee then sat back in the booth, resting his hands on the tabletop for a moment as he seemed to gather his thoughts. "I first saw Elise when she was waiting tables at this little eatery near campus in Boulder called Dickies. It's not there anymore, but they made the best nachos. Anyhow, I was doing my undergrad and was there with some buddies, and..." The smile that slowly spread across his lips was unlike anything Faith had ever seen with him. "I just knew I had to meet her."

"Love at first sight?" Faith asked, charmed.

"Well, for me, but my buddy, Chris, was the one who had the guts to talk to her," he said with a sheepish grin. "I watched the two of them date for a few months, all the while lamenting my failure to speak to her."

"That had to be hard," she said softly, noting movement out of the corner of her eye. She glanced over at the breakfast counter and saw Wyatt making coffee, her back to them. A wave of nervous butterflies divebombed her stomach before she looked away, returning her attention to her father. "So, what happened?"

"I gave Elise a ride home one night, when her father failed to show at the end of her shift. We talked. Sat in my car and talked for a full hour outside of her house. Finally, her mother flipped on the outside light, letting her know it was time to come in." His smile grew, eyes looking beyond Faith into a past when she didn't even exist yet. "Our talks were magical." He cleared his throat and returned to the present, rearranging his silverware where it lay on the table as he glanced up at Faith. "I finally talked her into breaking it off with Chris and giving me a shot."

"Go you," Faith said, impressed.

"It wasn't until after we were married that I discovered her issues with depression. Unfortunately, back in those days, treating—even acknowledging—mental health issues was frowned upon, and little was available other than institutionalization. She didn't need that. I believe today your mother would be diagnosed as bipolar. She struggled mightily with it. Her mother begged us not to have children," he said, voice not much above a whisper. He seemed upset and grabbed his cup of coffee, perhaps sipping to take a moment from whatever he was feeling.

"It's not your fault," Faith said softly. "I really hope you know that."

After a moment, he nodded and put his cup down. "She adored you," he began again, the same smile returning, though sadness remained in his eyes. "She loved being a mother. I was working on my master's by that time and was working so she could stay home with you." He shook his head. "I think it just got to be too much. Her mood swings were becoming dangerously irrational and things were getting worse between us."

Faith listened, sad to hear about what sounded like the slow deterioration of her mother's mental state. In a way, she almost wished she didn't know, but recognized it was important that she did, to help understand herself perhaps in the woman she had little memory of. Faith had no mental health issues that she knew of, counting herself lucky considering her mother's history, but still, the woman was more than that. "What was she like?"

"She was very intelligent, curious. That woman could spark up a conversation about anything." He smiled, again seemingly caught up in a memory. "She was very kind, could be stubborn and tenacious. But, very loving. Probably her best quality."

Faith absorbed all that she'd been told. She had more questions for him for another time, but there was one she needed an answer to now. "Why did you marry Carrie?"

Ogden met her gaze, his unwavering. "I was weak." He sat back, crossing his arms over his chest. "I had not one clue how to be a single parent. Carrie came along and I all but begged her to save me." He looked away, reaching up to stroke his facial hair. "Most cowardly thing I've ever done," he murmured. "I'm so sorry. Neither you nor Dawson deserved that."

Faith felt a mixture of relief and gratitude for the apology and the fact that it truly seemed her father finally understood, but it also dredged up so many years of anger and resentment and profound abandonment. After a long moment, she let out a heavy sigh and looked at him. "The irony is, I went into law hoping that you'd finally be proud of me, notice me." She gave him a sad smile. "Never did I think all it would take was for me to help rebuild a few houses."

Ogden looked down into his coffee for a moment, his expression pained. After a long moment, he glanced up at her. "First of all, I've always been proud of you, Faith, proud of who you are as a person and the young woman you've turned out to be. I credit Elise with that, as short a time as she had with you. Second of all, you haven't just rebuilt a few houses." He indicated the bustling café around them, people talking excitedly, laughing, and calling out greetings to each other. "You've rebuilt a town, given a people hope and their future back."

She gave him a small smile and nodded. "Well, I need to use the restroom," she said softly. Truth was, she'd heard a lot and needed a moment to herself.

Sliding out of the booth, Faith glanced over to the breakfast counter. Through the window she could see Wyatt in the kitchen. Like a burglar in the night, Faith zoomed to the hallway where the restrooms were and the other door to the kitchen. She was relieved nobody was in the women's restroom, and ducked inside. She was about to lock the door behind her when it was pushed open.

"Someone's in here—" Faith began, pushing back on the door, but lost her grip when Wyatt pushed inside, closing and locking the door behind her. Faith just stared at her, able to see the anger in those turquoise eyes that haunted her, but what got her the most was the hurt she heard in her voice.

"Why have you been avoidin' me?" Wyatt asked.

Faith could only stare at her, her mouth agape.

Wyatt crossed her arms over her chest, her gaze boring into Faith as her anger seemed to build. "I know you're busy an' all, but there ain't no reason why y'all can't respond to a text. Even you, Mizz Mayor, have to take a dump." She indicated the small single-toilet bathroom they faced off in. "Thus, where we find ourselves."

Again, Faith could only stare. She opened her mouth to speak, but nothing came out. The realization of her cowardice was beginning to feast on her gut, making her feel nauseous. Wyatt's next words didn't help.

"I've not heard from you in nearly a month, Faith," Wyatt continued, the anger in her eyes turning to match the hurt in her voice. "I've texted, I've called, and nothin'. If I've done somethin' wrong, I wish you'd just end the suspense and tell me so I can fix it." She looked away for a moment, but not before Faith caught the glisten of a tear in her right eye. The waitress took a moment and seemed to gather herself and her emotions. She turned her gaze back to Faith. "I just felt like we were buildin' somethin' special, our friendship, and I guess it's possible I just misjudged you, the woman you are."

Faith felt panic ripple through her when Wyatt turned toward the door. "You didn't misjudge," she blurted out, relieved when Wyatt turned back to look at her, the hurt and pain Faith had caused her plain as day on that beautiful face. Faith wanted to cry. "I shouldn't have done what I did." At Wyatt's look of confusion, she clarified. "You're a married woman," she whispered. "It was wrong."

Wyatt stared at her, looking incredulous. "The kiss?" she said. "All this fuss is over the fact that you backed out of a dream sideways and mistook me for whoever was in your dream?"

A bark of laughter erupted from her lips, though it sounded like it was more about relief than amusement. Even so, it raised Faith's hackles, as she was feeling more stupid by the second. She brought a hand up and cupped the back of her neck, which was warm to the touch. Clearing her throat, she repeated, "You're a married woman, Wyatt. I felt...bad."

Wyatt sobered and took a step toward Faith, her eyes softening. "Sounds to me like this is a bit of projection goin' on. You freaked out and kept your distance from me like I'm the one who did," she said, a hand on her own chest. The look in her eyes changed, and Faith couldn't quite read what the emotion was, though determined was certainly part of it. "You say you feel bad that you kissed a married woman, well, fine."

She reached out, quicker than a snake, and cupped Faith's face with both hands and pulled their lips together. The kiss lingered much longer than it needed to prove Wyatt's point, and Faith was pretty sure she felt the tiniest little nip at her bottom lip as Wyatt pulled away, but just barely.

"Now we're even," Wyatt murmured a hair's width away from Faith's lips. She stepped back, her hands slowly dropping away from Faith's face, making it feel like a caress. "Can we please move past this?"

Faith couldn't speak, so simply nodded dumbly. She watched as the other woman left the bathroom, leaving her alone to her thoughts. *Move past this? One of the reasons I stayed away from you was because I was worried it would happen again.*

Chapter Eighteen

Faith's smile was instant as she opened the front door, a beautiful Wyatt standing on the other side holding a large bouquet of sunflowers in a crystal vase in her hands. "Welcome."

"Why, thank you," Wyatt said with a smile and a small curtsey that made Faith's smile grow. As always, Faith was struck by just how beautiful Wyatt was. She was wearing the same outfit she'd been wearing in the bathroom earlier that day, but now the ever-present bandana was gone, her hair brushed down to a rich, auburn shine.

Faith looked past her friend and saw no car. "Didn't Pops drop you off?" she asked, stepping aside so the waitress could enter.

"He did not." Wyatt handed Faith the flowers as she passed her. "For the lady of the house," she said softly with a little smirk.

"Why, thank you, ma'am," Faith said with a chuckle, taking them. She closed the front door and led the way through the foyer to the kitchen where she set them on the counter by the kitchen window. Thus far, it was the only flat surface in the house near a window other than the floor since she had no furniture. "So, who dropped you off?" she asked conversationally.

"I decided to see how far it was to walk it," Wyatt said, leaning against the counter nearby as Faith arranged the big, yellow flowers. "It's just a little less than a mile, so I can come on over and bug you any ol' time I want to."

Faith sent her a side glance. "Fine, then. Maybe I'll let ya." Suddenly, the teasing in Wyatt's eyes vanished, leaving sadness behind. "What's wrong?" Faith asked softly.

Wyatt said nothing as she pushed away from the counter and bridged the couple steps between them to enfold Faith in a hug. Hugs from the waitress weren't unusual, but Faith could tell from the start this wasn't one of her tight but brief ones. Wyatt held Faith fully to her, their bodies of similar size and height fitting perfectly together.

Though they'd only known each other a handful of months, Faith knew a special bond had formed between them early on, and she now fully understood how her stubborn cowardice had affected Wyatt by staying away from her for the past month. Well, the past three weeks and not quite five days. Not that Faith was counting.

As she absorbed Wyatt's warmth, Faith relaxed into the embrace, burying her face into the softness of Wyatt's hair and her neck. Her eyes slid closed at the warmth and softness, the fragrance of Wyatt's shampoo and just a hint of her perfume underneath the smells of working at a café all afternoon. That perfume, a scent that had quickly become synonymous with Wyatt, was comforting, as well as quickly acting as an aphrodisiac for her.

As that thought crossed her mind—and shot down to burn low in her belly—she began to pull away, but Wyatt tightened her hold. She relaxed again into the hug and allowed herself to just enjoy it, to enjoy the feel of Wyatt against her, something that she would undoubtedly never feel again.

She nuzzled her face a bit more into the warmth of Wyatt's neck, feeling Wyatt's fingers begin to absently roam through Faith's hair in response.

"Faith?" Wyatt whispered.

"Hmm?"

"Please never walk away from me again." Though still in a whisper, the emotion, almost desperate in nature was clear.

Faith felt the words like a dagger to her heart. She tightened her arms around Wyatt's petite frame. "I promise," she whispered back. "Never again."

※ ※ ※ ※ ※

Faith stared at her, her heart racing. "You're serious?" she finally managed, almost holding her breath. "We got the emergency grant?"

"We got the grant," Meredith Green repeated, a huge smile on her face.

"Woohoo!" Faith banged on the table with her hands in her excitement and relief.

Feeling like a million dollars, she looked around the table in a conference room in the mayor's office. Every seat was filled by people she'd personally appointed to help get Wynter back on its feet. Meredith Green was a retired librarian who had spent most of her career working with local, state, and federal governments to get grants and programs for her patrons. Then there was the woman who'd been a doctor at the Wynter Medical Center before it had been shut down. Also in attendance were former police officers, the retired fire chief, business owners, and a couple stay-at-home moms.

Everyone's input was valuable, because each of those representing at Faith's table had needs that represented the needs of an entire community. It was a community that they needed to grow, be it bringing Wynter residents back home who had left to save their families or simply bringing in new residents, like Faith and her father.

"Okay," Faith said, slapping the table a final time before pushing to her feet. She walked over to the white dry erase board that was mounted to the wall behind her. Uncapping a marker, she quickly jotted down four bullet points. She turned to those gathered. "With this grant money, here's what I think is absolutely crucial." She turned back to the board, the fragrant tip of the marker gliding easily over the smooth white board as she wrote:

Police
Fire/EMS
School
Medical Center?

"Why the question mark after Medical?"

"Because I think the first three are of most importance right now," Faith said, facing the doctor who had asked the question. "It's of absolute importance, yes, but if we have EMS we can provide temporary help to our residents right now during transport to Tunston if that's necessary. Now," she said, raising her hands to forestall any arguments. "I have no desire for Wynter residents to ever have to rely on Tunston again. But, as wonderful as the grant is, we have to be judicious in how we spend the money, how we bring Wynter back and service her residents." She looked around the room. "What do you guys think?"

After a moment of silence, the members of her so-called Wynter Phoenix Board glancing around at each other, a few scribbling notes for their own perusal, Lionel asked, "What next?"

Faith grinned at him. "Recruitment, Lionel. Let's give this bitch her wings back."

※※※※

Together they walked in silence to the front double doors of the building. Their silence was very comfortable after the half-hour-long talk they'd just had. Reaching the front doors, Faith was stopped with a hand to her arm. She turned and faced the attractive brunette.

"I'm so glad you came," the woman said, her soft voice pleasant. "It gives me so much to think about. Have you spoken to my husband yet?"

Faith grinned, fishing her keys out of her bag. "That's my next stop. I came here to talk to you first because, come on now, Stacey," she said in a conspiratorial tone. "We both know who really makes the decisions in a family."

The teacher laughed, nodding. "So true." She gave Faith a quick hug. "Thanks again. I'll get back to you soon, okay?"

"Absolutely. I know it's a lot to turn over, but it's a very legitimate offer." She smiled at the Latina woman, then pushed the bar on the door to open it and stepped out into the beautiful day.

※※※※

She was fascinated as she arched her head back, looking up at the ceiling, high overhead. It had to be high in order for the garage-type structure to accommodate the massive fire engines. She hadn't been that close to one of those things since she was a kid and the fire department had brought a couple tankers to her school to wow the fifth graders with a water show from the powerful hoses.

She looked down when she felt a tap on her knee where she sat in a folding chair. When she'd arrived and stated her business, she'd been shown that chair to wait. An instant smile spread across her lips when she looked into the excited brown eyes of a Dalmatian. He sat on his haunches in front of her, one front paw on the polished cement floor while the other rested on her knee.

"Well, hello there," she reached out and lifted the dog's bone-shaped tag attached to his collar. "Fisher. How are you?" she said in the tone that seemed to come naturally to anyone speaking to a dog. She laughed when he raised the paw from her knee to shake. She took it in her hand and lightly shook it. "Aren't you a gentleman?"

"Don't let him fool you," said an amused-sounding man's voice a short distance from her.

Faith glanced over to see a somewhat short but muscular Hispanic man walking toward her. She smiled, pushing up from her chair after releasing the dog's paw. "Oh?"

"Yeah. He's a beggar, that one," the man said. He was dressed in dark blue BDU pants and a light blue T-shirt with the station's logo and number spread tight across his well-developed chest. "Aren't ya, bud?" he asked, roughhousing with the dog for a moment until the dog was over on his back, one of his back legs pedaling through the air as his belly was rubbed. With a final firm pat to the dog's side, the man stood to his full height and offered his hand. "Julio Lucero. Chief said you were looking to talk to me? You're from Wynter, right?" His dark brown eyes seemed to darken a bit, the skin between heavy dark eyebrows knitting together. "Is everything okay? My mom okay?"

"Oh yeah, everything's great," Faith said, wanting to put his concerns at ease. "She's as feisty as ever." She gave him what she hoped was a disarming smile. "My name is Faith Fitzgerald, the new mayor." She still wasn't comfortable with the title, but in this situation knew it was important and necessary.

"Oh yeah, yeah," he said, grinning. "Dad told me about you. Okay, what can I do for you, Mayor?"

"Is there somewhere we can talk, Julio?"

※※※※

Honk honk!

An hour later, Faith relished the loud double blast of the air horn that announced their presence driving through the neighborhood around the fire station. Again she felt like that fifth grader, impressed by the sheer magnitude of the size of the ladder truck she rode shotgun in, with all its modern technology paired with time-tested mechanics.

She glanced over to her companion and driver, Julio Lucero. He grinned at her, and she returned it.

※※※※

A muffled curse fell out of Faith's mouth along with the bit of pickle from the bite she'd just taken of her fast-food burger on the go. She'd stopped to grab something once she'd passed what was referred to as the Tech Center, which was an area of southern Denver with a cluster of large buildings that dealt with business from banking to the tech industry.

After she'd left Colorado Springs, she'd taken the hour and a half drive to Denver proper to make some calls for her next move. Now, as she wolfed down her lunch, she glanced at her phone, attached to a windshield holder, to check out the address located on Akron Way.

She had a meeting with Denver Police Sergeant Susan Weston, who was an instructor at the Denver Police Academy.

※※※※

Another jaw-cracking yawn nearly split Faith's face as she took the left turn that would lead to the farmhouse's gate. She shook her head vigorously to clear it, exhausted from a long day of traveling halfway across the state to make connections and, hopefully, recruit. She was surprised when, like a mirage, a figure appeared in her headlights, walking along the left side of the single-lane road.

Slowing her SUV, she pushed the button and the window whirred down. "Hey, little girl. Need a ride?" When she had her attention, Faith raised her eyebrow. "Didn't your mamma ever tell you it isn't safe for a pretty girl like you to be out walking at night?"

Wyatt grinned, walking over to Faith's 4Runner, placing the hand that wasn't carrying a picnic basket on her hip. "I got moves to protect myself," she said, her voice taking on the same playful tone as Faith.

"Yeah? I think I'd like to see those moves."

Wyatt shook her head slowly and replied sagely as she backed away. "No. Stranger danger."

Faith laughed. "Get in, you nut." She pressed the button to unlock the passenger-side door, and Wyatt climbed in. "Where to?" she asked.

Wyatt rolled her eyes as she got settled with her basket on her lap. "Brat."

"What were you doing out here so late?" Faith asked, all serious as she got them going. "Not sure how safe it is." She glanced at the clock on her dashboard. "It's almost nine thirty."

"Eh," Wyatt said, waving off Faith's words of concern. "Not in this town. I've actually never lived anywhere that I feel so safe."

Faith nodded. "Fair enough. Why were you headed to my house so late?" she asked, knowing the road had only one destination.

"Well, your daddy came into the café today and told me you were all over God's green earth today, and he was worried you weren't gonna eat properly. So," she added, patting the basket she held. "Here I am."

"So, you're saying you and my father are ganging up on me, huh?" Faith asked with a grin, admittedly touched. She turned the SUV onto the dirt road and reduced her speed a bit.

"No, silly," Wyatt laughed, swiping playfully at Faith's thigh with her hand. "Timing was simply meant to be. Lucas just left for duty, so I bugged outta there."

For reasons she wasn't comfortable admitting to

herself, it rubbed Faith wrong to hear Lucas's name. She gritted her teeth for a second before pushing it away. She pulled up in the driveway, noting her father's bedroom light was on. He'd asked if he could stay with her until the divorce from Carrie was final, as he wasn't allowed to buy any property while it was ongoing.

To her surprise, Ogden had drawn up a prenup and Carrie had signed it before they married. He was just beginning his business in those days and, from what he told Faith, wasn't sure the marriage would take. Now, it worked out nicely as it made the divorce a much easier process. Faith knew her father would be fair to Carrie, considering they'd been married for nearly thirty years, but she was glad that bitch couldn't take him to the cleaners.

In the house, Faith stood back and let Wyatt take control of her kitchen. Truth be told, it was adorable. Wyatt hummed her way through unloading the picnic basket onto the counter, revealing a small glass casserole pan that had been encased in a heating bag. Once she unzipped the bag, fragrant steam wafted out. She moved around the small space, opening cabinets and drawers until she found what she needed—a dinner plate and flatware. She knew she could ask or guess what Wyatt was looking for and direct her, but it was just too cute to watch her.

"Okay," Wyatt finally said, dishing out a huge portion onto the plate. "This was my mama's recipe."

Faith's mouth was watering as she looked at the slice of ketchup-topped meatloaf, generous scoop of mashed potatoes, and glazed carrots. She glanced up at Wyatt, who looked at her expectantly. "You know this portion would feed me for about three days, right?"

With only a smirk, Wyatt reached into the basket and pulled out an empty plastic storage container with a lid.

Faith burst into laughter, walking over to the fridge to grab a can of soda before the two headed into the dining room where her father had set up a card table and chairs. Faith sat down, Wyatt taking the chair to her right, her elbow resting on the table and her chin against her fist. Realizing how hungry she really was, her burger and fries long gone, she dug in.

Eyes sliding closed, Faith chewed slowly, savoring each flavor, the spicy, obviously homemade, ketchup and the creamy, buttery mashed potatoes. The meal was one of her favorites. She was in heaven.

"Oh. My. God," she finally managed, taking a sip of her drink to wash the food down. She looked at Wyatt and gave her an enthusiastic thumbs-up. "Excellent."

Wyatt's face lit up like a Christmas tree, making her ever more beautiful than she normally was. "I'm so glad."

Slowing down the shoveling after a few moments, Faith glanced at her friend. "What are your plans for tomorrow?" she asked, sitting back in the folding chair as she began to get full.

"Funny you should ask. I'm off tomorrow, and I was going to ask you the same thing, where you might need my help." Wyatt grinned. "Perhaps to continue peelin' off that hellacious wallpaper in the kitchen?"

Faith chuckled. "Honestly, all these walls are going to go," she said, using a finger to point in all general directions. "Once we're done with everything else, I'll get going in here. I'm going to be in town tomorrow, and now that we have the hot springs given the all-clear, I was going to start upstairs."

"Ah yes, I heard about these elusive hot springs," Wyatt said, sitting back in her chair as well. "You know, I had no idea that was there."

"No?" Faith asked, surprised. She'd wondered if Pops or Mr. Wynter would have told her.

Wyatt shook her head as she reached over and caught a little bit of creamy mashed potatoes that was on the edge of the plate with the tip of her finger. Faith was mesmerized as she watched that finger find its way to full lips and finally disappear inside that mouth she'd dreamt about far too often.

Clearing her throat, Faith looked away, pushing the plate away from her. "Tell you what. Why don't you meet me at Bessie's in the morning? Will that work?"

Wyatt grinned. "What time, darlin'?"

Chapter Nineteen

Faith could feel expectant turquoise eyes on her, but she allowed herself the time to truly taste what had just been inserted into her mouth.

"Super creamy," she managed at length. "Love the tanginess of the mango."

"Too much?"

She finally met Wyatt's gaze and shook her head. "Not at all. Honestly, this is a winner," she said, indicating the spoon Wyatt held in her hand. "I think this is definitely what we should give out as samples tomorrow."

The sun broke through the clouds as Wyatt's smile shone forth. She clapped her hands and whirled around, nearly skipping back to the kitchen. Faith would be lying if she said she didn't take an extra long peek at Wyatt's shorts-clad ass as she hurried away, though surreptitious about it as her other employees were present.

Clearing her throat to clear the gutter in her mind, she returned her focus to what she'd been doing before being approached to try Wyatt's newest concoction. She stood behind the bar filling old-school chrome napkin holders.

Only three months before, she'd brought Wyatt into the empty shell that was Bessie. Now it was properly plumbed, the electricity had been updated, and the hot springs had been discovered and checked out to be safe for use. The tile around it had been redone and the stairs outfitted with non-slick rubber tread. Handrails had also been installed for safe travels up and down the stairs.

When she brought Wyatt in, she had been hoping Wyatt would have some ideas, some insight on what the town would want or need. Lord, did she! Like a little B-52 bomber, Wyatt buzzed in, dropping little idea bombs everywhere. After a while, Faith realized there was no reason to try to get a word in edgewise, so she turned on the recorder on her phone. Besides, this was some good stuff.

By the end of that day, they'd taken Wyatt's ideas and grabbed Ogden for his years of expertise and came up with the little gem she stood in the middle of now. Bessie's was a multi-part business. The ground floor was an ice cream and confection shop splashed in fun colors on the walls and the plastic tables and chairs. Nothing matched, just a feast of fun for the eye and the palate. The new wood floor had an inlay of the ice cream cone scoop they'd come up with for the logo for the bottom level, *Bessie's* plastered across it.

The old mahogany bar had been moved upstairs, and a new, fun and festive counter had been installed along the back of the room, replete with a large glass case where tubs of the fresh homemade ice cream were displayed, the excited customer able to watch as the employee built their cold treat to order.

The back third of the room had been walled off and a kitchen fashioned. The ice cream machines were back there as well as the equipment necessary for Wyatt to create her amazing lemon cake and banana bread. She was also branching out to learn more about candy making. Faith had been concerned that Wyatt would be upset or reject her offer to run Bessie's and leave the café, but she'd jumped at the chance—literally.

The upstairs, on the other hand, was an homage to the original purpose for the building. The stairs to the second floor had been moved to the front of the building, so upon entering you could choose to go up the stairs to the left or straight into the ice cream parlor. At the top of the stairs were a pair of mini saloon doors that didn't block the vision of people coming or going, but set the stage for the room beyond.

The bar had been fully and lovingly restored, and made the room look like the patron had stepped back in time. It was a miniature version of the original saloon setup on the main floor, but with all the modern conveniences. Old tintypes from the saloon had been blown up and festooned the tabletops under a protective layer of lacquer. Lots of wood and darker colors added to the more adult atmosphere.

During the day, the upstairs served as a coffee shop, complete with some of the baked treats served downstairs. At night, it became the saloon it once was, with extra seating downstairs in the closed ice cream shop. A second small kitchen had been installed upstairs to make the modest bar menu. The finger food wasn't enough for an entire meal, but enough to increase ticket totals and keep patrons happy.

The biggest complaint Faith had heard from the people in the town was there was nowhere for adults to go and meet for a drink or hang out and read, get a good fru fru coffee. They had to go all the way to Denver for that. Sure, there were bars and liquor stores in Tunston, but nothing for Wynter to call her own. And, getting a piece of pie at Pop's was the closest thing any kid had to a fun treat out.

Faith hummed to herself as she ripped open a new package of napkins to fill another napkin holder. She heard the front door of the building open just before she heard the hard, heavy footfalls of whomever had entered. Looking up, she saw the looming figure of Lucas Pennington, his deep blue eyes fixated on her.

Feeling her stomach roll, she stiffened her spine and stood up straighter, head slightly cocked to the side. "Afternoon, Deputy. We're not open until tomorrow when the festivities start." To hide the fact that her hands were shaking, both from pure disdain and from intimidation, she returned her focus to her napkin holder, shoving the wad of napkins in far harder than was necessary. "I'm sure I can get Wyatt to give you a sample of what we plan to give out tomorrow during the parade," she said, hitching a thumb back toward the kitchen behind her, the huge window in the wall showing Wyatt working diligently on making an incredible amount of ice cream. They'd installed the window so people could watch in wonder as their treat was created.

Thumbs hooked into his utility belt, he smirked as he looked down at her. "I don't need you to get anythin' from Wyatt for me," he said, reaching down to finger a few napkins that were left in the package. "I get all the free samples I want from my wife."

She glared up at him, torn between wanting to shoot him with his own gun and wanting to throw up.

"Every night," he finished, a dimple winking at her when he grinned.

Jaw muscles clenching and unclenching, Faith asked, "Is there something useful I can actually help you with, Deputy? All my licenses and permits are up to code and up to date," she said, nodding her head over to the brick wall next to the ice machine where they were framed and hung for all to see.

He never took his gaze off hers as he slowly shook his head. "Naw, don't care nothin' 'bout that," he drawled, shifting his weight to a hip.

"Then I'd say you have no business here, Deputy. We're closed," Faith said, managing to not clench her teeth.

"I got plenty of business where my wife works, ripped from a perfectly good job at the café for what?" He picked up the napkins and tossed them up in the air only for them to slowly float back to earth, one sliding off the counter to the floor at his feet. "Scoop ice cream?" He smirked. "Sweeten' the boss's day, maybe?" He planted massive hands on the countertop and leaned down, Faith forced to look up to meet his gaze. "Ain't gonna happen, girly," he murmured, his tone almost sounding like a bedroom voice if not for the murder in his eyes. "The only sweet treats she's gonna be servin' is to snot-nosed ten-year-olds."

It was impossible to keep the outright disgust from curling her lip. She had no doubt it was shining in her eyes, too. "I have a business to get ready to open, Deputy, so if you don't mind, I'd like to get back to it."

He met and held her gaze for a long moment before pushing off the counter, a smirk on his face. He tipped his uniform hat and turned to walk away.

Enraged at his behavior, Faith found herself calling out to him. When he turned back to look at her from where he stood, about halfway to the door, she said, "You know, a lot of times dogs pee on their perceived territory to mark it. Some of us are housebroken. Why don't you go piss somewhere else?"

His smirk turned into a snarl, but he said nothing and simply left the building, leaving Faith shaking in his wake. She was partly afraid of him, not entirely sure what he was capable of, but also absolutely filled with rage.

Normally not remotely a violent person, she couldn't hold it in. The napkin holder she held in her hands went sailing across the room with a roar that erupted from her throat. As the loud CLANG! rent the air as the holder slammed against the brick wall, she immediately regretted her action.

"Shit," she muttered, hurrying from around the counter to where it had fallen beneath one of the tables. She fell to her knees and gathered the pieces of the destroyed napkin holder, feeling terrible for the destruction of an innocent object. She was also angry at allowing a bottom-dweller like Lucas make her that angry.

"Faith?"

She turned to see Wyatt standing just beyond the table she knelt under. "Hey," she managed.

"Honey, what is it?" Wyatt asked gently, squatting down next to the table, concern on her face.

Faith stared down at the pieces she'd collected. Luckily, it had come apart in large chunks. She was too ashamed to meet Wyatt's gaze. "I'm fine. Sorry."

"What happened?" Wyatt reached out and ran her fingers through Faith's hair. "You're tremblin'."

Faith looked at her, able to feel Wyatt's concern coming off her in waves. With the tight space beneath the table, there was very little daylight between them, and, as it always did, Wyatt's perfume wafted over her. It was so comforting, yet so deeply tempting.

"There's only one person I know that can make a body tremble so," Wyatt whispered, her hand sliding from Faith's hair to rest against her cheek. "I'm sorry, darlin'." Tears glistened in her eyes. "So very sorry."

Faith reached up and gently grasped Wyatt's hand with her own. "Not your fault," she whispered back. Her heart began to race, and the trembling took on a whole new meaning.

Time stood still for a moment, just one perfect moment, before reason returned and Faith lightly squeezed Wyatt's fingers before pulling away.

※※※※

The warm, early August night air smelled fresh and clean. Faith sat on her porch swing, gently moving it to and fro with the bare foot that was on the floor, her other leg tucked up against her body.

She sipped from her glass of iced tea, looking out over the night. She smiled as she heard the very distant practice of the school marching band, their attempts the only sound in the quiet late evening. School would be starting in a week, the very first class of the new and improved Wynter Mountain Elementary School, Wynter Mountain Middle School, and Wynter Mountain High School—known collectively as Wynter Mountain K-12 School and all in the same building due to the very small class sizes—and the kids were so excited to be representing their new school in the morning at the parade.

As she looked out over her property and the lights of Wynter beyond, she felt a mixture of emotions: great pride and exhaustion, yet a deep sadness, a loneliness that she'd felt more and more over the past couple months. She knew that asking Wyatt to run things at Bessie's was absolutely the right call, but it had a really stupid, unthought-out consequence. Spending ten hours a day with her, nearly every day for the past three months, had been equal parts wonderful and painful.

She brought the cool drink up and took a sip, the night disappearing for just a moment as she saw Wyatt's face slip before her mind's eye. She saw her smile, she saw the way Wyatt looked at her that, in Faith's mind at least, seemed to be just for her. Her laugh, her brilliant mind, and sweet kindness to any and everyone. And, she'd gotten to see a very different side of Wyatt in the past months—quite the business mind she had. Her ideas were insanely creative, yet smart and practical.

Faith smiled, thinking about some of the conversations they'd had. Over the months, as she'd felt her attraction grow into full-on feelings, feelings she refused to name, she'd started to distance herself. Either she'd found work on the opposite floor or had gone to her office to work out the details of the building next to Bessie, which the two had acquired. They'd found that it had a tunnel that also led to the hot springs, though had been walled off at some point in the past.

She'd spoken to her team and they'd decided it would benefit the town to turn the building, or part of it, into locker rooms and showers for those who wished to go into the hot springs. It would be a project down the road a bit, but at least the building was deeded to the town. Records of prior ownership couldn't be found, it had been vacant for so long.

So, it had been nice to stay away from the

business to work on that, even on days when there was no reason for her to oversee anything. She'd done it just to keep her distance. One day she found herself sitting in her office playing a game on her phone, nowhere else to go but the shop.

That was the day she'd realized that the town wasn't paying her to play games or to hide, so she'd put her big girl pants on and gone back to the shop, and met with the other shop owners to coordinate their grand openings the day of the Wynter in August parade and festivities. The empty buildings all up and down the main street had been picked up and turned into a small grocery store, a shipping store—even a gas station was coming in the fall, among others.

So, as she sat there, enjoying the night while sitting on her porch swing on the porch of her house, she had everything in the world to be grateful for. She had everything in the world to be proud of. So why was she so sad?

❧❧❧❧

Faith yelled out in excitement along with the crowds lining both sides of the street. She cheered and clapped louder as the Wynter Police Department made its slow crawl down the street, the squad cars all newly serviced and painted. Two officers per car, the five-car squad had their lightbars rolling. It was a small police force at the moment, but by god, at least they had one.

Following the police cars were the two ladder trucks, also painted and pretty, with the water tanker and EMS trucks of the Wynter Fire Department behind it. The front truck blasted its air horn, exciting the kids in the crowd. Uniformed firefighters hung on the trucks or walked alongside, waving to the crowds on either side.

"That's my son!" Ana Lucero exclaimed to anyone within earshot from where she stood with her husband not far from Faith. "The new fire chief. That's my son!"

Faith smiled, pretty sure Ana hadn't stopped smiling since the day she'd taken a stroll down to the DMV to tell Ana the news about the new fire chief and the new fifth grade teacher. Ana had screamed and nearly climbed through the small hole in her window to get out of her booth to hug Faith.

Following the fire department was the group of K-12 kids that would be filling the halls and classrooms of Wynter Mountain K-12 School. They all wore matching T-shirts in the blue and silver school colors, the school name and mascot emblazoned across the front. Behind the giant mass of kids, from five years old all the way to eighteen and ready to graduate, were the teachers and faculty in their own matching shirts.

Faith raised a hand to wave when she recognized Stacey Lucero in the group. The school district had tried to fight them that Wynter's population was now too small to support a school, and that the kids should continue in Tunston, but they were able to prove how many days of school the kids had had to miss over the harsh mountain winters when passage to Tunston at a higher elevation was impossible. They'd won, and besides, Faith had no intention of Wynter's population staying as small as it was. It had shrunk due to mismanagement and corruption. No longer.

After the kids was a flatbed trailer that was being pulled by a truck covered in a banner that made her heart do a flip, caused by the woman who was dancing on that flatbed as the classic "Louie, Louie" began to blast out of the huge speaker anchored onto the trailer. Wyatt was joined by all the employees of Bessie's, clad in their uniforms for both upstairs and downstairs.

Faith could sense the crowd around her getting into the song, dancing, many singing along, but she only had eyes for Wyatt. She was dressed in short denim shorts, strong, tanned thighs beautiful. She wore her Bessie's Scoops T-shirt, which was white and looked like it had been splattered by various colors of ice cream. Her hair was swept up in one of her bandanas, and she'd never looked more beautiful. Something in her movement, in her expression, was a pure joy that Faith had never seen before. She wondered what was behind it.

Two huge freezers had been anchored to the flatbed as well, plugged into the same generator as the speaker system. Still dancing, the employees gathered by the freezers and started handing out pre-scooped paper cups filled with the mango ice cream Wyatt had come up with the day before. The truck was going slowly enough that they were able to reach down to people who ran up to the truck, or jump down to give out samples farther back in the crowd.

Faith saw Wyatt hop down, her hands filled with sample cups. She was surprised when Wyatt ran up to her, shoving the last one she held into Faith's hands.

"Want a sweet treat, little girl?" she murmured, wiggling her eyebrows suggestively before sticking her tongue out at Faith and running back to the truck.

"Hiya, Mayor Faith!"

Faith smiled and raised a hand in the general direction of the man who had called out to her on the street in front of the café, which was closed for the day due to the parade. As her employees were finishing up with closing duties, she'd gathered all the bags of trash and hauled them over to the massive dumpster they'd had placed in the parking lot at Pop's—with his permission, of course—and was headed back to Bessie's.

The main street of the town had been blocked off to vehicular traffic after the parade to continue the festivities. An area had been roped off as a dance floor and a local band had set up, blasting country hits, pop hits, and some of the classics to the throngs of townspeople. All the new stores had their grand openings, as well as vendors from near and far with booths of their wares for sale, anything from homemade candles and jewelry to artwork and caricature artists.

It had been a total success, and something she wanted to talk to her group about making an annual event. For now, it was late and most of the booths had been folded up, many completely gone already, leaving empty spaces behind. The music was still going, some fun, upbeat country song.

Her head bobbed along to the beat as people danced, some sloppily from a few too many beers, but all seeming to have a good time. What stopped her, however, was when she spotted her father. Hands tucked into the pockets of her shorts, she watched, amused then charmed.

Ogden Fitzgerald was doing his level best to keep

up with organist and, as it turned out, very capable dancer Miss Vicky. Faith laughed a few times as he continued to step on Vicky's booted feet, but what got her the most was the smile on his face. In all her life, she'd never seen such a smile of pure, unadulterated joy. Why, if she didn't know better, she'd say he was having...fun.

Not wanting to chance him seeing her, as she feared he'd be embarrassed and go back to being a reserved stick in the mud, Faith walked on. "Night, guys," she said, passing two of her employees as they headed out.

Reaching for the door, Faith paused as the country song ended and the piano notes of the next began. She smiled; one of her favorites. Humming softly along, she entered the building, noting the main floor was mostly dark, save for the safety lights. Chairs were stacked on the tables. She decided to head upstairs.

As she climbed the long, narrow staircase, she could hear soft singing that matched the song that could be heard loud and clear from outside in the street. Reaching the top of the stairs, Faith stopped, hands resting atop either side of the saloon doors, to watch Wyatt, who was taking her time sweeping with a broom and singing along.

"You've got a great voice," Faith said, pushing through the saloon doors, which swung gently behind her as she entered the room.

Wyatt glanced over at her and smiled. "Nah. Now, Daddy, he's the one who had a voice." She stopped sweeping, wrapping both hands around the broom handle and resting slightly against it. The smile on her lips was soft and wistful. "This was Mama's favorite song of Patsy Cline's, though."

"I love this one, too," Faith said, hands going back into her pockets.

Wyatt said nothing as she walked over to the bar, carefully resting the broom against it before walking over to Faith. "What about you, darlin'?" she asked, reaching out and lightly tugging one of Faith's hands free. "Are you 'Crazy'?" she asked softly, alluding to the title of the song that was being beautifully covered by the band outside.

Faith smirked, stepping forward as Wyatt stepped backward, leading her to a spot at the center of the room where there was more space between the tables, the chairs stacked on top. "That all depends on who you ask."

Wyatt smiled. "Dance with me."

Faith's hands went to Wyatt's waist as Wyatt's arms slid up around her neck. They shared somewhat awkward smiles as they got settled, then Wyatt's head went to Faith's shoulder as they began to sway together.

Faith's eyes slid closed as she marveled at just how right it felt to hold Wyatt to her, their bodies barely brushing together as they moved. Faith was getting lost in the sound of the music, the scent of Wyatt's hair so close to her nose, and the feel of her breasts pressed against her own, so soft yet so firm at the same time.

As Wyatt's fingers twined themselves into Faith's hair, Faith's hands moved from her slender waist to slide over her back, the cotton of her T-shirt made warm by the skin beneath. Faith's heart quickened as she felt warm breath against her neck. She wasn't positive, but thought she felt the softest touch of lips there.

She couldn't help but think how perfect Wyatt felt against her, how it felt as though she'd been in her arms for years, for lifetimes, even. As the song played on, she realized that they were moving less and less, the music no longer the glue that held them together in such physical intimacy.

Wyatt lifted her head. For a moment, their foreheads nearly touched, Wyatt's eyes downcast as her fingers continued to play in short, dark hair. Faith looked into the beautiful face that had haunted her dreams for months, so close to her own. She studied Wyatt's features, though she had each one memorized and the sound of Wyatt's voice tattooed across her soul.

Something inside Faith screamed at her to move, like a warning siren going off in her head. Without thought or warning, she jumped away, grabbing the broom and nearly throwing it at a startled Wyatt before leaping and clearing the bar top like a world-class athlete, only for her ankle to let her know it was a less-than-gold-medal landing...

Heart racing, Faith hurried over to the cash register, messing with it even though it had been counted down an hour before. A second later, she heard the final loud thud of a booted foot on the stairs.

"What the fuck?" Lucas's voice boomed into the room. "What the fuck's this?"

Faith glanced over at him, praying like hell she didn't look as guilty as she felt. To her credit, Wyatt, who had begun sweeping frantically at the sound of the footstep, glanced up, the very picture of innocence.

"Lucas, what are you doin' here?" she asked, walking nonchalantly over to where the upright dustpan was. "I told you I'd get a ride home—"

"Don't talk back to me," he growled, over by her side with inhuman speed as he grabbed her by the arm.

"Hey!" Faster than she'd jumped over the bar top she made it around, only to stop in nearly a cartoon-like fashion when Wyatt glared her way, arm outstretched and hand up.

"No," she exclaimed, eyes hard. "No." Her voice had lost its edge, but her eyes hadn't. "Go home, Faith."

Faith stared at her, deeply shocked and hurt. Her mouth moved, working to form words, but none came forth.

"Go home," she said again. "I'll deal with my husband."

Confused and stung, Faith said nothing, simply walked past the couple feeling like a kicked puppy. She made her way down the stairs, one step at a time, each thud against the hard wood echoing in the fog that was her brain. She couldn't wrap her mind around what had just happened, the two very different sides of Wyatt she'd seen. One minute her touch had been so gentle, loving, downright seductive; the next, a cold hardness in those eyes that she'd never seen.

Chapter Twenty

It was normally a sound she loved, that of a gentle summer rain, especially with the bedroom windows open to allow a nice cross breeze in. But, as she lay there on her mattress on the floor, all Faith could think about was how her night in town had ended.

She kept seeing those hard eyes looking at her. *Go home. My husband.* Unchecked jealousy raged through her. Lucas's comments to her the day before hadn't helped, bragging about what Wyatt did for him every night, which of course sent images haunting her, things she didn't want to think about. What his words had conjured up literally made her want to vomit.

"Stop it!" she yelled at herself, bringing her hands up to cover her face, more tears threatening to come. "This is stupid." She started to laugh through her tears, overwhelmed at the absurdity of it all.

She stopped short, thinking she heard something outside. Sitting up, she used the neckline of her tank top to dry her eyes and listened. Now that her father had moved into his house by the lake, she was alone in the house and her bedroom door was open. Staring into the darkness beyond was a bit daunting as she heard it again. Footsteps?

Crawling off the mattress—a bed had to be her next purchase—eyes still keening to see into the darkened hallway, she blindly reached for the mesh shorts she'd kicked off before bed, tugging them on over her panties. She grabbed her phone and walked in bare feet to the bedroom window that faced the front of the house. There was no car parked, nor one that she could detect in the limited view beyond the gate down the hill. Due to the roofline, she couldn't see the porch or the front door.

Her head whipped around back toward the hall when she heard definite footsteps on the wood porch floor. She headed in that direction, unlocking her phone as she went and bringing up the screen to dial so she could call 911 if necessary.

She hurried through the darkened house, deciding not to turn on any lights as she wanted to keep the element of surprise. That, however, proved to be a moot point as she cried out when a loud crack of thunder boomed over the house, the rain outside clearly worsening into an all-out thunderstorm, common late in the summer.

Hand to heart, she blew out a breath and continued on, padding down the stairs and to the front door, just as someone knocked loudly upon it. Again, her heart stopped. She walked up to the door, her hand sweating around the phone it held. As surreptitiously as she could, she moved up to one of the tall, narrow windows on either side of the door.

Relieved yet confused when she saw a very wet Wyatt standing on the other side, she set her phone down on the small console table nearby and unlocked the door, pulling it open. A flash of lightning sliced open the night, sending an eerie and very telling light across Wyatt's face.

"Oh my god." Faith could hardly breathe, staring.

"I came to apologize," Wyatt said, her words

nearly drowned out by the growling storm behind her.

Faith reached out and took her wrist gently before lightly tugging. Wyatt stepped inside the threshold and Faith closed the door behind her. Inside the dimness of the foyer, Faith didn't need light to see the afterimage of the angry black eye that the lightning flash had revealed. The accompanying bruise covered Wyatt's left cheek. Tears were instantly in her eyes again.

"Apologize?" She gasped. "For what?" She reached up a hand toward Wyatt's face but stopped before making contact, pulling her hand away. "My god, what did he do?"

Wyatt took hold of Faith's retreating hand, taking it in both of her chilled ones. "Apologize for how I had to speak to you." She tucked their joined hands to her chest, almost how a child would hug a teddy bear for comfort. "I could tell he was fixin' to let loose, and I had to get you out."

The tears came faster and harder. "I did this to you, then," she cried. "I left you to that monster."

Wyatt took a step forward, their hands nearly pinned between their bodies. "You didn't do this, Faith," she whispered. "He did." She lightly pulled her hands away from Faith's and brought them up to her face, using her thumbs to gently wipe at her tears.

Faith's eyes fell closed at the soft touches.

"I learned a long time ago," Wyatt continued, speaking so close to Faith's cheek that she could feel the whispered words as well as hear them. "He's not worth anyone's tears."

Faith nodded slightly, her eyes opening, Wyatt's so close. "No, but you are."

Wyatt met and held Faith's gaze for what

seemed like an eternity before her hand slid from the side of Faith's face up into her hair, using the leverage to draw Faith toward her. Faith's eyes closed at the first touch of those full lips against her own. She knew immediately this was going to be unlike any kiss they'd shared before.

She felt Wyatt relax into the kiss as their lips moved against each other, slow, testing. At the very first tentative touch of Wyatt's tongue against her own, Faith knew she was home, even as she stood in her own house.

As the kiss deepened, a small whimper was released from Wyatt as she tightened her grip in Faith's hair, her hips pushing insistently against Faith's. Faith's hands trailed down to those hips, holding them tightly against her.

After a long moment, the kiss broke, leaving them both breathing heavily. Wyatt rested her forehead against Faith's. "You have no idea how long I've wanted to kiss you like that," she murmured.

Faith looked shyly at her. "Me, or a woman?"

Wyatt caressed her cheek, a soft smile spreading across her lips. "Just you."

Faith looked deep in her eyes, her own adjusting to the dimness, and saw only truth there. She brought up a hand and brushed the backs of her fingers down the soft skin of Wyatt's cheek before continuing down over her throat and her right breast. She took Wyatt's hand in her own and, without a word, turned and led the way up the stairs and to her bedroom. Wyatt went willingly, hesitatingly only a moment to reach behind her and lock the front door before they left the foyer.

Once in her bedroom, Faith glanced back at Wyatt when she heard a small laugh. "What?"

"We really need to get you a bed, darlin'."

Faith grinned, backing toward the mattress. "It's on my to-do list."

The storm amped up outside, thunder once again cracking open the night. Faith could see the sheer curtains dancing as they were being pelted by wind and rain. She hurried to one window, slamming it shut before moving to close the other. When she turned back to the mattress, she nearly had a heart attack.

Her wadded Bessie's T-shirt in her hands, Wyatt stood there in all her perfection, like a goddess, in a bra and the shorts she'd had on earlier that day. She met Faith's gaze, her own a bit shy. "My clothes are damp," she explained softly. "I don't want to get your bed wet."

Faith walked slowly over to her, her gaze falling to those breasts, lovingly cupped in satin and lace. She took a deep, steadying breath. She brought her hands up, lightly running her fingertips up along the smooth, chilled skin of Wyatt's sides until she reached the rounded sides of her breasts. She met Wyatt's gaze again, the shyness now turned twin oceans of want and need.

The kiss Faith initiated was slow, teasing, yet filled with promise of pleasures to come as she trailed her nails around Wyatt's sides to her back, unhooking her bra. Wyatt's mouth was incredible, just as Faith had dreamt it would be. Her lips were soft, her tongue warm and sweet, as no doubt the rest of her would taste. She burned to find out.

Bra falling away, Faith's hands found Wyatt's bared breasts, the nipples hard enough to tickle her palms as she ran them in small circles, coaxing a soft whimper from the woman she kissed. Her hands moved downward, unbuttoning and unzipping the denim shorts before her fingers snaked their way over that sexy behind, pushing the material down with them, her hands cupping a satin-covered bottom.

Wyatt broke the kiss with a gasp as one of Faith's hands found its way between Wyatt's thighs, the volcanic warmth emanating through the saturated material, nearly singeing her hand as she squeezed.

Something seemed to switch in Wyatt, her shy, uncertain touches becoming bold as she reached for the hem of Faith's tank top. With one violent tug, the garment was up and over her head and flying to the floor. As if a desperate race began to get to the bed, shorts went flying, panties, socks, and shoes. Finally, Faith was flat on her back, Wyatt on top of her.

Their kiss was passionate and sloppy as hands found any purchase they could on bare skin, months of bottled need and desire unleashed. Finally, Faith got hold of Wyatt's hands, holding them still just long enough to roll them over, their roles effectively reversed.

Wyatt looked up at her, daring in her eyes. Faith smiled, leaning down to place a soft, loving kiss on her lips before she rose to her hands, pushing herself up so that her breasts dangled over Wyatt's face. From the way her hands kept finding them, Faith knew Wyatt was deeply curious and, perhaps like herself, a breast woman.

She watched as Wyatt's hands reached up, her expression that of awe as she cupped up and explored the soft firmness. Faith's eyes fell closed and her head back as Wyatt's mouth engulfed one of her nipples, her tongue exploring the shape and contours. A long, languid groan escaped her throat, her arms becoming shaky as her need began to overcome her strength.

Pulling away, Faith stole a deep but quick kiss before she left her mouth and moved on to explore her neck and throat. She insinuated herself between Wyatt's spread thighs, lavishing praise upon Wyatt's flesh with tongue, lips, and teeth, giving ample attention to both perfect breasts. She could feel Wyatt's hands in her hair, which seemed to be a favorite for them. The wonderful sounds of Wyatt's moans and whimpers urged Faith downward.

As she got nearer her goal, her mouth watered at the wet heat she could smell, so close now. It was all of Wyatt's need, all of her desire wrapped up in that smell. It was a whole new kind of perfume for Faith to become addicted to. Moments later, she discovered no matter what she thought of Wyatt's scent, it had nothing on her taste.

Arms wrapped around strong thighs, Faith feasted, her tongue finding every sensitive spot, sucking the very places that made Wyatt's hips buck or her fingers tighten in her hair. She could tell by the quickening of Wyatt's breaths and the loud, sensual noises, Wyatt was getting close.

Getting a strong grip on her thighs to keep her hips still and legs spread, Faith concentrated her mouth where she knew Wyatt needed her most and began to suck and bat with her tongue mercilessly. She hummed in satisfaction as Wyatt's hips tried to buck against their hold, her whimpers and moans turning into cries of pleasure as her body released its desire like lava.

Holding her tongue hard against Wyatt's pulsing clit, she waited until the woman she held began to calm, her passion spent, before she lifted her face after leaving a kiss between Wyatt's legs.

Wyatt's taste still thick on her tongue and her lips, she made her way back up until she lay atop Wyatt's body, strong arms encircling Faith and pulling her close. Their kiss was passionate, sharing Wyatt's desire as Faith adjusted her own hips between Wyatt's legs. Like white lightning, a bolt of pleasure shot through them both as their clits came into contact, just as a bolt flashed across the heavens above outside.

Their kiss continued as Faith's hips moved in a slow thrust against Wyatt, their combined wetness making her movements fluid and smooth. Wyatt's knees raised and spread wider, pushing her clit up into better contact with Faith's, both rock hard and sensitive to the softest of touch or hardest of thrust.

Finally, they were both breathing too hard to continue kissing, so Faith pulled back just enough to feel Wyatt's heavy breathing against her face. She opened her eyes and looked down at the woman beneath her, marveling at this magnificent creature who gave her the gift of showing her how she felt through touch.

She could feel her pleasure rising, but she kept her thrusts slow and firm against Wyatt. She hugged her to her, their naked breasts pressed together as they moved together. Faith's mouth opened and her eyes squeezed shut as her orgasm flowed over her like a warm bath of honey. Wyatt held them together almost painfully tightly as she dissolved into her second release, gasping for air.

It took a moment for Faith to get her bearings back, but she was worried she was crushing Wyatt, so she disentangled herself, their lower stomachs stuck together by sweat and desire. She chucked at the sound it made as she pulled them apart. She flopped over on her back, chest heaving as she took in lungfuls of air and cooled down. She smiled when she felt her hand taken into Wyatt's.

Looking over to her right, she found the serene, very contented face of the most beautiful woman she'd ever known. "Hi."

Wyatt let out a soft sigh. "Hey there."

Faith rolled over to face Wyatt, who also turned, mirroring her position. "You're so beautiful," Faith murmured, reaching over and lightly tucking auburn hair behind Wyatt's ear.

Wyatt leaned up on an elbow over the short distance to Faith and left a lingering kiss to her lips. "Getting cold," she said softly before sitting up just long enough to reach down and gather the covers Faith had discarded before getting out of bed an hour before. She pushed Faith to her back and snuggled up to her, resting her head on Faith's shoulder as she pulled the sheet and light blanket over their bodies.

Faith pulled her close, reaching down under the covers to pull Wyatt's top thigh up and over hers. "I love the feel of your skin. So soft," she murmured, lightly running her fingertips over the thigh.

"Is it always like this?" Wyatt asked, her fingernails absently tracing patterns over Faith's stomach.

"Being with a woman has always been a good time," Faith began. "Even wonderful. But, it's never been like this for me before," she added truthfully.

Wyatt lifted herself to a forearm, looking down at Faith. She smiled, bringing the hand up that had been on Faith's stomach. She traced the features on

Faith's face, lips kissing the fingertips as they passed. "Now I know," she whispered.

"Know what?" Faith asked, almost put into a trance by the soft touches.

Wyatt lowered her face toward Faith's. "What it's like to truly make love," she whispered against Faith's lips before taking her in a slow, exploratory kiss. She lowered herself a bit, her hand gliding down from Faith's neck where it had rested and down beneath the covers as she moved her leg off Faith's.

Faith's heart began to race and her arousal grew as once again Wyatt's hand rested on her stomach. She could sense Wyatt wanted to do more, her fingers just barely tapping the top of her bikini line, but felt unsure of herself. As the kiss deepened, Faith moved her right leg so that it draped over Wyatt's hip, opening herself up. She brushed the backs of Wyatt's fingers to let her know it was okay.

Wyatt moved out of the kiss, looking deeply into Faith's eyes, again seeming to need that reassurance. Faith leaned up and placed a light kiss on her lips before resting her head back down on the pillow.

Wyatt's fingers trailed down farther until they finally rested in the heat between Faith's legs. "So wet," she whispered.

Faith smiled. "Can't imagine why."

Wyatt gave her a sexy little grin before her fingers began to move, exploring the soft, velvety terrain that made Faith a woman. Her eyes fell closed and her other leg lifted, her foot coming flat to the bed, offering more space to Wyatt's questing fingers. She could feel Wyatt's gaze on her, so she opened her eyes and looked up into that face, her own gaze drawn to the ugly black eye and bruising of her cheek. Instantly, tears once again began to gather.

"Shh, baby," Wyatt whispered, leaning down to rain light kisses over Faith's face until she finally stopped at her mouth. "Don't think about that right now," she murmured. "It doesn't matter anymore."

Faith accepted the kiss that was initiated, finding herself getting lost in it. Her body relaxed once more, the sadness that had begun to build released with every touch and stroke of Wyatt's fingers. And when those fingers slowly entered her, the world narrowed down to just the two of them, lying entwined so close they were nearly one.

With a few silent directives by Faith's fingers to Wyatt's, Wyatt soon found her footing as she touched Faith, gently moving inside her. Faith's hips began to roll with the gentle thrusts. She'd never been touched by anyone the way Wyatt was touching her. Her gentle yet deeply passionate nature was evident in every look, every touch, and every kiss. Somehow, she managed to reach not just inside of Faith's body, but into her heart and her very soul.

With Wyatt's lips so close to her own, Faith cried out as her second orgasm crashed over her, her back arching and fingers clutching the sheet covering the mattress beneath her. Her head snapped back with the intensity, her world exploding in light and color behind closed eyelids.

It took several moments, but finally she began to come back to earth, the soft murmurs and kisses on her face and lips helping. She reached for Wyatt, pulling her back down to her, her body snuggled up into Faith's side. They shared a loving kiss before settling in.

Chapter Twenty-one

She drove through the streets of Wynter, deeply satisfied to see people out and about, cars coming and going. She knew they had a long way to go to get Wynter back to what it once was and beyond, but she was proud of the momentum that had begun.

It was a bright, beautiful Sunday morning, and she was enjoying her drive to work. After waking up alone, she'd have thought she'd had the most vivid, wonderful fantasy-dream yet, if it weren't for the incredible soreness between her legs. After falling asleep initially, Faith had woken up to wandering hands and lips, which had sent them into a second round of lovemaking before again sleep called. Though she wasn't entirely surprised to find Wyatt gone when she awoke, she'd been very sad. She'd have been worried if it weren't for the text she'd received:

Mornin', beautiful. Coffee's brewin' for y'all at the shop.

The text had made her feel better, for sure, but she was still nervous. Last night had been the single most amazing night of her life, the most amazing experience with a woman she'd ever experienced. She knew where her heart lay, what she wanted, but was scared to even consider what Wyatt was thinking.

Pulling into her parking space, she sat behind the wheel for a moment. She glanced into the rearview mirror to make sure she looked okay, which she knew was stupid. Clearly Wyatt was attracted to her, but she still had the silly schoolgirl butterflies ramming at full speed into her rib cage anyway.

They'd decided to not open the ice cream portion of their business until eleven, but their coffee shop opened at seven on weekdays, eight thirty weekends. It was seven thirty, and she cursed herself for running late as she'd planned on being there thirty minutes ago. She'd set her phone alarm before going to bed, but had been so wiped out by her active night that she'd slept right through it.

Heading inside, she smiled, already able to smell the coffee brewing upstairs even as the downstairs remained dark and roped off. She trotted up the stairs, greeting Sam, one of their employees, and a local high school kid as they passed in the stairwell. At the top of the stairs, she felt her heart do a little flip in her chest when she spotted Wyatt standing at the bar. She was opening boxes that contained bottles of their various flavored syrups for the coffee and drinks. The unboxed supply had been utterly wiped out from the seemingly unending stream of people during the previous night's festivities.

Wyatt was freshly showered, her hair up in its Rosie the Riveter bandana. She was stunning. Faith also, however, noticed the horrible bruising for the first time under light. She was surprised, as Wyatt had clearly made no attempt to hide it under makeup. The black eye and cheek bruise were there for all to see.

Faith took a moment, then swallowed and pressed the Start button again on her heart and stepped forward. She knew they had to keep everything totally on the down low, especially from their employees and customers.

"Hey."

Wyatt glanced up at the sound of Faith's voice, a smile spreading on the lips Faith remembered so well. "Well, hey there, sleepy head. Wondered when you were gonna wander on in," she added with a wink.

Faith smirked. "Yeah, well. Funny that." She stepped up to the bar, slapping her hands lightly on it. "I thought you wanted a ride in this morning," she said, keeping her voice light and conversational even as all she wanted to do was grab Wyatt and give her a very proper hello.

"Well, I did," Wyatt admitted with a small nod, sparing Faith a glance before returning her focus to what she was doing, box cutter in hand. "But, I decided ta give Miss Vicky a call and come in with her. I know she always gets breakfast at Pop's every Sunday before church. Of which," she added, eyebrow raised. "She met your daddy for breakfast."

A little stung and confused on why Wyatt had chosen to go in with the church's organist, she pushed it aside for a moment and smiled. "They were dancing last night."

"Really?" Wyatt asked, leaning forward slightly as though about to hear good gossip. "How do you feel about that?"

"You know," she said softly. "I've never seen my father happy, my entire life. You see a picture of him throughout the years, it's obvious he's there because someone told him to be. He's smiling because someone said, 'Say cheese.' But," she continued, her voice growing softer yet with a tinge of emotion. "In the months since he's been here in Wynter, I've seen real joy in his eyes, in his smile. He's smiling because there's something to smile about. I saw that last night, too, when he was dancing with her."

"Finding yourself," Wyatt murmured, a finger daring to brush the back of Faith's hand for just a moment. "It seems to be the magic of Wynter. You find yourself, you find your faith." She smiled at what seemed to be an unintended double entendre as she looked Faith in the eye. "I need to talk to you," she said softly.

Faith nodded. "Sure."

"Libby, Faith is here, so we're gonna head down to the office for a sec," she called out to their weekend opener, who was back in the kitchen.

"'Kay," was called back.

Wyatt quickly finished what she was doing, then they headed down to the main floor and back to the door that led to the basement where the manager's office had been set up. Once inside, Wyatt closed the door behind the two of them and grabbed Faith in a deep, passionate kiss that left them both breathless.

"Do you have any idea how amazin' it is to be able to do that any ol' time I want?" Wyatt said with a grin, still holding Faith close with hands on her hips.

Faith returned the smile and nodded vigorously. "Yup." She left a lingering kiss on soft lips before taking Wyatt in a tight hug, needing to feel her close. The two women didn't speak as the hug went on for many moments until finally Wyatt pulled away, lightly caressing the side of Faith's face before she moved to sit in one of the two chairs at the desk.

"I'm sorry I wasn't there when you woke up this mornin'," she said. "I had to get back to the house.

Had me some decidin' to do, some plannin' to do, and a call to make."

"Okay," Faith said, moving to sit in the other chair, spinning it to face Wyatt. "What did you decide, what's the plan, and who'd you call?" she asked, light humor in her tone but nerves in her gut.

Wyatt reached over and took Faith's fidgeting hands in her own, resting them on her leg. "I decided I've had enough. I can't do this anymore," she said, shaking her head, suddenly looking very tired. "I can't live a lie for my daddy anymore. He's gone. I can't live for him no more," she repeated softly, sadness in her eyes as they met Faith's steady gaze. "I have to live for me. That's why I didn't cover this up," she said, indicating the bruising to her eye and face. "Ordinarily, I'd cake on the makeup or just not come into work, hidin' at home like the scared little girl I've been for too long."

Faith said nothing, just sat and listened, marveling at the strength of the woman sitting before her.

The sadness left her eyes, replaced by what Faith saw as nervousness. "Now, I'm about to really put my heart out there, but I got to," she said, letting out a heavy breath. She looked Faith square in the eye. "I already knew I loved you, Faith," she continued softly. "Hell, I think I've loved you since the first day I saw you eight months ago when you wandered into the café." Her smile was instant, making a beautiful face absolutely breathtaking. "But after last night, I now know I can't live without you, and I don't wanna try."

Faith felt her heart flip for the second time that morning. She let out a long, slow breath, part relief and all love, and nodded. She could see the determination in Wyatt's body language to get through what she had to say, so she didn't interrupt with her own declarations.

"So, this leads me to the plannin'," Wyatt continued. "I'm leavin' Lucas, Faith. I don't love 'im, never did. I stayed all those years out of some..." She looked away, as though searching for the right words. "Some misplaced duty, I guess." She met Faith's gaze again. "And, I was afraid. I had nowhere to go, nobody to care what happened to me. Once Mamma and Daddy died, he was it."

Feeling that sadness returning again, Faith ran her thumb gently back and forth over the back of Wyatt's hand, letting her know with the touch that she was there for her and she was listening.

Wyatt looked into Faith's eyes, her fingers tightening around Faith's. "I'm not alone anymore. I've got support, and most importantly, I've got the reason I've needed to finally be free and be myself."

Not saying anything, Faith cupped Wyatt's face and brought their lips together for a long, lingering kiss. "I love you," she finally whispered against them. "If you want me, you'll never be alone."

With a small cry, Wyatt grabbed Faith in a painfully tight hug, as though she'd been holding her breath, worried what Faith's response would be. "Thank god," she whispered into Faith's ear. "I was so afraid you wouldn't want someone so broken."

Faith brought up a hand and cradled the back of Wyatt's head in a loving hold. She smiled. "Broken? Are we talking about you or me here?"

Wyatt laughed and pulled away slightly. The sadness in her eyes was gone, the slightly lost look that Faith had noticed from time to time was gone. In its place was a love and adoration Faith had never seen aimed at her. She had no doubt the same shone from her eyes, because she certainly felt it.

"So, what next?" she asked. "Are you going to stay with me?" she asked, wiggling her eyebrows to try to lighten a heavy situation.

Wyatt took Faith's hands again. "That takes me to the phone call." Faith got the sense she was hedging, but didn't know why. "My phone call was to Miss Vicky. I asked her if she could pick me up because, yes, I needed a ride to work, but I wanted to talk to her. She had a little apartment above her garage that her son lived in for a minute after he graduated from college. I asked her if I could rent it from her during this divorce situation."

Hurt and confused, Faith's eyebrows fell. "Why wouldn't you just stay with me? I have another bedroom if you didn't want—"

"Baby," Wyatt said softly, bringing up her fingers to forestall what Faith was about to say. "You're the mayor of this town and a business owner. You're beloved and respected. There is no way in hell I'm gonna let that son of a bitch drag your good name through the mud by claimin' you broke up his marriage." She studied Faith for a moment, as if to say, *Trust me, there's a method to my madness.* "I'm not gonna let him say I left him for you because I didn't. I'm leaving him for me. I'm leaving him so I can be free to heal and be the best me I can for you." She smiled, briefly cupping Faith's cheek with her palm. "I've been with him for almost nineteen years. I've wasted enough of my life."

Faith could only stare at her, amazed at Wyatt's strength and courage. Again, that steely determination shone through. As much as she'd love to take her home with her, the plan made sense, as did the reasoning. "We still get to see each other, right?" she asked, eyeing the beautiful woman sitting less than a foot away. "Like, we get to kiss and stuff?"

Wyatt burst into laughter, part of which sounded relieved. "You silly thing," she murmured sexily, right before taking Faith in a passionate kiss.

❧❧❧❧

It was a house, a house like any other. It had all the expected things: furniture, a large television, kitchen table, and bedroom furniture in the bedrooms. The house was neat and clean, but the furnishings were worn, mismatched, tired-looking. There was nothing on the walls, no family photos, no artwork. Not even a hanging clock. It almost seemed like a house that could be rented fully furnished, all the basics included but none of the heart of a home.

Not sure what to do with her hands, Faith shoved them into the pockets of her track pants as she waited for Wyatt to return. Standing in the middle of their living room, she felt a wee bit conspicuous, even if she was the only person in the house.

"Sorry, baby," Wyatt said, rushing into the house from the back door. "Couldn't find what he'd done with the damn garbage bags." She held up a roll of large black trash bags before hurrying into a darkened hallway. "Come on."

Taking one last glance out the front window to make sure they wouldn't be surprised, Faith hurried after. They ended up in the back bedroom upstairs, where Wyatt switched on an overhead light. Faith assumed it was the bedroom Wyatt shared with Lucas, which instantly made her feel sick to her stomach.

The bed was a simple queen with a plain wood headboard. The two dressers were simple, scarred and mismatched from the bed and each other. Like the living room and kitchen, nothing on the walls, no knickknacks, nothing. Only an intricately carved wooden jewelry box, a single perfume bottle, and some paraphernalia for Lucas's uniform were scattered on top.

Wyatt already had the closet doors folded open and was grabbing clothes by the armful, hangers and all. She glanced over at Faith, who stood by the opened doorway. "Baby, my dresser is the one by the window. Just empty it." She nodded toward the roll of yard bags that she'd tossed onto the bed.

Nodding in acknowledgement, Faith tore off a few bags from the roll and hurried over to the indicated dresser. She wanted to be respectful of Wyatt's things, but she knew they just didn't have time. Her heart was racing, her blood pounding in her ears. She unceremoniously stuffed armfuls of panties, socks, T-shirts, and sweatpants into the bag. She filled one with half the dresser's contents—not wanting to chance the bag ripping—and began to fill a second.

She glanced over at the other dresser when she heard the sound of squeaky hinges. Wyatt had opened the top of the jewelry box and was sorting through it, removing a bracelet, a watch, and a necklace, leaving them on the dresser top before closing the box again and moving it over to the bed where a few pairs of women's shoes had been tossed.

"You're not taking those?" Faith asked, nodding toward the three pieces on the dresser top.

"No, ma'am," Wyatt said, walking back over to the dresser. She brought up her left hand and used her right to tug and twist at her wedding ring, making amusing faces of concentration as she tried to work the ring off. "All I want is Mamma's jewelry, which is in there," she said, nodding toward the jewelry box. "He gave those to me," she said with a grunt of exertion as the ring came off. She studied it for a long moment before dropping it into the circle the bracelet made.

"You could sell them," Faith suggested with a shrug.

Wyatt shook her head. "I don't want nothin' from that son of a bitch." She met Faith's gaze. "Never did."

Faith met her gaze and grinned. "That's my girl."

※ ※ ※ ※

Faith stood behind her SUV, hands on hips. After a record-setting game of pack-up and Tetris in the back of the 4Runner, she looked at the results. They'd crammed a bag or a box into every square inch of the cargo area and back seat. The only thing left, which wouldn't be possible that night, was Wyatt's mother's hope chest, which was in the garage and held the last of her parents' belongings after they were killed.

"Okay, this is it," Wyatt said, hurrying down the walkway to Faith, a stuffed backpack slung over one shoulder. "This is what I'll take to Miss Vicky's," she explained, dropping the pack off in the front passenger seat before meeting Faith at the back. "My goodness," she said, meeting Faith's gaze. "All my earthly possessions. How sad is that?"

Faith completely understood. "You know," she said softly. "The day I met you, everything I owned was crammed into the Element I'd bought before I left New York. I felt like such a failure. Here I was, almost forty, and my entire life fit in a handful of boxes." She gave her an understanding smile. She wanted to reach out to her, but she knew they still needed to be careful. Anyone in the surrounding houses could be watching. "But you know what?" she continued, trying to display all the love she felt for Wyatt in her expression and in her quiet tone. "It ended up being the most liberating thing to ever happen. Led me to you."

Wyatt reached over and took Faith into a hug, though she clearly was mindful, as it was far more of a hug to a friend than a lover. "I love you," she whispered.

Faith smiled. "I love you, too."

Faith reached up to pull down the cargo door when the sound of an approaching car alerted them both. The car was moving very slowly, its headlights on high, blinding them. Faith raised her hand to shield her eyes, the pit of her stomach clenching. Pure instinct had her lightly nudge Wyatt behind her.

The car stalked up to them, reminding Faith of a shark or a big cat toying with its prey. It came to a stop about thirty feet from them when a spotlight turned on, shone right on them. Faith didn't believe in guns, but in that moment she wished she had a weapon. By the size of the person getting out of the car, only seen as a silhouette in the curtain of light, she knew exactly who was staring at them.

"What's goin' on, here?" he asked, sauntering toward them, a hand resting on his utility belt.

Faith took a step out from behind her SUV, feeling bold by her building anger. "Looks like your wife's leaving you, Deputy," she said casually, unable to believe the words that seemed to just jump out of her mouth as they always did when talking to Lucas Pennington.

"That so?" he asked, stepping up to them, close enough that they could see him as more than just a black figure in the light. He looked down at Faith, then past her at Wyatt, who had stepped a bit farther behind the 4Runner. "That true?"

Faith glanced back at her. It absolutely incensed her to see Wyatt so afraid of him. What kind of man does that to anyone, let alone the one person you're supposed to love and cherish? Her attention was pulled back to Lucas when he spoke again, his deep voice raising in volume.

"You fixin' ta leave, huh? For the dyke, here?" He smirked at Faith. "If'n you think you gonna get somethin' outta her," he said, nodding his head in Wyatt's direction. "She's a cold bitch. Ya ain't gonna get nothin' for your trouble." The look he gave his wife was blood-chilling. "You gonna go live in her shit palace on the hill? Huh?" he barked when Wyatt didn't respond.

"She's not coming with me, Deputy," Faith said loudly, voice firm. She now understood fully why Wyatt had arranged things the way she had. "I'm here to help her move this stuff because she doesn't have a car."

His lecherous grin returned when he looked at Faith. "You may have the people of this town fooled, *Mayor*, but I knew you was trouble the minute I saw ya."

She returned the smirk, taking a step forward into his personal space. She was deeply satisfied when he took a partial step backward. "We're leaving," she said, reaching for the driver's side door and pulling it open, the move banging the door into his side. He jumped out of the way with a growl.

"Cunt."

She smiled at him through the window as she waited for Wyatt to climb into the passenger side after she'd closed the cargo door. She started the SUV.

All of the sudden, Lucas's handsome face contorted into rage. "You ain't getting' nothin' from me, ya bitch!"

Faith was shaken. She could see in that moment what a monster he must have been with Wyatt all those years. She put her hands on the wheel, ready to get them out of there, but stopped when she felt a small touch to her leg. Glancing over, she saw Wyatt subtly shake her head before she looked Lucas directly in the eye. Clearly, she had something to say, so Faith buzzed the driver's side window down.

"I don't want anythin' from you, Lucas. I never did. I'll be by tomorrow to get the rest of my things," Wyatt said, her voice deadly calm. She looked at Faith. "Let's go," she said softly.

The hatred in Lucas's deep blue eyes as he stared at Wyatt then Faith was heart-stopping. Finally, Faith pulled away from the curb, Lucas taking a step back out of the way. She glanced in the rearview mirror to see him standing in the middle of the street watching them go.

Chapter Twenty-two

Her nose and brain registered the smell. She was in the middle of a dream about barbecuing steaks when her ears got in on the game and the sound of sirens popped her eyes open. Sitting up in bed, she looked around the darkened bedroom, trying to figure out what she was smelling and hearing.

"Oh crap, a fire!"

Throwing the sheet aside, she scrambled off the mattress, nearly doing a header into the wall in her haste, as she hurried to a window that overlooked the front of the house. Seeing nothing but smelling the smoke so strongly it burned her nose, she tore out of the bedroom and down to the front door, hurrying out onto the wraparound porch. It was then that she saw the blaze off to her right.

"Oh…" She breathed deeply, realizing it was a house fire, probably a mile away from her house.

In the darkness of night, no real streetlights in the area, it may as well have been a massive bonfire. Instantly, her mind went to her business. No, that area of town was much farther east. Next her mind went to Wyatt, but relief was almost instant as Vicky's house was toward the outskirts of town closer to the church. Something else occurred to her, and after a moment of mental calculation, she raced back inside.

Throwing on a pair of shorts and tennis shoes without even taking the time for socks, Faith was back downstairs and storming out of the house to her SUV. Moments later, it was skidding onto the dirt road.

As she made her way down the road and toward the blaze, she felt as though she were driving right into the mouth of hell. The night was painted with heat in colors of orange and yellow, black smoke, as well as the dizzying array of lights from the fire trucks and police cars.

Sitting in her car, she watched, tears beginning to stream down her cheeks at the nightmare that was Wyatt's house completely consumed by flames. It was clear that it wasn't salvageable. She started when something exploded in the attic, a fireball shooting into the air before it disappeared into black smoke.

She reached to the seat behind her and grabbed a hoodie in the back seat and used it to wipe her eyes and face before she grabbed her phone from the passenger seat. Wyatt needed to know, but Faith was not looking forward to making the call. She also knew they needed to speak to the police.

❧❧❧❧

She couldn't get it out of her mind, the sound of Wyatt's sobs. When Faith said on the phone that, yes, the destruction looked to be total, Wyatt had said it felt like losing her parents all over again, because what she had left of them was in that house. That was what had killed Faith the most.

She pulled up to the police station, where she was told Wyatt and Vicky would meet her. The fire department guys at the scene said it would be best to go straight there to make a statement, and, Faith surmised, get out of their way. She recognized Vicky's car and saw that it was empty, so the women were clearly already inside.

Killing the engine, Faith took a deep breath and glanced at herself in the rearview mirror, worried she'd see a woman staring back at her with puffy red eyes. It wasn't as bad as she'd feared, so she climbed out and made her way to the front door of the brick building, attached to the larger building that was the jail.

The lobby was very small, and had a polished tiled floor with the Wynter Police Department crest inlaid. The wall straight ahead was the front desk, though most of it was walled off, the rest glassed off by a bulletproof window that the front desk clerk sat behind. To the left was a painted cinderblock wall with a line of plastic chairs to sit, Vicky occupying one, and the opposite wall had public restrooms.

"Hey."

Vicky looked up from her phone, peering over her reading glasses that were perched on her nose. She smiled, removing her glasses and setting them and her phone on the chair next to her. She stood and accepted a hug from Faith.

"Are they already talking to her?" Faith asked, glancing around the small lobby, noting the steel door next to the front desk clerk's window with a keypad next to it.

"Yes, they took her back pretty much as soon as we got here," Vicky said, retaking her seat, Faith taking the chair opposite Vicky's belongings.

"I truly appreciate you bringing her in, at…" Faith glanced at the clock that was mounted above the drinking fountain between the two bathroom doors. "Four seventeen in the morning."

"Oh," Vicky said, reaching over and patting Faith's knee. "I'd do anything for you girls, especially Wyatt." She placed her hands in her lap and let out a tired sigh. "I've so badly wanted her to leave that turd, but honestly wasn't sure what would finally give her the strength to do it." Vicky glanced at Faith, a knowing smile on her lips. "I'm glad it was real and true love that finally gave her the oomph she needed."

Surprised, Faith raised her eyebrows. "She told you?"

"Didn't have to," Vicky said, glancing toward the steel door which, after a long, harsh *buzz*, opened. "It's not hard to see the beauty between the two of you," she concluded.

Faith glanced toward the noise and saw Wyatt appear, a uniformed officer standing behind her. Immediately her heart nearly erupted out of her chest as she hurried over to Wyatt, who met her halfway across the room.

The hug they shared was tight, almost desperate, as Wyatt clung to Faith, the tears coming hard and fast. Whispering words of sympathy in her ear, Faith held her, mindful they were not alone, also very mindful of the alarming information Vicky had just given her. Perhaps they weren't being as clever as they thought.

Finally, Faith pulled out of the hug. "Are you okay?" she asked softly, raising a hand to brush some hair out of Wyatt's face that was stuck to a tear streak. "Want to head on home with Vicky? Get some rest?"

Wyatt shook her head, taking several deep breaths as though to center herself. "I want to go with you," she said softly, for Faith's ears only. "Is that okay?"

Faith nodded. "Of course." Faith glanced over at

Vicky, who was already nearly to them.

"I'm sure they'll want to talk to you," the older woman said. "I'll run home and grab her overnight backpack and drop it off back here."

Turning back to Wyatt, seeing her looking so exhausted and defeated, Faith changed her plan. "You know what," she said, flipping through the keys on her key ring and working to detach her housekey, which she placed in Wyatt's palm with a gentle smile. "Vicky, would you mind grabbing her backpack then taking her to my place so she can relax?"

"Of course." Vicky turned to Wyatt. "You and me again, kid."

Wyatt smiled weakly but said nothing.

"Thanks so much, Vicky. I truly appreciate it," Faith said. Her attention was grabbed when the uniform officer caught her attention. "Want to talk to me, now?" At the officer's nod, Faith turned back to the two women before her. She accepted a quick hug from Vicky, then another from Wyatt before walking over to the waiting officer.

She was led down a long hallway of the same painted cinderblocks as the lobby, interrupted by doorways, some open to reveal uninhabited offices, others closed with signs on them that read things such as: *Evidence Room, Interrogation 2,* and *Roll Call.* Finally, the maze of hallways ended in a small, plain room painted light gray with a rectangular table and three chairs. She was escorted into *Interrogation 1.*

"Detective Montez will be in in a second," the officer said, leaving the door open as he walked away.

Looking around, Faith took one of the seats, a simple plastic chair with thin foam padding. She set her keys and phone on the table and lightly tapped the table with her fingers to deal with some nervous energy. She'd never been in trouble and didn't practice that kind of law, so sitting in an interrogation room was a new one for her. Five or so minutes later, Faith's attention was garnered by footfalls walking down the quiet hall outside the room and stopping at the interrogation room.

"Good morning, Mayor. Sorry to keep you waiting." The woman entering was of average height with short, blond hair cut into a sporty style, her gray eyes alert and a bit intense. She looked to be in her thirties and was dressed in a women's-cut suit. She dropped a notepad on the table along with a pen before she took the chair across from Faith's. "I just got in and got the twenty-five-cent rundown on what's going on. I understand Mrs. Pennington has already been interviewed, so I'm here for you." She adjusted her body in the chair before glancing at Faith. "I'm Detective Grace Montez, by the way."

"Nice to meet you, Detective Montez. Please call me Faith."

"Faith it is." The detective flipped open the notebook and grabbed the pen, uncapping it as she met Faith's gaze. "Tell me who you think set the fire at 18 Songbird Lane?"

"Lucas Pennington," Faith said simply.

"Owner of the house and sheriff's deputy with Wynter County, Lucas Pennington?" the detective asked.

"One and the same."

The woman studied Faith for a moment, as if sizing her up. "You know, we tried to track down Deputy Pennington to alert him of the fire, and he's nowhere to be found. According to the sheriff's office, he arrived back at HQ around two thirteen this morning, turned in his badge and his resignation."

Faith stared at her, shocked. "Wow. Just after two would have given him plenty of time to get home, pack up whatever he wanted to take, then start the fire and leave."

The detective tapped her pen on the page where she'd written a few notes. "What's your history with Lucas Pennington? I understand you and his wife, Wyatt, are close friends, and that now she works at your business."

"Yes, this is true," Faith responded, her heart skipping a beat. She knew she couldn't lie to the detective and wasn't afraid to tell the full truth should it be needed.

"I know Wyatt is well known in town," Detective Montez said, sitting back in her chair. "She was well loved at the café. But, I'm not aware of close friendships like she has with you. How did the husband take to this? Do the two of you get along?"

"I've only met Lucas a few times and it's never gone well," Faith explained. This seemed to draw the other woman's attention as her eyebrows lifted.

"How so?"

"I'm not sure if you've seen Wyatt since Saturday night, but she's sporting a nasty shiner right now, courtesy of Lucas Pennington, and it's not the first, either. I can't tell you how many times I've seen bruises covered by makeup. Plus," she added, resting both hands on the table as she leaned forward a bit. "I've seen him manhandle her with my own eyes." She shook her head. "I don't take lightly to insecure males who feel it's okay to beat up on women, children, or animals to soothe their own twisted feelings of inadequacy."

"Have you said as much to him?" the detective asked.

"Not in so many words, but I've made it clear I know what's going on and it's not okay."

"When's the last time you saw Lucas Pennington, Faith?"

"Last night around nine thirty," Faith responded. At the other woman's questioning look, she explained. "Wyatt decided she'd had enough and was leaving him. So, we left my business after closing and headed to the house on Songbird. We were there for maybe thirty minutes or so, maybe forty. Wyatt packed up what we could fit in my SUV, then her plan was to go back today and get a couple pieces that belonged to her parents. We were about to leave when Lucas showed up."

"How was his demeanor?"

"Furious."

"Did he make any threats? Toward you, toward Wyatt, anything?"

"No, no threats. I don't remember exactly what was said now, but no threats. We saw him for a few minutes, I'd say. Less than ten, for sure, then we left. I dropped Wyatt off at Vicky Gallagher's house, where she was when I called her to tell her about the fire."

The detective rested the pen on the pad and interlaced her fingers as she leaned forward a bit, studying Faith. "Where were you when the fire started, Faith?"

Faith met her gaze, noting the change in tone from fishing to more focused. "I was at home, asleep."

"Were you the one who called in the fire?"

"No. I was awoken by the sirens of the fire trucks

and the smell of smoke. The fire was well underway when I woke up," she answered, keeping her tone even and conversational.

"Can anyone vouch for you?" the detective asked, picking up her pen again, as though waiting for a name or number to write down.

"No, Detective, I live alone. Just moved into the house a few weeks ago." Faith tried to keep any anger out of her voice, as she felt the woman sitting across from her was turning those gray eyes on her.

"If you two are such good friends, Faith, why did Wyatt go to stay with Mrs. Gallagher instead of with you?" She raised a honey-colored eyebrow. "You just said you're living in the big ol' house by yourself."

"In truth, I initially suggested that. It was Wyatt that thought better of it, as she knew Lucas didn't know where Vicky lives."

The detective's eyebrows fell. "Does she feel she's in danger?" she asked.

Faith met and held the woman's gaze. "Look what he did to their house, Detective."

※※※※

Faith showed up at her gate twenty minutes later, finding it very sweet that it had been left open for her. She climbed out of the car to close and lock it behind her, the sleepies definitely creeping back in after the adrenaline had petered out. The house was dark, but with the same consideration, the front door had been left unlocked for her. Like the gate, she closed and locked it before heading upstairs to her bedroom.

The sweetest sight met her, and one she realized she definitely wanted to see more often: Wyatt curled up in her bed. She lay on her side, Faith's pillow hugged to her chest. Unable to bring herself to take the pillow, Faith quietly set her keys and phone on her new dresser, then tugged her lightweight sweatshirt over her head.

Slowly, she lowered herself to the mattress and removed her tennis shoes before scooting over to curl up behind Wyatt, folding her arm beneath her head in lieu of a pillow. She smiled at the little moan that escaped Wyatt's lips just before she wiggled her shorts-covered bottom back into Faith, who wrapped her arm around Wyatt's middle, holding her close.

"Sorry I stole your pillow," Wyatt murmured, releasing the pillow and moving away from Faith's embrace.

"No, you were fine," Faith said, sad that Wyatt moved away. She chuckled as Wyatt worked to carefully put the pillow under Faith's head after she'd been pushed to her back.

"I've got the real thing," Wyatt murmured with a smile, lowering herself back to the mattress, resting her head on Faith's shoulder. "How'd it go for you?"

"It went well, I suppose. I spoke with a detective, and I halfway think she thinks I did it," Faith said with a rueful laugh.

Wyatt raised herself so her head rested against an upturned palm. She looked down at Faith. "He took off," she said softly.

"She told me. What a coward," Faith said, staring up into Wyatt's beautiful face. She lightly traced the proud jawline with her fingertip. "Where do you think he went?"

"Back to Savannah, I'd wager," Wyatt responded, her eyes closing at the soft touches. She let out a heavy sigh, her eyes opening again. "With him doin' this, this divorce could get super messy."

"We'll get you a good attorney," Faith said, accepting Wyatt back at her side as the other woman snuggled in. "I'd do it myself if it weren't a conflict of interest. I also think we should apply to get you a temporary restraining order while you go through the divorce process, just in case that piece of shit is still around somewhere."

"You really think I need that, Faith?" Wyatt asked, her voice sounding sleepy.

"I do," Faith said softly, her fingers very lightly touching the bruised cheek that wasn't against her shoulder. "Let's get some sleep."

"I love you," Wyatt murmured.

Faith smiled. "I love you, too."

"Baby?" Wyatt slurred in her exhaustion.

"Hmm?" Faith hummed, beginning to fall into sleep.

"Can we get a real bed?"

Chapter Twenty-three

"My god," Faith whispered, hand to her mouth.

She was horrified as she followed the fire investigator through the soot-covered remnants of the house. The entire second floor had collapsed, the heat of the fire weakening the supports holding it up. The main body of the house was a heap of jumbled beams, partial walls, scorched appliances, and torched objects that used to be furniture.

"Let me take you into the garage, Mayor," Lieutenant Bill Wakes said, leading the way. "After my investigation this week, I can say with confidence that it's where it all started."

The garage only had two walls standing, the back wall and the wall to the right. The large, fiberglass garage door had been destroyed, as well as the wall connected to the house.

"Jesus," she murmured, eyes wide as she took it all in. She'd never seen anything like it. It was a nightmarish image and the smell was still so strong: burnt wood, rubber, plastic, and near-choking fumes from chemicals and insulation. It was overwhelming at times.

"So," the investigator said, brought up from Chief Lucero's former department in Colorado Springs. "I feel confident to say it started here." He walked her to an area of the garage that would have been against the back wall. It was strange—a perfect rectangle of charred wood covered in a heap of ash roughly four feet long and a foot and a half wide, a few items poking out, including what looked to be a large, cowboy-style belt buckle. "I do believe an accelerant was used," he continued. "You see here," he said, indicating the heap of ash. "I think this was likely a trunk or wooden box of some sort."

"A hope chest?" Faith asked, dread clenching her gut.

He met her gaze from beneath the brim of his fire department-issued baseball cap. "Absolutely, entirely possible. Was there one in the garage?"

"There was," she said, blowing out a long breath.

"Well, likely this was it," he said. "I think the accelerant, likely gasoline, was poured directly into it and then a trail of it was poured this way," he said, pointing toward a scorched trail on the cement floor. "And on into the house. That's what the burn patterns tell us."

Hands on hips, Faith looked around, disgusted and angry as all get-out. "So, this was arson, then?" It was more of a statement than a question, but she wanted to hear a definitive from him.

He nodded. "Absolutely."

"And, Lucas Pennington is responsible for it?"

"Well," he hedged, removing the cap and running his fingers through somewhat-sweaty gray hair. "You'll have to talk to Detective Montez about that, Mayor. My job is to find proof a crime has been committed. Her job is to prove who committed it." He gave her a smile.

Faith watched in silence, trying not to react. This moment was about Wyatt, not her own inner feelings of anger and grief. Wyatt turned the partially melted belt buckle around in her fingers, her thumb rubbing over the smooth metal.

"You know," she said softly. "Daddy used to tell me that Wyatt Earp himself gave it to him." The beautiful redhead looked over at Faith where she sat next to her on the porch swing. Her turquoise eyes glistened, but tears had yet to fall. "Imagine my confusion when I found out that he'd been dead for seventy years."

Faith smiled, though remained silent.

"Daddy and his Old West tales," she whispered, her thumbnail lightly rubbing the horse racing across the belt buckle. Taking a deep breath and letting it out slowly, she met Faith's gaze. "Did your daddy like those spaghetti Westerns?"

Faith shook her head. "No. He was a sci-fi man. In fact, I'm grateful he wasn't into the name thing like your parents, or I may have been Spock." The smile that earned her was worth every bad moment she'd ever lived. Faith reached out and lightly caressed Wyatt's cheek with the backs of her fingers. "I'm so sorry about this, baby," she said softly. "We can go by the house if you want—"

"No," Wyatt said, voice firm. "I have Daddy's belt buckle and Mamma's jewelry. Got my books," she added with a small smile, Faith easily able to see the collection of lesbian novels and erotica she'd moved from Bessie to what would become her home office. "There's nothin' more I ever could want from that house, which doesn't even sound like it survived, anyway. Diana said that, even though my name wasn't on anythin', I'm culpable for half of that damn house."

"Which that piece of crap had allowed to go into foreclosure," Faith added. She and Wyatt had gone to Denver to speak to Diana Lopez, the attorney Faith had hired for the divorce. "And, since he allowed the homeowner's insurance to lapse, it won't be covered." She looked out over the property, her hand reaching out blindly until she felt Wyatt's, their fingers automatically twining. "Not like it would've mattered," she added, looking back to Wyatt. "Arson by the homeowner."

"Ma'am?"

Faith went to pull her hand away from Wyatt's, but Wyatt held tight. She met those determined turquoise eyes, then relaxed, turning to the man standing inside the house at the open screen door.

"I got all the cameras connected and the monitors set up, including the camera down by the new electric gate you had us install." He hitched a thumb over his shoulder back into the house. "If you wanna come in, I can show you how it all works."

"Absolutely."

※※※※

"So," Wyatt said, laughing. "This poor kid is like, 'Mom, brain freeze. I can't think! I can't think!' And the mom looks down at her coffee she'd just gotten from upstairs and hurries over to junior. 'Drink! Melt it!'"

Faith laughed along with her as she dried the freshly washed dish she'd just been handed. She hadn't gotten around to replacing the broken dishwasher she'd inherited upon purchasing the house "as is." On her own she didn't generate that many dishes in the first place, so handwashing wasn't a big deal for the time being.

Wyatt pulled the plug in the sink of soapy water after handing the pan she'd washed over to Faith to rinse and dry. She glanced shyly over at Faith, who met her gaze. "I wanna ask ya somethin'."

"Sure, baby. What's up?"

Wyatt was silent as she dried the counter and sink with the dishrag before wringing it out and slapping it over the sink divider. "I'd like to get a car," she finally said, her voice almost little-girl soft. Her eyes downcast, she added, "I think it would make things easier."

Faith's heart broke as she set the pan and towel aside on the counter and took the few steps over to the woman who was nearly trembling. "Hey," she said gently, a hand going up to brush loose auburn hair out of Wyatt's face while the other rested on a womanly hip. "Wyatt, look at me." When she had Wyatt's eyes on her, she smiled. "I think that's a great idea. You still have your driver's license, right?"

What looked to be a bit of relief, though still guarded, entered Wyatt's eyes. "Technically, but I need to renew it. When I wanted to before, that's when Lucas sold my car."

Piece of shit rat bastard. "Well," Faith said cheerily, despite her dark thoughts. "I just so happen to know a really nice lady down at the DMV who I'm sure would be thrilled to help you out."

Wyatt let out a little cry of relief as she rushed into Faith's arms, holding her tight. Faith returned the hug, burying her face in soft, auburn hair.

"Baby," she said gently, "I'm not Lucas. I'll never tell you what you can and cannot do." She left a kiss to the side of a warm neck before continuing. "I think it's wonderful that you get a car. You are a grown woman and deserve to have your independence." She left a second kiss, this time at the corner of her jaw. "I want you to be who you are," she whispered into Wyatt's ear, smiling at the little shiver she felt wash through the other woman. "I fell in love with the strong woman I always saw inside you." She left a kiss on the corner of Wyatt's mouth. "He couldn't take that from you," she murmured against full lips. "And I don't want to."

Their kiss was slow and exploratory, but Faith made her intentions known, her hands moving down to cup an incredibly shapely behind.

Left a little breathless, Wyatt said, "I was thinkin' somethin' else, too."

"Oh?" Faith murmured, pulling Wyatt's hips harder into her own. "What's that?"

"Well," Wyatt began, tracing the fingernails of her two pointer fingers teasingly over the rounded sides of Faith's bra and shirt-covered breasts. "Tomorrow is Thursday, and since we're closed on Thursdays, I thought I might trouble ya for a bed tonight."

Faith smiled at Wyatt's choice of words. "Trouble me for a bed, huh?"

"Uh-huh," Wyatt responded in her sexy little way that drove Faith crazy. She could feel her panties already getting saturated and Wyatt had barely laid a finger on her.

"I don't know," Faith responded in a teasing voice, even as her hands came up to the buttons on Wyatt's short-sleeved women's-cut blouse, taking her time to unbutton it. "It's gonna cost ya."

Wyatt grinned against Faith's lips. "I'll pay double," she whispered.

※ ※ ※ ※

After her meetings downtown, Faith and Wyatt had spent the morning at Vicky's house where Vicky had drawn up a contract for Wyatt to "borrow" the nine-year-old gray Ford Taurus that had belonged to her husband, who had died nearly seven years before. She'd never been able to part with it until now. Faith had to wonder if meeting Ogden had anything to do with that.

The three women had sat down at the kitchen table and made up the contract for the car as well as a "lease" for Wyatt's renting of the small efficiency above Vicky's garage. Truth was, Vicky flat refused a dime for the space, but asked that Wyatt contribute to the utilities and groceries. However, according to the "lease," Wyatt was paying $1000 a month, a steep price for the area and such a small apartment, but it was simply a ruse. Only $200 of that was going to Vicky, starting with Wyatt's next paycheck, to go toward paying under the table for the car. The rest Vicky was stuffing into an account she'd opened up, every cent to go back to Wyatt once the divorce was over. Effectively, they were embezzling from the "marital assets."

In Wyatt's words, "I hate to lie, but that rat bastard can burn in hell. He's taken enough from me all these years. Fine time for me to keep what's mine and get the life I deserve."

Faith couldn't agree more.

Presently, they walked hand in hand along the

16th Street Mall in downtown Denver, which was an outdoor space that spanned several blocks for pedestrians to walk safely to shop and visit various restaurants. City busses ran along the length of the mall to pick up and drop off shoppers closer to their desired destination.

Faith glanced over at Wyatt, who looked more beautiful than she'd ever seen her, dressed casual for summer, her hair down around her shoulders. Wyatt was naturally a very beautiful woman, but today it was something very different. She seemed to be vibrating with happiness, a freedom in her every movement, every tone, and easy laughter that Faith hadn't seen before.

"What?" Wyatt asked, Faith seeing her reflection in the dark lenses of Wyatt's sunglasses.

Faith smiled, her chest swelling with the incredible amount of feeling and emotion she felt in that moment. "I love you," she said simply. Though it wasn't new for them to say it, there was something else behind it this time, perhaps a stronger feeling and meaning. Wyatt seemed to sense it as well.

"I love you, my sweet," Wyatt said softly, her fingers tightening around Faith's. "With all my heart."

They shared a long, loving smile as their pace slowed for just a beat, both seeming to be caught up in the moment before they continued on. "You seem very happy," Faith said at length, lightly tugging Wyatt toward her to get out of the way of a woman with a gaggle of kids that were taking up the entire sidewalk.

Wyatt didn't answer right away, as though pondering the observation before finally she responded. "I am. I'm happier than I've ever been."

She nearly blinded Faith with the smile she sent her way. "The only thing that could possibly make my world better was if Mamma and Daddy were around to see this. Mamma would have absolutely loved you."

"What about your father? Would he have hated me?" Faith asked with a grin.

"Well," Wyatt hedged, laughing when Faith shouldered her good-naturedly. "I think it woulda taken him some time to understand that I'm gay, but he woulda loved you."

They walked on in contented silence for a bit when finally Faith gathered the courage to ask what she'd wondered about ever since finding out Wyatt was attracted to women. "Can I ask you something?" she said as quietly as she could and still be heard above the noises of fellow shoppers and traffic around them.

"Of course. You know better than that, darlin'."

"Do you... Did you..." She bit her lip, trying to figure out the best way to ask without making herself throw up. "With Lucas—"

"Never."

Faith met her gaze at the blunt, firm word. She wasn't sure if Wyatt understood what she was, quite unsuccessfully, trying to ask. "You know what I'm trying to get at?"

"You want to know about Lucas and I and sex."

Faith shook her head in wonder. "How do you do that? You always seem to know what's in my head."

Wyatt grinned, covering their joined hands with her other one for a moment, adding an extra bit of her warm affection. "You're easy for me ta read, Faith. Always have been. What exactly do you wanna know? And, don't worry, I don't mind."

Faith nodded, taking a deep breath. It was information she needed, needed to better understand Wyatt and her life married to a man. "Were you attracted to him? Like, sexually?"

"Never," Wyatt said, not missing a beat. She did, however tug on Faith's hand and pulled her over to a bench where the two sat. "When I first met Lucas, I thought he was a handsome fella, because he is. But, there's a huge difference between findin' somebody attractive and bein' attracted to them. Like," she added, nodding toward a young African American man that rolled by them on a skateboard. "I think he's a nice-lookin' kid, but that doesn't mean I wanna have sex with him." She looked at Faith. "Make sense?"

"Sure. I can understand that." Faith nodded. "You know, when he came into Bessie's one day, he made a snide remark about you, said you were a cold bitch. His innuendo, of course, was you were bad in bed." She studied Wyatt's face for a moment, which remained mostly expressionless. "Such a shitty thing to say."

Wyatt smiled. "Well, it's true. I was utterly repulsed by him." She smirked as she looked out at the passersby. "Honestly, I just laid there and waited for it to be over. I was so glad when he wanted it less and less."

Though it was hard to hear, Faith still felt like she needed this information to fully understand. Unexpectedly, she also felt Wyatt needed to talk a bit about this as well. "Why do you think that happened?"

"Oh, Lucas was always sleepin' around. I think he finally found himself a girlfriend and they'd go to the cabin."

"Hunting, huh?" Faith asked with a raised eyebrow.

"Or somethin'." Wyatt smiled. "So, how did you know? When did you know?"

"Oh geez, I was really young. Third grade." She smiled, thinking about the woman who had caught her attention and imagination. "I had a teacher, Mrs. Wegner. She was a wonderful teacher, really good person, and wouldn't ya know it, mighty pretty."

Wyatt burst into laughter, once again taking Faith's hand into hers as she got to her feet, Faith following. They began to walk again. "Did ya realize ya had a big ol' crush?"

"I did not. She was a mother figure, don't you know," Faith said with a grin. "No, I really thought that was it, though. I mean, my mom had died a year or so before that, so I truly thought she'd just kind of slid into that role for me. That was a tough one to explain to myself when I had a dream we'd kissed."

"Oh my," Wyatt drawled. "Didn't know you were inta the older ladies."

Faith laughed, shaking her head. "I'm not." She leaned in a bit. "I'm into sexy little redheads with a great laugh and a great ass."

"Are you now?" Wyatt's tone shot straight between Faith's legs.

"Yup." She was silent for a moment as she took a few deep breaths to try and calm her body, which was suddenly very much awake. "So, now that you've experienced it, did sex with a woman match up to what you thought it would be from all your books?"

Wyatt didn't respond until they'd stepped up to the corner, a few other people nearby as they waited for a traffic light to change. She lowered her voice a bit. "I don't know about sex with any random woman, but making love with the woman I love is more than I ever could have fantasized or dreamed about."

Faith's smile froze in place when Wyatt leaned in closer, murmuring into her ear in that low, sexy voice of hers used only in the bedroom. Faith blushed at what she was being told.

"Tastes better than any honey you can get." Wyatt moved away as she began to cross the street on the green light. When Faith stayed where she was, nailed to the spot, Wyatt stopped halfway across the street and turned back to her. "You comin'?"

Faith shook herself out of her profound arousal. "I sure as hell hope so," she muttered, then hurried to catch up.

Chapter Twenty-four

Wyatt nodded, letting out an irritated sigh. "Yeah, I get it." She looked up from the checkbook ledger to Faith, who waited patiently for Wyatt's thoughts or questions she may have. "You must think I'm beyond pathetic." She tossed the pen down on the desk and sat back in the desk chair, which squeaked under her weight and movement.

"No, baby, I don't." Faith reached over and caressed Wyatt's cheek. "Honey, you were with that controlling bastard since you were sixteen years old. The years you would have been learning to do all this stuff was basically confiscated by him. Hell, the only reason you're able to drive… Isabelle—sorry, it'll take me a second to remember you name everything—is because your parents had already taught you how."

A small smile came to Wyatt's face. "Hey now. No givin' me lip on Isabelle. She's a good little car."

"I'm sure she is." Faith agreed with a nod, a teasing tone in her voice.

Wyatt let out a heavy sigh and closed the checkbook and ledger before putting it into her purse. She blew out a breath, which ruffled her hair. "Adultin' is hard."

Faith smiled and leaned over in her chair to initiate a kiss. "Yes," she said against her lips after. "But damn am I grateful you're an adult." A knock on the closed office door sent Faith sitting back in her chair.

"Come on in," she called out.

The door opened and Libby poked her head in. She was a college student and one of their barista/bartenders. "Wyatt, that vender is here, the dude with the sugar. You asked me to come get you."

"Yes, ma'am, I sure did." Wyatt hung her purse back up next to her jacket and sent a quick smile to Faith before she hurried out the door and toward the stairs, giving a quick squeeze to Libby's arm as she passed her.

Faith turned back to the desk and the computer to work on the next two weeks' worth of schedules when she turned back to Libby at her name.

"I was going to tell you," the college student said, plopping down in the chair Wyatt had vacated. "With Halloween coming in a couple weeks, there's this really amazing Halloween party over in Boulder for gays and lesbians." She smirked. "Not that I'm gay or anything, but my aunt is, and she and her wife go every year."

Faith studied the cute little blonde. "Why did you tell me about it?" she asked, curious to see what her employee would say, what she knew or thought she knew.

"Um, duh! Because you and Wyatt would be like the most gorgeous couple there." She gave Faith a wide smile before hopping up to her feet. "You should totally go," she said as she headed for the office door.

"Libby?" Faith called out. She waited for the younger woman to turn around and face her again. "What makes you think Wyatt and I are in a relationship?"

Libby stared at her for a moment, brown eyes looking at her suspiciously, as though weighing the question. "Well," she began. "Because you guys are. Aren't you?"

Faith pushed up from her chair and walked over to the barista, gently nudging her away from the door before closing it and returning to her chair.

"Uh-oh. Am I in trouble?" Libby asked, reclaiming her vacated seat.

Faith smiled and shook her head. "No. Not at all." She chewed on her bottom lip for a moment as she decided on what tack to take. "Libby, even though we still can't find Lucas to serve him—"

"Or arrest the piece of shit for the fire," Libby muttered.

Faith smiled. "That, too. But, even though Wyatt's filed for divorce, she's still in the middle of this situation, and Wynter is a pretty small town."

"But, Faith, everyone here loves Wyatt," Libby exclaimed passionately.

"I know. And Libby, I know you're young, but you don't understand. Sometimes people—"

"Okay," the barista said, holding up her hand in iconic talk-to-the-hand fashion. "First of all, don't patronize me. I may be young, but I'm not stupid. Second of all, *you* don't understand." Those brown eyes bored into Faith until Faith relaxed a bit, realizing how serious the young woman was. "I've known Wyatt since she moved into town, but I really got to know her four years ago when I started working at the café when I was still in high school. She was so sweet to me," Libby continued, her tone softening. "Treated me like a big sister or an aunt or something."

Faith smiled, very easily able to see Wyatt taking a precocious young girl like Libby under her wing.

"She was so beautiful, and she just always

seemed to have this..." Libby screwed her face up as she seemed to consider what word to use. "Ethereal quality to her. You know?"

Faith's smile grew. "I do," she said simply.

"As I got to know her better, I noticed that, no matter how good a mood she seemed to be in, or how silly she was being, or how sweet, there was always something missing in her eyes. You know? Like, like the smile or the laugh didn't reach them. And then," she added, her tone falling a bit. "I began to notice the bruises."

Faith nodded, swallowing hard as old anger rose once again at how the woman she loved was treated.

"Now, Wyatt is one of those ridiculously naturally beautiful women who don't need a lick of makeup, so when she came in with that stuff caked on, we noticed. If she wasn't covering a black eye, she was making up excuses for a split lip or bruises on her arms. Five perfect finger bruises," she said, demonstrating a hand grabbing her upper arm. "I was so confused, you know? My dad would slit his own throat before he'd touch my mom like that, so domestic abuse from Lucas never even crossed my mind."

"How'd you find out what was going on? Did Wyatt tell you?"

"Nope. Pops did. He was so protective of her. Honestly, I think the only reason he let her go from the café with his blessing was because he knew she was with you."

That surprising bit of news actually brought unexpected emotion to Faith's eyes. She blinked rapidly to stop the tears from forming. "Wow. I thought he hated me. Never had a nice thing to say."

Libby grinned. "It's when he does that you have

to worry. Naw," she said, reaching over to a tissue box at the end of the desk close to her chair and snagged a tissue to hand to Faith. "Pops adores Wyatt. He never had any kids, so I think he kind of adopted her, like from day one. Him and Billy. Word has it that Pops is trying to raise funds to help Wyatt pay for that house, since the bank's gonna take it, and since it burned down, clearly the bank won't get out of it what's owed." She met Faith's shocked gaze. "Don't say anything to Wyatt. My mom just mentioned it, so…"

"That's unbelievably sweet of him, if he is. We'll figure it out no matter what, but, incredibly kind," Faith said softly, touched.

"This is what I'm trying to tell you, Faith. I mean like, do you realize that this is the first time in six years I haven't seen Wyatt with a bruise somewhere?" She gave Faith a disarming smile. "Like, seriously, I can only dream of having someone love me the way that she loves you, or how much you love her. It's so obvious. Faith, we all love Wyatt, and honestly, we all love you, too. Look what you've done with this place in less than a year!" She leaned over and gave Faith a quick hug before standing. "What you guys have is really beautiful. Don't hide it."

Faith watched her leave, then let out a long, heavy sigh, thinking about what she'd heard.

☙❧

Faith stared at the little speaker box connected to Wyatt's phone via Bluetooth, her playlist keeping them company as they worked. She looked at Wyatt, who stared back at her, a question in her eyes. "You have Sarah Brightman on your playlist?" she asked, incredulous.

"Hey," Wyatt said, hand to hip. "I may be a redneck from Georgia, but I know the voice of an angel when I hear it."

"Huh." Faith walked across the expanse made from the wall that had been knocked down several weeks ago and left a lingering kiss on Wyatt's lips. "I knew there was a reason I loved you," she murmured.

"Better be more than one." Wyatt smacked Faith on the bottom with her hand as Faith headed back to her side, both women taking a portion of the huge expanse to paint.

It had taken months, both for lack of time and that Faith was trying to be careful with her savings, but she, Wyatt, Ogden, and some of his boys had made steady progress. Walls had been taken down or moved, floors redone, and kitchen reimagined. It would be a little longer before the bathrooms could be renovated and the yard landscaped, but Faith was thrilled with what they'd achieved thus far. Her father and Vicky were upstairs painting the guest bedroom and the hallway.

Faith's phone chimed, alarming her that someone was passing through the gate. A camera hidden there showed her it was the pizza delivery guy. She pressed the button on her phone to open the gate.

"Woohoo! Lunch has arrived."

Twenty minutes later, the quartet sat at the kitchen table eating their pizza after a long day's work. Chewing on the bite she just took, Faith looked around at the people who had come to mean the most to her. Never had she thought her father would be on that list. But, there he sat with the woman that he obviously adored. Vicky brought the human out of him, the man. Gone was the reserved, stiff architect who seemed to have a circuit board instead of emotions. She'd even seen him wearing jeans one day.

"Your house is coming along beautifully, girls," Vicky said, picking up her can of Diet Coke to take a drink. "Just beautiful."

Faith had to admit it gave her a little thrill that she included Wyatt in that remark. She glanced over at the woman sitting next to her, who was smiling at Vicky, eyes aglow. She'd thought long and hard about what Libby had said to her a few weeks before, and had mentioned it to Wyatt, minus the part about the fund Pops was supposedly trying to put together.

"When do you think it'll be done?" Ogden asked, grabbing a napkin to wipe greasy fingertips.

Faith looked around, noting all that had been done but knowing there was so much more she knew she wanted to do. She was about to say as much, but Wyatt spoke first.

"Not sure we ever will finish, Mr. Fitzgerald," she said with a little laugh.

Ogden glanced up, looking at her over the rounded lenses of his glasses. "Wyatt, please call me Ogden," he said gently. He sat back and glanced over at Vicky, his daughter, then back at Wyatt. "After all, we're all family here now, aren't we?" He looked back to Faith and gave her a small smile.

※※※※

Darkness had fallen and Ogden and Vicky had left long ago. Painting was finished and now it was time to wind the day down. Faith loved this time of night, the time when she and Wyatt were settled in, be it watching TV, soaking in the claw-foot tub upstairs, or doing what they were doing now—relaxing on the couch with a fire in the fireplace as the only light in the room, just the two of them, no other distraction. What made it difficult, however, was that it always felt like borrowed time.

The two sat at opposite sides of the couch facing each other, Wyatt's legs stretched out with her bare feet in Faith's lap, being rubbed by strong, assured fingers and hands. The long days up and down the stairs were taking their toll on her feet.

"We need to get you some insoles or something, baby," Faith said, focusing her firm touch at the toes of Wyatt's left foot. "Maybe some of those big white chunky shoes that nurses wear."

"A nurse, huh?" Wyatt's voice dropped a couple octaves. "Now, baby, I thought you preferred it when I dressed up in the French maid costume, no?"

"Oui," Faith agreed, playing along. "Ooh la la!"

Wyatt grinned and, pulling her legs up, moved her position to her knees on the couch, lightly slapping Faith's legs to stretch out. Movements like a lioness on the prowl, Wyatt crawled over Faith's body, lowering herself to lie atop her. They'd decided against making love as it was Wyatt's time of the month and she admitted her cramps weren't complying with her wishes to go away. Faith didn't mind, just wanting to be with her, no matter what they were doing.

Wyatt initiated a slow, deep kiss but broke out of it before it could get out of hand. She rested her elbow on the throw pillow beneath Faith's head and looked down at her. Faith studied the beautiful face above, noting the flickering shadows from the flames that danced across delicate features.

"Hey, gorgeous," Faith murmured, hands resting on a shapely behind, one of her favorite places on Wyatt's body.

"Hey yourself, darlin'," Wyatt responded, bringing up her free hand to trace Faith's features. "Your daddy sure looks happy, doesn't he?"

"He does. They both do," Faith agreed, one of her hands sliding up underneath the back of Wyatt's shirt to trail over the warm, smooth skin of her lower back. She thought back to all the years prior to having Wyatt in her life and wondered how she'd gotten along without her affection, her touch, her very presence.

"How do you feel 'bout that?"

"I think it's wonderful. Just goes to show that you're never too old to find love again," Faith said, wrapping her arms around Wyatt as the younger woman readjusted her body so she could rest her head on Faith's upper chest, their bodies flush.

"I agree," Wyatt murmured, her voice sounding tired. After several moments of contented silence, she sighed and raised her head. "It's gettin' late. I'm openin', so have an early start." She left a lingering kiss on Faith's lips before carefully climbing off of her and the couch. "I gotta git."

Almost wanting to cry, Faith simply nodded as she sat up. "Yeah."

They embraced at the front door, an embrace that seemed to last longer and longer each night they had to part. Saying goodbye was getting so much more painful each time, even if they would only be apart for the time they slept.

Faith buried her face in Wyatt's neck, her eyes closed as she inhaled Wyatt's scent, a fragrance that had become such comfort to her. "I love you," she whispered, leaving a kiss first on Wyatt's neck, then on her lips. "Please text me and let me know you got home safe."

Wyatt studied her for a long time, then nodded. "I will. I love you, my sweet."

Bundled up in her jacket, Wyatt headed out into the cold late October night to Isabelle, who sat patiently waiting to take her mistress home. Faith stood at the open door and watched until Wyatt was stowed safely in the car and it started up. With an echoing wave, Wyatt drove off into the night, her car equipped with a remote to open the gate, just like Faith's.

Taillights of the Taurus fading into the late night, Faith closed and locked the front door with a heavy sigh. She walked to the living room and used the poker to douse the flames so the fire would burn down safely to embers. As she knelt before the fireplace, the warmth of the fire on her face, she fought back the loneliness that began to descend upon her like a heavy blanket.

Pushing to her feet, satisfied the fire would burn itself out, she walked to the kitchen to take care of the coffee cups she and Faith had used for their "before bed" coffee. New appliances finally installed, including the dishwasher, she rinsed the cups and loaded them on the top rack.

She froze, hearing the sound of tires crunching on the snow as they came up the drive. She walked to the front door and glanced out the side window. Isabelle had returned. Concerned, she quickly disengaged the locks and opened the door just in time for Wyatt to hurry over to the front porch steps, taking them quickly before running into Faith's arms.

"Whoa, baby, are you okay?" Faith asked, holding Wyatt close. "What's wrong?"

"I can't do this anymore," Wyatt whispered, her words partially muffled in Faith's neck. She pulled away and looked into Faith's concerned face. "For the first time in my life, I have a place of my own, a home. But," she added, shaking her head. "It's not. They say home is where the heart is, and it ain't in four walls tucked above Miss Vicky's garage." She brought a hand up and cupped Faith's cheek. "It's with you. It's absolutely absurd that I found the woman I want to spend the rest of my life with, yet I'm livin' across town, leavin' here every night only to get there, where I should wanna be. But all I want is to be back here with you."

Faith's heart quickened its beat at Wyatt's passionate words, some rambling on together. She took the hand upon her cheek in her own and cupped it against her chest. "What are you saying, Wyatt?" she asked softly, not wanting to assume anything, no matter what her own heart was screaming for.

"I'm sayin' that Libby is right. What we have together is so beautiful, and for the first time in my life I'm livin' my true life, bein' my authentic self. But am I?" she asked, eyes pleading into Faith's. "Are we?"

Bringing Wyatt's hand up to her lips and leaving a lingering kiss there, Faith whispered, "What do you want, baby?"

"I wanna be with you every night, in that big ol' bed we picked out together. I wanna wake up with you every mornin'. I wanna get a dog. I wanna fill this big ol' house with the love it so desperately needs." She took a small step closer, their bodies brushing against each other. "I desperately need."

Faith smiled. "I desperately need it, too," she whispered, her tone filled with emotion. "I need you."

Wyatt said nothing as she took Faith in a tight hug, no words exchanged, none needed as everything they felt and needed were magically conveyed to the other in that embrace. "I wanna come home," Wyatt said at length.

Faith's eyes squeezed shut as she held Wyatt tighter. "Yes. God, yes."

Chapter Twenty-five

Faith's eyes fell closed and her back arched as her fingers tightened in long, auburn hair as Wyatt's head began to quickly bob between her legs, the pressure building into a crescendo of pleasure that was unstoppable. Wyatt held on to Faith's spread thighs as Faith's hips bucked wildly with the violent release that rushed through her body.

Her cry was loud as it erupted from her throat, deep and guttural. She fell back to earth, both physically and mentally as Wyatt's tongue gave her some reprieve, soft lips leaving a gentle kiss where her tongue had just been. Faith felt the warmth of Wyatt's body move atop her own. She wrapped her arms around her, her breath slowing somewhat. She sighed into the kiss Wyatt initiated, her lips and tongue covered in the slick warmth of Faith's spent desire.

"Merry Christmas, baby," Wyatt murmured against Faith's lips.

Faith grinned, eyes finally opening as she looked up into Wyatt's beautiful face. "Indeed."

They lay on the living room area rug, the house lit only by the twinkling lights on the massive Christmas tree and the popping flames of the fireplace. It was Christmas night, and after a wonderful day celebrating with Ogden and Vicky at his lake house, they'd arrived home, not even unloading the car of gifts and leftover food before Wyatt had Faith in her favorite position to have her: on her back and open to her voracious appetite.

Wyatt had sweetly explained that her incessant need to make love to Faith was based in both the fact that Faith was "hotter than a tin roof in the south," and that she had "a lifetime of makin' up to do." Faith, for her part, didn't mind at all.

"So," Wyatt said softly, brushing her hair behind an ear as it had fallen into Faith's face. "I'm thinkin' we take this upstairs." Kiss. "I want you to." Kiss. "Bring out our little friend." Kiss, kiss, kiss. "And make love to me."

"Oh, I see. So, now I finally get a turn, huh?" Faith teased, her fingernails trailing up and down the smooth warmth of Wyatt's naked back.

Wyatt grinned. "It is not my fault that you make the most scrumptious noises when I'm inside you, darlin'."

"Uh-huh." Faith slapped a naked behind playfully before lightly urging Wyatt to move off her, which she did. "I'm quite okay with your plan."

"Should we just close up for the night, baby?" Wyatt asked, indicating the house around them.

"Nah," Faith said, grabbing Wyatt's hand and tugging her toward the stairs. "I know I'll want some water later, so I'll take care of it all then."

Once upstairs, they split up, Wyatt heading to their master bath and Faith to their armoire, where they kept their small collection of toys. She found what she was looking for and strapped it into place around her hips, then walked over to the beautiful Elizabethan-era four-poster bed they'd picked out together. She loved Wyatt's taste in furniture and décor, always with a flair for the historic. It brought tastes out of Faith that she didn't even realize were there.

She tossed aside the throw pillows onto the small padded bench that ran along the foot of the bed, and pulled down the comforter, blanket, and sheet before climbing onto the mattress. She lay on her back on her side of the bed, hands behind her head as she waited. She stared up at the ceiling and felt utterly complete and satisfied with her life as she heard the toilet flush in the other room and water turn on. Wyatt had moved in two months before, and she'd never been happier.

The bathroom door opened and a goddess stepped out. Faith watched Wyatt, in all her naked glory, walk over to the bed. Her skin was creamy perfection. Her hips swayed just so as she walked, just enough to catch the eye and make the mouth water. Her breasts were proportionate to her size and perfectly shaped, the nipples a dusky rose when hard, as they were now. Her hair was down and brushed to a shine, the deep auburn in stark contrast to the paleness of her skin, that of a true redhead. Her face was so beautiful, lips naturally full and rosy.

She embodied everything that poets and artists had been celebrating for thousands of years, what men had killed for and what women lived in the shadows for, to admire in their most secret thoughts. Wyatt was desire personified.

Once Faith began breathing again, she began to sit up, but Wyatt stopped her. She climbed onto the bed then on top of Faith, straddling her hips. The phallus, which stood erect where it was attached and snuggled up against Faith's crotch, was just in front of her. The bright purple shaft was just barely pressed against the neatly trimmed triangle between Wyatt's thighs.

Hands on Wyatt's thighs, Faith watched as Wyatt's hands roamed over Faith's torso, nails trailing down her stomach, making the muscles beneath the skin twitch in response. She circled Faith's belly button before moving back up to cup her breasts, thumb and forefinger lightly tugging on hardening nipples.

Faith's eyes were heavy as warm waves of pleasure made their way from her breasts south. She could already feel Wyatt's own wetness on the skin of her upper thighs from where she sat, and that alone turned her on.

Wyatt leaned her upper body down, her lips wrapping around one of the nipples she'd just been teasing, replacing her fingers with her tongue. Faith's eyes fell closed as her breathing picked up slightly. Her hips jerked a bit as her arousal began anew.

She smiled at her predicament. "Who's supposed to be seducing who, here?" she murmured, bucking her hips slightly to make the dildo known.

Wyatt chuckled sexily as she kissed her way up from the breast to Faith's lips. "Yes," she murmured against them.

Faith grinned, then reached down between their bodies, her fingers easily finding Wyatt's clit, already hard and slick. Wyatt stayed where she was, lips in the breathing space of Faith's as Faith stroked her, Wyatt's hips slowly rocking with the touches. "Lift for me, baby."

Wyatt stopped her movements and sat up, lifting up on her knees as Faith wrapped her hand around the phallus and guided the tip to the slick opening of Wyatt's most private place. It easily slid inside, Wyatt lowering herself as Faith gently pushed upward. Completely inside her, Faith felt flushed, her arousal on high.

Hands sliding up to Wyatt's hips, Faith gently began to move the phallus deep within Wyatt before slowly withdrawing a bit, not fully. Wyatt braced herself with her hands on Faith's sides. Her hips rolled in tandem with the movement of the hips beneath her. Her eyes closed and her head fell back as Faith glided her hands up to cup her breasts, lightly tugging on the hard nipples, squeezing and tweaking them. Her mouth watered to taste them.

Sitting up, Faith took the nipple into her mouth, suckling the rigid flesh as Wyatt's hips continued to move, the phallus easily sliding through the incredible wetness inside her, which Faith could hear. She left the breast and raised her head, only to be met by Wyatt's mouth finding her own. She'd only been inside Wyatt for a few minutes, but already Wyatt's breathing was increasing, as were her movements against Faith.

Wyatt buried her hands in Faith's hair, deepening the kiss. Her tongue rubbed against Faith's in time with the phallus thrusting inside her body. Finally, Faith pushed Wyatt off of her and to her back, Faith following. She rolled on top of her between Wyatt's legs, which opened wide for her. She resumed the kiss as she reached down and once again guided the phallus tip inside Wyatt, using her hips to push it home.

Their breathing became too hard to continue kissing, so Faith pushed up to her hands and used the power of her body to thrust into Wyatt, their hips slapping together with the quick, short thrusts. Wyatt clung to Faith, her cries loud and constant, joined by Faith's own groans as the pressure of the flat side of the dildo pushed against her with every thrust, as well as the psychological excitement of what she was doing to the woman beneath her.

Finally, Wyatt grabbed Faith's shoulders with claw-like fingers as she gasped loudly, almost holding her breath as her body shuddered. Faith's own body let go as she thrust in one final time, teeth gritted as she rode out the intensity of the orgasm.

Several moments passed before Faith finally got her bearings back. She gingerly pulled the phallus out of Wyatt and climbed off the bed. She unstrapped and walked into the bathroom to leave the harness and dildo on the sink to be cleaned later before returning to the bed, Wyatt welcoming her with literally open arms.

Faith snuggled up against her, her head resting on a naked breast. She sighed in contentment as Wyatt lovingly ran her fingers through her hair. "Did you have a good Christmas?" she asked, her hand resting on Wyatt's stomach.

"The best I've ever had as an adult," Wyatt said softly.

Faith smiled. "Sadly, that was a pretty low bar to meet."

"True," Wyatt acknowledged. "But, it was a wonderful day, baby. I really loved our Christmas party at the shop, too."

Faith's smile widened, thinking of the fun they'd had with their small but tight crew. Music, silly games, and giveaways. "We have so much left to do for our New Year's in Wynter celebration," she added, switching gears from the past to the immediate future.

"I think it's wonderful y'all are gonna have somethin' for the whole town," Wyatt said, fingers moving from Faith's hair to trail over her upper back and shoulders.

Faith's eyes closed, a contented hum vibrating from her throat. "Pretty handy that Libby is going to school for graphic design," she murmured. She was vaguely aware of Wyatt's reply.

"I agree. She showed me some mockups last week for the signs we'll put all around town... Baby?"

Faith felt herself shaken slightly, which snapped her out of the sweet, intoxicating sleep she hadn't even realized she was falling into. "Oh crap, sorry." She pushed up to a sitting position, a loud yawn nearly cracking her jaw. "Okay, I'm going to head downstairs and close everything up." She left a kiss on Wyatt's lips.

"Baby, y'all look like you're about ta crash." She sat up. "I'll go—"

"No, baby, it's okay." Faith left another lingering kiss on soft lips. "Be right back," she murmured. "I love you."

"Love you, too, darlin'."

Faith climbed off the bed, her stomach muscles sore from their very active night as she tugged on a T-shirt and flannel pajama pants. Her woman had no issue walking around the house buck naked, claiming there was no way anyone could see in. Faith acknowledged that was true, but she'd never felt comfortable being naked unless there was a reason.

She trotted down the stairs in bare feet, first going to the fireplace and dousing the flames before she reached behind the tree and unplugged the lights. She always hated turning them off. Even when she was in her tiny apartment back in Brooklyn—which seemed like a lifetime ago, not merely just under a year—she often left her Christmas lights up long after she'd taken her tiny tree down. She'd string them around the window in the bedroom and leave them on at night.

The back door was locked, never having unlocked it from when they'd left earlier in the day to head to Ogden's house. She made her way to the front door, which she knew they hadn't gotten around to locking when they'd gotten home. It had amused Faith, really. Wyatt already had making love on the brain, and having to be a good girl all day with the family festivities had almost been too much for her. They hadn't even gotten out of the car when she made her intentions very known.

Front door locked, she walked over to the kitchen. She was thirsty, and figured Wyatt, if still awake when she got back upstairs, would be as well. She'd grab them something to drink then arm the security system, since she'd pass the security panel on the way back up the stairs.

Opening the fridge door, Faith chewed on her bottom lip as she looked over the selections, trying to decide if she wanted a bottle of water for them to share or the raspberry-and-banana smoothie Wyatt had made the day before. Deciding on the water, she grabbed a fresh bottle and stepped back to close the door.

"Who's pissing now, bitch?"

For just a split second she saw the tall figure standing on the other side of the door before out of the corner of her eye she caught something swinging. She barely correlated the horrid *crack* she heard with the explosion of pain in her head before she hit the floor, darkness falling.

The first thing she noticed was the pain. Excruciating pain. The next thing she noticed was that her face was sticky and wet. Trying to move herself from her position lying on her side on the floor, she gasped as pain shot through her head and body anew. Holding still, she held her breath, praying it would pass. When it didn't, she knew she just had to push through it.

She tried again, managing to push herself to her knees only to succumb to the pain and vomit where she knelt, which made the pain worse. Gasping for air once she finished, she closed her eyes for a moment, then with gritted teeth braced against the kitchen island.

It seemed to take forever, but finally she made it to her feet, as unsteady as she was. Her vision was hazy and seemed to be only out of her left eye. Dazed and very confused, she tried to listen, but all she could hear was a horrible ringing in her ears and, it seemed, in her head.

"Jesus." She slurred the word, and nothing seeming to work right.

She held on to the island top as she staggered her way over to the wall, using it for balance as she continued forward. She had no idea why she'd been on the floor, no idea what had put her there or why her head was hurting so badly. She was even more confused when she saw that the front door was open.

"I locked that," she muttered, her words thick. It felt like her tongue was about three sizes too big for her mouth. It was then that she noticed the staircase and saw that one of the banister dowels was missing, leaving a gap like a missing tooth in a row of teeth.

Suddenly, it all hit her.

"Oh my god."

She tried to call out to Wyatt, but her head exploded in a new round of pain. She grabbed her head, and her hands were instantly covered in warm, wet stickiness.

She tried to think through the fog in her head where her phone was. She vaguely remembered it being up in the bedroom. That's where Wyatt was. Again, she began to move, forcing herself up a step at a time until finally she reached the second-floor hallway.

"Wyatt?" she managed. Though it sounded like she'd screamed it at the top of her lungs in her head, she knew it had been not much more than a whisper. "Wyatt?"

Stopping to throw up again from a fresh wave of pain, Faith forced herself to keep going. Reaching the halfway-closed door, she crawled inside the large bedroom. The bedside lamp was still on, though it lay on its side on the floor next to the nightstand it had been on. The bed was empty, sheet and blanket draped onto the floor, halfway off the bed.

"Wyatt?" she said again, looking to the bathroom, the light off and the door wide open.

She saw her phone on the floor near the lamp. She crawled over to it and was so grateful that it turned on even though the screen was cracked. Barely able to make out the numbers on the screen as she got to the dial screen, she squeezed her eyes shut, still only one eye with any vision. As hazy as her sight was, she managed to find the three numbers she needed.

At the sound of the woman's voice on the other end, Faith managed, "Please, help me."

Then all went black.

Chapter Twenty-six

Wings, like dragonfly wings. Angel wings? Above, round and round they went. And a sound, she knew that sound: thwap, thwap, thwap...

Darkness...

"Who did this to you, Faith?"
"Lucas..."
Was that her voice? Did someone else speak for her?

Darkness...

Groaning. She was groaning as she was jostled, even as her head felt like it had been cemented to whatever she was lying on. She was moving. Nauseous, so nauseous.

Darkness...

Kind, familiar dark brown eyes.
"I've got you, Faith. We'll make it all better, hon, don't you worry."

Darkness...

Peace. It was so peaceful. The cabin around

them was small, one single room, more rectangle than square. A fireplace took up one entire wall, the surrounding area made up of large river rocks. The fire popped cheerily, the flames dancing, far brighter and far more vivid than she remembered them ever being before.

She was being cradled in a lap, the person sitting in a rocking chair which slowly and gently lulled her into calm. She recognized the smell of the person, knew it in her soul even if she couldn't place it. A hand cupped her head, holding it still against the softness of a full bosom, a motherly comfort filling her.

Soft humming drifted down from above where her head rested. It only stopped long enough for the sweet whispered words to be heard: "I'm so proud of you, Faith. You have to go back."

"I don't want to go back," she responded, feeling a bit petulant.

"You must."

"Why?"

"They need you. She needs you."

"No." She went to pull away, but the hand resting against her head held her close. "I want to stay with you."

"You can't, my love. Not yet. You have more to do," the soft female voice said reasonably. Like the scent, so familiar yet unplaceable.

"But, I don't want to lose you again." Her eyes closed when she felt the gentle pressure on the top of her head, a kiss.

"I'm always with you, my sweet little angel. Always."

Darkness…

Slowly, oh-so-slowly, the darkness began to recede. She could feel the coolness of the air on her skin, could make out the light of the room through closed eyelids. The fogginess in her brain began to dissipate, leaving the serenity of the fog to clear into confusion.

Her eyes slowly opened, though only to half-mast as the natural sunlight coming in from the window was too bright after such complete darkness. She adjusted to it before looking to her left, noting a presence there. A woman sat, reading. It took her a moment to formulate the image into a name.

"Vicky?" The word came out as a raspy croak, her throat dry and burning.

Vicky looked up from the book she was reading and immediately removed her reading glasses, her face beaming with the instant smile that came to it. Setting the book and glasses aside, she got to her feet and moved the short distance to her. "Oh, it's so wonderful to see those beautiful eyes open," she said softly. "How are you feeling, sweetheart?"

"I don't know. Where am I?"

"You're in the hospital, Faith." Vicky reached over to the rolling table next to the bed and grabbed a plastic cup with a bendable straw in it. "Here."

Faith gladly took sips of the room-temperature water when the straw was put to her lips, which felt chapped and raw. The water felt like heaven as it slid down her throat, the Sahara getting a much-needed rain. "Thank you," she whispered, feeling much better. "How long have I been here?"

"This is your fourth day. We've been so worried.

Your father literally just left about ten minutes ago. I made him go get some food. I'm honestly not certain he's eaten since that wonderful doctor in the ER called us." She smiled, taking one of Faith's hands in her warm, soft ones. "I'm sure at this moment that eleven-dollar burger down in the cafeteria is the best one he's ever had. Want me to call him to come back?"

Faith tried to shake her head but found that was a mistake. Her eyes closed as pain rushed through her head in a massive wave. She stilled and nearly held her breath until it crested and slowly began to fade away. "No."

"Oh, sweetheart," Vicky said, her thumb running over the back of Faith's hand. "Dr. Smith said it would be up to ten days or so for the pain to really subside."

"And, I'm on day four?" Faith managed, proud of herself for remembering that little detail. "Oh boy. What happened?"

"What do you remember?" Vicky asked, setting the water glass back on the table when Faith whispered a no when it was offered to her again.

Faith contemplated that question for a moment, trying to run back into her memory banks, which at the moment were clouded due to medication and injury. "Dragonfly wings," she murmured. "It made a lot of noise."

Vicky was silent for a moment, as though trying to figure out what Faith was talking about. "I'm not sure about a noisy dragonfly, but they did airlift you here to St. Anthony. You have a fractured skull, sweetheart, and your left orbital socket was cracked."

Faith stared at her for a long moment, stunned at the information. "How?" She slowly moved her head to look around the hospital room, finding it empty.

"Where's Wyatt?"

Instantly pain entered Vicky's eyes, which made Faith nervous. The older woman looked as though she were about to speak when the door to the hospital room opened.

"Can you believe this thing cost me nearly thirteen dol—" Ogden stopped his complaining mid-sentence and seemed to forget about the Styrofoam to-go boxes he carried as he set it aside and rushed to Vicky's side. The look on his face was pure relief. "Hey, kiddo."

She looked at him. "Hey. You look like a werewolf."

Confused, he looked to Vicky, who brought her hand up to his scruff. "Oh," he said sheepishly, running his hand through his overgrown beard. "One of those men who can grow a beard in a day. I've had other things on my mind other than maintenance."

Vicky tugged playfully at the shaggy growth. "My very own Sasquatch."

Faith smiled weakly. "Where's Wyatt?" Ogden glanced over at Vicky, which made Faith's heart drop. "What?" she asked, panic beginning to fill her. "Is she okay? Is she hurt, too? What happened?"

Ogden cleared his throat, then wrapped his fingers around the guardrail on the side of Faith's hospital bed. Taking a deep breath, he spoke. "I'm just going to be straight with you, Faith. The night of Christmas, Lucas Pennington got into your house and attacked you with a Louisville slugger before abducting Wyatt from the premises."

"A baseball bat?" Faith whispered, her brain running slow on reaction and absorption.

Vicky nodded. "He left it behind at the scene."

The most painful part of the news finally hit home, and as much as she wanted to dispute what her father had said, somewhere deep inside it felt correct, like an echo of something she already knew. She suddenly felt very nauseous, and it had nothing to do with the pain in her head.

"Sweetheart." Vicky took Faith's hand again. "The detective on the case has been here every day to see if you've woken up yet. She's been like a dog with a bone."

"The state police have been brought in," Ogden added. "And there's been talk of maybe bringing in the FBI."

"I know it's a lot to deal with after your injury, just waking up and everything," Vicky said. "How about we get Detective Montez over here now that you're awake? Maybe she can give you an update."

Faith considered it a moment, but the truth was she had so much bouncing around in her head that she needed time to think. There wasn't a lot she could tell the detective at the moment that would be helpful, anyway. She cleared her throat and looked at the couple looking back at her expectantly. "I think I'd like to be alone for a little while."

Ogden and Vicky exchanged a quick glance before nodding in tandem. "Okay. We'll be down in the cafeteria eating our thirteen-dollar burgers if you need anything," Ogden said with a teasing tone. He lightly squeezed her forearm before he and Vicky left, picking up the food containers on the way out.

Left alone, Faith let out a heavy breath and stared out the window. She could see the sky darkening as a storm gathered. She knew the hospital was in Lakewood, which was a town southwest of Denver proper, less than twenty minutes away, depending on traffic.

As she watched the clouds gather, she tried to think back as far as she could, tried to remember the events of that night. Anything. All she kept seeing in her mind's eye was Wyatt's beautiful face, her smile. She was surprised to feel the tickle of a tear roll down her cheek to her ear. She hadn't even realized she was crying.

She brought up a hand to wipe the tear away and wipe at her ear when the door to her room opened. A woman stepped inside, turning to make sure the door closed behind her, which it took its sweet time doing on its tight spring hinge. Finally, she turned to look at Faith.

She was beautiful, her hair dark brown and long. It was straight and parted down the middle. It reminded Faith of the entertainer Cher during her Sonny Bono days. She looked young, twenties, and was dressed in faded blue jeans and a filmy blouse that billowed as she moved.

As the woman walked over to her bed, Faith noticed that the colors of the woman's clothes and her features were extremely vivid, even though none of them were colors that would normally pop. She wore no loud colors, no neons, and her large eyes were chocolate brown. But still, it seemed wherever she went, everything around her became vivid, alive.

The woman climbed onto the bed next to Faith, gathering her to snuggle into this strange woman.

"Hello, my sweet little angel," the woman murmured into Faith's hair, Faith's head tucked against the woman's chest.

Faith's eyes slid closed at the soft voice, a smile spreading across her lips. She relaxed into familiar comfort. "I hoped you'd come," she murmured, not even sure why she'd said that.

"I'll always come." She left a small kiss on the crown of Faith's head, which amazingly no longer hurt. "I need you to watch something," she murmured. "Will you do that for me?"

"Of course."

The TV mounted to the wall flickered on. Faith maneuvered herself so she could see the screen easier yet stay in the comforting arms of the woman beside her. She had no idea who the woman was, but felt she'd been with her recently. Her presence was incredibly comforting, almost making her feel like a little girl wrapped up in a blanket fresh from the dryer, warm and soft.

On the screen suddenly appeared Lucas, dressed in the sheriff's deputy uniform that Faith had always seen him in. She felt instant hatred and anger fill her, and her body began to tense. The woman beside her ran her fingertips up and down Faith's arm, and immediately the anger drained from Faith.

Lucas was in what seemed to be a locker room of sorts, metal lockers running along the wall, much like what would be found in a middle school or high school. He was talking to a woman, also dressed in uniform. She had long, black hair, which was pulled into a tight French braid that reached about two-thirds down her back. A pretty girl, looking to be in her mid-twenties. They were standing close, in the other's personal space, their body language looking flirty, very familiar with the other. It was made totally clear when the two kissed.

"Was he cheating on her?" she whispered, anger

again bubbling up.

The scene faded, a new one beginning, much like a scene fade in a movie. The new scene was outside of a small cabin tucked into the woods. She saw the familiar huge truck that belonged to Lucas and an SUV of some sort parked behind it. It was nighttime, and a light in one of the windows gave her the quick silhouette of two people the size of Lucas and the woman in an intimate situation of a sexual nature.

The scene faded again, and the new one was of the cabin burning, Lucas standing off to the side watching.

The scene faded again to show a different cabin, Lucas and the same woman with dark hair in a braid fighting, yelling at each other, though no sound came from their mouths. Faith gasped when he delivered a harsh backhand, nearly knocking the woman off her feet. The woman stormed out of the cabin as the screen faded to black, remaining so. The show was over.

"You must find her," the woman Faith was snuggled against whispered. "Find her, my sweet little angel."

Faith gasped, eyes popping open. She winced as her head let her know in no uncertain terms that it was there. She was in her hospital bed, alone in the room. She looked up at the mounted TV to see the dark screen reflecting the white linens covering her and her bed.

She tried to figure out what had awakened her when she heard it again: a firm knock to the heavy room door. "Come in," she called out as loud as she dared.

The door eased open and a woman stepped in wearing blue scrubs. Her dark hair was pulled back into a somewhat messy ponytail. She smiled and raised a hand in greeting as she pushed the door fully open.

It took a moment, but finally it clicked. "Cameron!"

Her smile widened as the doctor walked over to the bed, stopping beside it. "Hey, lady. You have no idea how good it is to see you awake." She stepped to the foot of the bed and grabbed the chart tucked into the holder there, flipping open the metal top and reading the material written beneath it. "Well then," she said, glancing up at Faith. "Doc says once you awaken naturally, which you have now done, they'll be able to send you home." She slapped the chart shut and replaced it before moving back to the side of the bed. "Looks like you may be getting your walking papers soon, kid."

Faith smiled. "How did you know I was here?"

Cameron placed her hands on the siderail, like Ogden had before. "I was there when they brought you in, Faith," she said softly. "I was your attending physician in the ER."

Faith just stared at her for a moment. "Wow. Thank you, Cam."

The other woman smiled and took Faith's hand in her warm ones. "You gave me a scare, lady, gotta say. Working where I do, I've seen the work of some real monsters, but this guy is definitely up there. I'm so sorry all this happened. You and your partner are in my prayers."

"Thanks," Faith said softly, accepting the gentle hug she received as best she could.

"I need to get going, but I wanted to check to see if you were awake. I've been stopping by every day, chatting with your dad and Vicky. Really cool couple.

I thought you weren't that close to your dad?"

Faith smiled. "It's been a process over the last year."

"Well, he told me you've got quite the enterprise going on in that little town. A body can stop in and get a scoop of ice cream, a latte, or a margarita." She grinned. "Once you're back home and well, I'm gonna stop in and get one of all three, you got it?"

"I'll give you a five percent discount," Faith teased. She laughed when Cameron pointed at her as she began to walk backward toward the door, almost as if to say, *Behave*. No idea it was coming, Faith blurted out, "Do you believe in angels?"

Cameron stopped, her hand already gripping the handle on the door. She glanced back at the bed for a moment before walking back over to it. "Did something happen, Faith?"

Faith stared at her. *Crap.* "I...don't know."

Cameron studied her for a long moment before she said, "I've had a lot of people come through my ER that are literally at death's door, or that do slip away from us but we are able to bring them back. Some have come back to thank me and my team later and whatnot, and some have told me stories about things they saw, people. You were one of those people, hon," she continued. "We almost lost you, the swelling and bleeding was so bad. Once we got you somewhat stabilized, we decided it was best to knock you out of commission for a little bit, let the body take care of the swelling naturally. They just moved you out of ICU yesterday, Faith."

Faith listened, shocked at the severity of her injury. "Oh," she said dumbly.

"So." Cameron shrugged with a smile. "Maybe

somebody came along to help us out, huh?"

Faith nodded, not sure what to say. She felt like she had a lot to contemplate. "Thanks, Cameron. For everything."

Cameron smiled. "Anytime. You just remember that when I order my margarita."

Chapter Twenty-seven

Ogden slowed as they neared the gate to Faith and Wyatt's property. Faith leaned forward a bit, peering through the windshield. "What is that?"

Bringing his truck to a stop, Ogden pulled the brake and hopped out. He hurried over to it in his Ogden way, *The-Flash*-level quick for him but ambling for someone else. It made Faith smile. He grabbed the large white bundle and made his way back to the truck, climbing in with a whoosh of cold air.

"Polar bear?" he asked, handing her the fluffy white stuffed animal.

She took it, unable to stop the smile at the soft, furry little guy, which was of a very huggable size. "Very cute. Why was it there?" Faith asked, noting the slow progress of the gate swinging open.

"Wait until you see the house," Ogden said, sparing her a glance before moving them forward again. "Since the day after Christmas as word spread, people began leaving things here at the gate for you gals. They left flowers, plants, stuffed animals, cards, notes, even receipts." He gave a quick chuckle. "Your house is a veritable flower shop, should you wish to change your business plan."

"Receipts?" Faith asked, confused as she released the buckle on her seat belt as the truck pulled to a stop behind her 4Runner.

Ogden killed the engine and removed his key. "Your business has been overflowing all week. People there to support you gals. I think the purpose of the receipts left was to let you know that. Most of them have little notes written on them, too." He met her gaze, a little smile gracing his grizzled face. "Messages of support and love."

Faith wasn't sure what to think as she hugged the stuffed animal to her chest. She looked out the window at the house, mixed feelings swirling in her head and heart. Though she had no real memory of what had happened and was glad to be home, she knew Wyatt wasn't waiting inside for her, and nobody knew where she was. She couldn't allow her mind to go beyond the fact that she was missing.

Ogden held Faith at the elbow as they climbed the stairs up to the porch, the straps of his backpack slung over one shoulder and her polar bear held in the hand not helping her. Vicky opened the door, a welcoming smile on her face.

"Welcome home, sweetheart," she said kindly, holding the door open for the two to pass.

Faith smiled in gratitude but said nothing. She felt a bit like a zombie entering the house. Once her sanctuary, her safe place to share with Wyatt, it was now filled with a horrible void, memories she had no access to, as well as the emptiness of uncertainty.

Vicky closed the door and Faith was led to the living room. The Christmas tree was still up and the lights were on, as was a warm, cheerful fire in the fireplace on such a cold day. But what caught Faith's attention the most was the gathering of flowers put into vases, potted plants, stacks of greeting cards, some just the card, others still in their sealed envelope addressed to either Faith or Wyatt, or both. There were many stuffed animals, an entire zoo of them.

The house was filled with the strange mixture of fragrances, flowers and chicken noodle soup. Overwhelmed, she sat down on the couch, exhausted from the exertion of the walk from the truck to the couch. She wanted to sleep but was almost afraid to. Now that she was home, she wanted to start looking for Wyatt.

"Vicky came over this morning and washed and changed the linens on the bed, and put on her homemade—and if I may say so," Ogden added from where he stood by the fireplace. "The most spectacular chicken noodle soup you'll ever eat in the Crock-Pot."

Feeling drained, Faith nodded acknowledgement and looked down at her hands, which rested in her lap.

"Sweetheart, are you sure you don't want to come home with me or with your dad?" Vicky asked, suddenly standing next to Ogden.

Faith glanced up, easily able to see the concern knitting Vicky's brow. She gave her a weak smile. "Yeah, I'm okay. Honestly, I just want to sleep. There's so much to think about, so much for me to try to..." She shrugged and let out a tired sigh. "Feel, I guess. I just need some time."

"We certainly understand," Ogden said, walking over to her. He bent down and left a scratchy kiss on her cheek before Vicky gave her a gentle hug.

"If you need anything, we're just a phone call or a text away, okay?" Vicky said, squeezing Faith's hand before releasing it.

Faith nodded. "Thank you."

"The soup should be done in about an hour," Vicky added as the couple began to make their way toward the front door.

"Oh," Ogden said, shrugging the backpack off his shoulder. He set it down on the coffee table and unzipped the main compartment. Withdrawing a photo album, he set it down in front of Faith. "As you requested."

She glanced at it, noting its worn edges. "Thank you." She smiled at them both, feeling a strange mixture of sorrow to see them go, yet the need to be alone. "I love you guys," she blurted.

The couple turned, and, almost making Faith smile, Vicky's face melted. Ogden blushed "We love you, too," he said quietly, his voice a bit more gruff than usual.

She watched them go, the front door closing behind them, the locks engaging a moment later. She'd given her father a key to her house months ago, as she and Wyatt were considering getting a dog, and he'd offered to help out during the day when they were both busy with the shop and Faith's duties to the town.

She was about to push up from the couch when the door was unlocked and opened again, Ogden appearing. He hurried over to the security panel. He was about to push the button to arm it when Faith spoke.

"Dad?"

"Hmm?" he hummed, head raised a bit as he looked through the bifocal portion of his glasses at the buttons on the panel.

"Did..." Faith thought for a moment, trying to formulate what her question was in her mind, which was still a little hazy. "Did my mom have any sort of, I don't know," she said with a shrug. "Nickname or term of endearment for me?"

He glanced at her, then looked off into the past for a moment before responding. "As I recall, she used to call you her sweet little angel."

❧❧❧❧

Faith's eyes fell closed as the sweet, soothing warmth of the mocha breve with extra whipped cream slid down into her belly. "So good," she murmured. "Thank you, Libby."

"Yeah, no worries," the barista said, holding her own drink in a Bessie's to-go cup. She was looking around the kitchen, a pensive expression on her face.

"What?" Faith asked, standing at the island, her hand resting next to the third cup Libby had brought for Faith's guest, arriving soon. "What's wrong?"

"This place was pretty messed up." Libby met Faith's gaze, her own filled with sadness. "Your dad and Vicky came in and cleaned things up after the cops were done. They had to do some touch-up painting and your dad had to fix the banister." She looked around, letting out a heavy sigh. "They did a helluva job. You'd never know anything happened."

"Dad tells me you really took the reins down at the shop," Faith said softly. "You'll never know how much that means to me."

The younger woman nodded, pursing her lips as though trying to keep in unshed emotion. "Sure thing. Wyatt taught me a lot. I just thought, what would Wyatt do?" She sipped her coffee, looking away, but not before Faith saw an extra little glint of moisture in her eyes.

"They're going to find her, Libby," Faith said

quietly, no idea where the deep-seated belief she suddenly felt came from. "You have to believe that."

Libby was silent for a moment before saying, "Bet you didn't think this is how you'd spend New Year's Eve, huh?"

Faith smirked and shook her head. "No."

"Did you hear that the festival Wynter was gonna throw got turned into a vigil for Wyatt tonight instead?" Libby asked.

Faith nodded, again sipping from her drink, though more for something to do with her hands than because she really wanted any in that moment. What she wanted to do was curl up into a ball and cry. "Yeah, Dad told me."

"You gonna go?"

Faith's phone alerted her that someone was at the gate. She grabbed it and looked at the camera image, clearly seeing Detective Montez behind the wheel. She pressed the button to open the gate before setting the phone down and meeting Libby's gaze. "I don't know," she whispered. "I don't know if I can take it."

Libby walked over to Faith and took her into a tight but quick hug. "You've got this. We're all here for you. For Wyatt."

Faith nodded, taking a deep breath as the young blonde stepped away just as the doorbell chimed. She glanced in the direction of the front door before meeting Faith's gaze again. She gave her a smile that said it all: *I love you guys, we all love you guys. We'll fight for you.*

The two walked to the door, Libby giving her another hug before pulling the front door open. Grace Montez stood on the other side.

"Thanks for coming, Detective," Faith said. "Libby, this is the detective who's been working on Wyatt's case. Detective Montez, this is one of my employees, Libby."

"Nice to see you again, Libby," the detective said, giving the younger woman a curt nod as she removed her sunglasses.

"You, too. Brought your caramel macchiato, extra vanilla, no whip," Libby said, hitching a thumb back toward the kitchen. At Faith's confused look, Libby explained. "She's been in like almost every day since all this happened. Kinda know her order backward and forward."

"Oh," Faith said, amused. "Got it."

Libby turned to Faith, pleading in her eyes. "Please come tonight, Faith. The whole town will be there, and I think it'll do you good."

Faith nodded. "We'll see."

Libby gave her a final hug then turned to Grace Montez. "Detective."

Faith watched the cute little blonde leave, noting she glanced back at the detective before she trotted down the stairs, her expression hidden behind the dark lenses of her sunglasses.

"Come on in," Faith said, closing and locking the front door after Grace entered. At the detective's look, she gave her a sheepish grin. "Sorry." She unlocked the deadbolt. "I'm a bit paranoid now."

"Understandable," Grace said softly, relocking the door with a kind smile. "I would be, too." She reached out to put a hand lightly on Faith's shoulder. "It's really good to see you up and around. I came by the hospital hoping to catch you awake or lucid, but not to be."

Faith wasn't sure what to say, feeling small and alone even as this woman, such a warm presence, stood not more than a foot from her. "Well," she said at length, clearing her throat. "As she said, Libby brought you coffee. She called this morning to see if I was up for company and a mocha breve, and who am I to turn one of those down?" She smiled weakly and led the way to the kitchen, handing the other woman the cup, grateful for the cardboard sleeve as the brew inside was still quite hot. "Careful."

Grace took it with a quiet thanks. "So, are you up for this?"

Faith nodded, letting out a shaky sigh. She grabbed her own cup and headed to the living room, the detective following. The two got settled on separate pieces of furniture. Her heart was racing, nervous about what the detective would want to know. After her nightmare that had thrown her headfirst into her morning, she was eager to get this over with.

Grace grabbed one of the ceramic coasters from the wooden holder at the center of the coffee table and set her cup on it before she retrieved the notebook from the inside pocket of her women's-cut blazer. The detective was definitely a woman who carried herself well, an air of authority about her yet she was personable and caring.

"Okay, Faith," the detective began softly. "First of all, I want to say that I'm so sorry. I haven't lived in Wynter very long, just since getting on with the department here, but I want you to know that every single person I've spoken to, which is darn near the entire town, adores Wyatt and has nothing but glowing things to say about her, and about you." She smiled. "And, your barista is right. I've become quite addicted to your coffee," she said, pointing the pen she held at her cup. "You can definitely say I've become a regular."

"Well, I'm just sorry we don't carry any donuts," Faith said, her weak attempt at humor finding a home as the detective burst into laughter.

"No, but I'll take your lemon bread over a donut any day." She cleared her throat and seemed to get into serious mode. "What do you remember from that night? Did you see Lucas?"

Faith shook her head. "No."

For just a split second she saw the tall figure standing on the other side of the door before out of the corner of her eye she caught something swinging...

Squeezing her eyes shut, she curled in on herself, sock-covered feet pulled up onto the couch as she wrapped her arms around her shins. Faith heard a small whimper rent the air and it took a moment before she realized it had come from her.

Detective Montez moved from the chair to the couch next to Faith. "It's okay," she murmured, a hand on Faith's shoulder. "It's over now."

Faith nodded, blowing out a breath.

"Can I get you some water, Faith?" the detective asked. "Or something else?"

"Water, please. There are bottles in the fridge," Faith whispered. She was slightly jostled as her companion pushed up from the couch and left the room. She glanced up from where her gaze had been fixed on her knees, covered in snowman-covered fleece. She glanced over at the Christmas tree, the lights dark. She didn't have the heart to turn them on.

"Here you go," Grace said, reclaiming her seat, a fresh bottle of water in her hands. She twisted off the cap and handed the bottle to Faith. "We can wait until tomorrow—"

"No," Faith said, shaking her head as she took a long drink, the ice-cold liquid snapping her out of her fear and dark memories. "No. There's something…" She saw her mother's face before her mind's eye again, a combination of the woman who had held her and the one frozen in time in the pictures in her father's photo album. Again, she saw the television screen, the woman with the braid, the two cabins, all of it. She took a deep breath then turned to the detective. "There's something I need to tell you."

<hr />

She couldn't believe the number of people that had gathered. It had to be the entire town plus some. The streets were undriveable from the gathering of bodies, all a single speck of firelight from the candles they held.

"You okay?" Libby asked softly as she pulled her car to a stop along the curb.

Faith nodded though said nothing, her eyes riveted to the scene before her. The vigil had started outside of Bessie's, but from what Libby had told her, it had grown until it filled half the streets of the town.

The vigil had begun an hour before, but Faith couldn't do it. It didn't matter what her father said, what Vicky said, what Pops said, she just couldn't do it. But finally, something inside her told her she needed to be there, *had* to be there for Wyatt, to fight for her until her last breath. So, she'd called Libby, who'd come straight over to pick her up. Faith knew she was in no shape to drive.

"Here."

Faith looked over to see Libby offering a simple long, thin white candle with a little paper disk slid up its length to catch any hot wax before it could hit the holder's hand.

"Come on," Libby urged. "There's your dad and Vicky."

Faith looked up, relieved to see the couple walking over to them. Vicky came around to Faith's side of the car and opened the door. She gave her a loving, motherly smile as she held out her hand. Faith looked at the gloved fingers before she took them in her own.

As she got out of the car, she was surprised to hear the crowd singing as one unanimous voice. She allowed herself to be wedged between Libby and Vicky, her father behind her, a hand on her shoulder. Those closest in the crowd walked up to her and gave her huge, chilled kisses to the cheek, and words of encouragement and prayer.

Faith felt overwhelmed by the love. As her candle was lit by someone in the crowd, she knew she was safe, she knew she was loved, and she knew she had plenty of people there to put her back together when she fell apart.

Her eyes fell closed as tears slowly slid down her cheeks as she silently mouthed the words as the crowd sang Wyatt's favorite, "Crazy."

Chapter Twenty-eight

Faith's eyebrows fell in concentration as she rolled the flavors around in her mouth. The tartness of the raspberry concentrate was a bit much, but then it was tempered by the incoming chocolate, then it was completely taken over by the incoming chocolate, which turned into an avalanche of chocolate flavor.

She rinsed out her plastic sampler cup and shook her head as she glanced over at Libby and Tad, who waited expectantly for her score. "I'd give this one a four, honestly." She chuckled as their faces fell. "No, it's a great flavor combination, just way too much chocolate."

Tad, hip thrown out and hand perched upon it, raised a carefully shaped eyebrow. "I told you, Libbs."

"What?" She gasped. "I told *you!*"

Faith grinned, shaking her head. "When do you two go back to college again?" she muttered good-naturedly.

"You're so going to miss my specialness, Faith," Tad said, dumping the remnants of his concoction down the sink.

"I won't miss you wasting my supplies, I can tell you that," she quipped.

"Oh, burned!" Libby crowed, wiping down the counter where they'd made a small mess in their experimentation. "You need some aloe vera there, Tad?"

Faith grinned. It felt good to smile for a moment. Now that the high school kids had gone back to school, she'd lost those workers during the day and they would be relegated mostly to weekends, as they couldn't work in the adult part of the business in the evenings. Her three college kids were still with her: Libby, Tad, and another young man named LaShawn, whom she'd be losing permanently when he started at CU Boulder in a couple weeks. But for now, their silly humor and antics were welcome.

It was four days into the new year, and though she wasn't even supposed to be there, she couldn't spend another day at the house. It had begun to feel like a prison. She needed to be useful, so she'd spent a couple hours at her office doing her mayoral duties, then headed to the shop to see how things were going, where she could help for a bit.

She was admittedly tired, her body using so much energy to heal. It was a full ten days since it had happened, and she was due to go see her neurologist in two days. The headaches had finally begun to ease, but she still wasn't sleeping, her stress high and anxiety level through the roof. Her regular physician wanted to prescribe her a mild antidepressant to take the edge off, but she didn't want that. She wanted to stay fully alert and feel every bit of this until it was over.

"Okay, I seriously think we need to come up with an amazing adult smoothie," Tad said, leaning back against the counter. The tall, slender carrot top glanced from woman to woman. "Whuddya think?"

"I think it would sell like gangbusters," Libby said with a shrug. "Maybe like a grasshopper smoothie with vodka?"

"You two figure that one out. I don't really

drink, so am of no real help," Faith said, waving them off as she turned to the main counter as her co-eds gathered the blender, spatula, and other things they'd used to make their earlier smoothie to take back into the kitchen to wash.

Faith readied herself for the customer who was climbing up the stairs, their footfalls quick but not loud as they made their way up the wood stairs.

A moment later, a woman appeared through the mini swinging saloon doors. She wore casual clothing, fitted jeans with winter boots, and an unzipped Columbia jacket over what looked to be a red sweater. She wore a baseball cap with a professional football team's logo on it. It was pulled low, shadowing her face. Either she had short hair, or it was pulled up under the hat.

"Good afternoon," Faith said with a smile. "Welcome. What can I get you?"

The woman gave her a quick smile before she looked up at the menu board placed on the back wall over Faith's head.

Faith waited patiently, but she could feel more than see the woman's gaze on her from time to time. It made her a bit uncomfortable. Something about the woman was niggling at her, but she had no clue what it was, nothing even to put her finger on. But, something…

She was about to ask if she knew the woman when she heard Libby's voice call out to her from the kitchen door. "Yeah?" she called over her shoulder.

"Can you bring me a Band-Aid, please? Tad cut himself on the blender blade. Again."

Faith rolled her eyes and gave a sheepish smile to the woman, who was looking at her again. "Give me one second."

Faith hurried to the bathroom on that floor where the First-Aid kit was located and quickly grabbed what Libby would need to bandage Tad's boo-boo, dropping them off with the dynamic duo before hurrying back to the counter. The woman was gone.

Her stomach clenched, though she had no idea why. She hurried around the counter to the swinging doors and rested her hands on either one as she looked down the stairs. Nothing.

"Jesus, did I get hit that hard?" she muttered.

Suddenly, she gasped. She nearly took a header down the stairs in her haste to get down them. She glanced into the ice cream shop, but the woman was not one of the few customers that were waiting in line, and certainly not her employee.

She ignored the curious gaze she got from a customer as she burst through the front door, out of breath as she looked first one way then the other. No foot traffic on the frigid day, but as she watched, a blue Toyota Highlander pulled away from the curb, back end fishtailing slightly on ice as it made its way onto the main road from where it was parked just down from her shop.

"Everything okay, boss?"

She turned to see Stuart, an elderly man who worked in the ice cream parlor, standing next to her, still in his apron. "Did you see a woman leave? From upstairs?"

He glanced out to the street then back to Faith as he shook his head. "I was cleaning up an ice cream scoop oopsie from a kiddo on the floor. Sorry."

She let out a heavy breath, which came out in

a huge puff of steam. "Damn." She smiled at him as she pulled her phone from her own apron. "It's okay, Stuart. Go on back inside, sir. I don't want you to catch your death out here." Once he ambled back into the shop with a playful salute, she dialed Detective Montez.

※ ※ ※ ※

She lay on the couch, bundled up in the quilt Wyatt had brought with her into their home. She could smell her perfume on it, comforting. She'd begun sleeping on the couch a couple nights before as the bed upstairs felt like a canyon-sized pit of loneliness and sadness. Even the guest bed was too much space. So, curled up on the couch, she felt like she was in her own little cave. Her father, Vicky, and even Libby had offered to stay with her if she needed company, or simply to feel safe, but Faith found herself in the very strange headspace of feeling terribly alone and scared, but desperately needing isolation from anyone who wasn't Wyatt.

Feeling so helpless, she thought back to her conversation earlier that day on the phone with Grace:

"Listen, I could be crazy, maybe she was a ghost or I got hit harder than we all thought, 'cuz I seem to be the only person who saw her, but I think Lucas's girlfriend just walked into my coffee shop," Faith said into her phone from where she sat behind the wheel of her SUV to get out of the frigid temperatures.

"Wait, what? Why do you say that?" the detective asked, surprise and confusion in her voice.

Why, indeed. *"Gut feeling. As in, every-hair-on-*

your-body-stands-up kind of gut feeling. And, she kept looking at me, almost like she was trying to place me or something."

"Maybe she's seen you on the news. Lord knows the reporters have been sniffing around here enough in the last two weeks." Grace snorted. "So, what did she look like? What was she wearing?"

"Uh…" Faith ran a hand gingerly through her hair, completely avoiding the side of her head that was injured. No longer bandaged, it was incredibly sensitive to any touch. Washing her hair was fun. "Blue jeans, winter jacket that was dark gray and like a neon green or yellow, you know that weird in-between color? Red sweater, baseball—"

"Hold it, Faith," Grace interrupted. "Your ghost just walked in. Call you later."

The call had disconnected and Faith was left with a feeling of elation and fear.

Faith hadn't heard back from Grace, and had used any willpower she had left to not chain-call until Grace answered and told her what happened. She knew the detective had a job to do, and she'd been wonderful in keeping Faith in the loop as best she could.

≈≈≈≈

Sitting in a surprisingly comfortable chair for a doctor's office waiting room, Faith flipped through a magazine on neurosurgery, which admittedly she found dry and uninteresting. Tossing it aside back to the small end table next to her chair, she was about to turn to her phone for a game when she heard whispering. Glancing up, she saw the older woman and teenage boy sitting across from her staring at her, whispering back and forth to each other in Spanish. She couldn't understand the language, but certainly could tell it was about her.

Finding it rude but determined not to react, she turned her attention back to her phone. She heard them talking louder now, the teenage boy sounding excited. Now slightly concerned along with her confusion, she glanced up at him again. This time, he popped up in his seat and was pointing from Faith to something above her head.

"Lady, look!"

She looked from the excited young man up behind her to realize there was a TV mounted on the wall, which is what they were staring at. She gasped when she saw her face plastered on the screen, clearly a news broadcast. What stunned her the most was when it went from a picture of her—which looked like it had been taken from the brochure for Bessie's opening—to a live shot of a wooded area. It went from a reporter on the ground, his words silent as the sound was turned off on the flat screen, to a shot from a helicopter hovering over the area.

"How do we turn this up?" she exclaimed, her heart beginning to race when she read the banner along the bottom of the screen: FORMER SHERIFF'S DEPUTY SUSPECTED IN ESTRANGED WIFE'S KIDNAPPING LOCATED. She was about to step onto her chair but felt a hand on her arm. The teenager hopped up onto the chair and reached up to the TV, the sound easing up.

"...we can see this place is crawling with police, Jackson, and from what we can tell from our vantage point up here is that they basically have a trap set around the cabin, which is also heavily in the crosshairs of police," a woman was saying, her words narrating the video shown. Her voice sounded tinny through what was likely a headset, the *swoosh* of the helicopter blades slicing through the air disrupting the broadcast in a choppy fashion.

"Holly, has there been any sighting of the woman, Wyatt Pennington?" a man asked, apparently the "Jackson" the woman had referred to. He was dressed in a suit and sitting at the anchor desk in the studio.

"We haven't seen anyone as of yet, and to our knowledge police haven't said anything to Ryan on the ground," the woman responded. "Hang on, Jackson... Okay, we're being told we have to move out of the area. Back to you in the studio."

The shot went black for a moment before it was back on the anchor. "We're not entirely sure what's happening there, but just a recap of the situation. Back on Christmas night, Wyatt Pennington, Wynter woman and estranged wife of former sheriff's deputy Lucas Pennington, and her friend, mayor of Wynter Faith Fitzgerald, were attacked in their home after months of trying to track Pennington down to serve him divorce papers. Fitzgerald was left for dead and Wyatt was taken from the home."

"Faith Fitzgerald?"

Faith was snapped out of her tunnel vision of the news report by her name, not only just spoken over national news but then in real life behind her. She glanced over her shoulder to see her neurologist's nurse standing there with her chart in her hands.

"I, uh..." She turned her attention back to the

TV. There was no way she was leaving now.

"Apparently a mystery woman showed up at the Wynter Police Department a day or so ago and gave pivotal information that has led to the apparent location of Pennington. Ryan, any more information?" the anchor asked.

The reporter on the ground from before was back on a split screen with the anchor. He held his microphone with the CNN logo on it. He stood in front of what looked to be a barricade of police vehicles, including a large black tactical vehicle that read *SWAT* across the back.

"Yes, Jackson. The woman, who has asked to remain unnamed, apparently used to work with Pennington at the Tunston Sheriff's Department. She directed police to a cabin here in Guffey, which Pennington purchased over the summer after another hunting-style cabin he had in Gunnison, about two and a half hours from here, went up in flames. It was called accidental at the time, but after Pennington became the main suspect by Wynter police in the arson burn of his house in Wynter, that case has now been reopened."

Faith gasped, her hands balled together and held in front of her mouth as she watched. She couldn't believe it—exactly as she'd been shown in that weird… dream. Or whatever. She felt suddenly like she was standing in the middle of a busy street. A quick glance around showed her that the entire waiting room, plus the receptionist, nurse, and another nurse, had gathered to watch the news. If it weren't her life, she would have found it amusing.

"So," the anchor was saying. "This cabin where you're at now is the cabin he bought?"

"No," the reporter said, turning to indicate the area behind him, though nothing could be seen but police vehicles and the skeletal branches of winter-dead trees, a blanket of snow covering the ground. "About thirty yards that way is another cabin, one that locals say is only used during hunting season by an out-of-state family, so essentially Pennington has stumbled upon a small arsenal."

"Oh, goodness."

Tears stung the backs of Faith's eyes. She could barely breathe.

"Police have said that they suspect Pennington was holed up in his cabin until yesterday, when police began snooping around here after his former girlfriend came forward," the reporter explained.

"Any news on if Wyatt is with him?" Jackson asked, appropriate concern on his carefully expressed face.

"There's been no word on that so far, Jackson. It seems right now it's a bit of a standoff." Suddenly, an incredibly loud *BANG* rent the air, sending a startled reporter to hide behind a police car. "Whoa!"

Faith let out a little whimper, others around her reacting verbally. She even felt someone's hand on her shoulder. Silent tears fell down her cheeks as she continued to watch.

"What's happening there, Ryan?" Jackson asked with concern.

"I'm not sure. It sounded like a bomb went off here." The reporter slowly stood from where he hid, staring off in the direction of the trees behind the police vehicles. "There's a good deal of shouting now, though I can't make out what they're saying." The reporter sucked in his breath and fell back to the ground again as a second bang rocked the afternoon, followed by what sounded like a few shotgun shots.

Faith was full-on crying now, her shoulders shaking. She heard her phone ring and felt it vibrate in her pocket. She sniffled and used her sleeve to wipe at her eyes as she grabbed it and brought it to her ear.

"Hello?" she barely managed to say.

"Faith, it's Grace. We've got her."

Chapter Twenty-nine

Heart in her throat and doctor's appointment rescheduled, Faith flew down the highway. The police car in front of her and the one behind her with flashing lights and blaring sirens got her to Guffey in record time, courtesy of a favor from Grace Montez's former precinct in Northglenn, a suburb of Denver.

What should have taken just over two hours took about an hour and fifteen minutes. Finally, they pulled into the tiny parking lot of the tiny police department of the tiny mountain town of less than one hundred people. Her SUV squealed to a stop and she barely had the engine cut off before yanking the key from the ignition and shoving out of the vehicle. The two escorting officers whooped their sirens twice at her before heading off back to Denver, she imagined.

She ignored the news trucks that surrounded the area, the parking lot clearly blocked off to them by some of the officers who were standing guard. A couple eagle-eyed reporters began to yell questions at her, but she ignored them, too. She had one thing on her mind, and it was whatever Grace had to tell her in that squat brick building.

She had no idea if she was in for good news, the worst news of her life, or something in between. On the phone, Grace had simply told her she needed to get there immediately, that she had a couple friends on their way to escort her, and where was she? She said she needed Faith there in person to talk to her about what had happened.

Faith was scared to death.

She nearly ripped the door off its hinges in her haste to get inside. The building looked like a movie set: one large room, replete with three desks for officers, the front desk, a water cooler, and two doorways in the back, one marked RESTROOM with a door, the other an open doorway leading to another room marked CELLS.

The room was filled to capacity with uniformed officers from various departments and teams standing around, some talking quietly amongst themselves, though most were quiet. Buried in the sea of humanity, she caught a glimpse of Grace toward the back of the room in between heads and shoulders. She saw the EMS logo on the back of the jacket of the person standing next to her.

"Excuse me," she said to the first officer she came to. When he turned to look down at her in question, she explained, "I'm Faith Fitzgerald. Detective Grace Montez called for me."

He said nothing, simply moved aside, indicating that she should make her way through the throngs. With unending utterances of *excuse me, pardon me, oops, sorry about your foot, let me through, please,* she made it to two people away from Grace and the EMS worker.

"Grace?"

The detective glanced over at the sound of her name and quickly moved from where she'd been standing and stuck her arm through the small space between the two officers standing in front of Faith.

Her hand reached blindly until it located Faith's wrist, then yanked her between the officers.

The EMS man stepped aside, and Faith gasped.

Wyatt leapt off the desk she was sitting on while the EMS person attended to her, the wool blanket that had been draped over her shoulders falling to the floor as she threw herself into Faith's arms.

Faith wrapped her arms around her tiny body as tightly as she could, her eyes squeezing shut, the tears still managing to escape into the dirty and greasy auburn hair her face was buried in.

"My god, my god, my god," Wyatt whispered almost like a prayer as she clung painfully to Faith, her body trembling. "You're alive!"

"I can't believe it," Faith said, holding her even tighter to her. "I can't believe it. Yes, I'm alive." She felt Wyatt begin to go limp in her arms. "No!"

Grace rushed forward and together they stopped her fall, the officers moving away to make space for them.

"We need to get her to a hospital," the EMS man explained. "Her body weight is dangerously low, and so is her blood pressure and levels."

※※※※

Faith's phone was blowing up with texts from the people back home who had also seen the TV footage in Guffey. She'd turned her ringer off; people were calling as quickly as they were texting, but sitting in the waiting room in the hospital where Grace had instructed her to wait, she had very few answers to the unending questions. The most important bit of information she could give, however, was that Wyatt was alive.

Her eyes closed and her head fell back against the wall as the relief washed through her again. There'd been no time for Grace or anyone else to fill her in on anything. Right after Wyatt passed out she'd been gathered into the ambulance, and Grace had jumped into her service car and Faith into her 4Runner to make the forty-minute drive to Cañon City, another small town but one large enough to house a full hospital, St. Thomas More, where Faith sat now.

Grace was in with Wyatt and the medical staff, taking pictures for their case as Wyatt was given a thorough examination. Faith had fought to go with her, but Grace made it clear that was not advisable. So, she sat in the waiting room on an uncomfortable chair, her heel tapping a nervous staccato on the polished tile floor at her feet.

She let out a tired breath, as it was turning into a long day of nonstop heightened emotions, and the adrenaline had died down, leaving her feeling spent. She looked back down at her phone as yet another text came in and had to laugh.

Libby: What? What!!? WHAT?!!!! She's alive??!!! WHAT!!???

Faith responded in the affirmative, amused. She couldn't help but smile, thinking of the unbelievable, and likely overwhelming, welcome Wyatt was going to get.

"Hey."

Faith's head snapped up at the sudden voice in an otherwise empty waiting room, happy to see a very haggard-looking Grace walking over to her. She plopped down in the chair next to Faith. "How is she?"

Grace nodded, reaching up to run a hand through her hair. "Good as can be expected. They're getting her settled into a room now, so they sent me out here to get you."

"Great, let's go," Faith exclaimed, moving to get to her feet, but the detective stopped her with a hand to her leg.

"I want to talk to you first," Grace said, meeting Faith's confused look with a side glance.

Faith relaxed back into the chair, though nearly held her breath. "Okay."

"She's lost eleven percent of her overall body weight, due to dehydration and neglect."

Faith stared at her. "He was starving her?" Anger, like whips of fire, raced through her.

"We don't know the full extent of things quite yet. Pennington is on his way back to Wynter now, a much better facility to hold him than the Guffey situation. So, once I leave here, I'll head back for a full interrogation. But, you're going to be distressed when you see her, Faith," she continued softly. "I mean, *really* see her. I just wanted to give you the facts before you do."

Faith nodded, understanding. "Okay."

"She was chained or shackled in some way. When we got to her, she was naked, filthy, chained to the wall."

Faith's eyes closed, tears slipping out as she absorbed the information. She nodded in acknowledgement of what she was being told. She couldn't speak.

"She has some broken ribs, fingers, though they're mostly healed, it seems. Bruising," Grace added, handing Faith a tissue from the box on the table across from them.

Faith took it and nodded, the only thing she could do to respond as the tears came faster. She knew she had to get it out now, as Wyatt would need her to be strong.

"She had a sexual assault evidence kit done." Grace sighed, sounding exhausted. "Not easy for a woman to have to go through."

Faith let out a shaky breath, wiping her eyes as fresh tears began to come. "I have no doubt that monster did that to her," she whispered. "I wish you'd killed that fucker."

Grace patted Faith's thigh before sitting forward, indicating she was about to stand. "Don't worry. He's the most hated man in the entire county. No doubt the defense will have to ask for a change of venue to Denver or something. The DA will throw the book at that son of a bitch for what he did to Wyatt, and to you."

Faith accepted the hand that was offered to help her stand, which she did. She felt a bit weak in the knees, so much information in her head, so much emotion in her heart.

"Come on," Grace said softly. "Let's go see your girl."

The room was small, outfitted with the basics: narrow hospital bed dressed in white linens, a roller table off to the side, a small plastic pitcher and matching plastic cup with bendable straw sticking out of it. It looked like water in the cup. Faith assumed the closed door led to a bathroom.

What caught her attention, however, was the tiny figure lying in the bed, quiet and still, her eyes closed. She seemed to be sleeping peacefully. The medical staff must have gotten her to a shower, as her hair was now clean and brushed out, an auburn halo around her head and shoulders. She was dressed in a hospital gown, the thin blanket folded over the top of the sheet just below her breasts.

Faith walked into the room alone, having given Grace some money to head to a local store and buy Wyatt some clothing and shoes to go home in. She walked over to the bed, her eyes never leaving the form lying in the middle of it.

Wyatt was a naturally small-framed woman, but the body before her was downright tiny. It was easy to see the bruises that littered her arms and her face, some old, some new. Her bottom lip was swollen, a cut slashing across it to the corner of her mouth, leading to a nasty bruise that looked to be a couple of days old.

Faith grabbed the one chair that was there and brought it up next to the bed, sitting down as she reached over and gently took Wyatt's hand in her own. She looked at the delicate structure, the paleness of the skin, so soft. She noticed her pinky and ring fingers were taped together on her other hand, and figured those must be the broken fingers Grace had mentioned.

Her gaze went back to Wyatt's face, so beautiful even through all the abuse it had taken. The beauty was so much more than the physical features, it was the woman behind them. The heart she had, the love she was capable of, even for a perfect stranger. In their time together, she'd never known love like she was given from Wyatt, never known such passion, such kindness, and nobody had ever brought the best out of her like this precious woman did.

She leaned forward and closed her eyes as she brought the soft hand to her lips, leaving a lingering kiss on the knuckles, silently vowing to give her life before she'd ever let Wyatt be hurt again.

※ ※ ※ ※

Wyatt was dressed in the simple pair of sweats, sweatshirt, and tennis shoes Grace had picked up for her. She'd been quiet the entire drive home, yet she'd held a death grip on Faith's hand. Luckily it had been a fairly straight drive on the interstate, not a lot of turns or stops where she'd need her other hand for anything.

As they got closer to Wynter, Faith could feel her excitement grow, just wanting to get Wyatt safe and sound behind the fortified walls of their home. She'd spoken to Dr. Jill, the therapist Wyatt had seen off and on since the previous fall to deal with the traumatic years being married to Lucas, and she'd recommended Faith keep things quiet and intimate for now, just the two of them until Wyatt got her sea legs under her. She said it could take a few days or it could take a couple of months before Wyatt was ready to peek her head out into the world again. Let her lead, she advised.

As she took the exit that led to Wynter, she glanced over to the right to the farmland and the farmhouses. She smiled, squeezing Wyatt's fingers just enough to get her attention. "Look, baby," she said.

Wyatt followed the direction of her nod until she saw it. On the side of a huge red barn, someone had hung a huge sign that read:

WELCOME HOME, WYATT! WE LOVE YOU!

As they got closer to town, they saw random people standing at the side of the road, some waving, others holding more signs, all cheering them on. Faith couldn't keep the smile off her face, and as she looked over at Wyatt, she could see she was in awe.

"Why are they doin' this?" she asked softly, eyes wide as she met Faith's gaze.

"They love you, baby," Faith said. "This entire town was scared to death for you."

"I'm not worth this," Wyatt whispered, sounding shocked as they saw yet another group of people, this one a group of school-age kids with a few adults. As soon as Faith's SUV came into view, they were jumping and cheering with excitement, the adults waving.

It was once they got into town proper, though, that even Faith's mouth hung open. Much like the night of the vigil, the town in its entirety had come out to welcome Wyatt home. They were standing on the side of the street, in parking lots, sitting on their car hoods, leaning out of business doorways, including Bessie's.

Faith saw Libby and some of the other employees whistling and yelling out of the windows they'd opened on the second floor, in the coffee shop. Dogs barked in excitement at the end of leashes.

"This is just unreal," Wyatt whispered, turning as far as she could in her seat to see the other side of the street, raising a hand to wave at some little girls standing with a man.

"Baby, look," Faith said, pointing ahead to the foothills high above the town. Atop it someone had placed a massive red heart, painted on what looked like pieces of plywood put together. Their initials were painted at the center of the heart.

"It's all so much," Wyatt said, bringing her hands up to cover her face.

Concerned, Faith glanced over at her quickly before looking back to the road to make the turn for their road. She said nothing, simply reached over and placed her hand on a thigh. "Almost home, love."

Reaching the gate, Faith reached up to the visor and pressed the button, sending an electronic signal that swung the gate open. She passed through, the gate slowly closing on its own. She drove easily up the private road to the house, which her father had cleared of snow the day before. He'd bought a snowblower and found every excuse to use it he could.

Pulling to a stop in her spot next to Isabelle, Faith cut the engine and looked over at Wyatt, who met her gaze. Faith thought she looked so terribly tired, the normally vivid, lively turquoise eyes dull... dare she say, dead?

Faith reached over and ever so gently ran the backs of her fingers along an unbruised side of Wyatt's jaw. "I love you," she said softly.

"I love you, too," Wyatt responded, her voice soft but flat.

"Ready to go inside?" Faith asked, nodding toward the house. She wasn't sure what Wyatt was going to think, coming back, considering what had happened the last time she'd been there.

Wyatt glanced up at the house through the windshield, then let out a shaky breath. "I have to," she said, meeting Faith's gaze again. "It's home. Right?"

Faith nodded. "It's home. Our home."

Wyatt nodded. "He ain't gonna hurt us again," she said, though it sounded more like she was trying to convince herself than comfort Faith.

"No, baby. He's locked up in a cage like the animal he is." She unbuckled her seat belt. "Ready?"

Wyatt stared at the house again for a long moment before she, too, unbuckled her seat belt and opened her door, almost as though going before she lost her nerve. Faith hurried to catch up to her, sifting through her key ring until she found the house key. She trotted up the stairs to the porch, Wyatt already at the top, hugging herself as she waited.

Faith gave her the most loving, comforting smile she could before she unlocked the door but didn't open it. "Just so it doesn't startle the hell out of you, there's a mass of stuffed animals, cards and letters, and plants inside," she explained. "I had to throw out the flowers, but it's stuff folks left at the gate after... well, after."

Wyatt said nothing, simply nodded. Faith pushed the door open and stepped through first. Though she knew there was nobody inside, certainly not Lucas Pennington, her protective side kicked in instinctively. She heard Wyatt enter after her and the door slam shut, the locks being engaged aggressively. Turning to face Wyatt, she saw her hurry over to the security panel by the stairs and arm the system.

Faith hadn't fully dealt with the fact that it was her fault Lucas was able to get in. She knew she, too, needed to get in and talk to someone about the events of two weeks ago. "I'm so sorry," she said, not much more than a whisper.

Wyatt looked at her over her shoulder from where she still stood at the security panel. She turned and walked to her. "Why? For what?"

"It's my fault," Faith whispered. "You said we should lock up, and I said to wait, I'd do it later." To her shame, the tears came hard and fast.

She hated herself, as this time was about Wyatt, not her. She turned away, meaning to head to the kitchen to grab a paper towel to wipe her eyes, but Wyatt stopped her, pulling her into a hug. She allowed herself to be held, and to really feel, because it was Wyatt, the one person she'd needed to feel with throughout this entire ordeal. She could finally let go.

"I got'cha, baby," Wyatt murmured into Faith's hair, one hand finding its way to its favorite place—Faith's hair—the other lightly caressing Faith's back over her sweater.

They were silent for a long time, Faith's tears drying up as they simply held each other, breathing each other in.

"Darlin'?" Wyatt murmured.

"Hmm?" Faith said, sighing in relieved contentment.

"Why on earth did somebody leave us a stuffed pickle?"

Confused, Faith pulled out of the hug just enough to look over toward the gathered objects. Sure enough, a big, green gherkin was smiling at them. She burst into laughter, having never noticed it before in the mix of unicorns, polar bear, dogs, cats, stuffed rainbows, etc. It felt good to laugh, and it made her heart even lighter to see the small smile on Wyatt's face.

Bringing up a hand, Faith lightly tucked hair behind Wyatt's ear. "I can't believe you're here." Something popped into her head that she wanted to know.

"Why did you say that I was alive, back at the police station?"

"He told me you were dead," Wyatt said softly. "Said he killed you." She looked down, but not before Faith saw the glisten of welling tears.

"He gave it the college try, but I'm here, sweetheart." She lightly cupped Wyatt's face, mindful of her injuries, and left the softest of kisses just to the side of her lips, not wanting to hurt her.

"What did he do to you?" Wyatt asked, eyes closed as she leaned into Faith's touch.

"He hit me over the head with a baseball bat. Put me in the hospital for a week, but I'm okay, and now we're together."

Wyatt took Faith in a hug again, resting her head on her shoulder. "Together," she murmured.

Chapter Thirty

Faith gasped, heart in her throat as she shot up in bed. Her leg hurt where she'd been savagely kicked. Looking to her left, she saw Wyatt wrestling with her covers, legs kicking wildly at her nighttime assailant.

Getting her bearings, Faith reached out a hand, yanking it back when Wyatt turned from her back to her side, her eyes squeezed shut and her face screwed up in an expression of pure terror.

"No! Stop, stop!"

"Wyatt, wake up." Faith reached out again and touched Wyatt's shoulder, lightly squeezing. "Baby?"

Wyatt gasped, loud and terrified, as her eyes popped open. She looked at Faith—more *through* her, actually—as she scrambled away from her. "Don't touch me!"

"Okay, okay, I'm a statue," Faith said, hands up in supplication.

Wyatt's breasts heaved beneath the baggy T-shirt she wore, her breathing more like gasps of air being sucked in then forced out. It took several minutes, but finally Wyatt began to calm down, though she remained sitting nearly on the edge of the bed farthest from Faith.

"Are you okay?" Faith asked softly, wanting nothing more than to reach out and gather her partner in her arms, but learning already it was a mistake.

Wyatt glared at her. "What do you think?"

The words and tone stung, but Dr. Jill had warned her this would happen, the anger. Patience was her best friend, but man, it was hard. "This is the third time this week, sweetheart," she said gently. "Maybe that prescription Dr. Jill mentioned would be—"

"I'm sorry I interrupted your fuckin' beauty sleep, Faith." Wyatt shoved the remaining blankets away from her as she climbed off the bed. She stormed to the bedroom door, unlocking the lock she'd insisted Faith install, and slammed it shut after her.

Stunned to the spot for a moment, Faith shook herself out of it and slid off the bed before hurrying to the bedroom door. She opened it just in time to see the guest bedroom door slam shut. She took a moment to remind herself that this had nothing to do with her, this wasn't personal to her or their relationship, this was something going on inside Wyatt, part of the healing process.

Even so, a rush of anger erupted through her, making her want to tear Lucas's testicles off. Pushing that thought out of her mind, she walked over to the guest room door and lightly rapped on it with the backs of her fingers. "Are you okay, baby?"

"Leave me alone," came the muffled response, the words sounding thick with emotion.

Faith sighed with sadness but didn't let it enter her tone when she answered, "Okay. I love you and I'm here if you need me." When there was no response, she walked away.

༄༄༄༄

Hair still damp from her shower, Faith stood

at the counter preparing the Keurig maker for her travel mug. She had meetings all day downtown at the mayor's office, so she was getting ready for a full day. After the events of the previous night, it would be a good distraction, she admitted to herself.

Her flavor of coffee for the morning picked out, she tucked the K-cup into the place in the machine and walked over to the fridge to choose her flavor of coffee creamer. She was not ashamed to be a "froufrou" coffee drinker. That was part of the beauty of owning a coffee shop.

Walking back to the coffeemaker and her travel mug, she began to pour some of the thick, white chocolate and raspberry liquid into the mug when she heard Wyatt enter the room. She spared a quick glance at her before returning her focus to her task.

"Good morning, baby," she said, trying to sound casual. "Want some coffee?" When Wyatt said nothing, Faith glanced in her direction again to see her leaning against the island, closed off as she hugged herself. The expression on her face said she was mulling something over, so Faith said nothing, waiting for her to speak when she was ready.

"I'm not sure there're words ta say how sorry I am for talkin' to you that way, sayin' such horrible things." She tucked her lips in, eyebrows furrowing almost as though she were trying to contain her emotion. She wasn't looking at Faith, instead looking at the travel mug that was currently being filled with fragrant brew by the machine. "You're the best thing that's ever happened ta me, Faith. As hard as he tried, he couldn't take you away from me, he couldn't destroy us, but after how I treated you, seems like I'm fixin' to."

Faith walked over to Wyatt, who looked like she was about to break. "No, baby," she whispered, gingerly gathering the other woman in her arms, cognizant of any signal that her touch wasn't welcome. When she saw that Wyatt wasn't going to push her away, she tightened her hold, cradling the auburn head that rested against her shoulder. "I'm not going anywhere, Wyatt. I'm not you and don't pretend to understand what you feel or where you're at, but after what I experienced, I hated the world, was so angry that after everything we'd been through, after I'd fought so hard to get to you, it was all possibly taken away," she murmured. "My poor dad didn't know what to do with me, so honestly I think he kind of solicited the services of Libby to put up with me." She smiled when she heard a soft chuckle.

"If anyone can, it's that little tiger," Wyatt said.

"Exactly. All I wanted was you, but she was wonderful. Put up with all my moods and angry outbursts." She ran her fingers through the long, thick strands of Wyatt's hair. "She's just an employee and became a good friend, and she managed to put up with me. I love you with all that I am, and there's nothing or nobody that can ever take me away from you again." She left a kiss on an auburn crown. "Certainly not a completely understandable angry outburst. Okay?"

Wyatt pulled away from Faith but not out of the embrace. She studied Faith's face for a long moment, the tiniest bit of light returning to those beautiful eyes. She brought up both her hands and lovingly cupped Faith's face. She brought their lips together in a soft, lingering kiss that, for just a moment, deepened to a more intimate caress. Faith understood that it wasn't about sex or seduction, but simply Wyatt's need to reconnect, to rediscover what they'd temporarily lost.

"I love you," Wyatt whispered, stroking Faith's cheek. "With all that I am."

Faith smiled. For the first time since this nightmare had begun nearly a month ago, she could feel that just maybe the sun would come out from behind the storm clouds.

"I put in a call to Dr. Jill this mornin', so once she gets into the office she and I can talk. I'm gonna talk to her about the sleepin' medication or maybe even meditation, somethin'," Wyatt said, dropping her hands from Faith's face and moving over to the coffeemaker. She stirred the liquid in the travel mug, and as she continued talking added a bit more cream until it was the way Faith liked it. "I wanna go in to work for a few hours today."

Though surprised at the announcement, Faith was pleased. She wasn't an outright extrovert, but Wyatt needed to be around people to a certain extent. She needed the town and the town needed her. "I think that's a wonderful idea. Want me to drop you off on my way to the office?"

Wyatt sent a smile her way as she pressed the lid onto the travel mug. "No, darlin'. I think I wanna stretch me and Isabelle's legs together."

※※※※

Tired of bureaucracy and red tape, Faith needed a break, and there was no better break than to see her love and get some coffee. It was the beginning of March, and she was working with her city council on the year's budget. This was ordinarily something that was done the previous fall, but the rebuilding of Wynter had turned everything on its head, so the current year was one that Faith intended to use to get Wynter back on her feet, back on track, and running within the confines of other towns of similar size.

Her drive over to Bessie's wasn't just for a break. She and Wyatt had a phone call with the DA at one, and a little birdy told Faith that perhaps a wonderful surprise could be waiting for Wyatt, so she had an appointment for that, as well.

Arriving at her business, Faith was pleased to see the lunch crowd from across and down the street at Pop's heading to her place for a little dessert for themselves or to take back to work for coworkers. It was a lovely, symbiotic relationship.

Making her way through the crowd downstairs, accepting greetings and hugs along the way, she went into the kitchen where she knew she'd find Wyatt, working her magic on cranking out the sweet goods with a little of her love as the secret ingredient to their success.

Wyatt's back was to her as she entered the room, and over the last month, she'd learned the hard way that sneaking up behind her partner was the very wrong thing to do. Wyatt had gotten much better with affection, but surprise was not her friend.

"Hey gorgeous, what's shakin?" Faith said softly, announcing her presence before she hugged the redhead from behind, leaving a quick kiss on the side of her neck before moving away from potentially prying eyes. By this point it was no longer a secret that she and Wyatt were a couple, but Faith always tried to be careful with their PDA.

Wyatt reached back to cup the back of Faith's head and accept the kiss before the two parted. "It has been so busy today," she said as Faith moved away. "I think folks are gettin' a bit of spring fever."

"I'm sure. We've had so much snow this winter. Speaking of spring," Faith said, crossing her arms over her chest as she leaned back against the prep counter. "I was thinking of maybe putting together a contingency of people to clean up Miner's Hole. Now that we're starting to get people wanting to come here for the hot springs, and since Dad is renovating all those old miner's shacks for tourism rentals…" She shrugged her shoulders. "What do you think? That extra tourism income could pay for a total cleanup."

Wyatt eyed her from where she stood by the ice cream maker, the cold, gooey concoction slowly squeezing from the machine into the metal container Wyatt placed under it to catch it. "Do ya mean it? We could finally show that cemetery some love?"

Faith grinned and nodded. "Yup."

Wyatt squealed in delight and launched herself at Faith, who barely managed to catch herself an armful of excited redhead before she ended up with a counter-height bruise along her back.

"Thank you," Wyatt whispered into her ear. She left a lingering kiss on Faith's cheek before stepping away. "Can I be part of it?"

Faith gave her a sheepish grin. "Well, I actually kinda hoped you'd want to run it. I know what that place means to you, and I know that nobody can give it the proper love and attention like you can."

Wyatt gave her a sexy little grin, which made Faith's heart flutter for a couple of reasons. The obvious reason was that Wyatt was the sexiest woman she'd ever seen, but also it was the first time she'd seen the ghost of the woman Wyatt had been before everything had happened Christmas night. She'd been showing small glimpses of her former self over the weeks since she'd been rescued, but it had been slow and, in many ways, very platonic. It had been hard for Faith to not allow herself to fall down the rabbit hole of self-doubt.

"It would be my pleasure, Miss Mayor," Wyatt murmured in an exaggerated, and deeply sexy, southern drawl.

Faith took a slow, deep breath of air and let it out just as slowly. She so badly wanted to react to the flirtatious tone, and lord knew her body was reacting, but wasn't sure how far she could or should take it. "The pleasure's all mine, I assure you," she managed lamely.

Wyatt studied her for a moment, looking deeply into her eyes. She must have seen something there because she stepped a bit closer to Faith, a quick glance to the door and window to ensure they didn't have an audience.

She leaned in and murmured against Faith's lips, "It will be, baby, soon. I promise." She trailed her fingers down over one of Faith's breasts, making Faith's heart skip a beat.

"I don't want you to rush—"

"No," Wyatt said, meeting her gaze. "I miss you, too. Very much."

It meant everything to Faith to hear those words. She felt a great deal of healing done in that moment. The voice of their employee serving customers behind the counter coming closer caused Wyatt to quickly move back to the ice cream maker. Faith cleared her throat, hoping that would help to dry her britches, too.

"You ready for our call?" she asked, hoping her voice sounded normal.

"I am," Wyatt said with a nod and a smile over her shoulder as she used a rubber spatula to help guide the last of the ice cream out into the metal pan. "Gimmie just a sec."

∂∂∂∂

"Okay, Patrice, we're both here and we're ready," Faith said, her phone on speaker and sitting on the center console in her SUV, the engine running and heat on. She glanced over at Wyatt, who sat in the passenger seat, their hands clasped next to Faith's phone.

"Hey, y'all," she said.

"Good afternoon, ladies," the DA greeted, her voice that of the strange, tinny tone from a speakerphone. "So, I have to tell you, Detective Montez and her team have done one helluva job on this case. I mean, this sucker is airtight. And frankly," she added in her dry, naturally sarcastic manner. "He knows it. So, I had a little chitchat with the public defender, and they want to cut a deal."

Faith felt her heart do a little flip-flop. She glanced over at Wyatt, whose eyebrows were drawn in deep thought. She lightly squeezed her fingers to get her attention. Wyatt met her gaze and held it for a long moment, the silent communication of the truly connected passing between the two. Faith nodded. "All right, Patrice, what's on his mind?"

"Lucas knows he can't beat this in a jury trial, they'd nail his nuts to the wall, though I think all present question the validity that he possesses any. So, he's willing to plead out. Let's see here…" The sound of pieces of paper being rifled through could be heard. "Guilty to the arson of the marital home. Guilty to kidnapping in the first degree and sexual assault. Here's the kicker, though," she added.

"All right," Wyatt drawled. "And, what made him admit to the fire?"

The DA snickered. "Neighbor's doorbell cam caught the whole thing. Not real bright, this one. Faith, this affects you. He flat refuses to plead to any crime against you. He said, and I quote, 'The bitch don't exist in my world, so I ain't guilty.' End quote."

Faith shook her head. "Piece of shit," she muttered.

"Pretty much. What do you gals want to do?"

"Honestly," Faith said, "I don't really care about what he thinks of me or what he pleads to regarding me." Again she looked at Wyatt. "This is about Wyatt. Everything she's had to endure from that son of a bitch all these years. Besides," she added with a smirk. "I already won. I get to spend my life with his wife."

"Shall I add that into our response?" Patrice asked dryly, making Faith laugh.

"What kinda time is he lookin' at, Patrice?" Wyatt asked.

"Let me put it this way," the DA explained, "He's a relatively young guy, but he'll never be getting out. We're talking well over sixty years here."

Wyatt met Faith's gaze, reaching out and gently caressing her jaw, so much love in her eyes. "Will I get to tell him what I think?"

"What, like visiting him in prison?" Patrice asked.

"No, in court. I'm not testifyin', so, will I get my

chance to have my say?"

"You can make a Victim Impact Statement in open court, yes."

Eyes never leaving Faith, Wyatt said simply, "Let's do it."

❧❧❧❧

"What're we doin' here?" Wyatt asked as Faith unbuckled her seat belt.

Faith grinned over at her. "It's a surprise. Come on."

The two walked up the path to the front door of the small house, a woman that Faith knew Wyatt would recognize opening the front door as they reached it.

"Hey, Lisa!" Wyatt exclaimed, sharing a quick hug with the woman. "How's Tad likin' bein' a college man?"

"He's been whining about doing his own laundry." Lisa laughed. "Welcome to adulthood, big boy."

Faith followed behind the two women, who chattered on like two monkeys in a tree as they were led through the house and down a long hallway to a closed door. She smiled, her heart beginning to race when she heard the whining on the other side.

"Okay, here we are, ladies," Lisa said, hand on the doorknob. She turned it and pushed the door open before stepping aside.

Inside the room that looked as though it had perhaps been a home office was an area walled off by a series of baby gates lined up end-to-end. A desk, chair, and lamps were shoved into a corner outside the baby gate perimeter. Inside the makeshift prison was a chocolate Lab adult resting on her side, looking utterly exhausted as six tiny bodies whined and squeaked as they vied for a teat for lunch. One little one was sitting in that awkward little way that puppies do, looking like it had no idea how it had ended up out in the world. An eighth puppy was doing its level best to waddle its way toward the baby gate wall and the humans standing just on the other side. It took a wrong step and did a face-plant in the blanketed floor that covered the area, earning a round of "Awws" from the humans.

Faith, who was already in love eight times over, looked over at Wyatt, nervous at what her reaction would be. "Cute, aren't they?"

Wyatt looked like a little girl again, giving Faith a look that made her smile. Wyatt literally looked as though she were about to burst with joy. "Oh my goodness, yes! Why are we here?"

Shoving her hands nervously into her pockets, Faith shrugged. "You've spoken so much about the Labs you had growing up, and you always wanted a dog, so…"

Wyatt nearly bowled Faith over with the intensity of her hug. "Oh my gosh!" she gushed into it, shocking Faith when she cupped her face and left a lingering kiss on surprised lips. "Yes. Lord, yes."

Faith grinned. "I figure maybe it's time to add to our little family. I mean, we have plenty of stuffed ones at home, but…" She grinned. "Not quite the same thing."

Wyatt's smile was more radiant then a thousand suns.

Chapter Thirty-one

Blowing out a breath, she turned this way and that, examining herself in the standalone mirror. She chose the nicest women's-cut suit that she'd kept—one of a couple—from her days in Manhattan. She knew she cut a nice figure in that suit, feminine yet radiated, "Don't fuck with me." It was a power suit, and that was the point.

"Holy smokes."

She froze, unable to take her eyes off the reflection of the woman who entered the bedroom. Slowing turned from the mirror, she wanted to take in the real thing. They'd had to buy Wyatt a dress, as she was struggling to put that last four or five pounds back on, but she was utterly gorgeous in the emerald-green dress that brought out the green in her eyes. She wore a small bit of makeup, just enough to add an edge to her natural beauty. Her hair was brushed to a shine and flowed down past her shoulders, nearly to her bra strap now.

"Holy smokes is right," Faith said, walking toward her, borrowing Wyatt's own words. "My god, you are so stunning."

Wyatt's smile was slow and almost predatory as she snaked her arms up and around Faith's neck when they met in the middle of the bedroom. "Funny, I was gonna say the same about you." She buried her fingers in dark hair as she initiated a slow, thorough kiss.

Faith responded, her hands moving to rest on Wyatt's hips, gently pulling her against her. The affection had grown, but she still felt when Wyatt had reached her tipping point and drew back, never demanding more than was given freely. She let out a contented sigh as Wyatt slowly pulled away, leaving a soft kiss on the tip of Faith's nose that made her smile.

"Are you ready for this?" she asked gently.

Wyatt caressed the side of her face. "Darlin', I've been waiting for this for nineteen years."

Faith studied Wyatt's face for a long moment, taking in every feature, ending with those eyes, always her eyes. They'd caught her from the moment they'd first met and managed to stop her dead in her tracks ever since. "You deserve this. You have so many people in your corner today, baby."

"I know. But, all I need is you." Another kiss before Wyatt released her and walked over to the bed, using one of the four posters for balance as she stepped into her high heels. "I'm not a fan of these darn things, but today they are necessary." She glanced over at Faith, who was dabbing on some perfume before she added some simple gold hoop earrings to her outfit. "Did you know heels were made for men to wear in the tenth century?"

Faith glanced at her as she inserted the first earring. "Come again?"

"Yes, ma'am. Horse ridin' men. Put heels on their boots so they'd stay in the stirrups then, golly, shocker, aristocrats took 'em over when they realized they could appear taller and more formidable."

Faith chuckled, putting the second earring in. "Why does that not surprise me?"

Wyatt smirked. "I'll grab the paperwork and

let's scoot."

※ ※ ※ ※

The courthouse parking lot was filled with cars, far more than Faith knew there should be. She looked around as Wyatt expertly maneuvered Isabelle into an empty space, which Ogden had so kindly managed to save for them by he and Vicky both driving a car in. Upon the text from Faith, Vicky pulled out, letting Isabelle slide in. After a round of hugs, the four of them walked into the building and took the elevator to the appropriate floor.

The courtroom was beautiful, from an era long gone when masons and woodworkers were used, true artists. The gallery was filled to capacity, all supporters of Faith and Wyatt. What surprised Faith the most, however was the figure that sat next to Pops. She walked over to them.

"Mr. Wynter?"

He smiled up at her, freshly shaven and his hair slicked back. He was dressed in a suit that was likely older than she was. He reached his hand out, which she took, his other hand covering hers before he used her hand to slowly get to his feet.

"It's so nice to see you, Mr. Billy," Wyatt said softly, affection in her voice as she held out her arm for him to use to stabilize himself.

He looked from one to the other before he reached up, one hand to the side of each of their faces, first pulling Faith down for a scratchy kiss of dry lips on her cheek, followed by Wyatt. "This," he said, looking from one to the other. "Is how it should have always been."

Faith smiled, always such a soft spot for him, which she knew Wyatt had, too. She glanced at Wyatt before turning back to him. "I agree, Mr. Wynter." They helped him to sit down again before they were escorted by the bailiff to the section reserved for the victims and their family.

Faith was nervous, her palms sweating as she sat with Wyatt on her left, Ogden to her right, and Vicky on the other side of Wyatt. Up in front of the bar, which in this case was an ornately crafted wooden railing and gate, were the defense and prosecution tables. Patrice was already there, the African American woman looking sharp in a skirt suit. The public defender sat at the other table with another man, Lucas not yet present. At the front, the judge's bench and witness stand sat empty, though the court reporter was at her station setting up.

"Miss Casey?"

Faith glanced over to her right to see the bailiff standing at the end of their row, of which Ogden was the end person. He looked past her to Wyatt.

"DA Lorrey told me you had some paperwork she'd keep at her table?"

"Yes, sir." Wyatt handed Faith the packet she'd brought, which was handed in front of Ogden to the bailiff. "Thank you, sir."

With a nod, the uniformed man left and headed toward the front.

Faith felt a touch and looked to her left. She was surprised when Wyatt grabbed her hand, entwining their fingers. She smiled at her, sending as much love and support her way as she could.

"Look at that," Ogden uttered, garnering Faith's attention.

A side door opened and three uniformed officers entered, one in front, two at the back, a tall man between them. He was dressed in a bright orange shirt and pants, much like medical scrubs, a white undershirt under the V-neck orange top. He wore leg irons around his ankles, the chain between them just long enough to allow slow forward progress. His wrists were cuffed and attached to a belly chain, which was attached to the chain between the leg irons, keeping his bound hands tight against his stomach.

"Serves that son of a bitch right," Vicky muttered.

Faith felt Wyatt's fingers tighten around hers, so she responded with a little squeeze. She had to admit it was deeply satisfying to see Lucas chained up like the animal he was. His usually well-kept dark hair was shaggy, almost giving him the appearance of a little boy. A pathetic little boy, but a little boy, nonetheless.

Faith watched with interest as the court proceedings began, including the entrance of the judge and introduction of the case and what was about to happen. In some ways it took her back to her litigation days, and a small part of her missed it. Wyatt had once asked her why she'd opened Bessie's instead of her own law firm. Considering there wasn't one in Wynter, she probably would have cleaned house. Faith's simple response was, "At what cost to my soul?"

Finally, the time had come for Lucas Pennington to stand up and admit his guilt. The judge stated each crime, followed by a quiet, "Guilty." It amazed Faith. Where was that deep baritone? Where was that cocky, almost downright cavalier bravado?

"Sheep in wolf's clothing," she muttered under her breath.

After the final guilty plea, the judge had a few

more things to say before she stated it was time for the Victim Impact Statement, given by none other than the victim herself, Wyatt Casey. When her name was called, a quiet fell over the courtroom. It had already been quiet, as in nobody was speaking, though the occasional cough or softly whispered request for a breath mint made its way around, but now nobody seemed to be even breathing.

Ogden and Faith stood from their seats and moved out into the aisle for Wyatt to pass. As she stepped in front of Faith, the two shared a quick but meaningful look. Faith couldn't take her eyes off the redhead as she made her way to the gate, stepping aside to swing the door back, and stepped through.

"That girl is so strong," Ogden whispered as they retook their seats.

Faith nodded, unable to speak.

Wyatt made her way to the podium where she was directed to give her statement. Faith had never seen her walk with such confidence, such self-awareness. She was a woman on a mission, and that mission was to search and destroy. She took her place behind the podium, looking directly at Lucas. Faith couldn't see his face, but Wyatt's first words gave her an idea of his expression.

"I've seen that look before, the one on your face," she began, her words to Lucas, not the court. Her conversational tone spoke of a woman who planned to speak to the man, not the situation. "You see, you'd get that look right before you were about to strike. Remember?" she asked softly. She raised her hand, turning it so the back of it faced him, therefore faced the galley as well. "Right here," she tapped the center of the back of her hand and ran her fingers down toward the edge that ran up to her little finger. "This was the zone for you. Your perfect weapon to get me back under control, wasn't it?"

Faith felt her fury rising, her fists clenching at her sides.

"No," Ogden whispered, covering her fist with his hand. "She needs to get this out."

"The funny thing is, Lucas, when people saw you, they saw this handsome man, tall, broad shoulders, big hands, a working man's hands. Right? Wonder what they'd say if they knew all those callouses were from the hours you spent squeezin' and squeezin' that wooden club you kept around. Remember that? The one that broke two of my ribs and my wrist?"

Gasps erupted in the gallery, but Wyatt didn't even seem to notice.

"What kinda man beats the baby right outta his nineteen-year-old wife? Tellin' her that if she gets pregnant again, he'll kill her?" She pointed at him with a finger. "You. You also dragged me all the way out here, away from anythin' and everyone I knew, didn't'cha? Isn't that what abusers do? Isolate. It burned ya good when we got here and I began to really find myself, didn't it?" Her eyes squinted down into hateful slits. "You couldn't stand it." Her smile was one of gleeful revenge. "Now look at you, all trussed up like a Thanksgivin' turkey."

The three officers took a step closer as a growl escaped Lucas's throat.

"Getting' mad?" Wyatt continued casually. "Ya know what I find the most interestin' in all this is, the very cage you planned for me is gonna be yours. From what I hear, law enforcement isn't all that well received in prison."

"Order," the judge demanded as a few chuckles scattered about the audience.

"You beat the woman I love in the head with a baseball bat," she continued, the first real emotion in her voice since she'd begun. "Faith Fitzgerald," she said, pointing toward Faith. "Is the most innocent victim in all this mess. I hate you, Lucas, and I got lots of cause to, but what you did to her is at the top of the list. And then you take me like some fool burglar in the night, like the coward you are. Big, bad, and strong, right?" Her grin was downright evil. "When that first flash-bang grenade went off in Guffey, you flat-out messed yourself."

"Bitch!" he raged, the officers laying hands on him to keep him sitting.

"So, you wanna know the impact you've had on me?" She lifted her chin, stubborn and defiant. "Nothin'. I've always been stronger than you, always will be. You've proven to be just as insignificant as your daddy always told ya you were." She glanced back at the judge, who was looking at her with surprise behind those thick glasses. "Your Honor, would it be all right if the bailiff gave Lucas what I brought for him?"

The judge cleared her throat and said, "It's highly unusual, and strongly recommended such action is not taken, however this case is one of horrific dimensions, and I'm going to allow it." She nodded at the bailiff, who walked over to the DA's table and picked up the paperwork he'd left there at the beginning of the proceedings. He walked across the space to the defendant's table and set the paperwork down in front of Lucas.

"You've been served, you son of a bitch." Without another look, Wyatt turned and walked away from the podium, the judge slamming her gavel down for order as the room erupted in cheers and whistles.

≈≈≈≈

They hadn't even waited around to hear the sentencing. Wyatt had kept on walking, right out of the courtroom. Faith trusted that Wyatt had done everything she needed to do. She'd said her piece and was now finished with the entire thing.

The drive home was made in silence, but again, Wyatt had held Faith's hand, not daring to let it go. They walked into the house, Faith closing the door behind them and locking it, an unfortunate need and habit learned by them both.

"You know," Faith said, picking a topic that she knew would make Wyatt smile. "We still need to pick a name for our little furry monkey before we bring her home in two weeks," she said, meaning the puppy they'd picked out, too young to be weaned just yet. She'd been walking over to the kitchen as she'd spoken, intending to make some coffee. When she got no response, she became very worried.

Glancing over, she saw that Wyatt had kicked off her heels and was building a fire in the fireplace. There was certainly a chill in the air as a spring snowstorm was moving in, but Faith was a little confused, especially by the almost methodical way Wyatt was doing her task.

"Baby?" she said softly, from where she stood by the kitchen island. She walked over, stopping ten feet or so away, unsure. "Are you okay?"

Even more confused, she watched as Wyatt moved the coffee table out of the way, then grabbed the thick throw off the back of the couch that she'd crocheted for that very purpose, and spread it out on the area rug where the coffee table had been. A few throw pillows tossed on top of it, and Wyatt finally acknowledged Faith's presence.

Remaining silent, though her gaze never left Faith, Wyatt reached down to the hem of her dress and gathered the material in her hands until she was able to lift it up and over her head, tossing the garment to the couch. In panties and bra, she stared at Faith.

"It's over," she said softly. "It's finally over."

Faith nodded, stunned by the very unexpected turn of events, but she walked over to her. "Yes, it is."

"The last time we made love we began by the fire, by the Christmas tree," she said, her voice soft and almost hypnotic. "Do you remember/"

Faith smiled. "Been able to think of little else," she whispered, taking the last few steps to Wyatt, who reached for the lapels of her blazer, using them as leverage to push the garment off Faith's shoulders. It joined the dress as nimble fingers worked on the buttons of Faith's blouse.

"He took our beautiful Christmas and made it ugly," Wyatt continued, the blouse quickly gone as well. "Stole our first New Year's together, and for a time, stole my hope and my faith." She smiled, seeming to realize her unintended double entendre. As one hand worked on the belt of Faith's slacks, the other cupped Faith's jaw. "I want those things back," she whispered. "I want new memories."

Faith could feel the slow burn as her body began to catch up with what was happening. She'd had to force herself to slow down, to wall off her sexual desire and need for Wyatt over the last two months, and as hard as it had been, it was now just part of her day, the fear of scaring Wyatt great incentive to reprogram her body to behave.

Faith looked deeply into Wyatt's eyes, and all she saw there was pure, unadulterated need. The passion that she'd known her for had returned, and it nearly burned Faith alive where she stood.

The undressing of Faith was as methodical as the building of the fire had been, with the last of Wyatt's clothing finishing the task. Faith was guided to lie down on the blanket, a pillow under her head. She reached for Wyatt, who lowered herself to lie just beside her, all the grace and beauty of a living goddess.

When their lips touched, it wasn't their first kiss by a long shot, but it was. There was something different about Wyatt's kiss, something different about the way she touched Faith in that moment. As the bruises from her shackles had slowly disappeared from her wrists, she truly had become free and untethered. Wyatt had been a good lover from the very first time they'd made love, her natural passion guiding her every move, but the intensity she put into every touch, every lick, suckle, and stroke of her fingers was filled with the abandon that she'd spoken of with five simple words: *It's over…It's finally over.*

As Wyatt licked one of Faith's nipples, Faith felt wetness on her breast. Looking down along her body, she saw that silent tears were running down Wyatt's cheeks, baptizing Faith's body with the power of their release. She knew it was nothing to be afraid of or worried about, but a blessing to Wyatt. As she was accepting Faith's body and love, she was letting go of a past filled with darkness and pain.

As badly as she wanted to turn them over and

love Wyatt with every ounce of her being, body and soul, she knew that Wyatt needed to do this, needed to control the situation and show her gratitude while claiming possession and domination of her new life, of herself.

Faith's head fell back as Wyatt moved lower down her body, the wetness of her tears leaving a trail. As she gave Faith sexual release with her mouth, Wyatt also seemed to release something as a sob escaped her lips.

It took Faith a moment to get her bearings, but she reached for Wyatt, pulling her up until her head rested on Faith's breasts, the majority of her body weight on the floor between Faith's legs. Knowing there was nothing to be said, Faith simply held her, caressing her naked back and her hair as she left soft kisses to the top of her head.

After several moments, Wyatt brought her arms up so that her hands cupped the backs of Faith's shoulders. For several moments they lay in comfortable silence, the popping flames the only noise.

"I'm going to talk to Grace about another case I think Lucas was involved in," Wyatt said at length.

"What's that?" Faith asked softly, her fingernails running an absent pattern over the soft, warm expanse of Wyatt's back.

"The death of my parents," Wyatt said simply. "I've suspected for years, but what was I going to do, you know? He was law enforcement. A brother in blue. Who would listen to me?"

It hurt Faith's heart to hear those suspicions voiced, suspicions she, herself had considered. "I think that's a wonderful idea, baby. You parents deserve that. You deserve that. Answers."

Wyatt lifted her head and looked down at Faith for a long moment. "You don't have to go back to work today, do you?" she asked.

Faith smiled and shook her head. "Nope. Took the day off. Wasn't sure how all this would go today."

Without a word, Wyatt moved off Faith and got to her feet, helping Faith to hers. She moved the log around in the fireplace to dampen the fire by removing its fuel source, then, taking Faith by the hand, she headed toward the stairs.

"Wait," Faith said, tugging lightly on Wyatt's hand to stop her. She walked over to the security panel and armed the system.

With a smile, Wyatt led Faith by the hand up the stairs.

If you liked this book?

Reviews help a new author get discovered and if you have enjoyed this book, please do the author the honor of posting a review on Goodreads, Amazon, Barnes & Noble or anywhere you purchased the book. Or perhaps share a posting on your social media sites or spread the word to your friends.

About the Author

Kim has spent her life in Colorado and can't imagine living anywhere else. She's been writing since she was 9 and stumbled into her first book being published in her mid-20s. She's worked in the film industry as a writer, director and producer, but now enjoys the quiet, happy life of a professional author. She can be reached on Facebook and on her website at, www.kimpritekel.com

Check out Kim's other books.

Zero Ward - ISBN - 978-1-943353-19-4

Danny Felts grew up in the heart of the Midwest on a dairy farm, expected to follow in her mother's footsteps and marry a farmer and become a mother. Danny had other ideas. As World War II heats up, she makes a decision that will change her life forever as she becomes a lie, serving with the Seabees in the Navy as Daniel Felts.

Kate Adams is about to graduate high school in her prestigious and elite San Diego neighborhood when she's dragged to the USO for a dance with friends and servicemen. There, she meets the person that will catch her eye and her heart, only for jealousy and vengeance to tear her apart.

Are Danny and Kate strong enough to win the battle within and fight for their love?

Connection - ISBN - 978-1-939062-24-6

Julie Wilson lives a charmed life as a beloved teacher and aunt in the small town of Woodland. Close to her brother and guardian of two adorable Yorkies, she loves her life, the only negative being ex-boyfriend, Ray who can't seem to understand the phrase, "We're done." Believing that's her only problem, Julie has no idea what hell awaits her during a normal summer afternoon.

Remmy Foster is the quirky, friendly drifter who has

never found roots after a difficult childhood, as well as the difficulties her very special gift brings into her life. Though she may call it exploring, the truth is she's running from ghosts that haunt her every step.

After a chance meeting with Julie while hitchhiking, Remmy will be thrown head first into darkness she could never have foreseen, regardless of her abilities. As the clock ticks, life and death is on her shoulders to make the right connection.

Warning - *Some scenes may be too intense for some readers.*

1049 Club - ISBN - 978-1-939062-97-0

Almost two hundred souls, one plane, six survivors, endless heartbreak.

When flight 1049, headed from Buffalo, NY to Italy falls from the sky, a firestorm of drama, pain, angst and sorrow ensues. Can an author, a business owner, a teenager, good ol' boy, veterinarian and ruthless lawyer survive? Better yet, can those left behind?

1049 Club is a story of survival, love, deep regret and miracles. Can the living make peace with the presumed dead? Can the presumed dead make peace with the lives and loves they thought they had before?

Blinded – ISBN – 978-1-943353-53-8

After a horrible explosion sends local television news reporter, Burton Blinde reeling both physically and emotionally, she walks away from her life and the dream job she was about to start at a major news network.

For six long years she hides out in a small mountain town, working at the local library, though is haunted by the life she had, including mysterious messages and gifts she was receiving before her life was turned upside down, a veritable bread crumb trail leading to the unknown.

Unable to resist, Burton begins to follow the clues, which will lead her into the darkest places of human nature that she may not be able to return from.

Damaged - ISBN - 978-1-939062-45-1

Family. A group of people you are related to by blood or love.

Nora Schaeffer has come home to her family after twenty years working around the world as a photographer for National Geographic. She's welcomed into the open arms of her father and siblings.

Family. A group of people who support you, lift you up when you fall.

Shannon, the youngest of the four Schaeffer siblings, has vanished, leaving her five-year-old daughter, Bella, terrified and alone. To help find Shannon, Nora has no choice but to turn to the dark-haired specter who has haunted her for twenty years. Along the way, she finds her own long-dead heart and uncovers chilling family secrets beyond imagination.

Family. A group of people who will stick together to hide the rotten soul at its core at any cost.

Who will live? Who will die? Who will be the most damaged? And who will learn to love again?

The Gift - ISBN - 978-1-948232-47-0

The dead do speak. You just have to listen. Homicide Detective Catania "Nia" d'Giovanni is the only daughter in a large Italian family of six children. The backbone—a position not applied for nor wanted—she continues to create new glue to hold the dysfunctional group together. For Nia, family time feels more like herding cats than spending time with her brothers and feisty, aging parents. Her heart has always been in her career with the Pueblo Police Department, especially since it will never be okay with her very Catholic mother to openly give her heart to any woman, until she meets a secretive waitress who has her at, Can I take your order?

And then it begins...

Three murders that are so gruesome, so horrible, they rock the small town to its core. Nia and her partner Oscar are left to piece together a deadly puzzle to find the key to unlock the monster they hunt. Or, are they the hunted? As they dissect the murder scenes where not one shred of evidence is left behind, more bodies begin to show up, each cleaner than the last, the shadowy specter that is the killer vanishing without a trace, making the woman Nia loves disappear right along with it. When there is no evidence to follow, Nia must trust her instincts...or, is she being guided?

The Plan – ISBN – 978-1-948232-43-2

As the dark days of the Dust Bowl came to an end, the midsection of the United States tried to rebuild and revitalize. In the small, dusty farming town of, Brooke View, Colorado, teenager, Eleanor Landry and her mother were dealing with her father, a self-appointment fire and brimstone preacher to his congregation of two. A plan to survive.

As the dark era of the robber baron comes to an end, giants of industry and innovation emerged with fabulous fortunes manifested in the mansions that dotted the landscape across the country. Lysette Landon, the teen daughter of the wealthiest family in Brooke View, was everything a good, proper girl of privilege should be. Only problem was, she wasn't dreaming of finding a young man to raise a family with. A plan to be free.

One look, one touch, all plans are off.

Secrets deeper and darker than the grave would bring Eleanor and Lysette together, their families connected by a web of lies and broken promises. A plan to escape.

Be careful because, life has other plans…

The Traveler Book One: The Hunted - ISBN - 978-1-948232-91-3

A story so epic one book can't contain it.BOOK ONE: 1977: In the era between flower power and the yuppie, Sonia Lucas is a young wife and mother, just starting out in life. Without warning, a strange presence and dark force enters her life, clouds building .... 1917: .... and a storm brewing as the world reeled from the horrific events of World War I just before it was ravaged by a Spanish flu epidemic that would kill millions.

Sephora Lloyd is a 16 year old girl lost in the responsibilities of an adult world helping to support herself and her mother. A beautiful young nun-in-training enters her life, bringing love and hope with her. That is, until a force bigger than either of them threatens everything Sephora holds dear.four women - three deaths - two words - one house

THE HUNTED

The Traveler Book Two: The Hunter - ISBN - 978-1-948232-93-7

A story so epic one book can't contain it.

BOOK TWO: 1890: In the dying days of the Old West, Sally Little runs her booming brothel with the passion and tenacity the business of sex requires. Savvy and indulgent, there's one itch Sally can't let herself scratch. Afraid of hurting the woman she loves, she instead unleashes...

Present Day: ...her renovation crew and fixer upper

TV show on a dilapidated mansion that has known nothing but death since a murder there in 1977.

Samantha Leyton sees ratings gold in bringing the sagging old house to life, but instead she discovers only she has the power to unlock the mystery that hunted four women across time, leaving death and destruction in its wake. Can she release her sisters who came before her and finally be granted the gift of love that is stronger than any evil? Four women - Three deaths - two words - one house

THE HUNTER

CPSIA information can be obtained
at www.ICGtesting.com
Printed in the USA
LVHW111336261222
735896LV00026BA/505

9 781952 270161